THE
LOST
BOYS
SYMPHONY

THE
LOST
BOYS
SYMPHONY

A NOVEL

MARK ANDREW FERGUSON

Little, Brown and Company
New York Boston London

Copyright © 2015 by Mark Andrew Ferguson

Little, Brown and Company
Hachette Book Group
1290 Avenue of the Americas, New York, NY 10104
littlebrown.com

First Edition: March 2015

Little, Brown and Company is a division of Hachette Book Group, Inc. The Little, Brown name and logo are trademarks of Hachette Book Group, Inc.

The publisher is not responsible for websites (or their content) that are not owned by the publisher.

The Hachette Speakers Bureau provides a wide range of authors for speaking events. To find out more, go to hachettespeakersbureau.com or call (866) 376-6591.

Library of Congress Cataloging-in-Publication Data
Ferguson, Mark Andrew.
  The lost boys symphony : a novel / Mark Andrew Ferguson. — First edition.
    pages cm
  ISBN 978-0-316-32399-4
  1. College students—Mental health—Fiction. 2. Hallucinations and illusions—Fiction. 3. Time travel—Fiction. 4. Male friendship—Fiction. 5. Triangles (Interpersonal relations)—Fiction. I. Title.
  PS3606.E726L67 2015
  813'.6—dc23   2014025211

10 9 8 7 6 5 4 3 2 1

RRD-C

Printed in the United States of America

For Oliver

The fox pulled out his knife, shouting: "I'm going to teach you how to live!" Then he took to flight, turning his back. But he had no luck. The snake was quicker. With a well-chosen blow of his fist, he struck the fox in the middle of his forehead, which broke into a thousand pieces, while he cried: "No! No! Four times no! I'm not your daughter."

—The Fire Chief
Eugène Ionesco's *The Bald Soprano*

THE
LOST
BOYS
SYMPHONY

PRELUDE: ESCAPE

H ENRY LEFT HIS mother's house at two thirty in the morning. The sound of the bright green spastic low vibration emanating from the house across the street crescendoed when he opened the front door, and got louder still when he stepped down onto the lawn. It sounded like cicadas at the height of a seventeenth summer, or a dense forest being chewed apart by wildfire.

At first the dangerous journey ahead had been too daunting to properly consider. Now Henry felt he had no choice. For weeks the sound had made sleep an impossibility. His body felt papery and insubstantial, and at last he feared staying more than he did the uncertainty of escape.

The previous day's run-in with the cops had cemented it. It was really just an unfortunate misunderstanding. Cause and effect, once so reliable, were no longer correlated in any meaningful way, so Henry had taken to running little experiments. For instance: If he tossed an egg-sized pebble at the house across the street, would it stick or bounce off?

The rock ricocheted off the wood of the front door with a sharp crack and landed on the bright orange welcome mat. Feeling comforted by the normal response from rock and door, Henry walked to the house, peered into a ground-level window, and saw the woman who lived inside. She didn't seem to have noticed him, so he banged on the glass.

"How do you sleep?" he yelled, but only so she could hear him. "Where is it coming from?"

Henry just wanted to talk—to gather information about the vibration. But then he saw how scared she was and he got scared too. He ran back to his house. When the police arrived he watched through the living room curtains as the woman gesticulated wildly in his direction. A moment later, the officers knocked on the door. Henry opened it, then quietly stared at them in protest of what he felt was unnecessary and unlawful intimidation. They were afraid too. He could tell by the sound of their voices, though he couldn't make out what they were saying. He was too transfixed by the way the one cop's Silly Putty eyelid dripped slowly down his face, too confused by the confetti that spewed out of the other's mouth.

"All that confetti!" he said, and then he laughed.

They must not have liked that, because their incomprehensible racket got louder. Henry's mother joined him on the threshold, pill bottles in hand. They rattled pleasantly as she shook them in the cops' direction. The officer who'd brandished his handcuffs put them back in his special shiny handcuff holster, and they left.

The neighbors might have said how sad it was over their morning coffee, but sadness was not what they felt. Henry knew that. He heard them whispering from a block away, through brick and wood and open air. They were scared of the hairy antisocial teenager. Scared that he wandered, muttering, through their backyards on his way to the woods. They all wanted him gone and would find some pretext to get the police back to his doorstep. But Henry would not be caught, and he would not wait until that bright green mess of a buzzing window turned fluid and shook the teeth right out of his head before sucking the whole goddamn street out of existence.

He squinted through the darkness, searching for any sign of a patrol car at the entrance to his cul-de-sac. There was no moon that night and very few stars on account of the lights of the city nearby. Henry walked to the end of his lawn and stepped onto the street. It was softer than usual. His shoes sank into the pavement, but only slightly. He jumped up in the air and landed a moment later. No lag. No puddle splashes from the asphalt.

I must have chosen the right night, he thought.

He stepped forward, and by the time he reached the third house down from his own he felt lighter. The air felt good and the sky was big and clear. He was almost happy, the fear momentarily out of reach. Distracted, he could no longer recall the reason for his nighttime walk.

Wait, he thought. *What am I doing?*

I have no idea, said a voice.

He recognized that voice. It was his own, from before everything went wrong. Henry wanted to grab on to it and climb it like a rope out of quicksand, but it was already gone. In its place stirred a familiar sadness spiked with fear, a purple and black bruise of a sensation that caught at the back of his throat, drew his eyebrows down, swelled his tongue. He wanted to sit down and cry but knew it wouldn't do any good, so he forced himself forward. The first step was hard but they came easier after that until half a block later when he heard a click and was hit by a pure white light that surrounded him completely. He stared unblinking into its epicenter, and though it hurt he could not turn away. He saw concentric circles like solar flares—they grew and contracted as his pupils tried to find the right focus and Henry was suddenly conscious of his eyeballs in the most curious way. They were moving inside of his skull without his consent, just millimeters away from his brain, and the light was manipulating them, working its way inside. But just as that strange fear was threatening to overwhelm him, he heard the same click as before and the brightness disappeared.

In pieces, like the melody of an old song, a memory materialized. Henry and his best friend, Gabe, used to walk this road at
night when they were kids, and the light had come on then, too. It
was controlled by a motion sensor mounted to a tree trunk at the
edge of his neighbor's driveway. He and Gabe used to play spy and
try to move so slowly that their little bodies wouldn't trip the sensor. They always failed, but that was most of the fun, and when the
spotlight bathed them in blinding white light they'd jump in the air
as if from the force of an explosion. Henry could remember Gabe's
elongated yell, how he would deepen his young voice to mimic the
sound of slow motion. Then they would stand, brush loose gravel
from their clothes, and casually walk away while hoping that none
of the older kids on the block had seen them playing make-believe.

The memory made Henry miss the world he had left. It made
him miss himself in that world. It made him miss Gabe and Val
and nights spent in the impossible comfort of his dorm room. The
thought of all he'd lost was devastatingly painful and unbearably seductive. Like gravity it pulled him toward his home and his bed and
his mother, and he almost turned around.

Stoppit, he thought. *Stoppit stoppit stoppit.*

He had vowed that he would escape. This sadness, however real
it might feel, had been turned into a weapon in the arsenal of the
enemy. Henry could not allow himself to be prey to the spastic vibration. There was no more time to debate or to question. With
balled fists pinned tightly to his sides and teeth clenched to the
point of almost breaking, he marched forward. The asphalt turned
to soup, and strings of black elastic tar wound themselves around
his feet. He lifted his old sneakers higher with each step, shook
them to dislodge some of the goop. It felt awkward and his thigh
muscles burned with the effort, but it worked. When finally he
reached the end of his street, Henry smiled, eyes wide with wonder. The bushes that bordered the road rustled in applause, and the

streetlamps lowered their curious faces, burst open like flowers, and showered him with orange and yellow sparks of congratulation.

The hard part, he hoped, was over. He pointed his shoes toward the city. Val was there, somewhere deep in the labyrinth of Lower Manhattan, and he would find her. She would save him.

THE BLACK CORNER

G ABE'S FIRST MEMORY was of a game. His T-shirt was pulled up, pinned between chin and chest, and his pants and underwear were around his ankles. Henry was there, his clothes in roughly the same configuration. Henry was singing, and Gabe was listening. They would take turns making funny noises in the dark. They were both four years old, and though they would remain best friends throughout childhood and adolescence and beyond, they would stop taking their pants off in closets together shortly after the time of Gabe's second memory.

Gabe's second memory was of being caught. This time, he and Henry were together in a sleeping bag. All of their clothing had been left in a reckless pile down past their feet. They lay on their sides, foreheads pressed together. Henry hummed notes up and down a scale, and when he hit just the right one the air inside the sleeping bag seemed to come alive and tickle Gabe deep inside of his ear. When that happened they both laughed and Henry said, "Now you go." But Gabe could never find the right notes. His role in the game was to take his index fingers and try to tickle the inside of Henry's ears directly while singing a silly song. Henry giggled and fought back until one or the other of them gave up.

Henry's mother's voice was surprisingly clear inside the bag.

"What are you two doing?" she said.

Gabe froze. He wasn't positive that what they were doing was bad, but the fact that they'd always kept it a secret made him feel afraid. Henry, believing the bag to be magical, whispered that if they were quiet enough his mother wouldn't find them. Gabe remembered the blinding light when she opened the bag and the feeling of the cool air replacing the moistness of their breath. It made him feel small and cold. Henry's mother dragged her son out by the wrist. He cried and tried to get away, but she held on to his arm and spanked his bare behind as he ran in a circle around her. That image was clear in Gabe's memory. Henry was like the tail of a dog being chased by the snapping mouth of his mother's open palm.

Gabe doubted that she'd spanked him, too, but he couldn't recall. His mind hadn't recorded anything beyond the air and the light, her loud voice and the sound of the spanking.

Fifteen years had passed since that moment, but when Gabe was reminded of it the shame was still fresh. It opened up somewhere in his sinuses and spread down through his chest before pooling and hardening beneath his breastbone. He never told his own parents what had happened, and as far as he knew Henry's mother had never revealed their secret. Because of that, Gabe always felt like he was still hiding, even after having been found.

He never fooled around with another boy again, and he and Henry never talked about it. As he got older, as he came to understand how typical their early, unfocused impulses had been, Gabe resented having been made to feel bad about it in the first place. Even so, the shame remained like the phantom of a severed limb. It was there inside him whether it made sense or not, one of the many strange stones that formed his crooked foundation.

For reasons he could not at first understand, Gabe thought a lot about those memories when Henry disappeared. Eventually, after long consideration, the reason for their persistence became clear. In the blackest corner of his mind, the place where Gabe put sex and pain and fear and humiliation, this memory was king. And at the center of it stood Henry, singing, his pants around his ankles.

THE LIVING ROOM

I T STARTED IN the living room of Henry and Gabe's apartment at 215 Hamilton Street. The room was all mismatched couches and dark wood paneling. An old TV blared from a particleboard stand that had been sitting in the same fetid corner since before they moved in. Mounted into the ceiling was a fan that had never been turned on. Even the slightest breeze would have disturbed the delicate ecosystem of the big wooden coffee table that dominated the center of the room. It was perpetually covered in takeout menus; napkins, paper bags, and plates from Tata's Pizza; scraps of paper; loose change; dusty-looking Ziploc bags; empty Arizona iced tea cans with blackened joint roaches teetering over their sharp mouths; aluminum takeout tins long since emptied of tacos or french fries, now slowly filling with the refuse of convenience store purchases; a Snapple bottle, its lid twisted tight to prevent the stench of cigarette butts from escaping the scum-streaked topiary.

It was the coffee table of inveterate pot smokers, and its general likeness could be found in every New Brunswick house that Gabe had ever visited. Once every few weeks he would get disgusted enough to throw everything away and wipe that table down. It always took two or three passes before the paper towel came up an acceptable dingy brown. If the mess bothered Henry he didn't show it, possibly because he was barely ever home. He spent most of each day locked in a practice room at Rutgers's main music building, where he worked to perfect percussion instruments that he would seldom use even if he *did* become a concert musician.

Gabe was sitting on the periwinkle couch one night, scratching at the loose threads that formed one of its thousands of tiny white diamonds, when suddenly Henry started laughing.

"What?" said Gabe. He had an expectant smile on his face.

Henry responded with a vague shrug of his shoulders and then laughed again. It sounded sharp and thin and out of key.

Gabe thought it was strange, but their nights were always strange. Gabe and Henry designed their time together to counteract and forget the monotony of their days. They strung late hours together, lengthened them with pot and caffeine, and didn't go to bed until they'd already fallen asleep while watching late-night talk shows or old sitcoms. Neither of them chased sleep anymore. It was easier to let it chase them. The habit had begun when Henry's ex-girlfriend Val disappeared from their lives the year before. At first Henry suffered from the kind of insomnia typical of the broken-hearted, and Gabe stayed up with him out of solidarity. But even after the pain subsided, the habit persisted.

Henry laughed again.

"What's so funny?"

Henry smiled and closed his eyes.

Gabe didn't know what to do, so he laughed too. He laughed until the corners of his mouth burned and his chest ached. It was the forced laughter of awkward parties and run-ins with old acquaintances. It deadened Gabe's senses and made him feel far away. When he couldn't stand it any longer he said, "Dude. What the fuck? What are you thinking about?"

Henry acted like he hadn't heard it. His socked feet were

propped on the corner of the coffee table; his hands rested on the pouch of the charcoal-gray hoodie that had become his sophomore-year uniform. He kept laughing, louder and faster until he was almost out of breath.

Gabe just stared. He didn't care to ask any more questions, so he listened to the organ jazz that flowed out of the little iPod dock in the corner and allowed himself to be lost in the melody, to bounce to the beat. Minutes later Henry unlocked his fingers, waved one hand in front of his face, and nodded his head.

"Okay then," said Gabe. "Get some sleep. You're scaring the shit out of me."

Gabe's bedroom was right next to the living room. He stood up from the couch, waited for his head to stop spinning, crossed the threshold, and closed the door.

Perhaps the strangest thing about that night was that it didn't seem particularly strange at all. Not at the time. A lot had changed since their time in the dorms the year before. It was easy to blame that on Val's departure, but Gabe wondered if that was fair. Long before she showed up, he and Henry had been perfectly able to fill each other's time without getting high. It wasn't Val's absence that was the problem. Not directly, anyway. The problem was that she'd changed them. When they were kids, Henry had needed Gabe. He barely talked to anyone else, even before his dad died when they were in middle school. After that he dug even deeper into his own strange imaginary world, a world that even Gabe couldn't access with any reliability.

But they stayed friends even as their respective paths through adolescence diverged. When Henry successfully auditioned to be the replacement drummer for a local punk band called Upstart, most of his peers thought it was funny. They couldn't picture him as a hard-driving punk rock percussionist. Gabe knew it made perfect sense. Henry was defined by the music he played. He didn't relish performing—he didn't join Upstart for the notoriety. He did it because Upstart was good. The lyrics sucked and the other kids in the band oozed the faux angst that defined the scene, but they were not just another teenage noise machine. Each member was technically proficient. They were dedicated, well trained. And in that way Henry was a perfect fit.

The first time Valerie Mitchell came to a show, Gabe avoided her. She and Henry were in gym class together and somehow Henry had worked up the courage to give her a flyer. Gabe didn't want to tell Henry that he didn't have a chance with Val, so he resigned himself to waiting it out. She would eventually hook up with some other guy or ignore Henry at a crucial moment. Or she'd ask him to drop a hint about her to one of Upstart's edgier members and Henry would *actually do it* just to be nice. But then he'd quietly implode and Gabe would console him for weeks.

The second time Val came to a show Gabe had drunk two syrupy malt beverages and was practically wasted. He cornered her in the bright hallway outside the community room at the Wayne senior center. "Stop giving him hope," he said, and he slapped his palm against the wall in earnest emphasis. "You're killing him." He felt like crying. He felt like kissing her. He felt like throwing up.

If Val was insulted she didn't show it. "Take it easy on the hard lemonade," she said. And then she walked away.

A few weeks later, Val kissed Henry for the first time. In the months that followed she stuck around. Without really meaning to, Gabe grew to really like her. She was warm. She asked Gabe questions about things he cared about and seemed to actually want to hear his answers. She touched his arm when she greeted him and hugged him when she said goodbye. The last of Gabe's defenses told him that it was all a strategy, that she was simply trying to get him on her side. So he tried to outdo her. If Val was being big, he could be bigger. But what started as artifice became real over time, and his fondness for her bled into his friendship with Henry until he began seeing his old best friend the way Val did. Suddenly Henry didn't seem so weak or shy or insecure. He wasn't just the kid who maybe felt things too deeply and needed too much. In many ways that Gabe had scarcely noticed before, Henry was confident and funny, kind and strong.

The three of them grew closer. Their inside jokes evolved into a whole private vocabulary. There were, of course, certain kinds of intimacy that Gabe wasn't privy to, but over time he got better at ignoring the ache he felt when he considered what Val and Henry did in private. The thoughts that he couldn't ignore—stolen glimpses of Val's body and the way her laughter made him feel—Gabe reserved for when he was alone.

They graduated from high school, then all decided on Rutgers for college. The adults in their lives protested—Val's mother in particular was adamant that Val not make decisions about school based on love—but they ignored the advice, confident in the knowledge that what Henry and Val had would outlast the cynicism. Gabe was just as sure of that as his two best friends were. He felt lucky to be a part of it.

That faith was what made it so hard when Val ended it.

Now, a year after Val left and a week after that first strange night in the living room, Henry was quiet and distant. A perpetual smile sat fat on his lips without ever spreading to the rest of his face. One day Gabe came home from his morning shift at the Magic Dragon hungry and looking for company. He walked in the back door and rushed through the kitchen, willing himself not to see the filth. He dropped his shoulder bag on the couch and listened to the house, waiting for a sign that Henry was home.

"Hey," he yelled.

No response.

He launched himself up the dust-caked stairs, taking them two at a time. At the top there was a bathroom and Henry's tiny bedroom. Through the open door Gabe could see that Henry was sitting at his desk, intense focus evident in his slack mouth and unblinking eyes.

"Did you hear me?" said Gabe.

Henry didn't look up, and Gabe saw that he was drawing on a blue-and-pink-lined index card. He entered the bedroom.

"Do you want to go to Tata's? Pizza or something?"

Henry sniffled and kept scribbling.

Gabe sat on the bed. From there he could see that three teetering piles of index cards had been pushed to the side of the desk.

"What are you doing?"

Henry didn't answer.

"Henry."

"I'm drawing," said Henry. It sounded like an answer but it wasn't, not really, and Gabe felt a familiar anger, one that had been lurking all week.

Henry lifted his pencil and appraised his work. Apparently satisfied, he put the index card on top of one pile and grabbed a blank one from another.

"Do you want to see?" he asked. The question sounded as though it were rehearsed, as if Henry was trying so hard to sound natural that the opposite effect was perfectly achieved.

Gabe lifted a few cards from the top of the pile closest to him. They were covered in elementary shapes and mathematical symbols, arranged as if by accident. He flipped through them once, quickly, and then again more slowly, willing himself to see something meaningful. He stared at one card so long that the shapes started to shift. Two squares connected at their centers by a thick line spun like bicycle wheels. Squiggles swam by.

He shut his eyes tight and opened them back on Henry. "Cool," he said. "Um. What is it?"

A single labored exhale was the extent of Henry's response. Gabe dropped the cards on the bed and walked out.

Soon after that, Henry stopped going to class. He didn't practice. He stopped drawing cryptic symbols. As far as Gabe could tell, he didn't bathe or shave or eat, either. He just sat. He fidgeted. He mumbled. Sometimes on the couch, sometimes on the porch, sometimes in his room—but always the same.

Gabe left the house as much as he could, but that didn't mean he could escape. He spent most of his time curating a list of possible explanations for Henry's behavior. Maybe it was too much pot, but that seemed ridiculous. New Brunswick was home to some of the most dedicated cannabis addicts on the planet, and Gabe had never heard a single story about anyone losing it quite like Henry had. The music conservatory couldn't have helped. All year, Henry had spent the majority of his waking moments alone in a windowless practice room. But there were other kids—Henry's friends in the program—who were doing just fine. And anyway, Henry had practiced for hours each day for as long as Gabe could remember.

The only explanation that seemed feasible at all was Val, but the timing was all wrong. Gabe couldn't recall the last time either of them so much as spoke her name.

THE TRANSFER

AFTER THE WHITE cement blocks of her dorm at Rutgers, Val's new life in NYU's Greenwich Hotel residence hall seemed luxurious to the point of excess. Her galley kitchen was quaint and homey. In the morning, its single narrow window glowed with the reflected light of the building across the street. The institutional-white paint was offset by the deep gleaming brown of old wood floors. When it was nice enough, Val sunbathed on a pier that poked out into the Hudson River with the Statue of Liberty looking on. Even the names of the streets—the building sat between the tree-lined Morton and the cobblestoned Barrow—imbued the place with a patina of old-world authenticity.

Val's mom, Connie, was resistant to the transfer at first. No school was worth fifty thousand dollars a year, she said.

Val wasn't discouraged. She knew her dad might join in the melee if called upon, but he'd long been in the habit of leaving the difficult conversations to Connie. So Val set about testing her mother's defenses. She argued over class size and access to the greatest city on earth (a phrase she repeated as if it were the chorus to a long protest song). She researched NYU's award-winning faculty and emailed news articles that featured her fantasy professors.

Her mother was unmoved until one day, during winter break,

Val accidentally hit on the strategy that would eventually win the war. She was in the kitchen, dressed in the threadbare yoga pants and tank top she'd left in her bedroom drawer when she departed for Rutgers. Now that she was home she relished the opportunity to be completely, unattractively relaxed. Her comfort was disorienting in its familiarity. It made her feel as though her first few months at college had been a dream. When she awoke in her own bed in the home she'd grown up in, she couldn't quite remember who she was supposed to be.

Whoever was on brewing duty that morning had left the coffee machine on with one perfectly proportioned serving still hot at the bottom of the carafe. It looked gritty and smelled burnt, but Val didn't mind. She grabbed a mug from the cabinet and filled it.

Her mom came in, sweaty from a run.

"Good morning, love," she said.

"Morning," said Val. They jockeyed for position at the refrigerator. Val got the milk and Connie got a half-empty bottle of coconut water.

"You seeing Henry today?" said Connie.

Val poured milk into her mug and kept stirring long after it had merged. She liked the sound of the spoon hitting the ceramic, its tinny clink a comforting distraction from the weight of her mother's question. She let herself be lost in the sound. It was a habit she'd picked up from Henry. He was always tapping on things, and not in an absentminded way. His constant tinkering was completely focused, as though he was listening for something vital in the sounds he was creating. At first Val had found it annoying. She told him that once, early in their relationship, but Henry acted as though he hadn't heard her. He was a percussionist, after all, a serious one. He practiced for hours in the evenings, and that remarkable discipline and dedication was one of the things that had drawn Val to him in the first place. His obsessive tapping was a part of that, she figured. Her irritation softened into a begrudging acceptance, then gradually transformed into a full appreciation of the habit.

Once, at the beginning of their junior year in high school, Val and Henry were eating lunch in the school cafeteria when Henry stopped talking mid-sentence and closed his eyes. Val knew better than to ask what he was doing. She closed her eyes along with him and opened herself up to the sound of the room. At first she couldn't hear past the din of conversation, but she let herself relax into that constant babble until it settled into a uniform layer of warm, bubbling static. Then she began to hear the outliers. Trays being stacked. A sharp burst of laughter. The slightest trace of a background hiss from the central air-conditioning. The buzz of music from the kitchen, how the tinny soft-rock ballads pierced through all the organic noise. Everything grew so loud that she could hardly believe she and Henry had been able to hear each other just moments before. Then she opened her eyes again and the room seemed transformed. The colors of her fellow students' clothing were brighter, her vision sharper. It felt as if nothing had been real until that exact moment, as if her whole life had only just begun.

She looked at Henry. He was gazing back at her with that grin. It wasn't the first time she'd seen it. He liked to show her things that fascinated him—works of art, records from his father's old collection, drawings he'd made—just to watch her react. He would wait for her to be touched by his interest and to transform it into her own, and then he'd smile that same slight smile. It said he loved her and that the secrets of their shared experience were all he'd ever needed, that nobody but she had ever understood him and that nobody but she ever could.

"Val?" said Connie.

"What?"

"I said are you seeing Henry today? He hasn't shown his face here since you guys got back. I'd like to say hello."

"Yeah," said Val.

"Yeah?"

"I mean no, I'm not seeing him. We've just been talking on the phone."

"Hm," said Connie, her intonation calibrated perfectly to suggest a weighty prodding without any specific demand for information.

That single syllable was the sound Val hadn't known she'd been waiting for. She lifted the mug to her mouth. The coffee burned her upper lip. By the time it was back down on the counter there were tears in her eyes.

Connie approached slowly, as if afraid of scaring her daughter off, and as soon as she pulled Val into an embrace the silent tears became quiet sobs. Val held her mother tight, and Connie slowly maneuvered them onto the padded bench of the kitchen's bay window.

A few minutes passed. When Val's chest relaxed enough for her to breathe, she said, "I love him."

Her mother sighed and swept Val's hair up from her wet cheeks.

"I love him. I don't know what's wrong with me."

"What's going on?"

Val looked into her mother's eyes. She thought hard about what to say, worked her way through the limitless combinations of words that might describe what she was feeling. But to describe it she would first have to understand it, and that seemed painfully beyond her reach.

"I'm just confused," she said. "We're together all the time. It's what I wanted, or what I thought I wanted, and it's good. I know what to be when I'm around him."

"What do you mean, you know what to be?"

"I mean I can be myself, but it's weird. It's like there's this one version of me that I've been since Henry and I got together. He sees things so clearly, he's always just happy as long as I'm there. That makes me happy too. But then when I'm not there he gets weird and clingy. It's like he just needs me so much and even though that feels good I don't think I need him the same way, and then I just feel wrong, like I'm not the same as him. And then I just feel guilty."

Connie stood and went to the counter. "Do you have to be just like him in order to be with him?" she said. "You left the burner on." She flipped the tiny metal switch on the coffee machine and turned to face Val again. "It sounds unhealthy."

"It's not," said Val. It felt like a lie. Or not a lie, but just too simple of a statement to be fully true. "I just feel like everyone else in the dorms is figuring things out. Everyone's still doing stupid things and acting fake and making new friends and pretending to be cooler than they really are. I don't think I want to be like that, but it's weird. Henry and Gabe and me? We just hang out all the time. We have so much fun, and I'm so relaxed, but I'm not changing, you know? I feel like I should be changing."

"I think you're perfect," said Connie.

Val rolled her eyes and used the bottom of her tank top to wipe away the last of her tears.

"I'm sorry," said Connie, and she smiled. "I know that's not what you want to hear, but I just can't help it."

Val tightened one corner of her mouth into a begrudging grin.

"Why don't you just tell Henry what you need? He'll have to understand."

It was a question Val had been asking herself for a long time. When she was alone, walking to class or going to sleep on one of those rare nights when she wasn't in Henry's bed, she felt her isolation with complete clarity. Henry was an island. As a refuge from everything else, his world was ideal. But to live in it all the time—it was exhausting. What if she didn't need a refuge? What if she didn't want it? She couldn't tell Henry that. She feared it would hurt him too much. And anyway, as soon as she saw him again she'd forget her misgivings and fall back into the comfort of his presence.

And then there was Gabe. She and Henry had always spent a lot of time with him, but once they reached Rutgers he was a permanent third wheel. What bothered Val wasn't his intruding on her alone time with Henry. It was that she found herself wanting him there. He was a buffer against Henry's intensity. She could joke with Gabe. She could tease him. They could play. Gabe brought that out in Henry, too. That couldn't be right, she thought, to need her boyfriend's best friend around in order to stay balanced. More recently, Gabe's presence had another, more disturbing effect. Val saw how he watched Henry's face, how he often waited to see his best friend's reactions before forming and expressing his own. It made her queasy, not least of all because she wondered if she was doing the same thing.

Val couldn't say any of that to her mom. It was just too pathetic. More than that, it would be an admission that everything both of her parents had told her before she left for school was true. They'd warned her about how being in a serious relationship in college might limit her. Val had insisted that she and Henry were the exception to the rule, and to admit now that they were the rule incarnate? It was embarrassing beyond belief.

Val inhaled as if preparing to sigh or moan. But when she breathed out, her mouth formed words as if by its own accord. "I don't think I want to be with him anymore." She looked at her mother to gauge her reaction.

Connie sat back down in the window and leaned against the wall. Her expression was locked in a facsimile of deep concern and sympathy, but Val saw something else there too. The lines around her eyes, her pause, the shape of her pursed lips—it all betrayed a veiled relief. Val would later wonder at how naturally the rest had come. She questioned whether it made her a horrible person. But in that moment, she saw that look of relief as a crack in her mother's carefully constructed wall. She knew instinctively that she could bring the whole thing down with just a few taps of a well-placed chisel.

"That's why I want to leave so badly," said Val. "I just can't stay, Mom. I can't. It's too hard." She cried again. This time it wasn't soft and subtle. Connie sat with her again, rocking her as she gasped and moaned.

Through the rest of winter break and in the weeks that followed it, that painful conversation was repeated. Each time, Val grew more certain that she would have to leave Henry. Each time, Connie grew more supportive. Val didn't fake her pain or her fear. She didn't have to. But managing the timing of her more extreme breakdowns to achieve maximum empathy from her desperate-to-please mother was, in Val's mind, fair game. The key was to draw only one exaggerated comparison between her life with Henry and her possible life at NYU. Connie would no doubt prefer the latter given her view that Val's relationship with Henry was unhealthy. She'd have to accept that staying at Rutgers would make it much harder for Val to move on. So Val applied to a couple of Ivy Leagues she had no business even corresponding with, a few prestigious state schools west of the Mississippi, McGill in Montreal, and NYU. It appeared that she was diversifying, but she knew that NYU would be her parents' only real choice given its proximity to their New Jersey home. They would sacrifice a few thousand dollars if it meant seeing their one and only child more than twice a year.

Val felt a little guilty when the gambit worked, but not so guilty that she couldn't savor the victory.

A month after moving into her new dorm, she was in love. She loved the brownstone buildings in the neighborhood around Washington Square. She loved the dramatic arch that guarded the entrance to the park, how it seemed to reach higher and wider at sunset. She was proud to view herself as an insider among the gawking tourist horde. She loved her new friends, loved the fake ID that she'd gotten on St. Mark's Place and the bars it got her into. She loved that when she sat down in class she wasn't the smartest, most prepared pupil in the room. The drugged-out, catatonic stares she had grown accustomed to in most of her classes at Rutgers were replaced by faces alight with competitive enthusiasm.

Most of all, Val loved the ease with which she could find herself in situations that were completely novel. Even her mismatched suite-mate—a chipper, blond, Utah Mormon—only enhanced Val's image of herself as someone who was living the kind of extraordinary life that New York City was meant to provide. She was *interesting,* and not because she was paired with someone as unusual as Henry.

And as for what she left behind, Val mostly felt relief. In New Brunswick an evening out meant drinking Keystone Light with a bunch of kids from south Jersey and discussing how people from different parts of her home state pronounced words like "water" and "drawer." She didn't miss the ugly highways or the hollow school spirit. She didn't miss being appraised by the pimple-faced meatheads who got stuck with door duty at the frats.

She did miss Henry, though. And she missed Gabe. She wished that her freedom hadn't required her to give them up. But it had. In high school, the choice between Henry and a more open life was simple. There was so little to miss by allowing herself to be consumed by her love for him. But once she was in the larger world, that choice was significantly more complicated. She didn't regret ending it. She couldn't, given what she'd received in return. But in the time since she'd broken up with him in the spring, she had come to regret the way she'd handled the whole thing.

Henry was so rigid. He stayed solid in his belief that they had lucked out to find each other at such a young age. He said that all the exploration most people do, the exploration she claimed to want, was unnecessary for them. They had been chosen for each other by some unseen authority, and she either saw that and loved him and had a responsibility to fight for that love, or she didn't. Val, like always, agreed to Henry's premise but surprised them both by saying that in that case she guessed she didn't love him. He didn't believe her, forced her to enumerate the reasons why, and in a moment of anger and frustration she obliged him. She told Henry he was clingy. That they had both been naive to think that they could last. That she couldn't stomach being the one person on earth who could understand him, that she wanted to have lots of friends, to do all kinds of things that Henry thought were stupid or a waste of time. She said he was fragile and immature, that his tight grip on her and Gabe were signs of his childish fear of exposing himself to the world. Worst of all, she said he was too eccentric for his own good.

In reality, the weaknesses she articulated about Henry were the very things that had made him so easy to hold on to. His need for her taught Val that she was desirable. His obvious joy in her presence made her worth seem palpable and measurable. And as for his eccentricity, unlike every other teenage boy she'd ever met, Henry seemed not to think about the past or the future at all. He didn't posture, he didn't pretend. For him, the present was all-encompassing and overwhelmingly beautiful. Of course that made him strange. Sometimes it was even frightening. But Val respected that part of him. She envied it, even.

So when she asked herself why she'd used all those wonderful things about Henry against him, why she'd turned them into defects that had forced her to abandon him, there was only one answer that made sense. The truth about why she was leaving him would have been even more painful for him to hear. Her world was bigger than him, or at least she wanted it to be. The moment wasn't enough for her.

She ended it in March. The pain lasted long after she was accepted to NYU in May, but it was suffering of the most unremarkable and predictable kind. That was a comfort. Val did homework alone in her dorm at night and drove home every weekend. By the end of the school year, hours would pass when she didn't think of Henry. By the end of the summer it was days. Just before she left for NYU, she understood that she was okay. More than that, she was happy. She arrived in New York, unpacked her things, and cheerfully embarked on the life she'd been dreaming of. And that happiness made her wonder: Maybe all those things she'd said about Henry's neediness and childishness were true. Maybe he was just strange and lonely and would always be so. Maybe her clinging to him and trying so hard to see the world through his eyes was as sad and pathetic as it must have seemed to her mother and the girls she used to call her friends. She *liked* not having to be Polaris in Henry's otherwise darkened sky. She could go in search of her own stars.

But it hadn't turned out to be that simple.

Val really did love NYU, but it was love at a distance. Her new friends, though funny and world-wise and interesting, seemed like set pieces in some strange movie about her life. They gave her places to go, made her feel a part of the marauding group of reckless city kids that they all longed to be. They gave her funny stories about who she was and the kinds of things that she liked to do. But so far Val couldn't quite get those stories to fit her. Despite its downsides, Henry's suffocating reliance on her had been proof that she was someone important. His strange kind of affection, however isolated it had required her to be, had nevertheless given her a place that was uniquely and undeniably *hers*. Now that she had moved on, she felt like she was watching another girl's life unfold from some deep, passive place within her. And though there was nothing inherently wrong with this other person's life, Val longed for her own.

ALLEGRO: GEORGE WASHINGTON

HENRY'S EYES HURT. He rubbed them, but that only sent irritated, burning blood to his swollen eyelids. It made him want to blink the world away.

He was a few hours into his sojourn and he'd been walking nonstop since his escape. He kicked a stone as he went. It hadn't seemed important at first. It was jagged, charcoal-colored, speckled with bits of silvery white. It jumped unpredictably and he was always having to chase it down. But after a few hundred feet, a few dozen kicks up the hill toward the highway, the stone turned dark green and mossy-looking. It rolled more smoothly, then smoother still, until eventually it was a perfect sphere that moved forward before Henry's foot even made contact. It had become Henry's navigator.

Henry thought this was fine. He was glad for a guide that seemed so self-assured.

The stone led him to the base of the George Washington Bridge, then circled the main drag in Fort Lee, New Jersey. None of the banks or bagel places or Korean grocery stores were open yet, but the traffic coming in and out of the city never ceased. He spent an hour just strolling through empty parking lots, kicking weeds that grew up through cracks in the asphalt. Then, at six o'clock, the stone led him back to the bridge. Henry watched a police officer unlock and open the gate to the pedestrian walkway. The cop got back in his car, turned on the lights and sirens—a dramatic touch, thought Henry, and the stone seemed to agree—pulled a U-turn, and sped away. When the car was out of sight, Henry cautiously approached the now opened entryway.

He was the first to walk on the bridge that day. The sky was a calm shade of predawn blue-gray. The palisades towered over the Hudson River to the north and west. To the south and east was the great city, rising colorless and jagged from the water like a splintering mountain. The air was clear enough that Henry thought he could see the Statue of Liberty down at the mouth of the Hudson. The statue waved and her torch sputtered and smoked as the motion of her arm fanned its flame. Henry waved back. Cars passed in the twilight, their rear lights burning purple lines into Henry's retinas, lines that drew fantastic loops and arches, spelled out unspeakable truths that were just barely readable before they faded back into oblivion. It was a beautiful morning, Henry decided. Val was, perhaps, waking up. She would see the day and she would *know*, even if she couldn't quite understand, that it was special. That he was coming.

Henry grinned and inhaled deeply. The stone led him to the first great tower of the steel giant he stood upon, but then jumped ahead too eagerly and slipped underneath the guardrail. Henry watched it fall, as silent and slow as a feather, to the water below, where it broke the surface and sent multicolored circles rippling out and out from the point of impact. Henry shrugged, furrowed his brow, and considered whether the stone wanted him to follow it. He felt less sure of himself than he had just a moment before. Could he really be expected to jump? Perhaps, he decided, the stone's only goal was to lead him to this tower. He would have to find another guide.

He heard a long, far-off sound. It was ghostly, almost not there at all, and yet still somehow lush and full. He turned his head, searching for the source, then rested his forearms on the railing and closed his eyes to better focus.

His arms felt the noise too, and Henry understood: the sound was the bridge itself, vibrating in the gentle wind coming down the river. He was standing on a massive harp complete with hundreds of woven steel strings, and the wind was running across it like a bow. Henry smiled. It was a sign, he thought. The bridge was his guide now, and it was singing to him.

He kept walking. The thickly twisted ropes of steel, the surface on which he stood, the long sloping cables above him—each part of the bridge resonated with his every footfall, and those resonances combined to form a song. Joyful now, he began first to jog, then to sprint. The faster his feet landed on the walkway, the faster the music got. The faster the music got, the happier Henry became and the faster he ran. When he finally reached top speed, it felt as though the bridge was a massive orchestra and Henry's feet were the conductor. It had just been warming up before, but now it was playing a fugue so loud and haunting that he could no longer hear anything else. It was frightening and aggressive but breathtakingly powerful. Henry had never heard anything so incredible in his life. The song obscured the pain of his burning chest. It cleansed the spit flying from his mouth and buttressed his legs though they threatened to give out beneath him. It emptied his mind of everything but a single question: *Why hasn't anyone tried playing this bridge before? How long has it been waiting for me?*

Still running, he was almost at the second tower when a new noise disrupted the fugue. It sounded like the buzz of a mosquito and it went from mezzo piano to fortissimo in just a couple bars, nearly drowning out the bridge song completely. Henry tried to push himself harder to save the melody of a moment before, but his thighs were overworked. He collapsed forward and lay on the cement. The music was still there, but faintly, as if from a great distance. Henry's focus was now drawn to this new blast of sound, so strong that he was afraid of being torn apart. He saw the air ripple where the towers met the sky and knew that the bridge was singing by itself now. He'd awakened it and it was angry and would destroy the very atmosphere itself if Henry didn't find some way to stop it.

He panicked and got to his feet. When he was able to walk again, the repetitive melodies of the bridge song continued. The notes he chimed with his sneakers now mixed with the towers' sustain in a perfect harmony. Soon the harmony was no longer simply audible. It extended over everything around him. The early -morning sky, the purple headlight afterimage of the cars as they passed, the waving torch of the statue, the rainbow circles on the surface of the water, the sinking of the stone, Val in her apartment, the bright green spastic low vibration—they all merged and the whole world was singing-glowing and humming-looping and the joy and terror Henry felt were complete and total and utterly essential to his being and he felt sure that if they went away he would die. He let go. The boundaries of his body felt obviously, inevitably meaningless, and he opened his mouth to scream but his voice was lost amid the din.

He was all sound.

He was pure light.

And then it stopped.

The change was immediate. One moment a bright cacophony, the next dark silence.

He was comfortably cool. He lay on his back, though he didn't remember falling. The surface beneath him was soft, and his head was propped on a pillow. His throat hurt. He opened his eyes as wide as he could, hoping to gather enough ambient light to make sense of his surroundings, but it was useless. *Where am I?* The question left his mind as quickly as it had entered. There was something more important to consider, something much more pressing that would not be ignored. Though he didn't know how he had ended up in a strange bed in a pitch-black room in an unknown location, his world was more intact than it had been in months. There were no voices. There was no green light. It all seemed like nothing more than a particularly vivid nightmare. His body felt like it belonged to him and him to it, and it responded to his commands effortlessly as he stretched and curled his fingers and toes.

I'm Henry, he thought. *I'm sane.*

The tears started hot, dripped down his cheeks cold, and pooled on his neck and in his ears as he gazed up into the blackness. Suddenly the wall next to his body buzzed with the low baritone of a man's voice coming from the other side.

"I think he's awake," said the voice. Then, louder, "I'm pretty sure of it." The voice was familiar, though Henry could not immediately place it. It sounded ugly, but not in any obvious way. He simply didn't like it. It was wrong.

"Yes," said another voice. It sounded older, quieter. It was hard to understand what came after. All Henry could hear were hard consonants divorced from their context.

The louder voice returned. "We should go see, don't you think?"

Henry sat up, his ears straining so acutely that they actually moved, his lobes craning involuntarily like little satellites. He was confused but not afraid. It occurred to him that maybe he was dead, but this didn't particularly bother him. He was sane again, and nothing could be worse than the hell he had escaped. He giggled nervously.

There was more mumbling through the wall. Then he heard a loud screeching, like the moving of heavy furniture. Footsteps approached, then silence. A few moments later, Henry heard a small mechanical chink, and the outline of a doorway was painted in light somewhere off to his right. There was a knock, soft and sensitive, like the knock his mother would use to wake him up when he was a kid. It betrayed a reluctance to disturb, and it put Henry at ease. He did not feel threatened, merely curious.

"Henry? I won't hurt you. You have to trust me," said the older, quieter voice. "I want you to close your eyes until I say. Are they closed?"

Henry nodded in the affirmative with his wide-open eyes fixed on the spot where he supposed the doorknob to be. It glinted as the door opened further. The light coming in painted a triangle on the floor. His eyes adjusted and the figures that entered the room became clearer. Henry recognized them though he'd never seen them before, and the recognition forced an otherworldly sound from his throat. When all his air was gone he gagged, vomited, and passed out.

THE DISAPPEARANCE

IT WAS ALMOST spring break, though spring never came to New Jersey in mid-March. The last pebble-studded mounds of snow still stubbornly blocked sidewalks and narrowed roads. Henry was worse every day, but Gabe had not yet given up hope. He brought extra slices from Tata's and left them in Henry's room. He ignored the deep, dark smell that effervesced from the damp armpits of Henry's sweatshirt. He got used to starting conversations that were destined to be aborted, making jokes that were ignored.

Gabe had considered relocating to some Floridian beach party for the one-week vacation, but he never would have done that even if his best friend weren't coming apart before his eyes. Staying in town would give him the chance to work extra hours at the Magic Dragon. Though it was technically a tobacconist, most people in New Brunswick thought of the Dragon as a head shop—a store that sold glass pipes to potheads or worse. To the cops and lawyers who worked downtown, the Dragon was a decent if eccentric cigar shop. They came in to buy Dominican Cohibas and rag on Gabe when they wanted a laugh. It made him feel like a zoo animal: North American bearded pothead. To them, he was a walking joke, the living personification of the college burnout stereotype. The pay was good, though, and the work was easy, so he continued to show up despite his misgivings.

The Wednesday before break began Henry had a rare moment of lucidity and mumbled something about going home, so when Friday evening arrived Gabe came home from work and, not wanting to confront the stranger his best friend had become, went to his bedroom and closed the door. He ignored hunger and thirst, opting instead for periodic tokes from his one-hitter and a handful of cigarettes smoked out the window. When he had to pee, he held it until it burned with vicious urgency, then tiptoed to the bathroom as quietly as he could. He needn't have worried. Henry didn't leave his bedroom either. Gabe watched cartoons on his computer until his eyes began to close, then crept into bed slowly, as if not wanting to wake himself. He slid comfortably into sleep.

In a dream, he saw Val. She looked young, the way Gabe remembered her from when they'd first met. Silver clips pinned her bangs up and away from her forehead, and she was on the couch in her parents' living room, staring at a television. The living room was a forest. There were no tree trunks, but a canopy of leaves hung overhead, and it felt vast, as if beyond what Gabe could see there was an endless expanse of dense woodland in every direction.

Henry sat next to Val on the couch. He smiled and played with the zipper of his hoodie while humming a tune. Gabe recognized it. He looked away and saw that Henry was then in another chair, on the other side of the room—the recliner that Gabe himself had just been sitting in. A lovely warmth spread up from Gabe's own palm, and he looked to his right to find Val next to him on the couch. She held his hand and laughed. She was teasing him about something, and he laughed too.

Leaves fell from above, a peaceful green snow of big flakes, alive with light. Val let go of Gabe's hand to catch one right in front of her face. She brought it to her mouth and bit into it, then laughed as she chewed.

The television was gone. No more couches. Gabe and Val stood on a footbridge that crossed the stream in the nature center at the edge of their hometown. Henry was crossing the water below them. In reality the bridge was just a few feet off the ground, but as Gabe looked down he saw that Henry was far away; his tiny form kicked at the water with bare feet, and the splash they produced repeated and folded on itself in dense waves. Val was in the water too. She was naked. Henry reached out to her, and then Gabe's own hand was suddenly on her face. His feet were in the water. It was icy cold and moving fast. He felt Val touching him and he was afraid that he was going to lose control, and though he wanted to, he knew it was the *one thing he must not do.* The splashing grew louder as leaves fell fast like rain. They caressed Gabe's skin, licked and stroked him, and he felt a full-body pleasure that was all-encompassing and without precedent. Gabe knew he would give in and release unless he did something, so he lifted his hands to protect his head and he ran. He looked back to beckon Val to follow him, but the figure that was once her turned around as Henry. He was naked and crying and rocking and singing full-throated at the sky. The leaves came down harder, as thick sheets of water. Gabe looked up and his body locked. His mouth was open, he couldn't close it, and the rushing leaves filled his lungs.

He couldn't breathe.

He ran.

But he was locked in place.

And he ran.

He couldn't breathe. Or he could but the air did nothing.

The sound of the water was everything, so incredibly loud.

Gabe awoke in the dark, still hearing it. Even as he opened his eyes, the loud rush of liquid static echoed in his ears. As his senses returned to him he had the instant and unmistakable feeling that he was not alone. He heard the sound of measured breathing and the shifting of cloth. He opened his eyes wide and saw a dark silhouette of Henry's hair cast like a shadow against the wall on the other side of the room. He was sitting on the floor. The light from the streetlights outside was just bright enough that Gabe could faintly see his friend's open eyes.

"Yo," said Gabe. The word elongated into a sigh.

Henry's breathing stopped for a moment, then started again, softer than before.

"What the fuck, Henry? What are you doing?"

Henry's voice, when it came out, was unguarded and calm. It was a voice Gabe hadn't heard in weeks. "Can I just stay in here?" he asked. "Please?"

Though there was nothing outwardly threatening about the situation, Gabe felt panicked. He felt as if he was in the presence of a dangerous stranger. A diorama of sick fantasies flooded his imagination: Henry caving in his skull as he slept, his hands sticky with blood and gray meat, Henry throttling him while laughing and crying and screaming. Gabe imagined darkness descending over his own open eyes followed quickly by resignation and sad unconsciousness. Then he imagined fighting back, bludgeoning and cutting and tearing his way free, but that was even worse.

Minutes passed without another word. Gabe lay with his eyes open. He hated himself for fearing Henry, but he also hated Henry for being so fucking scary. With each breath he took, Gabe's heart beat slower. He felt the tension leave him in a wave that moved down his body, relaxing each muscle and joint it swept over. Henry wouldn't hurt him. He knew that.

"You can stay in here," he said, and he rolled to face the wall. "Just go to sleep."

Gabe didn't dream any more that night, and when he awoke to the light of mid-morning, he was relieved to be alone.

Spring break came and went, but Henry just went. His phone went straight to voice mail, and if he was checking his email he didn't respond. Gabe dreaded going through Henry's mom to get information, but there was no one else. It was a lonely Sunday in early April when he finally gave in. He found Jan's name in his contacts list and spent a minute with his thumb hovering over her phone number before pressing down.

Four rings, no response.

The result was the same the next day and each day for a week after that. Henry might have a good excuse for not returning phone calls, but Jan's silence was puzzling. She seemed to be saying something with her silence. Whatever it was, Gabe didn't think he wanted to hear it.

With little else to occupy his thoughts, Gabe brooded. He imagined Jan in her big, beautifully decorated kitchen. A skylight in the slanted roof illuminated an old-fashioned wooden table and benches. A big window above the sink looked out onto the wooded backyard. Jan used to wait up for Henry and Gabe in that kitchen when they were in high school. Not to see if they were slurring their words or if their breath smelled like cigarettes, but because she was curious. She wanted to make sure that if they were hungry there was food to eat, that she got to talk to them before they went to sleep. She wanted to *know* them. They'd appear at one in the morning after an Upstart show, their skin salty with dried sweat, ears still ringing. Jan would have a pan heating on the stovetop before they walked in the door. She'd make them quesadillas or eggs or a big bowl filled with "leftover" salad that couldn't have been more than half an hour old.

She always had questions for Gabe. She made him feel important and interesting in an adult way, a way he never got to feel with his own parents. Her lack of response to his increasingly pleading voice mails said that Henry was gone. More than that, it said that he wasn't coming back, and that maybe it was Gabe's fault.

May arrived and brought with it the choking smell of sun-warmed garbage and the buzzing of bass lines from open car windows. Gabe felt like the whole campus had sex playing in the background. So far he'd been generally unlucky with girls at Rutgers, but sometimes, at the very beginning of summer, when the first short cotton dresses of the season appeared as if in answer to some desperate hormonal prayer, it was enough just to look.

Cal was the perfect replacement roommate for Henry, mostly because he invited no comparisons with Gabe's lost friend. He was stubborn and opinionated, an unabashed and self-proclaimed contrarian who started arguments just for the fun of it. Gabe had met him in the dorms their freshman year, and always thought him too interesting to dislike despite his sometimes combative attitude. When Gabe learned that Cal was couch-hopping after having been kicked out of the house he'd been living in, it seemed like a happy bit of serendipity. They smoked pot and played music and talked politics and philosophy. With Cal, there was no need to dive into the muck of feelings and insecurities. Most of the time that was exactly what Gabe needed.

It was the warmest day of the year. To celebrate, Gabe and Cal shared a joint over their respective breakfasts—Doritos for Gabe and a handful of granola for Cal. Gabe took his guitar out to the porch. With bare feet resting on the wrought-iron railing in front of him, he plucked a melody out into the neighborhood. He liked how his music mixed with insect noises and traffic.

He heard the light shuffling of feet on the steps to the house and looked up. It took him a long beat to recognize that the thin bearded face he was seeing was Henry's. When he did recognize his friend, there was no relief or joy, no fear or anger. All the emotions that had accompanied his long wait for that moment were strangely missing. Instead, he felt a quiet sort of curiosity. He smiled and Henry smiled back, but it didn't look right. His lips disappeared in a line of tightly crimped white.

Cal came out through the open front door. "Hey, man," he said, his voice taking on the timbre of a kindergarten teacher.

Henry didn't answer.

Cal took a swig from his water bottle, then wiped his mouth with the back of his wrist and stared.

Henry stood still. "I need to get some things," he said. "My mom wants me to be at home." He walked past Cal and into the house. The sound of his feet on the stairs sounded impossibly quiet, as if he weren't substantial enough to make the wood whine and squeak as it did for everyone else.

Cal looked at Gabe, his mouth open with amused disbelief. But then he saw that Jan was walking toward the house and he spun around on his bare left heel and quickly stepped back inside.

Jan looked older than Gabe remembered. Her silvering hair shone as she leaned heavily on the splintered railing and climbed up the steps. Gabe was happy to see her, but he felt ashamed, too. He wasn't sure why. He tried to pin it on the pot, but that didn't feel right. This particular shame was too deep and hot to be the result of standard chemical paranoia. For weeks he'd wanted to talk to her, but now that she was in front of him Gabe just wanted her to go away.

Once on the porch, Jan made no attempt to get closer to Gabe. There would be no hug, no cheerful hello. Gabe could feel the depth and purpose of her gaze. He busied himself with leaning the guitar against the railing, shifting his chair back, scratching his upper arm—anything to keep his body focused on a discrete task.

"You should have said something," she said.

The words tore at a vital part of Gabe somewhere deep in his gut. He felt a surge of nauseous adrenaline flit from his scalp to his fingertips. She sounded more sad than angry, but the edge in her voice was unmistakable.

"He's going to live at home now?" It was all he could think to say.

"Yes," she said, and she breathed in so deeply that Gabe could hear the air cascade over her teeth and down her throat. "Henry's staying at home." She stepped closer, sat down on one of the canvas camping chairs that furnished the ash-covered porch, and squinted into the early-afternoon sun. "You really should have just called me, Gabe. Before it got as far as it did."

The words made Gabe feel something unexpected. It was the distinct desire to hurt her. He kept his mouth shut.

"Gabe," she said. "Why didn't you say something?"

He let the silence of his tree-lined block make its presence known, but despite his anger he knew she wasn't being rhetorical. He wanted to give her an answer. "I don't know," he said. It felt like the truth.

"Henry told me that you guys have been smoking pot together."

"Was that a question?"

"I don't care what you do, Gabe, I really don't. I smoked pot when I was a kid."

Gabe saw her turn toward him, but he didn't look back at her.

"Something happened to Henry," she said. "Something must have started all of this."

Gabe stared at the house across the street, examined the peeling tar and roof shingles, the light green mold on the siding, the dislocated gutter.

"There must have been something that set him off," she said. "You need to tell me whatever you know, right now. I need to know whatever it was that started him off like this, so I can tell his doctors. They said it could affect his treatment."

"Nothing happened," he said. He turned, looked her in the eye. "He's been smoking pot. Nothing else."

"Something had to have happened," she said.

Gabe knew she believed that, and it made him sorry for her.

"Henry was always really happy. He's so talented and kind and smart. There has to be a reason for this. You were living with him. You've got to know something."

Gabe didn't answer, and this time Jan was the one to look away. It felt like a victory.

"He just started acting weird one day. That's it," said Gabe. He wanted to tell her that Henry had always been sort of lost in his own head, that he spent ten hours a day hitting blocks of wood with padded mallets. He wanted to tell her that Henry had been different since Val left, that he was lonely and always had been, regardless of what he'd led his own mother to believe.

But he knew he'd regret all that, even if it was the truth. So he lied. "He was stressed out, I guess. I've been trying to come up with an explanation too, but you have to know that I would tell you if there was something I knew about, something that I thought made sense."

"Some people can do drugs and be okay. Some people can't."

"I suppose that's true, Jan," he said. "But it's totally irrelevant."

"I'm not blaming you," she said, her voice softening. "Is there anything else in this house? Anything that he might have taken without you? I just need to know every possibility. I won't tell anyone what you've done."

"What I've *done?*"

"That's not how I meant it, Gabe." She sounded more desperate with each word. "Please," she said, "if you told me, I could tell his doctor. It could help."

"You're not listening to me." He would have gone on, but he heard someone approaching from inside. Henry appeared. In his arms was a plastic laundry bin piled with clothes, books, a couple of posters. He stepped down to the sidewalk and meandered off. Gabe waited until he was out of earshot. "There are all kinds of things around here, but if you're asking if it's possible that he did some drugs without me, I've already told you no."

"Please don't act like I'm attacking you."

"I'm not *acting* like anything."

"Stop!" she said. "Please listen. You can't imagine what this is like for me, so stop acting like a child and answer the question. Were there any other drugs he had access to? Anything else he could have done?"

"Between the people we know—friends of friends, neighbors, people at parties—there's no limit to what he *could* have done, hypothetically." There was momentum to his rage now. If she wanted to blame him, he would be impervious to blame. "If he were really on a mission he could have found weed, coke, heroin, mushrooms, ecstasy, acid, opium, crack—he could have found anything, whatever he wanted, within five minutes of here."

She was crying, he saw. It was a low blow, he thought, but it still compelled him to back off. "When he wasn't at class he was home, and when he was at home he was with me. I never did any of those things with him. He didn't just trip on acid and not come down. I wish it were that simple."

Tears gathered underneath Jan's chin. Gabe wanted to touch her. It felt like the right thing to do. But then she said, "Just tell me, Gabe. Just tell me what happened," and his pity turned to dust.

Gabe dropped his head and stared at a spot of dirt on the blue-painted two-by-fours beneath his feet. The pot was making everything too bright and small, like the whole world had shifted into miniature. He felt stupid for being high.

Jan sniffled.

When Gabe looked up again, Henry was on the sidewalk in front of the house.

"Do you need any help?" said Gabe.

Henry said nothing. He rocked on the balls of his feet, zipping and unzipping the front of his sweatshirt.

Gabe stood up, brushed past Jan's knees, and went inside. It took his eyes a minute to adjust, everything bright green and vibrating from the sunlight, but he knew the stairs by heart and found his way up to Henry's room. He figured Henry would come back up to get some more things, that they'd have a few minutes to talk.

Gabe stared at the index cards that were still piled high on Henry's desk. He had to prepare. He didn't want to hear himself speak the way Cal had. He would have to fight to act like he always did, even if Henry couldn't do the same.

A few minutes later Cal walked in and said, "They're gone."

SONATA: THE WHITE ROOM

HENRY CRACKED OPEN his sleep-swollen eyelids and saw the same deep darkness as before. His body was awake but his mind was still in transition. It was a feeling he recognized but hadn't experienced since before his break. He stretched. Yawned with satisfaction and pressed his face to the pillow. It felt incomprehensibly good.

His awakening had interrupted a dream—one that didn't end in his evisceration or involve the green light or beads of blood condensing on the walls or pigeons pecking at the backs of his knees. The memory of it was already fading, but Henry knew he had been in a ravine. Sunlight warmed his skin. Above him, the high branches of trees swayed in a breeze. He heard water, so peaceful, and he wanted to go back so he focused on the slippery half-remembrance, tried to feel the comfort of the sun and see the vivid green of the leaves.

There was a knock at the door.

"Henry, I'm coming in," said a voice.

The older one, thought Henry. His skin tightened over his body like the head of a drum. He sat up, drew a pillow to his chest, and pushed himself back into the corner at the top of the bed. The recollection of what he'd seen in his last waking moment hit him like an icy wave. Henry hadn't recognized the older one, though there was something familiar about him, but the image of the younger one, the one that looked like—

"Did you hear me?" said the voice. "I'm going to come in now. Don't be afraid."

Henry considered whether he should hide, run, or stand up and fight, but despite himself he whispered, "Okay."

The door opened quickly. This time the man flipped a switch and Henry was briefly blinded. As his eyes adjusted, he found that he was in a small room with white walls and a beige plush carpet. All of the furniture looked brand-new, and Henry had the impression that nothing he was seeing had ever really belonged to anyone. It looked like an Ikea showroom, as if the only thing missing was a giant price tag. The man in front of him was old, maybe seventy-five—the same man who had entered the room before. He wore dark blue slacks with a thick cardigan. He had thick hair, nearly white with just a touch of brown left to tint it. The smile he wore was genuine and unthreatening, but still Henry was wary.

"What?" said Henry—a challenge, not a question.

"What, what?" said the man. He chuckled softly.

"What's so funny?"

"It's not a matter of being funny," said the man. "It's just—here we are. I'll never get used to it. You'll see what I mean someday."

Henry didn't know what to say, so he hugged the pillow tighter and clenched his jaw.

"Relax," said the man. Sympathy beamed down from his deep-set eyes. He stepped toward the bed and Henry tensed. "You look like you're ready to launch yourself off that bed and throttle me. But you won't do that."

"Where am I?" said Henry. "I was on the GW, I heard this music, and then—" But there was nothing more to say.

The old man reached a stool in front of a desk and took a seat, crossed one leg on top of the other. "I'll tell you in a minute, but you should come out of this room. We blacked out the windows to help you sleep, but it's a beautiful day outside. You'll want to see it." There was a reassuring worldliness to the man, a warm edge to his voice.

"Why am I here? Is this a hospital?" Henry's voice wavered. "What do you want?"

"I suppose I want you to forget everything you've ever believed. And I want you to stop acting like a cornered cat. I had half a day in which to harm you while you were asleep and yet here you are, alive and awake. Just relax already." The man uncrossed his legs and straightened his knee, stretched it with a wince. Even as he grimaced he never broke eye contact with Henry. "Your first question is much more interesting. *Why am I here?* One for the ages."

Henry leaned his head back against the wall, looked at the ceiling. "That's not really what I meant," he muttered to himself.

"To put it simply," the old man continued, "you're here because you have to be. Would you rather be back on the bridge? Running from some bright green vibration?"

Those words were a hammer, obliterating every thought in Henry's head save one. "How did you know about that?" he said.

The old man put one hand in his pocket and picked some lint off his sweater with the other. "I know more about you than you know about yourself," he said. "And if you'll let me, I'd like to start exploring the hows and whys of what you're doing in that bed. Unless you'd rather just stay there for the rest of your life?"

It stung Henry's pride to admit it, but the old man had his attention. "Am I...if I come with you, will I still be thinking like this? Feeling like this?"

"You mean will you still be sane?" The old man chewed his lip, gathering his thoughts. "Things will always be a bit difficult for you. I wish that weren't the truth. But you'll get through. And you're better off right now than you've been in months."

The man's evasions were only slightly less comforting than his assurances, but it made no difference whether Henry trusted him or not. His only real choice was to face the strangeness that awaited him, to do his best to figure out what was going on. He put down the pillow he'd been clutching and pushed the bedsheets from his legs. His clothes had been changed. In place of the jeans and sweatshirt he'd been wearing on the bridge, he was now dressed in simple cotton pajama bottoms and an extra-large T-shirt that dwarfed him. He shifted to the edge of the bed, put his feet to the soft plush carpet, and stood.

The man smirked, stood up, and turned to walk out the door. "Call me 80," he said.

"Like the number?" said Henry.

"Precisely."

RINGTONE

VAL AWOKE IN the dark, dimly aware of the sound that had interrupted her sleep. In the first timeless moment after coming to, she just listened. It was a bouncy jingle, one she knew by heart though she couldn't remember why.

She rolled onto her back as the short verse played, her eyes closing despite her insistence that they remain open.

The verse ended, and she understood. It was her cell phone. But that wasn't her ringer, or maybe it had been, but wasn't anymore? But she hadn't changed it since her parents bought her that phone when she first left for college almost two years before. She awoke a bit more and remembered. It was her ringtone for Henry. The one that played only when he called her. When they were together it had played all the time, but it had been so long that she'd nearly forgotten about it.

The song began again. Val felt like she'd been hearing it for minutes and wondered at how the phone could have continued ringing for so long, but then she recognized that elapse as an illusion, the result of her sleeping mind's strange understanding of time. She pushed herself toward the edge of the bed and let her hand drop to the ground. She groped in the dark until her fingers found the wire of the charger, then pulled until she could grab the phone itself. She lay back.

She and Henry hadn't spoken since shortly after the breakup. When she was still at Rutgers they saw each other around, but beyond brief moments of eye contact and mute recognition, they didn't communicate. Henry didn't call her. At first she had been hurt by his apparent lack of interest in talking to her, but as time passed she saw it as a mercy. Unlike so many other couples she'd known, their breakup would be without the long tail of confusion and false hope.

The fact that Henry was calling her at—*what time was it?* Val looked at the screen of the phone as it began its third verse, her pupils painfully dilating in its bright glow. Two forty-five—if Henry was calling her that late, it must be important. She cycled through all that might have gone wrong. Had someone died? Was he in trouble? She felt a funny little thrill thinking about the possibilities and wondered why that should be.

"Hello?" she said.

"Val," said Henry. He laughed. "Vaaaaal." His tone was playful. Not bad news then.

"Henry? What's—what's happening?"

"What's happening, my man!" he said, and he laughed again. It wasn't a laugh she fully recognized. It seemed too joyful and uninhibited to belong to the reserved boy she used to love.

"Henry, seriously. Is something wrong? It's—why are you calling me so late? I was sleeping."

"Oh?" he said. "It's Henry."

"I know."

"I just—um—how are you?" His words sounded forced.

She sighed. "I'm fine, I guess. I'm tired. It's the middle of the night. How are you?" She spoke slowly, her displeasure infecting each word.

"Good," he said.

Val waited in silence so long that she nearly fell back asleep. "Henry?"

"I'm awake," he said.

Val laughed and shook her head in the dark. "I know you're awake, but I'm not. I mean, I wasn't. What are you doing up? You sound weird."

"I'm thinking about you," he said.

Val wished that it didn't feel good to hear that, and it occurred to her to say that she was thinking about him too. But she wasn't. Or she tried not to. It had been more than a year since they broke up. So much time had passed that she'd almost stopped thinking of him as a living person, an entity that existed outside of her memory. But on the phone was the real Henry, the one still walking around Rutgers and playing percussion and hanging out with Gabe and seeing strange significance in the mundane.

"It's been a long time," she said.

Henry cleared his throat and hummed softly.

"Are you drunk?"

Henry laughed again, then stopped abruptly. "I said I'm thinking about you." The joy she'd heard in his voice was gone. He spoke louder, and an edge that Val had never heard before was creeping in.

"You're drunk," she said. "God. Henry. Please, just do yourself a favor and hang up. Tomorrow, if you still want to talk, call me. I wouldn't mind catching up, but it's late and you don't sound like yourself."

"Do myself a favor?" said Henry. He giggled and hummed, and the music of it irritated Val's tired ears. "I'm doing…myself…a favor."

"Henry, I'm hanging up."

"I look at your pictures online."

"Jesus, Henry. Don't do this."

"You have hot friends." He laughed again, mocking and cruel. "I look at them and I do myself a favor."

"I'm hanging up," she said, but she didn't. She waited until his laughter had stopped and hoped that the threat would be enough to get through to him. She just said, "Henry?"

"You left," he said. "You fucking left."

"It's been a year."

"A year?" he said. "You should have come back. There were things I was supposed to show you, things that only you could understand. I thought you were coming back."

"Why did you think that?" she said, and she really wanted to know.

"But now you're evil. You're with *them*. You're an evil cunt."

The word exploded into Val's consciousness and left her feeling physically stunned, as if she'd fallen on her back from some great height. "I'm not doing this," she said.

"Doing what? Doing what? What the fuck aren't you doing besides seeing me or talking to me? Is this what a friend does? Is this what you do? I do? I do I do I do." His voice rose into a distorted song, those two syllables repeating over and over until he ran out of breath. Val lifted the phone away from her ear and winced.

Henry laughed again. "I see you."

"I'm not doing this," she yelled back now. "Call me back when you're not acting like such a fucking lunatic!"

She ended the call and threw her phone down, but instead of landing next to her on the bed it bounced up and crashed to the floor.

Who was that? she thought.

She sat up and threw her feet over the side of the bed, then jerked herself upright and stomped her way toward the door, where she slammed her fist so hard against the light switch that it hurt. The room filled with light. She had to get on her hands and knees in order to find her phone, which had slid beneath the old radiator by the window. She logged in to Facebook and searched for Henry's name. His picture flashed in front of her eyes in the few seconds it took her to find the setting that would allow her to remove him from her list of friends. He looked different from how she remembered him. It reminded her that without meaning to she had been picturing him making the call from his and Gabe's freshman-year dorm room. She could see the walls, the big windows tinted with scum from the car exhaust coming off Route Eighteen. But he probably didn't even live in that room anymore. That made her angry too.

She put the phone back on the floor by her bed, then lifted the blinds and looked out at the small wedge of skyline that she'd memorized since moving in the previous fall. A few spires appeared from down in the financial district, but the view was dominated by the big apartment building across the street from her own. Most of the windows were dark. A few glowed intermittently, painted by the shifting rays of television screens. Even fewer were bright, their occupants busy with the business of being alive despite the hour. She stood and stared, waiting for the big black bubble of violence in her chest to dissolve into her bloodstream.

She replayed the phone call in her mind but didn't even make it to the painful parts that came after she'd answered. Instead, she focused on the way she'd felt when she first heard the ringtone, how it had stirred something in her. Longing? Hope? Neither seemed quite right, but whatever the feeling was, it came back to her now as she looked out her window. She let it blossom inside her and it turned into a fantasy.

Henry would call back the next day. She felt sure of that. He would have to. And after he apologized, they would talk. About what she wasn't sure, but she wanted it to lead to more. She allowed herself the brief glimpse of what the future might look like if Henry's hurtful, misguided plea for attention actually led to a rekindling of their connection. She walked to the light switch and pressed it softly with her finger, then sat down on her bed and once again gazed out the window. She wondered who was up and why. The strangers in their homes had lives like hers, she supposed. They had thoughts and feelings that, from their perspective, took up all the space that the world had to offer. Maybe they were all happy. They would have to be, she thought, if they were living in this neighborhood. They were older and more mature. They were rich. Their relationships were set and comfortably worn in. The youthful heartache, the melancholy and dissatisfaction—it was well behind them.

That idea didn't erase the hurt of the conversation Val had just endured, but it did make her feel less alone. She lay down again and tried to sleep.

ADAGIO: VERTIGO

THE DOOR TO the bedroom Henry woke up in was one of three in a hallway. He saw the other two to his left when he stepped out. 80 led him to the right.

"Look around," said 80.

Henry followed him into a kitchen lined with unremarkable wood cabinets. It smelled of fruit peelings and stale spices. He was relieved to confirm that he was not in a hospital. 80 sat down at a small table at the back of the kitchen. There was a seam for a leaf, but the room didn't seem big enough to accommodate it. 80 tinkered with some crumbs that had been left on the dark wood surface.

There was a small window over the sink and two larger ones behind the chair in which the old man sat. They looked out onto a bright day, supernaturally green, as if the grass and the leaves of the deciduous trees outside had soaked up their fill of the sun and were radiating it back up into the sky. Henry walked back toward the room he woke up in. Stepping left immediately after exiting the kitchen, he found himself in a simply furnished living room. There was a blue couch with a fine white diamond pattern, a worn-looking armchair, and a wooden coffee table on which sat two empty mugs.

It was quiet inside the house. From outside came the endless rolling sound of birds. It would peak as some unseen excitement caused a swell in the tittering, then decrescendo for a few seconds before rising again. Through the big bay window behind the couch Henry could see a lawn rolling down a short hill, ending abruptly at a dense wall of forest. All the way to the right of the window was a door that opened inward onto a slate-paved entryway and a staircase leading up. There were empty coat hooks on the wall and a shoe rack on the floor. The door was open and through the screen came the scent of honeysuckle mixed with something rotten and sickly-sweet that was not entirely unpleasant.

Henry stepped to the couch and turned around to sit down. On the wall in front of him were two large rectangles of lighter white on a background of dingy eggshell. 80 walked in from the kitchen with a plate of crackers, set them on the table, and sat down in the armchair to Henry's right.

"Where did the pictures go?" asked Henry.

"Previous owners. I've always felt I should put something else up there but I'm not sure what."

"That room I just came out of, it's weird," said Henry. "It doesn't fit with this house."

80 nodded.

"I thought I was in a mental hospital."

"Until you got here, we didn't know what kind of state you were going to be in. We had to make preparations. We knew you were sick." 80 waved a hand in the air as if in apology. "The moment I saw you I knew you wouldn't be any trouble, but we couldn't have known that before. Not for sure. Usually, what you went through—the music on the bridge—usually it sets you straight for a while. But we didn't really know."

Henry was famished. He grabbed three crackers from the plate and bit into all of them at the same time. It felt strange to eat crackers in someone else's oversized pajamas. He felt like a child. "This house is old," he said. "It feels familiar. Where are we?"

80 opened his mouth to speak, but the sound of a door opening upstairs interrupted him. There were footsteps and the sound of another door closing. Water ran through the pipes, a hollow sloshing that Henry found comforting. "Who's that?" he said.

"Do you remember vacationing in the Catskills when you were younger? There was a small cabin, a bit dingy—a diner downtown where your mom would buy you pancakes?"

Henry tried not to let the shock register on his face.

"That cabin," said 80, grabbing another cracker for himself, "is about fifteen miles from here. The diner is close by too, down in town. Unfortunately we won't be going there."

"No pancakes?" said Henry. "Why didn't you just say 'We're in the Catskills'?"

"We're in the Catskills," said 80.

"Where are my clothes?"

A door opened upstairs. Muted footsteps approached the top of the staircase and descended. Before Henry saw the man walking down the steps he heard his voice. "You puked all over yourself. Where do you think they are?" A pair of feet appeared first. Then a hand came into view. It held a pair of shoes, a sock hanging out from inside each one.

Henry blanched when the man's head appeared. Now, in the light of day, it was more obvious but somehow less frightening. The man looked like Henry to an astonishing degree, except older. There was gray in his big, bushy beard, and he had hair past his shoulders. His voice was darker and fuller, but undoubtedly Henry's own. Perhaps strangest were the man's hands. Henry recognized everything: the proportion of fingernail to finger, joint to joint; the dried, split cuticles aggravated by years of nail biting; the way the first knuckle of the right pinkie was raised up and oddly angled after a teenage break that he'd never had treated.

"Your clothes are in the wash, in the basement," said the man. "Nobody is trying to make you feel like a child. What you're wearing is just all we had. Keep thinking that way, though. Ask questions. Be paranoid." He leaned over to bring his face closer to Henry's, an aggressive look in his eye. "It'll make it harder for the old man to fuck with your head."

The man sat down on the coffee table, his back turned to both Henry and 80. He got his socks and shoes on quickly, then stood and turned around.

"Look at me," said the man.

"I am."

"Don't believe anything this man tells you."

Henry followed the man's pointing finger until he was looking at 80, who smiled in the way a parent of a misbehaving child might smile at his dinner guests. It was an embarrassed apology, but not for himself.

"You heard me, right?" said the bearded man. "Don't trust this man. He doesn't know who you really are. He knows a lot of details, but that's it. The details don't matter."

"That's enough," said 80, but Henry could tell he didn't really believe it would make a difference.

"You're right," said the bearded man. "That's enough for now. I'm hungry." He left the room.

Henry looked back at 80, who was staring at him intently, as if waiting for something. "Do you see?" said 80.

Henry nodded. "I see. But I thought I was better when I woke up. I still feel better."

"You're better for now," said 80.

"I don't think so."

Henry heard the suction of the refrigerator door opening in the kitchen, pans being rattled, a cupboard slamming shut.

80 stood up and walked out, but Henry didn't follow. He went to the screen door at the bottom of the stairs and stared through the mesh. A streak of red crossed the yard—a cardinal or something like it. He could hear conversation from the kitchen but couldn't make out the words. It didn't matter. He needed food, though. Real food. He couldn't remember the last time he'd eaten, and the crackers had only made him conscious of his hunger while doing nothing to sate it.

He walked toward the smell of browning butter, and when he was in the kitchen the bearded man said, "You're hungry. Like, unbelievably hungry."

"Yeah," said Henry.

"You've been out for a long time. We drugged you, you know."

Henry leaned against the doorframe.

"I guess 80 didn't tell you." The man cracked three eggs directly into the pan, then moved to cut three thick slices of bread off a big brown loaf. He arranged them on a baking sheet and put it into the oven. "It felt just like you closed your eyes on the bridge and opened them in the bedroom, but it didn't really happen like that. We found you totally knocked out, put you in the car. The one out front." The man was fiddling with the whites of the eggs in the pan, leaving the yolks untouched. "It's a good long drive up here; you would have woken up. I gave you something on the bridge. Then again last night. You've been out for a pretty long time."

"How long?" said Henry. He searched the kitchen for a clock but didn't find one. It seemed strange. Kitchens always had clocks. "What time is it?" he asked.

"Good question," said the bearded man.

"It's about eleven thirty in the morning," said 80.

"You see?" The man pointed a rubber spatula at Henry as he

spoke. "You ask a question and 80 answers it but he doesn't *really* answer it. He gives you the information you specifically ask for and no more. It's never the information that he knows you actually need."

"Why do you have to be so combative?" said 80. He seemed genuinely pained.

Henry felt awkward. He knew he was at the center of the cold war these two were waging, but he had no idea what it was about. He had no personal stake. He just wanted it to stop.

The bearded man picked up the frying pan and yanked it perfectly, a quick backwards jolt that sent the eggs up in the air to flip once before landing back in the pan with a wet slap. "Dammit," he said. "Broke a yolk."

80 snorted. "So you're going to just ignore me?"

The other man pointed at the pan. "I'll take that one, I guess. Toast needs a minute." He got three plates from a cabinet next to the window above the sink, portioned out the eggs, added salt and pepper. "I always do that. Just forget to heat the oven beforehand, or to cut the bread or whatever." He rested one hand on the counter, leaned into it with his hip.

"Who are you?" said Henry.

"You know who I am," said the man. "But you want to hear it. Need to. I remember."

Henry nodded.

"He's 80," said the man with the beard. "I'm 41. And that makes you 19."

PROXY

THE CALLS STARTED soon after Henry's visit. Sometimes Henry would go on about peace and love, speaking of those concepts as if they were tangible, as if they were the only things that existed in the world. In this manic state, he spun fantasies about how New Brunswick could become the new seat of artistic expression in America. Long habit had programmed Gabe to automatically empathize with his best friend, to try his best to find a way to agree with him. But the fact that New Brunswick had become Henry's best hope for salvation was just too sad to believe. More often, Henry went on about the wars in Iraq and Afghanistan and spun long monologues about the clandestine activities of the NSA and the CIA. Henry talked about war, torture, and death as though he were living all those things personally, as if he had the power to change everything if only he could figure out how. Gabe found this easier to take. At least Henry's paranoia was grounded in the real world, even if it was a bit extreme.

Then Gabe started ignoring the calls, but sending Henry to voice mail a few times would only feed his already healthy guilt until he felt duty-bound to answer again. Spending a half-hour listening to Henry's schizoid ranting was the least Gabe could do, he thought. But then the end of the school year approached, and

Henry, knowing that Gabe would soon be free of classes, started asking about a visit. Gabe didn't know how to say no.

It was a warm Wednesday morning when he packed an overnight bag and got on a train headed north. He transferred at Secaucus and soon arrived in the leafy suburb of his youth. Henry was in the parking lot across the street from their favorite coffeehouse. He was leaning against his car, skinnier than Gabe remembered, skinnier than it seemed possible for a person to be. Gabe moved in to hug him but then wished he hadn't. Henry smelled like death, but sharper, like roadkill soaked in apple cider vinegar.

Gabe stepped back. "Hey," he said.

Henry nodded and got in the car. Gabe hesitated. Was it safe to be in a car with his friend? He thought of Jan. She spent every day with Henry. If she thought he was safe to drive, then Gabe supposed he had little to worry about. He got in and held his breath until he could roll down his window.

"So what's happening?" said Gabe.

Henry smiled. "You know."

"Um," said Gabe. "No. I don't."

Henry laughed.

A few painfully silent minutes later, they arrived at the house. Despite the circumstances, Gabe was happy to see it. It reminded him of all those nights after Henry's shows. Of Jan's cooking. Of years of sleepovers when they were kids, how they would fall asleep while whispering about imagined futures taken straight out of the PG-13 action movies they'd seen on WPIX 11. They would both be detectives. They would marry twins. They'd share a house and have matching cars and fight drug dealers or evil ninjas or aliens.

When they walked in, Henry closed the door behind them and bent to the floor to pick up an aerosol can of air freshener.

He shook it, then sprayed in straight lines along the seams of the door. Gabe instinctively willed himself to believe that it was a perfectly reasonable thing to do. He tried to come up with some rationale that would explain his friend's behavior, but it was impossible.

"Hey," he said, louder than he meant to. "What's with the air freshener?"

"It's... Sorry," said Henry. "Should we play some music?"

"We could just talk or something."

Henry stepped out of the foyer and through the door to the basement. Gabe hung his head and took a deep breath. He had assumed that Jan would be around, but the house was quiet. Had she known he was coming and left in anticipation? Or was she upstairs, hiding? He hoped it was the latter, if only because Henry suddenly seemed much more frightening than Gabe could have anticipated. He descended the carpeted steps to the basement.

Gabe wasn't much of a musician, but he'd been friends with Henry for so long that he knew his way around lots of the instruments down in the practice room. In addition to the professional-grade gear that Henry had collected over the years, he had dozens of toys: a Fisher-Price glockenspiel; maracas hand-painted with a beach scene and the word COZUMEL; wooden turtle figurines that doubled as whistles. All the adults in his extended family had made a habit of buying musical tchotchkes for Henry whenever they were in tourist-trap markets or airport gift shops and he kept them all. Gabe grabbed an egg shaker and sat down on the futon in the corner. Henry lowered himself onto the stool behind his drum set and started playing, but every time he settled into a beat he would jump right out of it again. The arrhythmic din grew louder and more frantic, and Gabe stayed motionless. He watched Henry thrash.

Then Gabe stood and yelled, "I'm going outside."

Henry crashed his ride cymbal repeatedly as he stood up, so hard that he seemed to be trying to break it. Gabe backed away and Henry threw his sticks down on the carpeted floor and laughed.

"So you're coming with, then?" said Gabe.

"Hell yeah," said Henry.

"You sure? It's cool if—"

"Let's go!"

Gabe walked up the stairs. Once safely outside, he lit a cigarette. Henry stepped out behind him, the aerosol can in his hand, and resealed the seams of the door with a fresh layer of dried roses and cinnamon. They both sat down. Gabe smoked. Henry breathed through his nose, his mouth locked in that same tight grin.

"Henry," said Gabe, "I'm worried. This isn't—this shit with the air freshener? You look like you haven't eaten. Are you...have you been to a doctor or anything?"

Henry nodded. "They give me pills. They're dangerous."

"But you take them?"

"My mom's pissed at me, I think. Everyone's always mad. I'm moving back down to the house. Maybe next semester."

Gabe didn't want to encourage the fantasy, but he couldn't think of a good way to discourage it, either. He said nothing.

Henry occupied himself with breaking a twig into ever smaller pieces. Minutes passed. Gabe was lighting another cigarette with the burning butt of his first when he caught motion in his peripheral vision. He looked up to see a doe and her fawn emerge from the woods bordering the end of the cul-de-sac. The pair approached Henry's house and stopped when they were on his front lawn, mere yards from where Gabe sat. The doe seemed wary, never turning her eyes from the porch as she began to munch leaves from the bushes on the lawn.

Gabe watched, amazed. It wasn't uncommon to see deer in the area. They were something of a nuisance, actually, and the town had done plenty to try to thin their numbers. But never had Gabe seen them get so close.

He looked at Henry, who smiled and nodded his head as if to say, *You see?*

And for once, Gabe did. He sensed how dangerous it was to overempathize, but in that moment there was no escape. His vision widened. The green of the grass and blue of the sky grew more vivid and the quiet of the street felt tangible and alive, as if the whole world were breathing Gabe in. He let the feeling come. The deer seemed to be saying something with their presence, and a vulnerable part of Gabe sensed that it would be easy to just let go, to find mystical import in the moment, to float off into some other reality that was stranger and more beautiful than his own.

He stood up fast and the doe ran off, followed by her knob-kneed fawn.

"I have to go," said Gabe. "I forgot. I have something to do. I need to go."

"Now?" said Henry.

"Now. Yes. I'm sorry."

"I'll drive you."

"No. I'll walk."

"You're leaving?"

"I'm sorry." Gabe walked away.

Gabe didn't answer the phone after that. He'd been ruled by fear ever since the night Henry started laughing, but that fear had been vague and unfocused. He was never quite sure what he was actually afraid of. But now, after his visit to Henry's house, to Henry's world, Gabe understood. He didn't want to go insane. And to talk to Henry—to join him in whatever reality had supplanted Gabe's own—it was dangerous.

Voice mails piled up, but Gabe didn't listen to them. It hurt to admit that Henry was truly gone, but that pain was seductive. To have irretrievably lost something—it was like a badge of honor. It felt meaningful, like something *real* was happening to him for the very first time. There was truth in his pain, the kind of truth that he'd read about in novels and seen in movies. An adult sort of truth, rooted in suffering.

Gabe didn't leave New Brunswick for the rest of the summer. The guys he smoked pot with—mostly Cal's friends, though a few kids from the dorm came through too—they all wanted to know what had happened, and Gabe surprised himself by acting like he knew. Without quite meaning to, he put together a story. Through repeat telling he refined his tone and shaped a narrative around the parts of the tale that got the strongest reaction. And with Henry cloistered away in his house, Gabe was pitied by proxy. He was consoled. He was told that there was nothing he could have done. The attention was welcome for a while. It made him feel important, or at least less alone. But the longer it went on, the more troubled Gabe felt. Henry's story should have been his own. He was the one who'd lost everything.

MINUET: TRIO

HENRY WAS DEAD.
  Or so he thought.

It was the best explanation—the only one, really, that made any sense. Maybe he'd followed the kicking stone down to the water, or perhaps he'd jumped the railing and stepped in front of a car. In reality, at that very moment, he might be crumpled facedown on the asphalt, awash in the sound of sirens, his body painted in the blue and red of flashing lights. Commuters might be cursing their luck, wishing they'd left just a few moments earlier, telling themselves that of course it was horrible that somebody had died but *did it have to be right then? On the bridge, for chrissakes?* Henry didn't have to work hard to imagine his unseeing eyes gazing down at the sky as reflected in a pool of his own blood, this house in the Catskills no more than his brain's last big show. The ultimate dream.

But if it was a dream, he was impressed by the level of detail. He could smell the freshly fried eggs. The unreal green of the grass and leaves was so beautifully bright that he couldn't look straight at it. The cardinal that had just happened to fly by, that bright red streak—a nice touch. And as for the two men he was with, perhaps they were just his idea of a joke. His life was passing before his eyes, but it wasn't his past. It was his future. Which was good. His past was mostly boring or painful. Even the best memories could be so easily poisoned by the knowledge of what would eventually become of him once the sickness took hold.

Henry felt calm for a dead man. He believed that what he was experiencing was in some sense true, but he understood a more important truth. It didn't actually matter. He'd learned months before to surrender to the mysterious forces that were pushing him along. The *real* was entirely subjective, and the idea that he'd ever had a choice about his hallucinations was in some ways the most destructive delusion of all. This was no different. He was going to sit down at the table and he was going to eat eggs. Not because it mattered or because the eggs were really there or because his body needed the nourishment. He would sit there and eat eggs because that was his only real choice. It was what the moment was requiring of him. There was no escape.

41 took the toast out of the oven and buttered each piece from a thick slab. "This butter is fucking incredible," he said. "It's from this dairy farm like three miles away."

Henry crossed the kitchen and took a seat at the table.

"So you've decided then," said 41, his voice rising above the sound of the faucet as he rinsed his hands.

Henry nodded yes. 41 placed a plate in front of him.

"80?" said 41. "Do you want to begin?"

80 cast his eyes down to his eggs. Each word out of 41's mouth seemed to deflate the old man a little more.

41 stepped away, opened the silverware drawer. Metal sliding along metal, little fork tine finger chimes and butter knife splash cymbals. He placed a mound of utensils on the table and sat down. They all began to eat.

80 took a bite of toast, wiped the corners of his mouth with his fingertips. "41 and I would like you to tell us about the practice room," he said.

This time, 80 wasn't being ambiguous. Henry knew exactly what he was talking about. It had already occurred to him that what was happening was not entirely unprecedented.

"You must already know," said Henry.

"It doesn't matter," said 41. "This is how we start this conversation." He wiped some egg yolk from his plate with a bit of toast. "It's the Socratic method. 80's a fan, relies on it a bit too much for my taste, but I have to agree that it's appropriate in this case. So just tell us."

"I don't know exactly when it started." Henry's tongue felt weak and clumsy. He stood up and went to the sink, drank cold water straight from the tap, then sat back down.

"Val left us. Left me. The stuff in the practice room—it was a while after that, but I think I knew something was wrong for a long time. I was hiding it. From Gabe. From myself." Henry paused. He couldn't help but feel that he'd started the story in the wrong place.

"I always heard things," he said. "Things other people didn't hear. When I was a kid I thought it was a game. All these sounds, they'd fit together. I was always singing along to it. I'd tell people—my mom, teachers, Gabe. Nobody else heard it, or if they did they refused to talk about it."

41 sighed. "Until Val."

"It got…complicated. When I was in high school, I'd get distracted and the music would get really loud sometimes. Then I met Val. The music was still there, but I could ignore it when she was around. She distracted me. And when I couldn't ignore it, it felt like there was a reason, like the music was telling me things. Sometimes I could even get her to hear it. But then she left. There were so many things wrong after that, and nobody that could help me. My mom just got overbearing. And Gabe was weird about Val, like he didn't want to say the wrong thing or get too involved or something. It was just easier to be alone. To deal with it alone. So I spent a lot of time in the practice room. I just practiced so much. I told myself that's what I was there for."

"But then," said 41.

Henry slid his fork beneath a cold clump of egg and brought it to his mouth. He'd forgotten his hunger—it seemed immaterial now—but he couldn't figure out how to continue. "But then... There wasn't any warning or anything, it just happened."

He chewed the egg slowly. He forced himself into remembrance.

"I was working on my four-mallet alternating grip—a total bitch—it had something to do with the resonance of the room. There was this phrase in an arrangement of Reich, I think—it would make the room resonate just right. A long roll on the low b-flat. When I hit that passage for the first time it was like the room was moaning. Like it was...I don't know. Like I was fucking it or something." He laughed. "It sounds crude, ridiculous, but that's what it was like. I could feel it in my chest, like my ribs were made of the same thing as the bars of the marimba. Like I was playing myself, kind of. It felt so good that I just stopped playing the music on the page. I bowed my head and closed my eyes and just played that note over and over. And when I was zoning out to that b-flat, I saw the most beautiful things."

Henry smiled at the memory.

"I didn't tell anyone about it. I knew something was wrong, like I said. But I wasn't afraid. It felt too good. So one day I'm all excited to get to school early because there's a schedule and I've been pissing people off by hogging the practice room. I walk in, turn on the lights, ready my mallets, get everything just right, then I leave the room to go to the bathroom and get some water. I guess that was kind of my ritual at that point. And then I'm walking back down the hallway and everything's really quiet." Henry closed his eyes and breathed in deeply. He recalled the feeling. It made him want to cry.

He put his hands flat on the table and kept his eyes shut as he continued. "But when I get close, it's not quiet anymore. I hear the room ringing and my first thought is that I've brought the room alive, you know? I don't need to play anything anymore, I can just hear the room. It's just *being*. So I'm excited when I reach the door, touch the handle, and then I hear that it's not just a single tone. I can hear mallets hitting wood. I open the door and someone's there, bent over the marimba. He's got dark hair and its curly like mine—he's wearing clothes that I recognize. The hoodie. My pants. He's playing the b-flat with my mallet in his left hand, and I can see his right hand down at his side. I freeze."

Henry opened his eyes and glanced at 41.

"I'm looking at his hand the same way I was just looking at yours. It's unmistakable. It's mine. "

41 nodded.

"I lean back into the door, and the doorknob clicks as it closes and the guy in front of me turns. I kind of already know what I'm going to see, but it doesn't make it any less...freakish, I guess. His hair is different and he's skinny, but other than that we look exactly alike. He's not older like you two, so there's just no question. This guy is fucking *exactly like me,* and he's playing the room just like I've been playing it, and when he looks at me he doesn't stop—he just keeps ringing out that low b-flat. And then we're locking eyes and it feels like I've never, never made eye contact before, like I've found an answer to this question that I never even knew how to ask. It feels like proof that I'm real."

Henry leaned forward on the table. "Is that how you guys feel when you look at me?"

80 and 41 appraised each other. Henry could tell that something of significance was passing between them, though he couldn't tell

what. 41's face seemed to soften momentarily to reveal a kindness that Henry hadn't seen before.

"Not really," said 41. "Not for a long time. I remember the feeling, of course, but it fades just like anything else."

"I don't feel it now," said Henry. "Not like I did in the practice room, anyway. And even then it didn't last long."

41 nodded. "Because he started crying."

"Yeah," said Henry. "And I didn't know why. And that's just—it's monumentally unsettling. I'm looking directly into my own eyes, and *I* don't even know why I'm crying. Then he whimpers something I can't understand, so I say *What?* and the second time I hear him when he says *I'm sorry* and he drops the mallet. Both ends of it hit the marimba and play this funny minor fifth that echoes back and forth in that little practice room until there's nothing left. I feel like I'm going to scream. It's all gone wrong, I don't know this kid in front of me any more than I know anyone else, and the fear is so intense that I want to just dig my fingernails into my skin and start tearing. So I open the door and run out."

80 tapped the table with his fork. 41 stared at the last bits of dried orange yolk on his plate.

"You asked 80—before—you asked him if he wanted to begin," said Henry. "What are we beginning?"

80 stopped tapping. "To answer your stated question, 41 was referring to the difficult conversation we're all enjoying at this very moment. But to answer your *real* question"—and with this 80 looked at 41—"the moment we took you from the bridge a whole new universe was formed. If we hadn't picked you up you would have become someone else. 41 and I have been that person. We've lived whole lives as that person. But we're not him anymore because *that* Henry is gone forever. Our pasts have been replaced many times over, and as you might have been able to tell by 41's attitude toward me, those changes haven't all been for the better. But if we

can teach you how to control yourself, your travel through time, we can begin a new future for you and a new past for ourselves. One we can all be happy with."

"So what happened in the practice room was real," said Henry.

41 *hmph*ed in the affirmative.

"And if that was real, this is real. That's what I'm supposed to believe."

"You think you're dead," said 41, "that this is all some last-dance illusion. I remember. That's not the truth, but I won't be able to convince you. Not right now, anyway, and it doesn't matter. You're going to behave as if we're all sitting here, for real, because you have no other choice."

"That feels about right," said Henry.

"I also remember that you're pretty tired of sitting, that maybe you want something to do with your hands. So you're going to finish eating and then you're going to do the dishes."

Henry smiled gratefully. He was coming to prefer 41's rough cynicism to 80's cryptic positivity. He ate quickly, then stood and did as he was asked. 41 wiped out the pan he'd cooked the eggs in, and 80 dried as Henry washed. When they were done 80 carefully folded the towel in half and laid it over the handle of the oven.

He turned to Henry and smiled.

"Let's go for a walk."

BUCCLEUCH PARK

T HE START OF Gabe's junior year brought with it the cloudy nostalgia he recognized from every September of his life. Long habit had imbued early fall with a counterfeit poignancy, an excitement and sadness without reason or purpose. Gabe resented it.

Three days before classes began, he woke up to the vibration of his phone against the wooden shelf that was mounted above his head. The night before, he and Cal had passed a bowl back and forth until the difference between asleep and awake was more or less meaningless. Somehow he managed to reach the phone before it went to voice mail, but when he saw "Jan: Mobile" his stomach pooled with a thick, cold anxiety that yanked him from his burnt haze. He didn't answer. Her voice mail was brief. She asked him to call her back.

Gabe closed his eyes and imagined what might come next. Jan would say Henry was doing better, and that she was wrong to have thought that Gabe could have prevented Henry from losing it in the first place. Gabe would be magnanimous, tell her it was okay, that he understood how awful the whole thing was and how nobody could be expected to act reasonably. They would talk together about what kind of help Henry might need. She'd listen and take action. After weeks—months, maybe—Henry would start to get better. Gabe would eventually forgive Jan and vice versa. They'd be as close to family as they were before. Closer, even.

He found her number on his recent calls list and tapped it with his thumb.

"He's gone," said Jan. No hello.

"Gone? What do you mean, gone?"

"I mean gone. He's not here. He left the house sometime last night."

In the lengthy silence that followed, Gabe imagined Henry wandering and alone, and what he wanted to say was *Fuck, that's really bad,* but instead he said, "I'm sorry," though he didn't want Jan to think he had anything to be sorry for.

"He's been talking about going to New Brunswick, so I wanted to let you know. If you see him you have to promise me—promise me, Gabe—that you will call me and that you won't give him any drugs, okay?"

Gabe's fantasy version of the phone call was being shotgunned into oblivion with every word out of Jan's mouth.

"Jesus, Jan. I won't give him any drugs. I'll call you if I see him. I have to run to class."

He hung up.

By late September, New Brunswick was littered with the multicolored molting of deciduous trees. Henry had been missing for almost a month. Gabe wondered if maybe he was dead. It was plausible—three weeks felt like a very long time to be wandering without someone taking notice—but it just didn't sound right. Henry couldn't die. He would come back from the brink, and Gabe would be there for him. Gabe felt sure of that.

But if Henry was still alive, where was he? At first it had seemed obvious that he would show up in New Brunswick. Gabe was so convinced of it that Henry was the first person he thought of when the phone rang or when he heard the sound of a key scraping the tumblers at the back door. Countless times a day he caught glimpses of men that looked like Henry, heard his friend's voice in every crowd. He knew he should be hopeful for Henry's return, but all he felt was raw, ugly panic.

He kept himself busy. For the first time since his first semester he went to all his classes. He took more hours at the store, too. Gabe had never meant to work at the Magic Dragon for so long. He obsessed over it sometimes, how the borderline legal status of the store might affect him later in life. And he'd grown to resent the way his customers treated him. Some were in awe, assuming Gabe had reached the pinnacle of stoner achievement. They asked *How did you get this job?* as though they thought he was the luckiest person on earth. Others were quietly judgmental. They asked *How did you get this job?* the way a self-conscious john might ask the same question of a hooker.

It was Wednesday afternoon and as quiet as the store ever got. Gabe did all the chores he could think of, then sat down to wait out the day. He turned up the volume on the stereo, lit a cigarette, and sent squadrons of smoke rings off into the air. The door alarm chimed its digital *ding-dong,* and he looked up to see Joan.

The store's most loyal customers weren't Gabe's fellow students, and they didn't buy cigars or bongs. To the homeless of New Brunswick, the Magic Dragon was simply the cheapest place to buy cigarettes. Gabe's boss made sure of that by filling his Escalade with cartons bought in Delaware and scratching off the tax stamps. And of all the homeless friends Gabe made at that job, Joan was the most disgusting. Her massive hips supported the rest of her body reluctantly and only with constant effort. She rocked a full thirty degrees left and right of center with each laborious step, and with her walked an impressive smell: a putrid mix of crotch sweat, beer breath, stale cigarettes, and strong perfume that lingered in the air minutes after she left a room. Gabe rarely saw her without a base-ball cap pulled over her greasy curls, and the yellow skin on her face luminesced with a mixture of sweat and God knows what else even in the dead of winter. Her pièce de résistance was the bright pink lipstick that was caked on her cracked lips. It was an ironic punch in the groin, mocking the rest of her haggard ensemble while hinting strongly at a sexuality no one could possibly wish to confront.

Joan opened the door, propped it with her foot, and pushed out a "Hey" from deep within her gut. At high volume her wet rasp vibrated inside of Gabe's own chest. When low, it sounded like a death rattle from the movies.

Gabe smiled and said hello back.

"You work today?" she asked.

"Yup, I guess so."

"I was wondering if you were going to be here," she said. "I wanted to ask you something."

"What's that?" Gabe said, reluctantly. He'd learned from experience that giving Joan an opening like that could lead to some pretty scandalous shit.

She waddled up to the front display case, reached into her pocket, and pulled out her tobacco and papers. "Well, I was down at the Krauzer's on the corner and that Paki told me he likes blondes, said he'd give me a tin of Bugler if I find someone for him."

"That right?" said Gabe. He smothered one cigarette in the overflowing ashtray on the counter and took another from his pack.

"Yeah. So, you know anyone?"

Gabe lit the cigarette in his mouth and said, "Do I know any blondes that you could hook up with the owner of Krauzer's?"

"He's the manager, I think," she said. "And, yeah."

"I'm pretty sure most of the girls I know aren't really looking for that type of thing."

Joan laughed. It sounded like the engine of a capsized motorboat. "Yeah, well, figured I'd ask," she said. She took a too-large pinch of tobacco from her pouch and placed it into a too-small paper, rolled it loosely, and licked the glue. Her purple-red tongue looked like some vital organ that had migrated up into her mouth. Gabe offered his Bic, trying not to let her hand touch his as she shielded the flame and leaned in.

"Oh, and something else. There's a new guy in the park," she said. "Heard about him from Mike and Tim—those brothers who squat in that place on Drift Street. Went to find him—just curious, you know."

"Hmm?" said Gabe.

"Well, I can tell he doesn't know a fuckin' thing about New Brunswick," said Joan. "He's too young, first of all, and he's got this big hippie beard. He won't say where he's from or what's his name or anything. All cagey. Well, I start telling him all about what he needs to know. I tell him where he can get food, where the cheapest beer is. And of course I mention the Dragon. You know how much business I send over here."

"You're our best customer," said Gabe. Joan loved that shit.

"Well, so I tell him he's got to come down here and then all the sudden he's interested. Starts asking all these questions. He wants to know if I go here a lot, if I know the people."

Gabe was suddenly on his feet behind the counter, though he didn't remember standing up from his stool. "What kind of questions? Did he ask about me?"

"Well, kinda, but not in particular." The hard p forced a white speck of spittle onto the glass counter. "He just said something about how he knew someone used to work here. I said sure, I know everyone down here and who's he looking for? He says his friend used to work here, but I told him they only opened the place a couple years ago so he was maybe thinking of that other place on George Street."

"What did he look like?" said Gabe. His blood was sour with adrenaline, a rush so strong he felt prehistoric, fight or flight in full effect.

"Dark hair, kinda curly, big beard. Something weird about his eyes, like they were too big for his face or something. Clothes seemed pretty clean but he was definitely sleeping under that bridge, cuz Frank who stays up in that gazebo told me. Frank seen him walking up from that stream at dawn the other day. Frank don't sleep much ever since—"

"How old was he?" he asked.

"Oh, probably, I don't know—maybe thirty-five? Forty-five or something?"

Gabe sat down, disappointed but relieved. That relief felt like betrayal. Why should he be happy that it wasn't Henry? Why should he be happy that his best friend was still missing?

"He was probably pretty handsome, I think, under all that hair. Maybe I'll ask him out," said Joan with a lascivious grin. "What do you think?"

Gabe didn't say anything.

Joan shifted her weight from one thick leg to the other. "Anyways," she said, "just thought it was sorta weird, you know. You seen him here yet?"

Gabe shrugged, shook his head. "Tell me if you see him again," he said. Then, as if to explain his pleading tone, he said, "We don't like people asking a whole lot of questions about the store, you know?"

Joan grunted in agreement. She mashed the pink nub of her cigarette into the ashtray. "Gotta go, I guess."

"You got enough smokes?"

"I'm fine," she said. "See you tomorrow." She hobbled out onto the sidewalk.

Gabe grabbed paper towels and Windex from the shelf underneath the cash register, then set himself to wiping Joan's brown palm prints from all the cases and counters she'd touched. He tried not to think about how much older Henry might look with a few months' worth of hair, how maybe Joan was wrong about the guy's age, how maybe she was too drunk or just needed glasses.

He stopped cleaning and put his elbows on the top of the counter, held his head in his hands. "Goddamn it," he said.

He put the Windex on the counter and grabbed the BACK IN FIVE MINUTES sign from its spot next to the cash register.

Half an hour later Gabe entered Buccleuch Park through the main gate across from the big brick hospital. On the way, like always, he took a shortcut through the circular drive in front of the ER. It felt strange, like walking on a grave.

From the way Henry had talked on the phone back before their final visit, Gabe didn't think he'd be sleeping in some ditch at Buccleuch Park. He'd be home on Hamilton, trying to start a commune in the living room. But maybe Henry hadn't run away because of the good fantasies. Gabe assumed his friend would be chasing something by leaving his mom's house, but wasn't it just as likely that he was running away? Maybe even more likely, given that Henry had been obsessively using air freshener for protection against some mystical evil. And if he was terrified and looking for a place to hide, why not a secluded a bridge in a familiar park?

Buccleuch was an expansive property that acted as a buffer between the Raritan River and one of the nicer residential areas in New Brunswick. There were baseball diamonds for Little League games, playgrounds, makeshift soccer fields with garbage cans as goalposts, and a white colonial mansion sitting on a low hill above it all. It was almost charming, but Gabe had heard enough from Joan to know that this park was ground zero for some of the worst things that went on in town.

Huge stone lions guarded the entrance to the park, their features softened by decades of wind and rain, gray skin mottled with dried chewing gum. Near their bases, the lions were nearly black from the exhaust of passing cars. Gabe opened his cigarette pack and was grateful to remember the half-smoked joint he'd stashed at the bottom. Judging that he was far enough away from other pedestrians, he fished it out and lit it with shaking hands, using one of the lions as shelter from the soft breeze. He was glad for the familiar release.

In the middle of the park was a thin swath of old trees that followed a little stream at the bottom of a deep ravine. Gabe got it in his sights and started walking. The bridge Joan had referred to was made of wood and stone and was far too big for its purpose. It looked like it was designed for a river and then plopped down to make the stream look even smaller and dingier than it already was. Gabe knew the area well. Like anyone else in New Brunswick who smoked weed, he had a mental list of public places where it was safe to take a few quick hits, and this ravine had been one of his and Henry's favorites. It was deep enough to keep them out of sight and the trees gave additional cover. It was also quiet, and truly beautiful.

He reached the tree line and walked toward the bridge. When he hit the shade of the high canopy he felt the effects of the pot. It wasn't much, and the fresh air and sunlight were sobering, but it was enough to make the trees above seem abnormally vibrant. Gabe stopped and looked up, watched the space between the leaves until the background of blue sky and foreground of greenery inverted. As his peripheral vision opened up, the field above him shattered into a panorama of random motion.

The sound of a far-off car broke the illusion. He walked again, down into the ravine, leaning back and taking small steps to avoid pitching forward. Momentum caught up with him and he bounced the last few feet down onto the gravel that followed the stream. The bridge was nearly above him, casting on the running water a dark shadow interrupted by the thin lines of sunlight that slipped between the planks.

Once in the shadow of the bridge, Gabe let his eyes adjust. He studied the ground for clues, as if he had any idea how to do that. He knew that most homeless people didn't hang out where they slept and that they always hid their belongings in places where nobody could just happen upon them. He could see up the embankment to where the intersection of earth and bridge created a deep crevice, hidden in shadow. It seemed like the perfect place for a stash. Gabe stepped up the bank again, angling for a better look. As he got closer he saw a dirty black backpack, the canvas kind that every kid wore in third grade. It was jammed right into the cleft formed where the cement of the bridge's foundation met the wooden walkway above. It was as if it had been waiting for him.

Movement caught his eye downstream. He turned fast.

About fifty feet away stood a man. His long hair and bushy black beard obscured everything but his eyes, his nose, and the very tops of his cheeks. The too-big eyes—just as Joan had described them—were fixed on Gabe. He was far away, so it was hard for Gabe to know for sure, but it looked like the man was smiling. He crouched and shook a little, then stood up again and lifted his right foot behind him, held it with his right hand while he bent his left knee. He did the same on the other side, then jogged in place and turned to face Gabe once more.

He was definitely smiling now. He looked familiar. Gabe could see something in the eyes that reminded him of Henry despite the full, graying beard. It wasn't him, of course—it couldn't be—but just to be sure Gabe took a step in the man's direction.

The man turned and bolted. Gabe scrambled down to the gravel and ran after him. He didn't know why. The man had run. That seemed like reason enough, and each frantic step only strengthened

Gabe's irrational resolve. Up ahead, mounted into a tall cement wall, was a large-gauge pipe that brought the stream into the park from its source on the other side of the highway. When the man reached it he was forced to climb up the side of the ravine to get around it. Gabe took the same incline at a diagonal, using his hands to catch the trunks of trees, which prevented him from falling and whipped him back on course. He reached the top of the hill in time to watch the man leapfrog over the railing separating the park from the highway off-ramp that bordered it. Gabe followed, hurdling over the short railing and its twin on the other side of the road. Whoever this man was, he'd just made a mistake. The chase had now taken them to an asphalt walkway penned in by a twenty-foot palisade on one side and the Raritan River on the other. The only way out was about a mile ahead, up an old iron staircase that led to a pedestrian overpass crossing Route Eighteen and down into town.

Gabe ran until he was nauseous with the effort. The palisade to his right was a favorite spot for graffiti artists, and the bright portraiture and elaborate tags turned to riotous streaks as Gabe sprinted past. By the time he hit the bottom of the staircase at the end of the path, his knees were elastic, his flushed face tingling. He heard footsteps up above him, clanking against the metal, and though Gabe tried to take the stairs two at a time, his legs wouldn't play along. The change in pace sobered him a bit, as did the cramping pain at the base of his rib cage.

"What am I doing?" he whispered.

He mounted the next step.

"What the fuck?"

And the next.

By the time he reached the landing before the top, he was sure that the overpass would be empty, and he was glad. The bearded man wasn't Henry. A glance had been enough to tell that. Any resemblance was just Gabe seeing what he wanted to see, which meant that he'd chased after a homeless man for no real reason. Now that the whim was gone, he felt sad and empty and more than a little scared. There were only a few more steps to the top. Gabe took them slowly. When finally his line of sight extended past the top stair, he saw that the overpass wasn't empty.

The bearded man leaned against the railing, spitting down onto the road and gasping in an effort to get his wind. Gabe stopped and stared through an oxygen-deprived haze. He felt sick. The cars below were deafening, the sun too bright. Even his own body was too much for him to handle—he thought he could feel his own blood careening through his veins, prickling underneath his skin and pulsing in his temples and toes. He knew he should run in the other direction, but he was too tired.

The man reached his arms above his head and stepped to the center of the bridge. He turned in a full circle, stopped when he was facing Gabe, and closed his eyes.

Gabe became fearfully conscious of the iron staircase behind his back. With even a gentle push the man could send him tumbling down the steps. Gabe gripped the banister in preparation for an advance, but it didn't come. The man stepped back and marched steadily in place, his knees rising above his waist with each dramatic step. He kept a steady tempo, and then he swirled his arms, pointing above and below him.

Gabe was stunned. He wanted to laugh, but he didn't have the breath. This man might not be Henry, but he was almost certainly just as crazy as Henry was.

The rushing sound of the cars beneath Gabe's feet was now painfully loud. He closed his eyes and focused on his breath. In the darkness behind his eyelids, his ears took over. He could hear the tires on the road below hitting a seam in the pavement with a rich, throaty pulse. The honking of a V of geese overhead syncopated itself against that beat, and Gabe's own heartbeat, loud in his ears after the run, matched the space between goose honks. He opened his eyes and blinked a few times. The small wet noise of his eyelids making and breaking contact with each other was somehow audible, and it fit seamlessly into a complex rhythm, as did the far-off wail of a police siren and the rustle of leaves in the breeze and the distant clacking of an Amtrak express train screaming through New Brunswick station.

Gabe couldn't separate one sound from any other. He couldn't isolate even his own breathing. The world was a song, a singular anthem comprised of everything he could see and hear. The man stamped and twirled away, and as his fists curled closed and unfurled Gabe heard the fast percussion of a faraway helicopter timed to each twitch of the man's fingers. It was that way with every part of the man's body—each motion was linked to a different part of the music, as though he were the center of it all.

Gabe slid his back down the low concrete wall near the top of the stairs until he was seated. His vision was obscured by a film of tears, but he could still see the man dancing toward the other side of the bridge, twirling so close to the steps that he seemed bound to stumble onto them and fall down to the other side.

And maybe that's what happened. But what Gabe later remembered wasn't a stumble.

It was a leap. A rearward leap up and then almost horizontal. The man's back arched like a high jumper's, his arms and legs hung loosely from his torso. The hair on his head was suspended beneath him and around him and pushed up to frame his face. It looked to Gabe as if the man had fallen asleep in midair, as if he was descending through water. The music was relentless. The man's hair and clothing fluttered softly as he fell, and Gabe could hear that, too, as loud as any of the other noises and perfectly harmonized. A solo.

And then the man was gone.

Gabe sucked in as much air as his lungs could hold. His vision was clear again, and the music that had overwhelmed him just seconds before was replaced by the mundane sounds of a highway overpass. He tried to move, but he was too sore, as if he'd been asleep in the same position for hours, so he lay still. But there was no stillness inside him, only panic. The man had jumped from the bridge—backwards and totally prone—to the stairs on the other side. He would have to be severely injured if not dead.

Someone might have seen Gabe chasing him. And when they found the man dead, how would Gabe explain what he'd been doing? He couldn't even explain it to himself.

He toppled forward and pushed himself up off the concrete. Now on his feet, he hobbled to the other side of the bridge and braced for the gruesome scene he fully expected to see, the scene that would ruin his life forever. But when he glanced down the stairway, it was clear. Nothing on the steps. Nothing on the landing.

Gabe limped to the bottom of the staircase just to make sure, but there was no man. No blood. No sign of anything.

SCHERZO: THE RELIC

ENRY FOLLOWED 41 to the basement. His clothes were waiting for him in an old dryer, and he quickly changed into them. He wanted to feel the warmth from the machine before it dissipated.

41 watched him undress and dress again, and he smiled.

"What?" said Henry.

"It's just strange. I remember how good it felt to get into those clothes. Made me feel like myself."

"I guess," said Henry. He wasn't sure what it meant to feel like himself.

41 turned to go back upstairs and Henry trailed after him.

His shoes were waiting for him by the door, and 41 watched him put them on before leading Henry outside and down the lawn. Their destination was a mossy boulder that sat near the edge of the clearing in which the house stood. 80 straggled behind.

Questions looped loudly in Henry's mind, so many that he wasn't sure where to begin. 41 saved him from having to decide. "In another time," he said, "we didn't pick you up. When I was you—the first time I was you—I woke up on the bridge alone."

As they walked, 41 plucked long yellow foxtails from the ground. Henry reached his own hand down to let the furry stalks pass through his fingers.

"It felt like I'd only been out for a few seconds, but I could tell by the feel of the light that it was late afternoon. There was no pulsing universe of sound, no music formed from the combination of everything on earth." 41 laughed. "I've experienced some crazy shit since then. But compared to that morning on the bridge, it's all been kind of run-of-the-mill, to tell the truth. I can still feel it. I'm a little in awe of you, frankly. You just survived that."

"If I'm to believe you, you survived it too," said Henry. "Are you in awe of yourself?"

"I suppose I am." 41 laughed again. "The first time I was you, I woke up on the cement, got up, and started walking. I was about as lucid as you are now, but afraid to go back to my mom's. I'd been looking for deliverance from that green vibration and everything it represented, and the bridge gave me that. I thought I'd really escaped, that it was best to stay away. As for Val, I still wanted to see her, but I knew it was a bad idea. I looked horrible, smelled worse than horrible. So I figured if I could get to New Brunswick and find Gabe, I could hide for a few days while I figured out what to do next. I walked all the way to Penn Station—two and a half hours straight down Broadway. It felt like an eternity."

They reached the boulder. Henry climbed up and sat down on the edge so he was facing the house. He bounced his heels against the thick pads of moss that clung to the side of the rock.

"I got on a train to New Brunswick without a ticket and locked myself in the bathroom. People started banging on the door after a little while, but I was too scared to move. Somehow I made it all the way to Metuchen before a conductor unlocked the door from the outside and kicked me off. By then I was pretty close to Rutgers so I didn't fight it. I just followed the train tracks as best I could."

80 reached the boulder then, breathing hard. "Don't let me"—he paused to inhale—"don't let me interrupt."

"You remember this conversation anyway, don't you?" said 41.

"I wasn't picking a fight," said 80.

41 turned his attention back to Henry, then pulled himself up on the rock so they were sitting shoulder to shoulder. "So I got to New Brunswick. I was tired and I felt like shit, but it felt like a victory to make it there. It felt right in that way that a lot of things just felt right around that time. I found a place to sleep for a bit, an alley by that grocery store downtown, the C-Town. At dawn I walked to the music school."

"You went to the practice room," said Henry. He turned to look at himself, his other self, examined the long gray hairs of his beard, the sunken cheekbones. *This should be more strange,* he thought. Maybe this was one of those things that his mental illness was causing him to think *just felt right* despite how obviously wrong it was.

"To you," said 41, "that first experience in the practice room seemed like a particularly vivid hallucination. It scared you into believing that something was terribly wrong. But to me—as the boy you walked in on, sleep deprived from walking all night and stuck two months in his own past—it didn't prove that I was crazy. It proved that I wasn't, that something real was happening, something extraordinary and completely unprecedented. When I saw you I felt *sane.* Do you understand?"

"I think so," said Henry.

"Say it," said 41.

Henry chewed his cheek. His vocabulary felt inadequate, his words poorly designed. It was as if he was thinking in the wrong key. "There were two of me," he said. "Only months apart. They—we were experiencing the same moment. But it meant something completely different to each of us."

Henry knew there was more to say, but before he could find the words, 80 inhaled deeply and spoke them aloud. "We are all alone," he said, "even when we are with ourselves."

Apparently, 41 could think of nothing acerbic to add.

"I didn't know that when I first showed up in 41's life," said 80. "I had forgotten so much about what it meant to be him. I'm sorry for that."

41 jumped down from the stone and paced with his hands in his pockets and his eyes on the trees. His steps left imprints in the lush grass. Henry watched the blades rise in each depression. In a few minutes it would look as though 41 hadn't stepped there at all.

"So now we all understand this profound truth about ourselves," said 41, and he laughed through his nose, a rapid-fire chuckling, completely joyless. "I'm really glad for that, but unfortunately for all of us we'll be learning that lesson for the rest of our lives." He started walking. "Follow me. We're going on a little hike. 80 needs to show you something."

Henry jumped off the rock and proceeded to the tree line. 80 stepped after them with a sigh.

They walked silently into the woods. 80 moved faster now, spurred along, Henry supposed, by the same nervous tension that Henry felt. It was like a silent current, an undertow pulling them down toward something inevitable. The static sound of rushing water grew louder as they progressed. Henry looked back, but the dense forest had already smothered his view of the clearing and the house. He wondered if they'd ever been there at all, but this walk was lifelike in a way that no other hallucination had been. It was calm, sort of boring. The trees were only trees, the sky only sky. No terrible cosmic import. No high drama.

80 hopped past Henry in an awkward half jog, then slowed when he caught up to 41. They exchanged words, but Henry heard only the *esses* and *kays*. Some time later, 80 and 41 broke through the trees onto a rocky streambed. Henry watched the sun turn the men a staggering golden white. 80 put a flattened hand on his brow and turned back. 41 did the same, and Henry understood. They couldn't see him. He imagined sprinting full speed back toward the

house, but what then? Where could he go and not be found? If this was all an illusion, escape was impossible. If it was real, his captors would need only to remember where they had gone when they were him. He trudged forward.

When Henry reached the streambed 41 said, "This is the Esopus Creek. We've got a while more to go. You need to rest?"

Henry shrugged. "I'm fine."

They followed the water, usually stepping forward on damp gravel and smooth stones, sometimes dipping back into the woods to follow a parallel trail when the creek was wide enough to hug its banks and leave no room for walking. Henry knew he should be thinking about the deep philosophical implications of his current predicament, but he didn't care to. It was a beautiful day. He was out on a walk in the woods and he wanted only to think of normal things. Snippets of old songs and half-forgotten memories, internal asides, private jokes. It had been a long time since he'd luxuriated in that sort of prosaic thinking. His thoughts turned to the childhood vacations he'd spent up here in the mountains. Each summer, Henry and his mother had shared a cabin with his aunt and uncle. The first time they came was right after Henry's dad finally disappeared into the cancer that had defined him for as long as Henry could remember. He never really knew his father in good health, and for the last few months he barely got to see him. His mom later said that his dad hadn't wanted to be remembered as a sad pile of bones. Instead, Henry remembered his father as a moaning ghost behind a closed bedroom door. It didn't seem much better.

"19," said 41.

The voice barely made it through Henry's haze of deep concentration. He didn't react.

"Henry."

This time Henry stopped walking and looked up. 41 had turned to face him. 80 was a bit further up.

"I'm going to show you what you're doing here, but you have to be patient. We can't explain everything all at once. Some of it you're going to have to figure out for yourself and some of it you're going to help us understand."

41 checked to see that 80 was still walking ahead, then lowered his voice. "Your being here, it's changed everything for me—for us."

"I don't know what you mean."

"I mean, you've set yourself free just by being here. For right now, just open your eyes. Pay attention." He smiled. "This is the most important thing that's ever happened to you."

41 started walking again. Henry felt more confused but more focused, too. Ten minutes later he saw up ahead a sheer wall of rock, seven or eight feet high. The creek bent to the right to get around it. 41, walking faster than before, was well ahead and out of sight. 80 was clearly pained by the hike and had fallen behind. Henry was in the middle, and when finally he made it to the point in the bend where he could see what lay ahead, he stopped. Spanning the water just a little ways downstream was a long wooden suspension bridge. It's twin towers were composed of two telephone poles each, which had been sunk into the ground on either side of the stream. The towers were connected at their tops by metal cables, and hanging down from those long arcs were thinner cords that were bolted into the surface of the bridge itself.

41 had stopped to allow Henry to catch up, and when Henry reached him he said, "Wait here. 80 will need help up this bank. Just get up into the trees and follow the stream and you'll see the entrance to the bridge in a minute or two."

Henry nodded. It didn't occur to him to ask why 41 wasn't waiting, why he wouldn't be helping. 41 stepped ahead and Henry turned around. 80 was only twenty or thirty yards away, but he was moving slowly. Henry kicked a pebble toward the water and it bounced off a larger stone before plunking into the stream. The sound was satisfying. Henry focused on it as it echoed again and again. At first Henry didn't find that strange, but then it persisted, repeated, returned, and folded in on itself, a series of clicks and splashes that oscillated without diminishing. The sound of the water was louder too, its variegated tones more dynamic and rhythmic in their susurrations. 80 reached Henry, his chest heaving. His skin was damp and sickly yellow, his lips pale blue. "Move," he said. "We have to get up there."

"You look like you need a rest."

80 shook his head and motioned Henry forward with a frantic little wave of his fingers. He looked lost.

"We should stop for a minute," said Henry.

"*We are not stopping,*" said 80, his face curdled with angst and anger. It reminded Henry of 41, and for the first time he could really see them as the same man.

"Do you hear that?" said 80. He stepped past Henry and took a step up the bank before retreating. "That—the everything. That means we have to go. *Now.* Help me!"

Henry stepped up onto the bank and grabbed a sapling with one hand. With the other he took hold of 80's forearm and pulled. From the bridge came the dry, hollow, meaty tone of a wooden wind chime—first one note, then two more. A seductive sound, it seemed to cast a shadow over Henry's vision. His throat burned and his eyes began to close.

"Help me, damn it!" said 80, and the urgent sound of his plea flung Henry back into his body. He climbed a few feet up, found another tree to hold on to, and reached back for 80. By repeating that process a few more times he was able to inchworm the old man up to level ground. The wind-chime sound had multiplied into a soft, tinkling chorus, and without the physical exertion to distract him, Henry was again overcome. The pitter-patter grew and expanded, like an approaching storm, reaching out and up until it merged with the rushing of water, the swaying of branches, Henry's own breath and heartbeat, the chattering of birds, the dry shuffling of 80's steps on the earth as the old man trotted ahead.

Henry stopped walking. He wanted only to be taken in by the all-encompassing music of the forest around him, but 80's voice again pierced through the symphony, a single word, hoarse and incredibly loud, "Run!"

Henry did, his feet catching on fallen leaves and ropy ferns. When he reached the foot of the bridge, his body failed him and he hit the ground on all fours. His stomach formed a painful fist and pushed fried eggs and the mealy remains of toast into his throat. The crash of his vomit hitting the dirt trail assimilated into the larger song, and he was enveloped. Through half-open eyes he glimpsed 41 dancing ahead of him on the timber walkway, his limbs flailing, reckless and beautiful, but the image gradually melted into wood and water, sky and bile. Henry felt a powerful rise as everything turned to color and sound, all of it pushing toward the uncontrollable climax, an inexorable white din that washed the world away.

Henry's eyes were open. Amorphous blue, wisps of white, green leaves, and gray swinging branches. He blinked and could have cried at how good it felt. He slowly came to understand that he was lying on his back. He lifted his torso, supporting himself on his elbows. The back of his shirt was wet with something. He recalled the puke. 80 approached him from the base of the bridge. His face was knotted with a peculiar combination of confusion and rage. After every few steps he stopped to look back as if expecting to see 41 materialize in the same spot he'd disappeared from.

"What happened?" said Henry. He grimaced as his own voice sent a jolt of pain through the front of his forehead and deep into his skull.

80 rested a hand on one of the taut steel cables. "What did he say?" He took a deep, shuddering gulp of air and then, in one short exhalation, he said, "What did he say to you this morning?"

"What do you mean?" said Henry.

80 lowered his head, seemingly too exhausted to try again.

"What do you mean, what did he say? You know what he said. You remember. You have to know."

80 shook his head, then lowered himself to his knees.

"Where did he go?" said Henry. "You must know. You have to."

80 looked up. Silent tears had saturated the deep tributaries beneath his eyes. He looked back at the spot on the bridge where 41 had been dancing, and when he turned around he appeared to be even more stricken than before.

Henry stood up slowly. He held his hands away from his body, not wanting to touch the runny mess he'd fallen down in. "I don't understand," he said. "I'm not supposed to know what's going on. That's what you're here for."

80's only response was a miserable whimper and a shake of his head.

Henry screamed. "Why am I here?"

"It's over," said 80. "I'm a relic. I'm gone."

REACHING OUT

GABE'S DREAMS WERE so vivid and visceral that they bled into his days. In waking life, as in sleep, he interrogated his memory and questioned each detail. He searched for alternative explanations for what he'd seen, anything that might counter the only theory that seemed plausible: he was having a psychotic episode. Henry was somehow contagious and Gabe had been infected.

Compounding his fear of going crazy was his total solitude. Gabe knew he should tell someone what had happened, but he feared hearing himself say aloud all that he was thinking. Even worse, he didn't know who would care. His parents would only overreact. The bridge between himself and Jan was still smoldering. Cal would be sympathetic but too logical—he'd propose a solution, Gabe knew, but it was unlikely to be a good one and in the end the conversation would just be deeply unsatisfying.

Val was the only one left, and she'd purposely removed herself from Gabe's life more than a year before. She might not be able to help him, and she might even resent him reaching out, but once the idea of speaking with her took hold, Gabe knew he wouldn't be able to resist for long.

It was more than allegiance to Henry that had kept Gabe from getting in touch with her before. There was, perhaps, an element of pride. She'd broken up with him, too, in a way. He didn't want to go crawling back like some lovesick baby.

It also felt dangerous to think too much about her. It had never been easy for him to ignore the way she made him feel. Mostly he succeeded. He could always see and appreciate Val's beauty, but the pain he sometimes felt when he looked at her grew less intense over time. That pain belonged to a fantasy girl who had never existed, a mythical Val who never opened her mouth except to kiss and who didn't do things like trip and fall and laugh in embarrassment or force her friends to pause a movie while she went to the bathroom.

But then she left and Gabe wasn't confronted with the *real* Val any longer. And maybe, if he was being honest with himself, he'd allowed the fantasy version of her to take hold again. A few times, late at night, he imagined her calling him up to talk over all they'd been through, to explain to Gabe why she'd left and how she wished she could still see him. That was always how it started. What happened after that first meeting was variable. That was the fun part. It made Gabe feel guilty, especially now, to think about it. He hadn't ever wished for Henry to disappear, not really. But in his fantasies that disappearance had been a precondition for everything that he secretly wished would come after. Now that Henry was really gone, Gabe was stuck regretting all the ways in which he'd imagined his best friend out of the picture for the sake of some masturbatory delusion.

But he was desperate, maybe insane. He needed to talk to someone who understood him.

He was home when he finally called her. It was late afternoon, cloudy but dry, the sun's light wasted for no good reason. He'd spent most of the day looking in the general direction of the television. It was on, but it would have been fine with him if it hadn't been. TV had become little more than an excuse to stare at the corner of the room. Cal wasn't cool with cigarettes indoors, so Gabe went out on the porch to smoke his anxiety into submission. He found her name in his phone and breathed in. He'd learned to shoot rifles in Boy Scouts, and he pressed down on her entry in his contacts list the same way he'd been taught to fire a gun: breathe out slowly, focus on the target, and press softly, just enough to engage the trigger—don't jerk in anticipation of the kickback.

He lifted the phone to his ear and Val's line rang.

Gabe wondered how she'd reacted when she heard about Henry. He pictured her shrugging her shoulders, sad but detached, but that didn't seem right. Then he imagined her distraught, crying alone in her bedroom in New York City for days, destroying herself with regret for having left Henry to deal with his illness alone. That didn't make sense either.

It rang again. He imagined Val walking around deserted city streets at odd hours, confused and melancholic. Just like him. That felt better, but not quite believable.

"I was wondering when I'd hear from you," said Val. Gabe hadn't even heard her pick up the phone. She was teasing him. She sounded happy.

"Hi, Val." For a moment, he was happy too.

There was silence, awkward but not unpleasant. "I'm glad you called," she said. "I felt like I shouldn't call you, you know? Like I didn't have a right or something. I've wanted to, though."

"It's okay," said Gabe. It seemed like what she wanted to hear.

"So," she said.

"How are you?"

"I'm fine. Good. Um . . . how are *you?*" she said, and she laughed. "I'm sorry. This is just weird."

Gabe laughed too. "It's definitely weird," he said, wondering which of a thousand aspects of the conversation she was referring to.

Something about her reaction to the call didn't make sense. He sighed and his breath was amplified by the phone's microphone. It came through his own earpiece as a roar of white noise.

"Gabe, why are you so quiet? What's going on?" She was still bubbly, teasing, actually curious about why he'd called her.

Gabe understood then. She had no idea. Not even just that Henry was missing. She had no idea that there was anything wrong with him at all. He reconfigured all of his expectations for the conversation and nearly panicked at the thought of where to begin. "Jan didn't call you?" he asked.

"Why would *Jan* call me?" she asked. "What's going on?"

Gabe felt bad for leaving her in suspense, but he couldn't think of what to say. It sounded like she was outside; he heard a light swish of traffic punctuated by bits of voices and short honks. This would forever be the moment when she found out. Gabe's memories of Henry's transition made it seem gradual and ambiguous. But Val's understanding of what had happened would be immediate and certain, and Gabe would be the reason. He saw her walking down a crowded sidewalk. Probably wearing clothes he'd never seen before, which felt sad. She might have even dyed her hair or gotten some new piercing. Gabe didn't know, and it bothered him. He just wanted to be able to imagine the Valerie Mitchell he knew. He wanted to know how she would remember this moment, what she would recall about the second the world turned upside down. He wished he could feel it with her.

"Is Henry okay?"

Again, Gabe heard her, but there was no answer to that question that fit the circumstance.

"Gabe!" Her voice hit his eardrum in a digitized squall.

He focused, wet his lips, and lit a cigarette. "What was the last thing you heard from him?"

Forty-five minutes and two dropped calls later, Val knew what Gabe knew.

"I can't believe Jan didn't call you," said Gabe.

"Jan's too in love with her boy," she said. "She'll never talk to me again. But I kind of can't believe *you* didn't call me."

Gabe knew she didn't mean it to hurt, but it did. "Like you said. I wanted to. I just felt like I shouldn't. I figured you'd find out from somebody else."

"He called me," she said. "Once. I should have known. He was saying the worst things. He sounded crazy, like someone else. I hung up on him, I thought he was drunk. God—I'm so sorry, Gabe."

Gabe didn't respond. He'd heard *I'm sorry* from so many people. It was only slightly less disappointing and pointless when coming from Val.

But then, as if sensing how inadequate her words had been, she said, "I know how much you love him."

It felt like forgiveness to hear that, but his relief came with a real physical pain. Not the poetic kind that burns or purifies, the medical kind of pain made of blood and bile and shit. He wanted to run from it, to pound his hands into concrete and metal until they bled and shattered and fell apart. He muted the phone and emptied his lungs until he felt a deep, underwater kind of breathlessness. And then he cried.

Minutes later, when his sadness got prettier, Gabe unmuted the phone. Val had waited patiently. She was home by then. The connection was better, and she told him she'd gotten into bed. Gabe imagined flannel sheets and downy pillows.

"I must have ruined your day," he said, his voice still wavering.

"How are you doing besides all this? There must be other stuff going on for you."

"Not really." He thought of the man and the bridge. He had meant to tell her, but it suddenly seemed meaningless. Val and he had passed through something since he picked up the phone. He felt clearheaded. Her attention was like the light of day chasing away the odd nightmare of the bearded man and the bridge. Henry was not living in Buccleuch Park. He was not some vagabond or archetypal traveler. Wherever he was, he was speaking in non sequiturs, forgetting to eat, fearing everyone, and completely alone.

Another hour passed. They mostly talked about Val. School, the city, her parents, how different New York was from New Brunswick. Gabe left the porch and went inside to lie on the couch. He listened to her voice as the living room darkened around him.

When he asked if she missed Rutgers, she scoffed, then apologized.

"You don't have to be sorry," he said. "I feel pretty much the same. I'm just not smart enough to get myself out of here, I guess."

"You should come see me sometime," said Val. "If New Brunswick is so horrible."

Gabe knew that it was the kind of thing anyone would say, like the "Bless you" after a sneeze, but there was nothing he wanted more. "How about next weekend?" he said, and he felt his stomach float up into his chest.

In the brief pause before she answered, Gabe pictured appearing at Val's door, allowed himself to feel the thrill that had accompanied his fantasies.

"Seriously?" she said. And she laughed.

Gabe interrogated her tone for proof of his own stupidity. Had she seriously said *seriously?* Was that joy or awkwardness in her voice? He opened his mouth to take it back—to let her off the hook—but she interrupted him.

"That would be great," she said. "I can't wait."

FUGUE: 41

T HIS IS NOT my life.

The voice in Henry's mind—the voice that was *him*, he supposed—it sang this ode to his confusion on a constant loop. He did not feel his age. He didn't even know what it meant to be forty-one. It was a biological fact, nothing more, totally divorced from his identity.

This is not my life.

It was usually a whispered mantra, but there were melodies, too. Sometimes the song was bittersweet and schmaltzy. Sometimes it was frantic, repetitive. The tune depended on his mood, the weather, how empty his stomach was. But always accompanying the words was a sensation that Henry now accepted as an enduring amendment to his body's constitution: a nasty little rush that shot from his sternum to his fingertips and back and set all his muscles into rigor.

This is my life.

Coming to terms with his own strange flavor of immortality was his life. It always would be, forever and forever.

After his first break at nineteen, Henry had a handful of episodes. Each was unique in its severity and specific delusions, but there were four notable constants.

First, the voices.

Second, the fear. The voices fed on it, and they got louder, more sadistic, until they were fully grown—his own private monsters.

The third was his hallucinations of those monsters and the forces they used to carry out their will. Forces such as the bright green spastic low vibration. Or the music, that great song of everything.

The fourth constant was different. It was more seductive. If Henry wasn't vigilant, he would find himself meditating on what had happened to him when he was nineteen. His recollections felt one hundred percent genuine; they lacked the too-vivid sheen of the rest of his hallucinations. He *had* seen himself in the practice room. Twice. Taken together, his two memories of that singular moment fit seamlessly. And in order for those memories to be real, what had happened to him on the GW had to be real too. But there was so much he didn't understand, and that made it worse. The mystery was too compelling for him to resist. It dragged him under.

Most of the time he could manage his sporadic symptoms with little tweaks in his medication and lots of sleep, good nutrition, and exercise. Staying close to Val (and later, Annie) helped too. His family centered him, and the daily expectation of his sanity was a powerful force for the good. Val and Annie kept the voices from becoming monsters. They kept the questions from becoming full-blown mysteries.

But there were two episodes that he had not been able to avoid. Most laymen would call them breaks. Collapses, crack-ups, de-compensations, disturbances, deteriorations—the name meant little. Henry's favorite had always been *fugue*. He liked it best on account of its quaint baroque undertones and inherent musical connotation.

The first of these fugues occurred when he was twenty-nine and on tour with a rock singer. He slept at odd hours and ate like shit, and though he saw the warning signs he didn't heed them. He felt he had to press on. Val had just learned that she was pregnant with Annie and they needed the money. The tour was scheduled for just over ten weeks. Henry lasted two-thirds of the way through before he was forced to make his way home and then back to Lung-Ta Mountains, the Massachusetts treatment center that had seen him through the first time around. At Lung-Ta, he took the drugs he was given. He talked to a psychiatrist, a social worker, various residents and researchers. He talked until he felt emptied out, but he went to bed feeling as though he'd said nothing at all. When he wasn't talking he imagined Val and her growing belly. He pictured her doing soothingly mundane things: drinking herbal tea, reading a book, or laughing at the TV. He returned home excited to fuss over her in the final months of her pregnancy, but she was not as thrilled to see him as he had hoped.

Before Val let him unpack his duffel bag she sat him down at the kitchen table and told him that if he ever again refused treatment or put himself in a position to lose control, she would leave him. They were going to be parents. She would not allow their child to suffer on account of his stubbornness.

Henry believed her. It hurt, but he knew he couldn't fault her. He promised it would never come to that.

But, of course, it did.

Henry's second fugue began just after his forty-first birthday.

He had an idea for a composition inspired by the music he'd heard on the George Washington Bridge twenty years before. *Bridgesong,* as he named it, was something he'd always wanted to create, but the choice to pursue it at that particular moment was as cynical as it was artistic. They needed money and there were a couple of composition grants he'd been chasing for years. What judge wouldn't be taken in by the story of his musical hallucinations? It was a bit of a dirty trick, sure—people were intrigued by the mythology surrounding insanity, particularly when it came to artists. Henry's history of institutionalization gave him an unmatched patina. He'd never wanted to exploit it before, but now he was middle-aged with a child to support. He told himself that his years of suffering had earned him the right to use his mental illness to his advantage.

Bridgesong required that Henry travel around the city and gather snippets of found noise to be parsed and layered and looped in his home studio. Val warned him to be careful. She'd long before made peace with who he was, his particular challenges, but her concern was not unfounded. Henry told her it would be a useful framework for a piece of music, nothing more. To prove his good intentions he took Annie along on his sound-gathering trips. He packed a splitter and an extra set of big studio headphones so they could both listen to the feed coming from his microphone. They walked hand in hand through Times Square and along the Brooklyn, George Washington, and Fifty-Ninth Street Bridges. He took her to Broadway and Spring on a Saturday afternoon when shopping was in full swing, then to the Brooklyn Promenade and Hudson River Park and the High Line. They rode the subways together, and the ferries, and even a red double-decker bus. They stood at the piers in Red Hook, in the sand at Brighton Beach. They marched down Canal Street.

Henry liked to picture how they looked to strangers. A grown man and an eleven-year-old girl holding hands and standing as still as possible while the rest of the world moved around them, the oversized headphones making their shadows look like Mickey and Minnie Mouse.

After a few minutes of listening, Henry would remove his headphones.

"What do you think?" he would say, and then he would watch her face scrunch with concentration. There was nothing practiced or affected about her expression. The bright little orbs of her cheeks lifted, turning her eyes into deep crescents. Her mouth dropped open, revealing awkward gaps between adult teeth that still looked too big to be hers. It took effort not to laugh or scoop her up and squeeze her, but he didn't want to interrupt her. It would prevent him from hearing whatever incredible thing she was trying to figure out how to say.

"There's that guy calling out about water bottles," she said once. "He said the same words over and over and over and it sounded funny. Like they weren't words anymore."

Or, "The bus makes a *really loud*, like, *whooshing* sound right after it stops to pick people up. I can't hear anything else for a second and then? I can again." She laughed.

After collecting, Henry got to work editing and mixing.

He isolated the screech of the 4 train as it traveled along the curved platform at Union Square. It reminded him of how the bridge had screamed. He mixed the rhythmic thumping of rush-hour traffic over the seams of the GW with the blast of the Circle Line ferry's horn to evoke the driving foundation of the song he remembered. Then, to add depth, he recorded a low b-flat, played with a felt mallet on the marimba. He trimmed off the percussive inception of the tone and its gradual ebbing, which left only the solid resonance itself. When looped, it provided a mellifluous foothold for the mechanical ruckus of everything else.

It wasn't exact—it never could be—but when Henry played everything together for the first time he felt a jagged twitch of that distant but familiar thrill. He was back on the bridge, running for his life, spittle flying up from his burning chest as he pounded out deep primordial chords with the soles of his feet. The feeling drove him to work harder, and he spent hours alone adding, shifting, modulating. He skipped dinner, he skipped sleep. When Val confronted him he barely even bothered to defend himself.

"This isn't worth your sanity," she said.

"I know," he said. "But the money—"

"We'll find the money," she said. "But you need to stop."

"I know," he said. "I will," he said. And he meant it. She hugged him and he held her. She told him she'd been scared, he told her he was sorry. They talked about how he might find more students, get more studio gigs.

But then, the next day, Val went to work and Annie went to school, and Henry could hear the music from the basement. It begged to be completed, pleaded with him to be set free. Perhaps he could have resisted, but he didn't truly want to. So he worked throughout the day, then showered in time to pick up Annie from school and get dinner ready. He knew he was close to the edge. It was scary but empowering. He could do it, he knew—he was finally confident and mature enough to hunt down his monsters without fear of being overcome.

One day he dropped off Annie and got to work. No lunch, no water, no need for a bathroom break—he sat in his office chair and swiveled back and forth to the rhythm of the music. He tweaked the sound of ocean waves, added a light sprinkling of taxicab tickers, then sat back again to listen. He was so close. The feeling was there. All he had to do was refine it and give it shape. It needed a beginning. It needed an end. He listened again, and this time he heard a faint vibration that hadn't been there before. He took off his headphones and the vibration resolved into a heavy pounding on the door upstairs, so hard that it shook the walls of the house and set framed photographs buzzing against the drywall.

Henry threw down the headphones, angry at being interrupted, and ambled up the steps, his legs sore from sitting.

"What?" he yelled. Another knock came in response. He opened the door.

"Mr. Edwards?" Henry saw in front of him a bulky man in a

beige suit and shiny tie. One of the man's hands was resting on Annie's shoulder.

"Annie," said Henry. "What are you doing here?" Then, to the man, "Is she okay?"

"It's four thirty," said the man. Henry remembered him now. A principal, associate principal, something like that. "She's been waiting on the steps of the school for over an hour."

"Four—what? Annie, come inside, okay?" He knelt to her level and held out his arms. In the moment before she ran into them he saw that her eyelids had ballooned out from tears. Her nose was red. She looked frightened and angry, embarrassed and sad—her face a collage of all the things Henry couldn't bear to see her feel.

"Mr. Edwards, I'm obligated to—"

"Thank you," said Henry. He stood up, lifting Annie, and closed the door. He could hear the man speaking outside, the words *counselor* and *attitude* and *report* intermingled with a meaningless murmur. "It's okay," Henry whispered into Annie's ear. She was too big to hold, really—her sneakers reached all the way down to his knees—and Henry strained to walk while carrying her weight, but he didn't want to let her go. She held on to his neck with animal urgency and cried as he crashed down onto the couch with her still attached.

Eventually her wounded silence lifted. "Where were you?" she said, over and over.

She pounded his chest with a tiny fist and he laughed as he said, *I'm sorry I'm sorry I'm sorry…*"

She couldn't help herself, she laughed too, though she did a fine job of keeping the corners of her mouth turned down.

They made dinner. Henry let her cut the vegetables for salad, had her stand on a chair with an apron on. They were singing together when Val walked in from work. Henry moved to greet her but stopped when he saw the look in her eyes.

"I got a phone call," she said.

Henry started to speak, but she held up her hand.

They ate. Val didn't ask the usual questions about everyone's day. Annie jabbered on about her art project, a new boy in her class, a birthday party, her teacher, a cartoon she'd seen. Val and Henry directed all their attention to her.

And then Annie went to bed. What happened after that couldn't properly be called a fight. It was too one-sided for that. Val said she'd had a feeling Henry was still working on *Bridgesong*, but she let it go because she knew he would do the right thing. But now he'd forgotten their daughter. He looked like shit. He was distant. He'd lied to her and she'd let him because—she couldn't even remember why. But no more. She'd made him a promise before Annie was born, and now he was forcing her to keep it.

Henry said he could control it. That she needed only to trust him, to help him, to give him the room he needed. He tried to explain about the voices, the monsters, how he was finally going to tame them, but instead of reassuring her, his desperate sincerity scared Val into action. That Saturday, Val packed for herself and Annie. She told him she would be back in a week to help him if he decided to recover or to move some of his stuff out if he chose to continue driving himself into the ground. Then she marched Annie out the door, en route to her parents' house.

Henry worked even harder then. He slept only when it was a physical inevitability. Food and hygiene were distractions he had no problem ignoring. Rather than shaking him loose of his obsession, the temporary loss of Annie and Val only added new urgency to his quest. Once *Bridgesong* was complete he would clean himself up. He would do anything Val asked and they'd come back. But first he had to finish. It was his life's work, the only thing that would heal him once and for all.

On the fifth day, he addressed his empty house. "It'll be fine," he said. "I'll be done soon."

"Go for a walk," said the house, and Henry didn't think it strange. "Sometimes you need to get some distance. Good for perspective."

Henry bit his lip and nodded thoughtfully. It was a good suggestion, he knew, but he ignored it. He was too busy. He didn't mean to be disrespectful, but the house took offense and its encouraging tone was replaced with a bitterness edging closer and closer to violence. Soon it was yelling and Henry was yelling back until, exhausted and scared and wanting to placate his demanding new companion, he walked out the front door in his slippers.

It was daytime. Bright afternoon. Henry hadn't realized.

The neighborhood was still, its denizens at work or school or shuttered behind closed doors watching talk shows or twenty-four-hour news channels. Henry's slippers flopped softly on the sidewalk. Annie had given them to him for Father's Day. They were backless and lined with some synthetic version of sheep's wool. He hadn't really wanted them at first, but then he put them on to please her and found that he liked them after all.

He was very tired. He hadn't noticed it before, but now it seemed like the defining feature of his existence. He lifted a hand to rub his eye and got a strong waft of raw onion and dried mushroom. He was confused for an instant, unable to fathom that the stink was his own. It was like smelling salts for his psyche. In the light of the afternoon, his skin tickled by a warm breeze, he saw the truth of his situation with astonishing clarity. He was fucked up, and it was time to turn it around.

He kept walking.

Up ahead, the road crossed a nameless stream winding down from the Oradell Reservoir. It was little more than a ditch and a trickle, but the city had erected a fifteen-foot span of concrete to cross it. Henry moved toward it mournfully, each step strengthening his resolve. The bridge was a sad reminder of what he'd been chasing, what had made him willing to let go of the two people he loved most. He wanted to do the right thing, but he wondered if it wasn't too late. There was no guarantee that Val would take him back. Annie might forgive him, but her trust, the thing he coveted most, had suffered irreparably. Still, his choice was clear. He would go to his old psychiatrist and therapist. If he had to he'd even go back to Lung-Ta to be deadened, chemically lobotomized, depressed and cajoled into normalcy.

He approached the bridge as if it were the physical embodiment of his fate. It wasn't the source of some mystical power—it couldn't transport him to another life. It was metal and paste. Ordinary just like him.

A vibration passed through his body. It tickled each of his teeth at their roots. He thought it was just exhaustion, but then it became audible and Henry shuddered. The sound was dull and deep, unlike anything he'd heard before—the cement of this structure offered none of the romantic harmonies that the GWB had played so many years ago, but the feeling that grew inside of him was the same. The bridge was singing, and the moment Henry's foot landed on it he heard the sound he'd been hunting, that great merging of leaves and birds and cars and trees and the barking of dogs and a jet overhead.

It's so easy, he thought, and he closed his eyes and let the world dissolve around him.

He awoke on cold cement. At first he took the lightly glowing sky for dusk, but quickly reconsidered. It was too quiet to be evening. Had he really slept on the sidewalk through the night? Had nobody noticed? His got up on his feet and assessed himself for damage. Finding none, he started back to the house. The music, the very experience he'd been chasing through his experimental composition, he had found it. Not a digitized simulation, but the real thing. And yet as he walked, Henry felt nothing close to vindication. He felt sad. It was noise, that was all, and the mystery was no more solved than it had been before. It was just a high. It didn't change a thing.

He quickened his pace. The damp slippers made it difficult to walk fast, so Henry took them off and trotted on the rough sidewalk. He'd thought that finishing the piece would be a way to heal himself. In a way he was right, though the healing only came through understanding that the music itself was meaningless. It was simply his most persistent hallucination, no more or less real than any other.

Back home, he bounded to the door. The knob didn't turn and Henry rolled his eyes, chastising himself for his own stupidity. He stepped around to the side of the house. A key was hidden underneath a ceramic frog that was a foot high and deep green, a selection of Annie's that had helped ease her boredom the day she'd been forced to endure an hour in the garden section at the hardware store. The frog was at the back of a flower bed, leaning against the cement foundation of the house. Henry stepped gingerly onto the exposed soil, bent over, and paused when he heard a sound he recognized. Now that he was closer he could tell that one of the basement windows was glowing with a soft, shifting light. The glow came from his office. The sound was his *Bridgesong*. The window was just a few feet away, half blocked by a healthy little bush of rosemary. Henry pushed the bush out of the way and peered inside.

In the chemical glow of the computer screen sat a man.

Henry froze. He didn't need to open the door to his house and walk down the stairs, didn't want to see his own face staring back at him. The whole idea was so repugnant that his lip curled and his nose trembled. He sprinted from the yard and onto the street, back toward the spot where he'd woken up. He hadn't slept or eaten properly for days, and his body was far beyond its limits, but still he pressed on, holding tightly the spot between his ribs where a stitch like a burning stake throbbed and threatened to double him over. When the bridge came into view Henry felt nothing—no vibrations, no warm buzz—and the few sounds he could hear in the quiet dawn remained mundane and distinct. When he stepped onto the bridge's surface the cement remained unmoved, not speaking or singing or even so much as whispering. Henry pounded with his feet. He lay down and slammed its surface with his open palms. He kicked and banged his head and his hands against the rough sidewalk until spots of blood seeped slowly from small abrasions, then lost the will to fight and succumbed to cramped sobs.

A car engine crescendoed as it approached, then went quiet. Henry heard a car door open and close, quiet shuffling footsteps.

"Let me help you up," said a man.

"Leave me," said Henry, his words nearly indistinguishable from his pathetic burbling. "Please."

"Look at me," said the man.

Henry rolled onto his back, resigned that this Samaritan wasn't going to leave a crying man on the sidewalk. Using his already filthy T-shirt, Henry wiped sweat and tears and blood from his face. He breathed through his nose to calm himself, and opened his eyes.

"Thanks for stopping," said Henry. "Really. I'm okay, though."

"I said *look at me,*" the man repeated.

Henry, still flat on his back, took in the full image of the man above him and instantly understood. It felt like a memory—this vision of himself as an old man—and somehow he knew he'd long expected it.

He rolled onto his side and sobbed even harder than before.

"I don't want to know," he said. "I just want to go home. I want my girls."

The old man moved closer and bent, slowly, to one knee. He placed a hand on Henry's upper arm.

"If you come with me," he whispered, "it will be all right."

Henry didn't believe it, but he was too broken to do anything but stand and be led to the car. He didn't even ask where they were going. The man lowered himself into the driver's seat back first, his hands white-knuckling the handle above the door as he swung his legs inside with a grunt.

"Call me 80," he said. The old man looked almost as afraid as Henry felt, but he forced a smile to his gray lips before shaking his head and closing the door.

Henry turned from the man and closed his eyes, then rested his head against the window.

80 put the car into gear. "Let's go."

OLD FRIENDS

A VIBRANT SQUARE of October morning light pulsed through a window off to Gabe's left. It seemed to be assaulting him from an impossible angle. He shielded his eyes with his hand and peered out through the gaps between his fingers. There was a window, just a couple feet away, wide and tall enough to give the impression that the room was spilling out into the air instead of the outside being allowed in. Past his feet he saw an unfamiliar dresser and a closed door. To his right was the sleeping body of Val. She was pressed to the wall next to her bed, her bare arm on top of the covers, the gray strap of her tank top caught in the crease of her neck. Gabe examined her. He wanted to touch the little round bone at the tip of her shoulder, to put his arm over her, but though he and Val had always been affectionate when she was with Henry, it now seemed impossible that he would ever touch her on purpose. He closed his eyes again and breathed deeply. The faint scent of her sweat registered in his nose and warmth oozed through his chest, as if his blood itself was trying to pound out through his skin just to reach her.

Gabe dozed. A sliver of the dream that had awoken him reappeared in his mind. He had been gasping for air, holding Henry tight as they tumbled down a raging river toward a black hole in the side of a great stone wall.

They were supposed to have talked about Henry. When Gabe considered what it would be like to visit Val, he imagined a tearful conversation over takeout. She was owed a deeper understanding of what had happened, he thought. He wanted to confess to her all the ways in which he'd failed Henry. Gabe wanted forgiveness, and there was no one else who could give it.

He showed up at her apartment to the smell of garlic and onions. Val offered him a fruity, over-carbonated malt beverage in a bottle.

She talked fast. "There's this bodega on the corner—that's just a store, I don't know why I never heard that word before—right down the street, where even though they card all the time the one guy is totally obsessed with Kara, my roommate, so he never checks when I go in there, which is honestly kind of a letdown because I spent like two hundred bucks in the East Village on this amazing fake ID."

"Huh," said Gabe. He sipped his drink. It tasted like Jolly Ranchers dissolved in Mountain Dew.

Val talked about how different it was at NYU. Gabe told her how nothing had changed in New Brunswick. Val finished cooking the brown rice and chicken breast. She served it to Gabe on a real plate from an organized cabinet on a clean table in the cutely decorated corner of her small kitchen. He felt as though he'd come in from the wilderness. He unfolded the paper napkin she'd given him and placed it on his lap.

Val smirked. "Be honest," she said, and Gabe's heart beat faster. He had tried to prepare for difficult questions, but still he was afraid. "When was the last time you ate something that wasn't frozen in a box from that horrible little quote-unquote grocery on campus?"

Gabe laughed. It was spontaneous and unforced. It felt clean. He lifted his bottle of alcoholic candy and waited for her to do the same. They clinked. "You disappoint me," he said. "Their frozen burritos come individually wrapped in plastic bags."

The food was good. Gabe was at ease. He hadn't anticipated it, but Val's apartment felt more private and peaceful than any place he'd found in New Brunswick. He was still expecting his body to be thrown into disarray once their conversation turned to Henry, but they acted as though the phone call that brought them back together had never happened.

After dinner they cleaned up, and Gabe imagined Henry watching as they did the dishes, wondered whether they would act differently if he were there. Gabe hugged Val and thanked her for dinner, and in his mind's eye he saw the way Henry's hands used to rest on the small of her back when they kissed. They turned on a movie, and Gabe had to remind himself that it was now and not then, that Henry was gone. Even the earrings Val wore conjured him. They were a high school graduation gift. Henry had dragged Gabe to the mall two weekends in a row to help pick them out.

It was late when the movie ended. Gabe wasn't shocked when she told him that he could stay over. It didn't matter that the couch was too small and that the only place for him to stay was in her bed. The boundary between them was still firmly in place. It was safe. Gabe borrowed some oversized sweatpants and changed in the bathroom. When he came back out he saw that Val had put on loose, low-rise pajama bottoms and a tank top. Henry was in the room again, giving Gabe a look of warning, telling him not to gaze at her braless chest or the little hollows above her clavicle.

Gabe got in her bed and was glad when she turned off the lights and climbed in next to him. They traded memories and laughed quietly to each other. In the dark, Gabe could focus on her voice.

He could almost forget how the thin cotton of her clothing draped over her body.

The morning sun wasn't so merciful. It lit up her skin as if from the inside, cast shadows in beautiful places. The previous twelve hours had changed something, he knew. For five years he'd made himself forget what Val made him feel. Now, in a single night, all that work was rendered moot. He turned onto his side to face her back, then cradled his hands in front of his chest. He moved his right hand forward until the back of his fingers rested on the soft gray fabric between her shoulder blades.

He pulled back, chastened himself silently, then got out of bed with as little motion as he could. He changed back into his clothes and tiptoed out to the living room, where he grabbed a crisp copy of *Franny and Zooey* from the bookshelf and sat down on the couch. He couldn't muster the focus required to actually read, so he rested his eyes on the book's open pages and listened to the city. It was quieter than he expected.

Val came out half an hour later. Gabe watched her stretch in her doorway—arms reached up to the doorframe, face contorted, a long stale sigh. Her tank top slid over her breasts as it rose up on her shoulders, and a thin band of soft white belly revealed itself for just a moment before disappearing as she lowered her arms.

"Hey," she said. "You sleep all right?"

"Slept great," he said. His desire was forceful and insistent. He wondered how he had ever been able to speak to her without parsing each word.

She walked to the bathroom. Gabe stood up and gathered his things. He could hear her brushing her teeth. The water ran in the sink, the toilet flushed. He found his socks and hopped them on while still standing, then kicked his feet into his shoes.

Val came out of the bathroom, her hair bundled in an alligator clip. She looked even better than before.

"I gotta get back," he said. "Work tonight."

She squinted, questioning, then softened her face and said, brightly, "Well, thanks for coming."

"Thanks for having me."

They hugged. She gripped him tighter than he had expected, and he reciprocated. Underneath his fingertips the skin of her back rolled over her vertebrae. His lips were so close to her neck, and the tang of her sleep-washed skin urged him to bury his face deeper. The moment she showed signs of letting go, he released his grip entirely and stepped past her to the door.

"Talk soon?" she said.

Gabe nodded as he went through the doorway and out into the hall.

It took him three attempts to buy the right ticket to get back to New Brunswick. He could see the words on the touch screen vending machine but couldn't retain their meaning for long enough to follow the process from beginning to end. The first time he pressed Start Over, a man in a Giants jersey sucked his teeth. The second time, Gabe heard a plaintive "Come on now."

Ticket in hand, he went to the long corridor that served as a waiting area. He sat on the ground, back against a pillar, and watched the departures board. In front of him a glass wall protected a bizarre diorama of famous New Jersey locales. Miniature floats hung from an elliptical track in the ceiling that turned as if on perpetual parade: three women holding a giant piece of saltwater taffy above their heads, carousel horses, a dirigible, a cadre of revolutionary soldiers standing atop a freighter, an old courthouse. Gabe had been in and out of the city a handful of times since he started at Rutgers, and he wondered how it was possible that he'd never noticed it before. It looked like a papier-mâché hell-scape, fascinating only insomuch as it was grotesque. He wondered who had commissioned it and how long it had been intended to last. Even kids would find it stupid or scary or both, and yet there it was, the only attempt at making Jersey look special in all of New York City.

Its aesthetic qualities aside, it was a welcome distraction. Val had been Gabe's last hope for maintaining some normalcy. He'd expected to leave her place feeling clearheaded, but now that hope had sweetly been destroyed. He slept with her, and even though it was just sleep, the euphemistic significance of the phrase tingled through him.

The pillar on which he leaned was in the middle of a wide hallway with platform entrances on either side. Reflected in the glass that protected the mobile were all the people around him. He wondered whose problems were bigger than his, whose were smaller. Some walked left. Some walked right. He tracked these strangers in both directions until his attention was snagged by a skinny bearded man with a black backpack. His face was mostly hidden by a swoop of long hair, but Gabe recognized the man's gait. Suddenly his breath felt thin. He sat up to get a better look, but the bearded stranger turned a corner and disappeared from sight.

Gabe wanted to stand up and follow the man, but instead he closed his eyes, sank back down, and rested his head against the pillar. *It wasn't him,* he told himself. *It wasn't him wasn't him wasn't him.* Eyes closed, he breathed until his heart slowed. A voice came over the loudspeaker to announce that his train was boarding.

Gabe snagged a three-person bench in the middle of a mostly abandoned car and threw his shoulder bag onto the seat closest to the aisle, staking his claim. Once the train was speeding through the tunnel under the Hudson, he leaned his head against the window and closed his eyes.

Some time later he awoke to the sound of a man's voice. He assumed it wasn't directed at him, and he tried to drift back off into sleep, but then he heard it again.

"Hey. Wake up," said the voice. It was close. "Can you move your bag so I can sit down, please?"

Gabe wanted to pretend to still be sleeping, but he'd never been good at that sort of thing. He was resentful but not brave enough to show it. He opened his eyes just enough to get a sense of how far away his bag was, then tucked it under his arm and gathered the long strap in his fist. He leaned against the window again and felt the bench shift.

"Thanks. I didn't mean to bother you."

Gabe responded with a half nod.

"I was hoping we could talk."

Gabe looked toward the voice, preparing himself to say something brisk and dismissive, anything to get this lonely loser to leave him alone. But the sight of the man's face arrested his senses. He was smiling again; this time Gabe was close enough to tell for sure. He hadn't changed his clothing since the last time Gabe had seen him, when he was flying in slow motion over Route Eighteen.

"What the fuck?" Gabe's mouth formed the phrase almost involuntarily.

"I'm sorry," said the man.

"Are you following me?"

"Yes."

Gabe had expected the stranger to say no, had already done the instantaneous mental prep work required for the conversation that would follow a denial. Now he was left speechless. Looking into the man's eyes, this close up, Gabe was struck with a vertiginous déjà vu.

"I know you," said Gabe.

"Yes."

"How do I know you?"

"You chased me the other day," he said. "I'm sure you remember it."

"Yeah, but—"

"I know you, too," said the man. He was still smiling, but now it was toothy, specks of white shining out from the overhang of his bushy mustache.

"You're crazy," said Gabe.

"Not today."

"Leave me alone."

"Tell me what you saw on the bridge."

Gabe looked out the window. The train was soaring on elevated tracks out over the Meadowlands. Ahead was a huge tangle of highways. It would be a while before they reached another station, and he considered his options. He'd been followed all the way to New York, then watched when he went to Val's, then followed back to the train station and onto this train. Whoever this man was, he had worked very hard to have this conversation. There was certainly something scary about that, but it was intriguing, too.

"You knew I would chase you," said Gabe. "You wanted me to."

"Probably."

"Probably? You were stretching. Why didn't you just do your little dance right then? Why make me run after you for a mile?"

"That's just the way it happened," said the man. "What did you see?"

Gabe had no reason to trust in the man's intentions, but, inexplicably, he didn't feel afraid. "When we got to the top of that staircase you started dancing." He sat up straight and glanced around the car, gauging how quietly he should talk so as not to be heard. "It was like everything...came together."

The man nodded, his eyes and mouth crinkled with bemused expectation.

"It was like...everything around me was choreographed. On

purpose. Like some crazy musical number in a movie." Gabe knew he wasn't getting it right.

"I hate that," said the man. "Why does everything have to be like a movie? Try harder."

"I don't know. Jesus. You were there," said Gabe. "You obviously know more about it than I do. What does it matter?"

The man turned his body in the seat and fixed his eyes on Gabe. When he spoke it was fast, without hesitation, and almost monotone. "The entire world condensed into a tiny space that was simultaneously infinite and finite, eternal and momentary. All the elements of the universe pushed so close together that in order to squeeze through your mind they had to lock in to one another and finally merge."

The words flowed from the man's mouth in time with the *kachunk* of the train on its tracks, and for a moment Gabe couldn't distinguish between the disparate sounds.

"You felt no separation between yourself and anything else. Time came to an end and then restarted. The music you heard was of a kind that you hadn't previously known existed but that you can now hear everywhere if you're not careful to ignore it. It was the sound of all."

The last syllable of the man's little monologue was still vibrating the air around Gabe's ear when he focused back on his surroundings. It seemed like everything had been remade. The muddy brown of the seats was brighter than before, as if the sunlight coming through the windows was charged with new life.

"Don't do that again," said Gabe.

"I didn't do anything."

"Yes, you did. When you spoke—"

"Anything else?"

Gabe thought about it harder this time. He felt it was important to say something useful. "You were at the center of it. Even when

you were falling through the air, it was like your body was conduct-
ing everything else."

The man looked doubtful. Gabe wanted to convince him but
recognized that the impulse was strange. When had he started feeling responsible to this man?

"Where did you go?" said Gabe. "I thought you were dead. Or
that I'd just imagined it. When you jumped off, I thought you were
going to break your neck or something. Then you were just gone."

The man looked down and smiled. "Have you fucked her yet?"
he said.

"Who?" said Gabe.

"When it happens, I don't want you to think about me."

"Why the fuck would I think about you? I don't even know who
you are."

"I'm why you went over there, aren't I?"

"No," said Gabe.

"I'm sorry I messed you up by showing you what I did, but I had
to. Nothing else would have made sense."

"I don't even know what you showed me," said Gabe. "I was
freaking out or something. Hallucinating. Then you disappeared."

"I was still there," said the man. "You just couldn't see me."

"I looked everywhere."

The man shrugged.

"You can't be for real."

"I'm for real enough that I'll probably get kicked off this
train for not having a ticket in a few minutes. Unless you want
to spot me."

Gabe had the funny thought that he might be a victim of the
most elaborate panhandle of all time, the man just an existential con
artist, confusing his marks to near insanity over the course of days
before hitting them up for train fare.

"Let me out," said Gabe.

"I'm not keeping you here." The man gestured to the two inches of clearance in front of his knees as if it proved his point.

"You're in my way," said Gabe, and he stood up.

"You didn't answer my question." Then, slowly, each word deliberate and full: "Did you fuck Val yet?"

Gabe sat down.

Recognition came in quick waves after that: the slight movements of the man's eyes as he spoke, his gait, the shape of his eyebrows, his teeth when he smiled. The first thing Gabe felt was guilt at not having recognized Henry before. And then he felt like sobbing out of relief or sadness or something else that he couldn't articulate. There were so many things he could say, so many things he'd imagined himself saying if ever he saw his best friend again, but for some reason the only thing that came out was, "You look like shit."

Henry laughed, and it revealed the deep lines around his eyes. All the things that had prevented Gabe from recognizing him now looked totally incongruous. There was silver in his beard, long streaks that started halfway down his jaw on either side. His cheeks were sunken in, eyes dark in their sockets and as wide and strange as Joan had first described them.

"What happened to you?" said Gabe. "What's with the cloak-and-dagger?"

"It's been a long time since I've seen you like this," said Henry, smiling. "I feel old."

"If you don't want to tell me where you've been, that's fine, but stop pretending like you don't understand what I'm asking."

"Okay," he said. "I don't want to tell you where I've been."

Gabe let this sit, unsatisfied. He thought about how scared he'd been of encountering Henry. It seemed silly until Gabe remembered what Henry had been like on the phone. It was *that* Henry he'd dreaded seeing. As different as the man in front of him was from the Henry Gabe had always known, he was even further removed from the sad, raving, broken version of himself that had lived for weeks on the other end of a cell phone connection.

"You seem...Are you okay?"

"I'm not," said Henry. "But I'm sane. For the most part."

"Why are you sleeping in the park?" Gabe asked. "You know you can stay with me." But that was a lie. Had Henry appeared at the door Gabe would have called Jan and the police in that order, without delay. He'd been missing too long. It would have been irresponsible to hide him. "What are you doing out there?"

Henry shot him a sharp look. It seemed to say that Gabe should know better, or that there was something essential he had yet to understand.

"This is bullshit," said Gabe. "It's only been like two minutes and I'm already tired of asking you questions that you won't answer."

"Then stop asking," said Henry, "or ask better questions."

"Just come back."

"Nobody else can know that you've seen me."

"That's just stupid, Henry."

"Nobody else, Gabe. Not my mom, not Val, not anybody. I know it's a big demand, and that it's unfair, and that you can't exactly take for granted that I'm in the best state of mind. But if I can't trust you, there's nobody."

"I kept a secret for you before and it fucked everything up. You know how much your mom hates me right now?" Gabe could see that his words weren't penetrating. "This is fucking crazy."

"Careful how you use that word. And she doesn't hate you."

"I can't keep the fact that you're alive a secret from your own mother."

"If you tell her, I'll just disappear again." Henry's lack of hesitation and emotion was chilling. "It's not your responsibility to make sure I'm okay."

"Then what is my responsibility?"

"I don't know," he said. "You don't really have one, not to me, anyway. Not right now."

"Why are you sitting here if you don't want help? You could have stayed missing, and from what I can tell, you plan to do that anyway. So, what? What am I supposed to do with this?"

"I don't need your help. Not like that."

Gabe huffed and deflated, then tapped the side of his head against the window.

"Jesus," said Henry. "You have one break with reality and everyone is falling all over themselves to find you the kind of 'help' you need. Such a weird fucking euphemism. It's not me that needs help—it's you and my mom and everyone else."

Gabe's eyebrows formed the visual equivalent of *You've got to be shitting me.*

"It's true," said Henry. "You just want to get me help from someone else so you can feel like you did everything you could. You're just as powerless as I am. I don't want your capital-*H* Help. I know that what I'm choosing to do right now could be problematic. I just need to talk to you every once in a while. I need to work some things out. That's it."

The train reached Newark Airport. Travelers wrestled rolling luggage down the narrow aisle between the benches. Henry's ragged appearance afforded them a wide radius of empty seats. Gabe waited for everyone to sit before speaking. "I don't know if I can do this. Why don't you just go to your mom? You're fine now, she'll leave you to do whatever, and she won't be losing sleep thinking you're fucking dead."

Henry looked past him out the window of the train. "I had a question for you," he said. "A question I asked twice already. You haven't answered it."

Val. The sharp points of Gabe's right cuspids found a little pad of flesh inside his cheek.

"You haven't done anything yet," said Henry. He sounded calm.

"What do you mean, *yet?*" said Gabe. "I wouldn't do anything with Val." But he knew that if he wasn't sitting with Henry he'd be obsessing over what he'd felt that morning, telling himself it was okay to see Val how he'd seen her, to want to see her more.

Henry stared, unblinking, until Gabe felt compelled to say more.

"I went over there because of you." It felt just truthful enough to warrant the self-righteous tone that crept into his voice.

"I don't matter anymore," said Henry.

"Jesus, Henry."

"Jesus, Gabe," he said, employing the deranged baby voice he used whenever he wanted to mock his best friend.

Gabe fought with the corners of his mouth and bit his lower lip, but he couldn't keep from smiling.

Warm laughter gurgled from Henry's throat.

"I'm not agreeing to keep your mom in the dark," said Gabe.

Henry laughed again. "Bet you'll keep Val in the dark, though."

"Why would you say that? I didn't fuck Val, all right? Stop testing me."

"I was just curious," said Henry. "It's going to happen. And when it does, you need to know that I don't mind."

"Christ, Henry, just come down off your fucking cross, get some of that capital-*H* Help you don't want, and get over yourself. Just come back to the house. We'll figure it out from there."

"I can't," said Henry. He put both of his palms on the seat between them and leaned forward on his arms, his face coming to a stop inches from Gabe's own. "Look at me," he said.

The train passed through a covered section of track, and when they came out on the other side the yellow-striated brown of Henry's irises billowed out as his pupils contracted. The space between each of his eyes and temples looked like an aerial view of a river delta, the southernmost tributaries feeding deep, dark reservoirs underneath each eyeball. The rest of Henry's face was obscured by the big flowing beard with its random patches of gray.

"Your beard," said Gabe.

Henry cocked his head almost imperceptibly to one side and smiled. "How long do you think it took me to grow this bad boy?" he said, and he patted the bottom of his beard with an upturned palm. "And how long have I been gone?"

Gabe made no move to respond.

"So," said Henry. "Let's talk about the bridge."

SONATA: A HOUSE DIVIDED

HENRY SLEPT, DEEP and dreamless, until the crunch of gravel awoke him.

"We're here," said 80.

Henry opened his eyes. A small two-story house rose up from an ocean of green grass as they approached. At the edges of the clearing was dense forest, and a glance in the rearview told Henry that they weren't within sight of any road but the one they'd driven up on. 80 pulled into the roundabout in front of the house, killed the engine, and opened his door. Henry's ears strained at the sudden silence. The air felt thin in his nose, and it smelled of grass and dust and water.

80 lifted himself up out of the car and went around to the trunk, then passed by Henry's door with plastic grocery bags in hand. "Grab something before you come to the house," he said.

Alone, Henry looked at the grass and listened. Birds called from every direction, not the chattering of morning but the sporadic calls of afternoon. The sound of leaves rubbing against one another in the breeze swelled and then dwindled, their liquid whisper almost indistinguishable from the faraway sound of water over rocks. Inside the house, cupboard doors slammed against their frames. Henry opened the car door and swung his bare feet out onto the gravel, stepped gingerly to the trunk, and then up to the house and through the screen door, which squealed softly on its hinges as he passed over the threshold.

"Back here," said 80.

Henry followed the sound past a flight of stairs and through the living room. In the kitchen, 80 was carefully folding a plastic bag. He shoved it into a floor-level cabinet.

"You'll want a shower," said 80. "There are towels up in the bathroom. I put some clothes out for you in the room at the end of the hall to the right. I'll make lunch."

Henry placed the grocery bags on the floor, careful not to make any sound, though he couldn't have said why. He stared at 80, studied the shape of his hairline, his ears. He had no doubt about who he was looking at.

"Is this real?" he asked.

"I'm asking myself roughly the same thing," said 80.

"How—"

"I remembered where you'd be," said 80. "I wasn't certain that I had the right day until I saw you."

"But—"

"We can talk later," said 80. He looked like he might cry. "Just go upstairs and take a shower. Please."

Henry made the shower water as hot as he could stand it, then sat down in the tub and let the filth of the previous few weeks slough off him. He waited until the steam made it hard to breathe before turning off the tap and drying off.

In the bedroom, he dressed. He opened a window. He sat down on the bed then, just to enjoy the feel of the air from outside, the reassuring cooking sounds from below—clinking metal, the sizzle of a pan.

By the time he got downstairs the table was set with two plates, each covered in salad and a still-steaming chicken breast. There were checkered cloth napkins, forks and knives, and two glasses of water.

"You're not hungry," said the old man, who was already seated. "Neither am I. It just seemed like the only thing to do. Cook a meal. I'd probably throw up if I actually took a bite."

Henry sat down and rested his trembling hands on the table, palms down. "I feel normal," he said. "Well, not normal, but...sane."

"I remember."

"But you're here. So. I don't know what this means."

80 picked up his fork, pushed lettuce around with the tines, then set it back down.

"I can't really be seeing you," said Henry.

"You are. And you know that."

"The practice room."

"Hmm."

"All those years ago? It was real?"

"All those years."

Henry considered all that they'd said and in how few words. "It's not—I don't think it matters," he said. "Please. I was going to go get help. I'm ready to let go. I want to go home."

"I remember," said 80. "But not just yet."

"Take me back. Please. You can do that, can't you?"

"We have a lot to talk about. And for the sake of expediency, I'll do the talking."

Henry rankled at being shut up, but then it struck him. "You already know everything I might say."

"That's part of it. But I also know a lot about how you got here, and a lot about where you're going."

"So you know how this is going to work out," said Henry.

"I do, unfortunately."

Suddenly an intense square of honey-colored light beamed through the window above the sink. A cloud must have passed, giving way to the sun. The light gave the room a glassy feel, and it felt like a sign, but of what Henry wasn't sure. "And why is it unfortunate?" he said.

"I thought I could save us," said 80.

"And you can't?"

"Well, I haven't. Not yet. That much is clear."

"Save us from what?" he said, but he knew. Val had left and taken Annie. He had fucked it all up. "I can't get them back?"

80 shook his head.

Henry looked up at the ceiling, then closed his eyes. "What happens now?"

"We go to the living room and get comfortable. I tell you what I know. When I'm done, we figure out what to do next."

They rose and walked out of the kitchen, their food untouched. The old man took the couch. Henry lowered his aching body into a big plush chair.

"Are you comfortable?" said 80.

Henry nodded.

"The first time I was your age, I left the house just like you did. I passed out on the bridge, saw myself in the basement, and ran back. But nobody came to save me. Someone in the neighborhood must have called the police—you know how it is around there. Everyone's bored, paranoid. These two young officers came. They didn't arrest me, not officially, but I wasn't making sense. I cried and wailed until they put me in the squad car and drove me to the hospital. I told a nurse I wasn't where I was supposed to be, that I'd jumped into the past. She brought a doctor. He brought a psychiatrist. I said all they had to do was go to the house and they'd find me there, *another me*, I told them, the one who hadn't left the house yet.

"Then Val came—be glad I spared you the pain of seeing the

look on her face. *Just go back to the house,* I told her. I wouldn't give it up. Eventually she made a deal. She'd drive back to the house and if she didn't find another me there waiting for her, I'd do whatever she asked."

Henry could picture it, vaguely. Val would have said no a thousand times, would have refused to play along with his delusions. The fact that she gave in was terrifying proof of just how scared she must have been. "She didn't find you, I guess."

"No," said 80. "Much later, I figured it out. I passed out on the bridge in the afternoon, woke up there that same morning. I shifted just about eight hours into my own past. By the time Val got to the house I had already left again. She was too late. But at the time I didn't know that, I didn't understand. I thought she was lying, told her she had to be wrong because I'd seen myself with my own eyes. There was some violence. Not toward her, nothing like that. I just wanted to go check for myself. They restrained me and I fought. Later, after all the meds had had time to build up and I was a good, obedient patient, I *still* wouldn't deny what had happened to me. I hated Val for not believing me. It wasn't fair, but I did."

"And Annie?" said Henry.

"She was too young to understand. After I came back and Val and I split, I got 'visitation' rights. An awful word. You don't visit your own blood. I was living alone, doing well, but it didn't matter to Annie. When she turned fourteen she asked to be freed of her weekend obligation to me. She said it was too hard to go back and forth. I felt like I was losing her, so I sat her down and tried to... I started from the beginning. I thought if I could only explain—"

"Jesus—"

"I wanted her to know the truth. And I don't need you telling me how bad a decision *that* was. From then on all I got from Annie was begrudging pity, and all I got from Val was disdain."

"You deserved it," said Henry.

"And imagine how much worse that made me feel. Before you think of scolding me, consider that you would have done the same. I just picked you up to *stop* you from being as stupid as I was."

"You want to undo this," said Henry.

"And you think it's impossible."

"It doesn't matter if it's possible or not. It's over. This is dangerous. It's crazy."

"Annie is grown now," said 80. "She's incredible. A woman cast in the mold of her mother. Sometimes she comes over on holidays. I give her no joy—I've known that for a long time. She has kids of her own, a boy and a girl, and I see the way she watches me when I'm with them, like I might break them. They like their grandpa, but when they get old enough she'll tell them what she knows about me. I'll watch them catch her fear. And then? When I'm gone? I'll be remembered but not missed. It will be a relief to everyone who knows me. I'll finally be the disembodied subject of family lore. Crazy old Grandpa. A joke."

"And Val?" Henry asked. "She never forgave you?"

80 shook his head. "She's been gone a few years."

"Gone?" said Henry. He was about to ask to where but then he understood and was overcome with a feeling like drowning.

They sat in silence again. The room grew darker around them as the sun slipped farther down on the other side of the house.

When Henry could finally speak again, he said, "Why am I here? What do you want?"

"It seemed obvious. If I had never relived those eight hours, never raved at the doctors and Val, everything would be different. So when I got out of the hospital I started walking. I rented an apartment up on Kinderkamack Road. It was close enough to make Annie's visits easier, close to that little concrete bridge, too. I visited that bridge once a day for several years, but I never heard the song again. Eventually I started feeding my drugs to the garbage disposal, thinking that could help. I spent nearly every waking moment listening for the music, searching it out."

"You wanted to hear it? Even after what happened the last time—even after you lost everything?"

80 shrugged his shoulders. "I'd do it again. You would have done the same."

"And eventually you heard it," said Henry.

"A long *eventually*, but yes. I stopped trying just the one bridge, bought a road atlas of the tristate and highlighted all the bridges I could find—countless crossings, I never realized how many there were. I visited them one by one, spending whole days driving from one to another to another. I'd find a place to park the car, walk to a particular site, stand with my eyes closed. It wasn't a very good method, but I didn't have any other ideas. Eventually it was little more than an eccentric hobby. Lots of old men have them. Truthfully, I didn't have much else to live for. Then one day, right on the other side of the reservoir over here, it happened. It was only a few years ago. I parked the car at this little country diner and ate lunch. As I was walking toward the bridge I started thinking about the vacation we took up here just after Annie was born. I pictured Val nursing in the little motel room, remembered Annie's feet, those little drumsticks, so fat she could barely flex her ankles. And Val's face, just open, beautiful, happy, and proud.

"I forgot about my surroundings, I forgot to listen. I was just an old man reminiscing like a pathetic fool—walking on a bridge meant for cars like some senile runaway. And then it happened. After searching for thirty-five years you'd think I'd have been prepared, but I wasn't. The song swelled up and absolutely exploded and overtook me so fast that next thing I know I'm sitting on my bony ass, my back resting against a metal railing so cold that it burns when I touch it. It was summer when I passed out, but I open my eyes and everything is a winter gray, completely quiet and still, no cars on the road. Even the Esopus Creek down below me is near silent, almost completely frozen over. Adrenaline is the only thing that gets me up on my feet, and I start to think I've made a huge mistake. The last time I shifted was when I was you. That was only a difference of hours, and I couldn't ever get right again. Now I'm displaced by months? Years? So I take a few deep breaths and to calm myself I picture walking across that bridge when it was warm, my car just down the road, my stomach full of something fried and awful. And by focusing on that, ignoring the pain and the panic, I hear the music again. It's faint at first, but then that white-noise rush just comes and takes me away, and the next time I open my eyes it's afternoon and I'm warm again.

"I walked back to the diner. My car was there, just as I'd left it. I got in and just shook and shook."

"So you can control it?" asked Henry.

"I need to focus on something, some time I want to be in. It's not like in a comic book—I can't go back and visit the Continental Congress and I can't go into the future. I can't focus on something I don't remember, and I can't remember something that hasn't happened yet. And I can't travel to just anyplace—I wake up on the bridge I passed out on. Really I'm quite limited."

"Limited," said Henry. He squinted. "Why bridges?"

"I'm not sure. Maybe there is something special about them, something acoustic or mystical, but I doubt it. It's probably a self-imposed necessity. A result of our experience. An association, nothing more."

"You seem to be enjoying this," said Henry, "the chance to talk about your method, how you did it."

"I've never spoken about it with anyone before."

"I don't care how you did it. I was about to let go of all this. I finally got to a point where I could—and then you—I just want to go back."

"And I can take you back, but if we follow the course of my memory—how can I explain? There are things I've known only since this morning. I waited for you down the road from the bridge. I saw you arrive, winded and crying. I watched you collapse and I drove up. Through all of that I remained myself, but then you saw me and you understood and in that instant a whole world of memory was thrust into my mind. The memories are brand-new and yet I've had them for forty years. It's hard to make sense of."

"I don't care how hard it is. I want you to take me back."

"And if we follow the course of these new memories, I'll oblige you. From this room we'll walk to a nearby footbridge that crosses the Esopus. I'll call forth the music, and when I awake you'll be there next to me. That in itself is rather incredible. I don't quite know how it's possible to take you with me, but my new memory tells me that it is. When you get home you'll call your doctor and pack your bags for Lung-Ta. For a while, you'll feel good. Things will get better between you and Val, but it won't last."

"It will," said Henry. "I'll do anything. I'll get them back."

"You won't."

"I will."

"I'm sorry, Henry, but this house, your time with me, this moment right now? This is real. There will be no question in your mind. You'll try to forget your certainty, or at least keep it hidden, but it will be much harder than you think. A few years from now the music will return and you won't be able to escape it. The rest will play out much as before."

"So you failed."

"I wouldn't say that."

"You still lost Val. You still lost Annie."

"There are other considerations."

"Like what?"

"A silver lining—"

"To what? Total fucking desolation? The loss of the only people that love you?"

80 huffed in frustration. "I know it doesn't seem—"

"No," said Henry. "There is no bright side."

"Fine. Not for you. Not right now. But before I came to get you I didn't learn to control this until I was in my seventies. After this morning, after this meeting, you'll do it earlier. A decade earlier."

"That doesn't really speak to my concern, does it?"

"Not directly, no, but you're missing the point. I agree. There's no bright side, not really and not yet. Your future, my past—it's mediocre at best. But we can change that."

Henry hated being sold to. His instinct was to fight back, but it seemed futile. 80 knew everything about him. If the old man wanted to convince him of something, was it even possible for him to resist? There was something else, too. Besides the fear, the anger and sadness, Henry knew that he was a little excited, too. He resented 80's manipulations but he couldn't deny that they were in an extraordinary position. The great mystery he'd carried with him his entire life—this was as close to a solution as he was ever likely to get. Could he really throw that away?

"I can tell you all you want to know about your future," said 80, "but you'll never fully understand it until you live it for yourself. I *have* lived it. I'm telling you that we can learn from it. The situation I'm in today, having lost Val, my own daughter like a ghost to me—that's not the life I was meant to live. We can have more."

Henry was on the edge, but something kept him from jumping into the unprecedented unknown. He wet his lips. "Where does it end?"

"That question," said 80. He shifted in his seat, leaned in to Henry. "It's a red herring. In my new life I've been thinking about it for forty years, and the only conclusion I've come to is that it doesn't mean anything, not really. I admit that we can't control everything.

We're bound to make mistakes—I already have—and it's good to be wary. But we *can* control ourselves. It stops precisely when we want it to."

Henry's skepticism remained, but 80's presence weakened his resolve. In forty years, Henry would agree with everything the old man was saying. More than that, he would *be* the old man. To disregard everything 80 said would be absurd.

Henry stood and walked to the bay window by the door. It was dusk. In the distance a mountain peak glowed with the amber light of the setting sun. Henry wished he were up there, alone. "What are you proposing?" he said. He didn't turn around. He didn't want to see 80's face.

"We push back the point of first contact."

Henry turned from the window and sat down again. He leaned all the way forward in his chair, his eyes focused on the floor.

"These experiences," said 80, "they have a way of interrupting our illness, correct? At least momentarily. So we intervene at a time when we need that cure. One way or another, that should do us some good."

Henry thought of his last fugue when, approaching thirty and with a baby on the way, he'd headed out on tour. Things got weird fast. The band's tour bus evolved into a microcosm of the eternal, epic struggle between good and evil, and his fear of that struggle grew with every passing day. The music echoed everywhere, ever present but just out of reach. Voices threatened him and his unborn baby girl.

Why wouldn't he try to save himself from all of that?

"It just seems so dangerous," said Henry.

80 cleared his throat. "It is. It always will be."

"And what if I say no? You could do this without me."

"Whatever choice I make from here is yours to make as well."

"That doesn't make sense," said Henry. "You can do whatever

you want. I can't stop you, and if I disagree, what difference does it make? You'll just console yourself with the knowledge that someday I would have come to agree with you."

"*A house divided against itself cannot stand.* I know you've heard the idiom, but you don't know where it's from. I just found out. I was thinking about you, about this meeting, and this saying came to mind, so I looked it up, and like so much else that's trite and self-evident it comes from the Bible. Mark, the New Testament. The scribes are debating with Jesus—really they're just jealous of him—and they start saying he's possessed by the devil. Jesus says, 'How can I be possessed? I exorcise the devil out of others. How can Satan cast out Satan? A kingdom divided can't stand. A house divided cannot stand. If I'm Satan,' he says, 'how come I'm fighting Satan?'

"Personally, I think whoever wrote the book of Mark was a little confused on this point, or maybe Jesus was, because you'd have to be a piss-poor student of human nature not to see that we fight against ourselves all the time. Countries, houses, individuals—we all struggle with ourselves. It's not a logical inconsistency, it's a precondition for humanity. But for us—you and me—we can't afford that."

"So you want us to be in agreement?" said Henry. "That's it?"

"I don't want it just for the sake of wanting it. It's absolutely crucial. When I change my past I change yours with it. And if, through our effort, you ever gain the ability to control your own travel through time, you'll be playing with my life along with yours. If we don't act together, as the single person that we in fact *are*, who knows what kind of damage we could do to ourselves? At some point there may be many versions of us, each with the ability to do whatever he pleases with his past. Our lives will multiply faster than we can understand them; our passage through time will tangle like a string. That's when your question of where it all stops becomes much more urgent. We need to be united," he said. "Completely.

And to that end, there are three things you need to know before you decide."

Henry assented with a blink and a blank stare.

"First, I remember hearing exactly this same argument when I was you. I remember how you feel, and it's for that reason that I want so badly to change your mind. Take this for whatever you think it's worth, but I deeply regret that I didn't listen."

Henry didn't know what that was worth. He hadn't decided yet. It seemed unwise to assume that 80's advanced age made him right, but it seemed just as unwise to mistrust advice from the man Henry would one day become.

"Second—we're in a loop. I remember being you and eventually you'll live this moment as me. You'll try to convince a forty-one-year-old *you* to take a chance, and you'll remember being *him*. He too will get older and try to convince another younger *him*. Objectively, this moment will happen only once, but in some real way you and I will repeat it for eternity. It is always happening. So, you've said no to this proposition maybe millions of times before. And you'll say no to it a million times more."

"Or maybe this is the first time," said Henry.

"Or maybe it's the last." 80 coughed. All the talking seemed to have sapped his energy, and with the fading afternoon light deepening the shadows in his lined face, he looked exhausted.

"If this will only happen once," said Henry, "then you already know it's impossible for me to change my mind. It happened the way it happened."

"In a sense, that's true," said 80. "But my life *happened the way it happened* once before. Then, when I met you this morning, I came to inhabit an entirely different life. There was one immutable truth, and now, paradoxically, there is another. I don't know what will change if we do this, but I've just remembered the life we'll live if we don't. And soon I'll die, knowing that forever and ever an endless procession of yous and mes will sit in this living room, debating each other. It's too depressing to bear."

80's talk of deathbed heartache was overwrought, to be sure, but Henry felt less certain than he had before. It wasn't necessarily that he believed the old man, or that he thought 80 was right. It was that Henry didn't want to *become* 80. He couldn't stand the thought of ending up so lonely and pathetic, and whatever else the old man might be plotting, he was offering Henry a possible way out.

"We could change things," said Henry, "and you could end up with regrets much worse than the ones you have now."

80 bobbed his head, his lips pursed and his brow pleated.

"You thought you could save yourself starting with me," said Henry, "but nothing much has changed. If I agree and we go find ourselves on that tour bus, why would it be any different?"

"Well. That's the third thing. When I found you on the street this morning, it was apparently already too late."

"Too late for what?"

"Val. She had an affair."

Henry's first reaction was to laugh, but the nervous chuckle was washed away by a wave of heart-thumping nausea.

"I'm sorry," said 80. "I thought by reaching you when I did we could stop it from happening, that we could get her back. I would have come earlier, but I needed you to reach the bridge. I needed you to hear the music, to shift again. It was the only way to make sure you'd believe me. It was only after that I realized. We were too late."

For minutes Henry sat, dumb and paralyzed, seeing nothing through his open eyes as he succumbed to pain and fury. Pain at the betrayal. Fury at himself. He'd never thought it possible that Val would want anyone else, but now it seemed so obvious. Why *wouldn't* she?

"Who?" asked Henry.

80 didn't answer. He didn't have to. Henry's intuition had already kicked in. He didn't speak Gabe's name, but when he saw pitying affirmation in 80's eyes, a jagged moan tore at his throat.

He sat in bleak silence as the room turned dark around him.

THE MORNING AFTER

Y OU SHOULD COME *see me sometime.*
  Val hadn't planned to invite Gabe to visit her. The words had just tumbled out of her, a kind of a joke, really. But then he assented, and Val was surprised by the pleasure it gave her.

I can't wait.

She cringed when she thought of how she'd said that. It felt wrong. Henry was insane. He'd run away from home. That was why Gabe had called her in the first place, and it was sad. So, so sad. And yet she felt happy—giddy, even. It bothered her so much that she had sat alone in her room and picked it all apart until finally she had an explanation that felt right. Her happiness was just an unsettling symptom of her loneliness. A sign of just how much she was craving something that would feel like home. It was proof of her brokenness, and for some reason that made it okay.

Over the week leading up to Gabe's arrival, she planned and replanned the menu, gave careful consideration to what clothing she might wear. It seemed important that she appear to be doing better than ever. Part of her felt she owed that to Henry—and, by extension, to Gabe—after what she had sacrificed to come to the city. Another, less generous part of her whispered that she wasn't doing well at all, that her attempt to prove otherwise was a sad ruse indicative of just how deeply confused she was.

It had been six months since the phone call from Henry. Her anger had lingered for a while, surprising her from time to time with a sudden burning contraction beneath her clavicle. But more consistent than her anger was the hope that Henry would call back. Val knew she was owed an apology and expected to receive it. But the hope was stronger than that simple need for closure should have warranted. Val wanted that call to be the beginning of something, not the end. She imagined how the apology would lead to a discussion of all that had gone wrong between them. That conversation would in turn lead to more. She and Henry would reclaim their common ground. Val didn't give much thought to what would happen after that. She just regretted having lost him entirely, regretted having lost the part of herself that felt at home with him. That, she was sure, could be undone.

Val had spent the summer in the city. She worked at a Tex-Mex restaurant a few nights a week to pay for the room she sublet in the East Village. The other two occupants of the apartment were twentysomething men who, as far as she could tell, had figured out a way to make a living by smoking pot and watching nature documentaries. By the end of her first week there Val had learned how to slip in and out without attracting attention. That strategy was worth pursuing for how much awkwardness it saved her, but it required her to spend hours alone in the tiny space that passed for her bedroom. It was just big enough for a bed and the wicker dresser that was her closet, vanity, desk, and filing cabinet.

When she was working or out with friends, Val looked forward to her time alone. Then, as soon as she was safely ensconced in her private corner of the world, she yearned to be outside and surrounded by people.

The sound of the air conditioner obscured any noise from the street. It blanketed her thoughts and left her feeling sort of weightless, as if the whole room were her body, the girl inside it just another piece of furniture. It made her feel vulnerable. At first she didn't know what she was afraid of or what it was that she wanted. The yearning that churned up from deep inside her was vague and shiftless. After a few silent days followed by hectic nights, Val figured that all she really wanted was to connect with someone to whom she mattered. Her mom didn't count. The girls she hung out with didn't either. More than once she scrolled all the way through the contacts list on her phone, as if she had simply forgotten who it was that could make her loneliness disappear.

She worked. She went out drinking. She tanned by the Pond at Central Park or on the steps of the fountain at Washington Square. She laughed when things were supposed to be funny and shook her head in sympathy when things were supposed to be sad or unjust. When food was supposedly good she made herself look as though she was savoring it. When the supposedly right kind of guy hit on her, she showed interest. When the supposedly wrong kind of guy talked to her, she feigned indifference and laughed about him with the girls later on.

The summer ended. She moved back into student housing with Kara. They weren't best friends or anything, but they'd lived well together and there was no one else Val wanted to live with more. By the time she'd finished putting her clothes away and setting up her computer, Val felt almost as if the summer had never happened. It reminded her of the sensation she'd first experienced with Henry—that disconnected familiarity that made her feel as though she'd just awoken to her surroundings for the very first time. As if her memories were incidental to the being that inhabited her body.

How had she gotten to be twenty years old? How was it possible that she was living in New York City?

Then Gabe called. She laughed to herself when she saw that it was him. And despite what he told her about Henry's sickness and disappearance, when finally she hung up she felt good. She knew that was wrong, but still she prepared for Gabe's arrival with a juvenile excitement she hadn't felt in years. It was an excitement laced with fear. Gabe might fill her mind with the unforgettable details of Henry's decline. Val would listen because she had to, because there was nobody else, but she didn't think she wanted to know.

Then he arrived, and her fear disappeared. His face was bright with ill-contained joy. He was just as glad to see her as she was to see him, and Val understood then that he was lonely. Perhaps even lonelier than she was. They never even mentioned Henry's name. There were a few allusions and euphemisms, but that was all. And Val was fine with that. The hours passed effortlessly, just as they had before. Val felt like the person she remembered being. Gabe wasn't the answer to the big unspoken question she'd been living with since leaving Rutgers behind. His presence simply made that question irrelevant. She didn't care what kind of life she was *supposed* to be living when she felt that free and at home with herself.

When it came time for her to get into bed, she invited him. It would have been a bold move had it been a move at all. Val just thought they would both be more comfortable. She couldn't remember when their whispers had ended and when sleep began, and the next time she opened her eyes it was just barely dawn and she saw Gabe's face just inches from her own. She very nearly pulled herself close to him. She wanted to place her open palm on the curve of his chest. She imagined lifting her leg and resting her inner thigh against his waist, imagined how easy it would be to hook the back of her heel into the space behind his knee, to touch her forehead to his sleeping lips. And with those thoughts in her mind, she fell back asleep.

It hadn't felt like a betrayal of Henry until later in the morning, when she came out of the bedroom and stretched in her doorway. Gabe's face showed signs of the same pained hunger that she'd felt for him in the light of dawn. A familiar thrill ran down the length of her body, then settled into a cold pool of confused regret.

She went to the bathroom, looked at herself in the warped mirror that Kara had found on the street and hung behind the door. She repeated the stretch and appraised herself. Seeing what Gabe had seen, she understood his reaction.

She clipped back her hair and washed her face, inspected her eyes and turned her head to each side, testing all angles for imperfections. Then she gave herself a confused look in the mirror, as if daring her reflection to attempt an explanation. Had she done the wrong thing, she wondered, inviting Gabe into her bed like that? She had abandoned Henry, who hadn't necessarily deserved it—she might have even driven him crazy. And now that Gabe had come to her for comfort Val had quickly turned it around. She had found comfort in him. There had to be something wrong with that, wrong with her.

She walked out of the bathroom. A few awkward moments later, Gabe skulked out as if he were a stranger. Val closed the door behind him and tried to locate the regret and confusion she thought she should be feeling. But as she scanned her body looking for the telltale signs of her curious depression, all she felt was the residue of excitement. It felt like hope.

In the kitchen, she put away the dishes from dinner. Kara pranced into the room in socked feet, full-length pajama pants, and an oversized T-shirt from Disneyland. She leaned against the refrigerator door and glared at Val expectantly.

"What?" said Val.

"What do you mean, *what?*" said Kara. "I've been stuck in my room all night and now you're not even going to tell me what for?"

"I don't know why you were stuck in your room all night."

"Well, I didn't want to bother you. So, what happened?"

Kara went to church every Sunday—in fact, she would be spending the next hour and a half getting ready to do just that—but she affected a self-realized worldliness. In her own mind, she was just another modern, normal, feminist, independent college student in the big city. Her lack of a poker face belied the fact that she was just as sheltered as she claimed not to be.

Val entertained herself with the thought of saying *Yeah, we totally fucked all night. I forget his name but he said he's allergic to condoms so I was like, whatever, you know?* But messing with Kara suddenly seemed boring. "I didn't ask you to stay in your bedroom," she said. "It's your apartment too—you should have just come out. It wasn't a date or anything."

"Oh really," said Kara, teasing.

"Really," said Val, her face ruthlessly straight. The dishes put away, she grabbed the kettle from the stovetop and filled it with water for the French press. "We're old friends."

"Friends who sleep in the same bed together?" Kara stepped to the cupboard. She was enamored with Cinnamon Toast Crunch, her only apparent vice. She opened the box and found a bowl. "That doesn't sound like the kind of friends I have."

"No, it does not sound like the kind of friends *you* have," said Val. She hoped that would be enough. When Kara sensed that she was acting uncool she usually shut down and waited for a cue as to what to do next.

"I mean, you know, I'm not like that," said Kara. She poured her cereal and got the milk from the refrigerator. "But I've never known anyone who sleeps in the same bed as a man and doesn't fool around even a little bit. My friend Tracey got herself into a lot of trouble once, sleeping on the back three seats of a bus—you know, that bench next to the bathroom? This guy Skylar was all over her."

"Trouble?" said Val, and she laughed. "Did you have to stone her or something?"

"No, not *that* kind of trouble." Kara sat down at the table and popped a heavily laden spoon in her mouth, then crunched as she spoke. "They didn't have sex or anything, he just felt her up. It was just, you know—moral trouble. I guess you wouldn't understand."

"No, I'm not acquainted with these 'morals' you speak of."

"You know that's not what I meant." Kara slurped whole milk through her teeth.

Val leaned against the counter next to the stove. She could feel the heat from the burner radiating dangerously close to her elbow, but she didn't move away. "I guess I can see how it might seem weird," she said. "But, honestly, it didn't *feel* weird."

"So you guys didn't..." Kara raised her eyebrows and puckered her lips into a tight approximation of a kiss.

"No. Nothing like that. We just slept."

"Well, I know I'm not, like, the authority on this kind of thing, but, seriously, I think that's a little weird." Kara punctuated her words with jaunty waves of her spoon. Val wanted to tear it out of her hand and throw it across the room. "People don't just sleep in the same bed together unless something is going on."

"Sometimes they do, though. I just did."

"And isn't he, like, your ex-boyfriend's best friend or something?"

Val thought about that. In the simplest terms, that description was true, but it was so inadequate as to sound almost meaningless. And if it was complicated before, it was even more so now with Henry missing. She and Gabe were the only two people aside from Henry's mother who really knew him. That bound them together, especially if he never came back.

"Henry's missing," said Val. She sat down.

Kara stopped chewing.

Val continued. "He kind of…lost it, I guess. Had a mental breakdown at school. Stopped eating, started saying crazy things. And now he's gone."

Kara dropped her spoon into the bowl and reached across the table to take hold of Val's wrist.

"How long's he been gone?"

"Three weeks."

"Oh my gosh!" said Kara, and the alarm on her face made Val feel self-conscious. Why wasn't *she* that distressed? What was wrong with her?

The kettle emitted its first plaintive whistle. Val broke Kara's grip and stood up to turn off the stove. "It's not as bad as it seems," she said, though she wasn't sure what that meant. Nobody knew how bad it was. "At least Gabe doesn't think so. Henry's sick, but he was talking about running away for a while before he actually disappeared. Based on what he was saying to Gabe before he took off, I think he doesn't want to be found right now."

"And that's a good thing?"

"Well, I guess it just means that his being gone this long doesn't necessarily mean he's dead." The word left Val's mouth like an artillery shell, then expanded like a cloud of gas. She closed her eyes, took two breaths, and opened them again.

Kara looked disturbed, but if she had anything to say it stayed locked behind her sugary lips.

"His mom must be flipping out," said Val. A startlingly clear picture of Jan flashed into her mind. She was alone in that big house, cooking elaborate meals for nobody but herself, carrying the house phone in one pocket and her cell in the other out of fear that she'd miss the call that would bring Henry back.

"Why aren't you?" said Kara.

"What?"

"Why aren't you, you know, flipping out?"

Val couldn't ignore that question, though she wanted to. She trusted Gabe's explanations for why he thought Henry was fine even as she saw that Gabe was worried. If his rationalizations weren't even working on himself, Val had to wonder why they were working on her. She poured water into the press and returned to the table. "I guess I just feel like he'll come back when he wants to."

Call me back when you're not acting like such a fucking lunatic.

The words came back in a torrent, made her feel the kind of anxiety she recognized from her worst nightmares. It was the knowledge that she had done something horrible, the absolute and suffocating certainty that she was indelibly stained. If Henry never reappeared, those last words to him would be chiseled into the stone of her life. She would have to read and repeat them until she died.

"So what are you gonna do?" Kara asked. "I mean, you have to try to find him, right?"

"No. I don't think I do."

Kara's mouth opened but no sound emerged. She closed it again.

"I don't think I want to talk about this any more right now," said Val.

Kara nodded and stood up. "I need to get ready for church," she said. Her bowl and spoon rattled together when she dropped them in the sink. On her way out, she placed a single fumbling hand on Val's shoulder and squeezed. "It'll be okay," she said.

The sound of water running through the pipes in the wall mixed with the faint and sporadic hum of traffic from the West Side Highway. Val thought about all that had happened since she left Rutgers, and the question that Gabe had pushed from her mind returned. It was as big and scary as ever, but she still couldn't articulate it. Her thoughts were moving too quickly to be turned into words.

The blast of Kara's blow-dryer returned Val to the present. She was a junior in college, living in an apartment in New York City.

Henry was missing and she'd just shared a bed with Gabe. It was incomprehensible.

She pressed the coffee and poured it into her mug, but the smell made her realize that she didn't want it anymore. She stood up and poured it in the sink, then scoured the sticky residue from Kara's cereal bowl.

MINUET: ESOPUS

WHEN HENRY AWOKE the next day the sun was high enough in the sky to paint red-walnut trapezoids on the floor of his bedroom. He struggled to reconstruct the world he'd left behind while sleeping. First came his body's painful understanding that Val was not with him in bed, followed by his conscious mind's recollection of why. That led him to recall 80 and what the old man had told him about Gabe.

Henry held his breath and waited for the pain to ebb.

It took so long that he had time to wonder if anyone had ever managed to kill themselves like that, just by sheer force of will. His diaphragm spasmed. He gasped for air while multicolored pixels of light floated in from the periphery of his vision.

He propped himself up on his elbows.

This is not my life.

He extended the mantra, filling the room with it.

These are not my clothes. This is not my bed. These are not my sheets. This is not my room. This is not my house. And then, strangest of all: *This is not my time.*

He flipped the covers from his body and placed his feet on the floor. It was warm from the sun. He walked to the window, and when the light was directly on his face he closed his eyes and relaxed into what he saw behind the lids: a field of pulsing red blood split by a bright yellow horizon. Did 80 remember this moment, Henry wondered? And what if he did? What if he didn't? There were so many inconsequential hours and days between the great movements of his life. In some ways, the minutiae were everything. They were the stuff he was made of. But Henry didn't remember most of it, so he had to assume that 80 didn't either.

Eyes still closed, Henry cataloged all that he had lost. Annie. Val. Gabe. His home. His marriage. His life.

The cliché questions—the *how could they*s and the *how dare they*s—couldn't be asked with any seriousness. He was of course tempted to be outraged, but that would have been a farce. Val had seen Henry through so much and he'd repaid her by breaking their one sacred rule. As for Gabe, it was out of the question to be shocked. When Henry disappeared the first time to wander the highways and back roads of New Jersey and Pennsylvania, Val and Gabe had sought each other out. Later, when Henry was better and Val came back to him, she told him about the night Gabe had come to see her. They shared a bed, she said, and though they didn't actually touch, not in that way, something changed between them. She said that they saw each other more after that, that they both grew more confused. But then Henry was found. Gabe and Val were both so relieved that he was alive that the fog lifted. They were friends again and nothing more.

Henry knew that Gabe loved Val. He'd even learned to enjoy the shape that love took. Gabe was the third point on a triangle that changed its proportions but never broke. Val loved Gabe too. She expressed that love by being Gabe's sounding board when he felt lost or confused. She built him up, shared her intimacy freely. For better or worse, that dynamic continued, even when Gabe got married. It got stronger still when he divorced a few short years later and asked if he could move in with Henry and Val for a couple of months. He helped take care of Annie during the day and cooked meals for Henry and Val at night. With Annie, the triangle became a square. Henry had loved it at the time. All of the people that mattered to him were under the same roof.

That memory was ruined now.

Their affair would have started as a kind of mourning, innocent but intense. After Val left the house with Annie, she certainly would have reached out to Gabe for advice and support. And she would have needed help with Annie, which Gabe would have happily given. Then, after Henry went back to Lung-Ta, they would have shared late nights and long weekend days. Annie would have loved the doting attention of her uncle, and Gabe would have told himself—and it would have been mostly true—that he was unselfishly acting the father figure, smoothing Annie's path to a time when Henry could be the real father that she desperately needed.

But then...what? Gabe would have crossed a line, Henry supposed, but perhaps he was just being generous with himself. Val may have started it herself. Perhaps they'd fallen asleep on the couch while watching a movie and woken up in an embrace. Maybe a kiss on the cheek was slightly off the mark and their lips touched, awakening a strong desire for more. Or maybe it wasn't innocent at all. Years of pent-up desire may have been unleashed, not in a moment of weakness but in one of pure, visceral strength.

Henry opened his eyes. He would not imagine that. The sun burned through his pupils and the pain made him forget.

Once out of the bedroom, Henry took his time in the shower. He brushed his teeth so long that the mint of the toothpaste numbed his tongue. He could have further delayed his descent downstairs by shaving his already thick beard—he'd stopped grooming when the obsession first took over a month before—but if he shaved that day, he'd only have to shave again the next. It seemed like a waste of effort. The smell of bacon greeted him as he walked down the stairs. He didn't actually remember when last he'd eaten. His hunger was of a lazy, unpracticed sort.

80 was already at the table, reading a book. "Morning," he said. He picked up a half-eaten triangle of toast and bit into it without looking. The crunch told Henry it was dry and hard—the way he liked it. Still, the sound was irritating.

There were three limp slices of bacon curling in the cast-iron skillet, and an open bag of bread on the counter. Henry got a plate from the cabinet and put the bacon on it, then placed two pieces of bread in the toaster. His stomach still warming to its desire, he turned on the burner underneath the skillet and opened the fridge for eggs.

80 read on. The toaster clicked a few times. Minutes passed and neither Henry spoke a word. The elder picked up his toast again and crunched. "You're annoyed by the sound of my chewing," he said. "It's a cumbersome pet peeve, really. People can't help making some sound when they eat. Not that I've been able to get over it any better than you have." He put down his book and smiled brightly. "It's kind of funny, though, isn't it? You being irritated by your own chewing from across the room?"

"Not really," said Henry. He turned toward the stove and cracked an egg into the sizzling bacon fat. It spit, sending a cascade of tiny, burning needle-pricks from Henry's fingers to his elbow.

80 crunched his toast again.

Once everything was ready, Henry sat down and ate in silence. Then he cleaned his dishes, dried them, and put them away. "I'm going for a walk," he said.

"I'd offer to come along," said 80, "but I know you'll say no."

"Don't do that," said Henry.

"What?"

"You don't have to tell me what I'm thinking or what I'm going to do just because you can."

"I'm sorry," said 80. "It's difficult to resist. I know it makes you feel powerless, like you have no choice in anything, but that's an illusion. Me knowing what you're going to do is not the same thing as you lacking the will to decide. In fact, our conversation yesterday should have made clear that I think you have the capacity to surprise me. I'm counting on that."

Henry wasn't in the mood to talk philosophy, and he heard the last of these words as a murmur as he walked through the living room and out the front of the house. The screen door creaked and then clapped against its frame. There was a satisfying finality to it.

He wished Annie were by his side, picking her careful way through the ferns and tree roots. They'd lift up rocks together, talk about potato bugs and poison ivy. She would have prepared for the trip by visiting the library and asking the reference desk for help finding a wilderness guide. Then she would have pulled a backpack from her closet, one with a pocket the exact right size for the book. That would have pleased her. On the car ride up, she would have read about first aid and finding water and different kinds of insects and plants. But rather than letting that information define or limit her own experience of the forest, she would have used it to fuel her wild imagination. She was kind of magical in that way. Henry pictured her running between the trees, the skin on her bony kneecaps imprinted with the shapes of twigs and needles. He might never have deserved Val, but with Annie what he deserved didn't come into it. He couldn't live without her. To 80, Annie only served to make him feel bad about himself. The old man had long since stopped expecting her to trust him or to want to be near him. 80 didn't even seem to think that she loved him, really.

Henry couldn't imagine being so closed off. But someday he would be. 80 was proof of it.

The stream, when he reached it, was smaller than he'd expected.

It was late spring. The water level seemed low but compared to what, Henry didn't know. He slid carefully down the bank and walked along the pebbled bed. When he'd gone just far enough to feel alone he stopped to rest on a massive tree root that had grown down from its trunk on the steep bank above. He watched the water and tried to relax.

80 was obsessed with changing the past. His bitterness drove him to believe that everything would be better *if only this* or *if only that*. It seemed impossible that they could control the change 80 sought. Henry considered the stream. He could build a little dam from sticks and mud, but he couldn't predict how that would change the water's flow a hundred yards down. 80 was deluded if he thought otherwise.

Even so, the old man had a point. They were in an extraordinary position.

Henry stood up and continued his walk along the bank.

He wouldn't have to limit himself to a single intervention. If he built a dam and it didn't do what he wanted it to, couldn't he just destroy it? Or build another one even higher upstream? With enough time he could reroute the water entirely, and time was exactly the thing he had in excess. 80 had already started that process, and though it hadn't worked perfectly, that was to be expected. Henry had been a guinea pig. 80 was inviting him to become a lab technician. At the moment, Henry was disinclined to accept the invitation. He resented 80's intrusion and the burden he'd placed on their shoulders. The old man carried out his manipulations with an attitude of patronizing pity, as though he were the shepherd and Henry the flock. He professed to care about Val and Annie and the betterment of Henry himself, but his actions seemed so calculated as to leave little room for emotion. And this, finally, was what bothered Henry the most. He was currently destined to become that sanctimonious, unfeeling asshole, to be plagued by loneliness and desperation until he became a pathetic old man. But therein lay the strange, paralyzing paradox. In order to avoid becoming the kind of man who would coldly manipulate his younger self into agreeing to a rash and dangerous action, Henry had to agree to that same rash and dangerous action.

It was too big an idea to properly contemplate. He couldn't find a way in.

He imagined Annie again, pictured her with her guidebook open to a page with leaves on it. She'd have told him what tree he was resting his palm on. She would have identified the soft ferns that had brushed against his shins in the woods. Without her there, Henry could only look, fascinated, at the green mossy stuff, the little white flowery things, the bushes with the pink flowers, the beautiful thin trees with the weird bark that peeled off like skin from a blister.

When he reached a bend in the stream, Henry saw a crossing farther down. It looked like someone had taken a child's drawing of the George Washington Bridge and transformed it into a design for a long hiker's footbridge. The banks of the stream were too steep and close to the water now, so Henry climbed up to level ground and walked on.

A few minutes later, he was at the very center of the bridge, sitting with his legs dangling beneath the lowest of three guardrails. He rested his elbows on the middle strut, his forehead against the top one, and looked down at the water rushing out from underneath him. He had the fleeting feeling that he was in fact moving backwards. The loss of equilibrium felt good. For a while, he thought of as little as he could. He wanted to simply breathe and sit, but just as he was thinking how glad he was to be alone, a light tapping announced that 80, walking stick in hand, was coming toward him. When he arrived at the center of the bridge, he stood with his left palm resting on the top of the stick, his right on top of that, and his chin atop both of them.

"I wanted to be alone," said Henry. "You said you knew that."

"You resent me, and I understand that perfectly. You don't want to become me. But what you fail to understand is that I don't want to *be* me, either."

"Stop selling me," said Henry.

"I'm not going to stop. This is what we do now, forever and ever. I will pitch you and you'll decline."

The music started, very faintly. The song was woody and watery with just the slightest inorganic twinge coming through the steel suspension cables. It settled into Henry's ears as though it had been there all along, so effortless that he wondered how he could ever *not* hear it.

"Even after I'm dead and you're dead, we'll still be here, endlessly locked in the same argument about nothing, and then we'll die again. And again."

80's voice bubbled into the song, played off the burble of the water over the stones below. It hit the steel cables with a pizzicato pluck and repeated. *And again. And again.* The song got louder. Inevitably, Henry was stupefied. The sound was everything, nothing was separate, and he forgot himself just as he had before and before, and then he was compressed along with everything else into a space the size of nothing but with limitless white depth in all directions. The rush came so loud, impossibly bright. Henry's last remaining bit of consciousness told him that it was good, so good, but then that was gone too, and everything was everything.

Some timeless time later, he again understood that he had a body. The transition wasn't as abrupt as before. The song lingered, its ghostly diminuendo like the sweet echo of a concert hall. The white receded and Henry noticed that his eyes were already open. He was looking down at running water—a stream surrounded on either side by a cacophony of red and orange. It was suddenly fall.

There was a tapping from behind him, close enough that it vibrated the hard wood he was sitting on and buzzed his tailbone like a tuning fork. He was cold. As his memory returned, he pulled his feet up from where they'd been dangling. He rubbed his ankles until the pins and needles subsided, then stood to face 80.

"We're here," said the old man. "But we don't have to go anywhere."

"I think we do," said Henry, and he started back toward the house.

THE MESSAGE

I T WAS EARLY afternoon by the time Gabe got back to his house on Hamilton Street. Cal was gone and everything was quiet. Gabe lay down in his bed, pulled the filthy comforter over his face, and fashioned a little hole just big enough to breathe through. The sound of mid-morning traffic on Hamilton soothed him. It had rained a little, and he liked the sticky noise that car tires made as they rolled over the wet asphalt.

He wanted to sleep, but the previous eighteen hours had been the strangest of his life. His mind wouldn't let go, so he ended up in a strange in-between place where his memories of that morning and the previous night were louder and more visceral than usual, like waking dreams.

Henry had said he was forty-one years old. He said that he was nineteen the first time he'd accidentally shifted himself through time. He said that the version of himself that Gabe was used to knowing was recovering someplace safe. He'd been removed from Gabe's time in order to save his life. Gabe had just listened, dumbstruck and scared.

They got off in New Brunswick. Gabe's senses felt unfiltered, as if his brain were trying to construct the world around him for the first time. As the train pulled away the rhythm of cars clunking over seams in the tracks meshed with the sound of feet descending the steel stairs. He tried to ignore the consonance, but it was impossible. Henry walked Gabe as far as the intersection of Easton and Hamilton. The walk was quiet. It was only about noon on a Sunday, late enough that the sidewalks in front of Cluck-U Chicken and Giovanelli's Pizza had been cleared of empty beer cans and Styrofoam takeout containers but too early for there to be much activity.

"Don't make me regret coming to you," said Henry. The words themselves could have been made to sound threatening or caustic, but his tone was clear. It was a genuine, almost pleading, request, as though he had too many regrets already. "I'll get in touch." And then, probably because of the look on Gabe's face, he said, "I'm all right."

Gabe bit down on his cheek hard enough to hurt a little. Henry was not all right. He was sad and lonely, possibly delusional. He was hallucinating, believing insane things. But Gabe was, too, and he felt robbed of any authority to disagree with this new Henry.

It was getting hot under the covers, but Gabe needed the peace of the dark to concentrate.

Henry had asked him to accept the impossible. His only proof was that he looked like shit and that he could somehow force Gabe to hallucinate. Even still, Gabe believed him immediately and instinctively. But if Gabe believed that the Henry he had just been with was truly from another time, then he would also have to believe that this Henry knew things about Gabe's own future. And then, though he knew it was trivial, Gabe's mind wandered back to Val and her creamy white stomach, the way it tightened over her middle as she stretched. The image had impressed itself on Gabe's brain with a crispness and clarity that caused a dull pain low in his gut. He tried to remember the smell he'd woken up to—he even lifted his T-shirt over his nose, hoping to find some remnant of her. And then he heard Henry's voice. *It's going to happen.* He was talking about Gabe having sex with Val like it was a foregone conclusion. *And when it does, you need to know that I don't mind.*

Two sentences, each one so simple, but when combined they formed a complex equation. He didn't really care about that second sentence, or at least he couldn't find the part of himself that cared enough to focus on it. That first sentence, though. *It's going to happen.* The words stirred in Gabe a sexual frustration so profound that he could practically feel his testicles ascending into his abdomen. He had been holding the fantasy at bay since talking with Val the week before, but now he let it take over. He was back in her bed, looking at the spot on her shoulder revealed by the loose gray strap of her tank top. He touched her skin with the back of his finger and then went deeper. He imagined parts of her body that he'd never let himself imagine before. She'd always been off-limits, but now that he was lifting the ban, he explored her in his imagination with an almost grotesque fervor.

Then it was over and the realization hit him hard. He was a bad, backward person. Instead of pondering how he and Henry had gotten locked in the same delusion together, and rather than trying to figure out what it all meant, Gabe had gone home and jerked off while thinking about Henry's ex-girlfriend.

When it happens, I don't want you to think about me.

There was nothing Henry could have said that would have better cemented his presence in Gabe's mind. Gabe wondered if that was on purpose, and thought back to one of the questions that he'd been pondering on the walk back from the train station. How much did he trust this Henry? He'd followed Gabe and confronted him after he left Val's apartment. His actions seemed designed to disorient Gabe, to threaten him, and yet he acted as though it was all fated, thereby absolving himself of any real responsibility.

And then there was the very real possibility that the Henry he'd seen on the train and in the park wasn't really there. Gabe was insane. The only alternative explanation was that Henry had traveled back through time to fuck with him, and that was no explanation at all.

Gabe laughed to himself under the covers, then threw them back. The cool air on his skin made him feel more present, more substantial. He stood up and took off his clothes, careful to keep the front of his boxer briefs from touching his legs. He heard the sound of his phone vibrating in the pocket of his pants. The pocket was twisted and the pants were inside out, so by the time he was able to get to his phone he'd missed the call.

It was Val. Gabe's blood turned warm and acidic. He stared at the phone, wondering if he should call her back. She couldn't see him, of course, but he was naked and he suddenly felt exposed. He put down the phone and picked up a mildewed towel, wrapped it around his waist. The phone vibrated again, just once, announcing that it had received a message. Gabe played it back.

"Hey, Gabe."

His skin tingled at the sound of his own name.

"Listen, I wanted to talk to you, but maybe this is better. I guess I just felt like you left kind of abruptly, and I wanted to tell you that I'm sorry, you know, if it was weird. That you stayed over.

"I mean, okay, now this is turning into an epic message. But whatever. I just feel like you came over here for help, you know? But then we barely talked about Henry. And I was thinking, since you left, that maybe that wasn't fair. Because I'm lonely here. I'm having fun, but when I saw you it made me really happy, like I was home and I could be myself, and I can't do that with anyone else around here right now. But you came over to talk about

Henry, and I guess I didn't want to, and that was just weird. And unfair."

Gabe looked down at his toweled body and recalled the way he'd been imagining her just moments before. He still felt ashamed, but it was obvious that she was confused too. It was a kind of absolution.

"So, I don't want things to be weird. Think about this and call me, okay? Or don't. If you don't want to talk about it I understand. I just...okay. Well, I'll talk to you soon. Or, I guess, whenever you feel like it."

Gabe imagined Val curled up on her bed, eyes rolling in frustration, biting her lip and shaking her head.

"Okay."

She took a short breath, but a deep one from the sound of it.

"Bye."

Gabe pondered what he'd heard. By instinct, they hadn't spoken about Henry. Maybe Val's message meant that she felt bad about that, that Henry was the real foundation of their relationship and that in avoiding him they'd just been kidding themselves. But she hadn't actually said that she wanted to talk about Henry, only that she thought Gabe did. She was apologizing for not giving Gabe that chance.

But what if Gabe didn't want to talk about Henry either? Would Val see him differently? Would she lose respect for him, having always seen him as the loyal friend? Or would it be a relief?

Gabe listened to the message twice more before getting in the shower. Then, when he was out and dressed, he listened to it again. It felt good. He didn't want to call her back yet. He was too afraid that the intimacy would dissipate if she were actually on the other end of line.

He felt almost normal. The same way he'd felt when he was with her. All the doubt and confusion caused by the bearded man just disappeared. If it was really Henry, then Gabe had been given permission to think about Val however he wanted. And if he was just a figment of Gabe's own imagination, then spending time with Val, hearing her voice—it seemed to make his burgeoning insanity disappear. The choice between trying to spend time with her and steering clear was therefore no choice at all.

DA CAPO: 19

"WHAT DO YOU mean, you're *gone?*" said Henry. "You're right here."

"No," said 80. He was still on his knees, crying through clenched teeth.

Henry looked up at the bridge, its wooden planks brightened to a fiery golden hue by the bright sunlight above. Henry himself was still in the shade of the canopy. In his mind's eye he could see 41 dancing to the woody clamor. He couldn't see any vomit on the front of his clothing, but it was going cold on his back, adhering his skin to the fabric of his shirt.

"I'm not here," said 80. "Not truly, not in this world."

"Stop."

"He's—God, what is he doing? What has he done?"

Henry wanted to kick him. Just a day before, the bright green spastic low vibration had driven him from his mother's house to the George Washington Bridge, where he'd experienced a hallucination of such intensity that it had knocked him out. He'd then been drugged and abducted by men whom he genuinely believed to be future versions of himself. Without even a moment alone to ponder any of that, he'd been paraded through the woods to this other bridge and abandoned by the one of his two companions whom he was beginning to trust.

Henry felt like a prop in some absurdist play, and the only person who could possibly help him make sense of what was happening was now kneeling on the bare earth, crying and muttering.

"I can't keep it straight," said 80. He sat up a little, raised both hands out in front of him, palms turned down as if bowing in praise. When Henry finally understood the meaning of the gesture, he grabbed the man's wrists and lifted him to his feet.

"Stop," said Henry. "Stop crying—what happened?"

"I need to sit down," said 80. "I need to think." He walked back toward the bridge. Then, using the guardrails for support, he slowly lowered himself to the walkway.

"But I just helped you up," said Henry. He followed 80 out onto the bridge. "Where did he go?" he said. "Please. Think. You have to know."

An asthmatic whistle mewled out of 80's wide-open mouth.

"Hello?" said Henry.

"I can't hear it."

"Where did he go?"

"I can't... But how?"

"He said I had set myself free," said Henry. "What did he mean?"

"I can't hear it," said 80. "It's gone, but how—"

"What did he mean, 80? Focus! What did he mean? He said I'd set myself free. Free how? From what?"

80 directed his fearful gaze at Henry. "From me. Free from me."

"But I'm here with you, right now. I'm here and he's— What did you do to him?"

80 stared down at the water. "It doesn't matter."

"Really? You don't think so?" said Henry. "Because to me? Right now? It seems like maybe it does. It seems like it matters a lot, actually."

"No," said 80. "It was a different time. It's over."

"This is what he was talking about, isn't it?"

"If you knew—"

"You'll just hide shit from me, you'll lie to me, right? No straight answers."

"I'm not lying," said 80. "It doesn't matter what happened."

"Bullshit," said Henry. He walked farther out onto the bridge and looked upstream. He imagined jumping into the advancing water. It would clean his clothes, at least. It would carry him away. Better yet, there was a car at the house. He could leave 80 where he sat, get the keys, drive until he found a highway, and head back home.

But what would he find when he got back to his mom's house?

What would he find if he went back to New Brunswick?

He charged back toward 80. "Where am I?" he yelled. "What time is this? Take me home."

"What time?" said 80. "It's...We didn't..." He rubbed at his face with both hands. "You can't go home. It's—You need to stay here. We need to fix this."

"Just tell me! If I find someone, ask them what day it is, *what will they say?*"

"It doesn't matter anymore. Not to you. You can get yourself to wherever you want to go, can't you?"

"I don't know what you're talking about."

"Not yet, then. Good. We have to fix this. We can fix it."

"Fix what?"

80's eyes were adrift, his face disturbing in its dispassion. "You need to understand. We need to be together on whatever comes next. 41, he'll ruin everything. It's you and me. You can learn. You can hear the music. You can do it, I know you can. 41 is proof of it.

You have to listen. Listen for it, and then when you hear it, we can fix this."

As Henry listened to the man's sputtering barrage, the discouraging truth became clear. "You don't understand what's happening," he said. "Not any more than I do."

80 placed one foot beneath him, bent a knee, got the other onto the ground. Piece by piece he lifted his body first to all fours and then up to standing. He squinted, his mouth taut in a grimace as he straightened his back. Henry watched, and though he felt compelled by courtesy to offer to help, he kept his distance and enjoyed the satisfaction that came with watching the old man struggle.

"We can fix this," said 80. "You need to stay with me."

"And if I don't? If I just leave?"

"41 knows what you'll do. He remembers it all. He remembers this very moment, this conversation. He left you here to have it. If you leave, he'll find you. He knows you'll know that. He wants you to stay here for a reason, and we just have to figure out what that is."

"But *you* don't remember this," said Henry. "You don't remember me. If this is real, that's—it's not possible."

"It's not possible, no. But it's the way it is. That's what this is all about." 80 took a step, but his knee buckled and he gasped as he fell forward. Henry reached out and caught the man's upper arms, pushed him upright. 80 looked him in the eye, and as Henry looked back he couldn't stop himself from marveling at the odd familiarity of the irises. Unlike every other part of 80's body, the years had done nothing to change them. They were a mirror image of a mirror image of Henry's own, and they held compassion and sadness and fear in equal measure.

"Help me back to the house," said 80.

THE FEVER

CAL RETURNED FROM his girlfriend's in the late afternoon and rolled a blunt, but Gabe refused it. Pot seemed dangerous. The music that Henry had told him about, the all-encompassing soundscape that he'd been warned he could never unhear—it loomed on the periphery of his every moment.

He went to bed early that night and slept late the next day. It had been months since he'd gone to sleep completely sober, and he awoke feeling painfully alert. The first thing he did was replay Val's message. Once, and then again.

He dressed for work.

The walk downtown started normally enough. It was good to be out in the fresh air. The houses and cars and people provided some distraction from Gabe's thoughts of Henry and the image of Val stretching in her doorway. But the closer he got to downtown, the stranger he felt. The big ugly McDonald's billboard, the men who sat in front of the train ticket vending machines begging for dollar coins, the bright red signage in the Rutgers bookstore window—Gabe felt like he was remembering all of it into existence. He had the sense that if he turned away it would all disappear. An express train shot through the station, and the pounding of its wheels jostled his joints in their sockets.

The crashing rumble reminded him of watching that older Henry float through the air.

He felt unmoored. Not momentarily disoriented but deeply disconnected. The massive parking garage that rose up next to him on Spring Street seemed otherworldly, its cavernous, wide-open sides like the crumbling walls of an alien ruin. The sky felt too close, the air too thin, and the sound of his surroundings was like a muddy brown soup that had been cooked for too long. Gabe wondered how he had ever been able to separate individual sounds from one another when they were simultaneously vibrating the same little set of bones in his inner ear.

Soon he reached the short block where the Magic Dragon stood. All he wanted was to turn off the music and sit in the darkened office, but when he stepped in he heard voices in the back and saw foam packing peanuts near the door to the showroom. His boss was there, and Dave, the guy who usually worked when Gabe was off. It was a shipment day.

Gabe astonished himself with his ability to act as if nothing was wrong. He pulled small boxes out of massive ones and opened them with care so as not to scratch the glass inside with his box cutter. He poured out peanuts, lined pipes up on the counter, talked over the prices, labeled, swept, vacuumed, cataloged. He went about accomplishing each task with a resolute focus, fighting the whole time to ignore the sound of tearing tape and paper, the clink of glass hitting glass, the way that tiny pieces of foam curled into eddies or puffed up in bursts when someone threw an empty box on the ground or walked by in a hurry. It all seemed a startlingly accurate, hyper-real facsimile of a normal day. At last he broke down all the larger pieces of cardboard and tied them into stacks with twine. A half hour later he was alone. He shut off the stereo and flipped the knob on the air conditioner. It ticked as its insides settled.

He didn't feel much like smoking, but the hours ahead of him needed to be filled with something, so he grabbed a pack of Camels from the display case, slipped an IOU into the register, and tore open the cellophane. The smoke felt good but the crackling of the moist tobacco was unnaturally loud.

He wondered if this was how it had started for Henry. When had *thoughts* become *voices?* How would Gabe even know?

He put out the cigarette and leaned his elbows against the counter, crushing the heels of his hands into his eye sockets until his vision was filled with dark, roiling clouds. Had it only been the day before when he'd awoken in Val's bed? When he'd spoken at length with a man who claimed to be Henry from the future? How had he let that happen? It had been frighteningly easy to abandon all reason and simply *believe,* but why?

He replayed the ride in his mind's eye. Nobody ever came to collect Henry's ticket. Had anyone noticed him on the train? Had anyone moved out of his way as they walked up Easton Avenue? And what about his insistence that Gabe tell nobody of his existence? It seemed like something a hallucination might say to protect itself.

Joan had seen him in the park. She'd even talked to him. But even that was no more than an assumption. Joan had spoken to *somebody,* and though her description of the man was dead-on, it didn't provide any comfort. She said he had a big beard, long curly hair, and deep, sunken eyes. Those features were the *only* things about the man Gabe had noticed when he'd first seen him, as if he'd conjured exactly what Joan had described without any further embellishments or additions.

The clock on the wall above Gabe's head was louder than he remembered it. Each tick sounded like a few dozen insect legs striking a wet surface at the same time. It was a meaty sound, and its rhythm began to frame the building noises that surrounded him. The click and whoosh of water in the pipes behind the drywall. The creaking of the floor of the apartment above. The humming of the fridge in the office in back. The idling engines of the cars outside.

A nauseous wave rose up to the middle of his throat. Deep in his abdomen, he could feel the weight of the pizza he'd forced himself to eat when they were unpacking the shipments. He stood up from the stool, grabbed the keys, and stumbled forward, but stopped when he heard a tapping on the glass followed by the ugly electronic chime of the motion sensor at the front door.

Joan's breathing announced itself to the room like a flat tire flapping on asphalt. Gabe took a deep breath through his mouth, not wanting to test his weak stomach with her stench.

"Whatsamatter?" she said, stopping in the middle of the room. "You look pale." All she carried was a plastic shopping bag. Judging by the fumes Gabe guessed it contained a fifth of vodka and some Diet 7Up.

"I'm fine," said Gabe, but his diaphragm wobbled as he spoke and he suddenly felt weightless.

He didn't remember running for the door, but he was outside when the vomit burned up through his throat and landed on the sidewalk. The sound of it, so specific and unmistakable, started a new movement in the fugue he'd been hearing ever since the bridge. Whatever relief he felt at having cleared out his system was overshadowed by the fear of what was happening to him.

He went back inside.

"Sorry," he said, though he didn't know what for.

"You better go to the doctor," said Joan.

Gabe didn't answer. He leaned against the wall.

"My mother died of stomach cancer," she said. It sounded like she was trying to be helpful.

"I gotta go home."

"Better get checked out," she said. Her face was alight with pity. "Probably nothing, but you don't know until—"

"Joan. Get out. Please. Now."

She shuffled in place, then retreated out the door. Gabe went to the back, rinsed out his mouth in the bathroom. He turned off the lights and locked up without balancing the drawer.

He was slick with sweat when he finally stepped through the back door of his house. The walk home had been terrible, each of his senses assaulted mercilessly. He felt as if his body had been ground into paste. His skin felt fiery, his insides cold. His only goal had been getting to the house, but once he was there he understood that it held no comfort.

Cal was in the living room. He said something, but Gabe could barely hear him and he didn't respond. He felt capable of speaking—he just really didn't want to. Maybe that was how Henry had felt. Gabe sat down on one of the couches, covered his eyes. Cal was watching some sepia-colored war documentary, the kind of thing that was always on one channel or another. A few seconds of it was enough to spur the nausea again, but Gabe breathed deeply and swallowed hard. He stood up, stumbled into his bedroom, and closed the door. Then he shut off the lights and stripped. He fell into bed, cocooned himself as he had the day before. But it offered no relief. He prayed for help. For deliverance. Silently at first, and then aloud. His whispers only added a new melody to the clamoring song that had enveloped him. Baritone voice-over and artillery on TV, the rustling of covers close to his ear, cars on the street and the dim, tinny radio at Tata's. His whispers floated on top of it all. The song was a staticky, driving thumper, and it vamped and vamped, over and over, as if waiting for some cue that would drive it all home. And then, as if descending from above, there it was—the melody that the music had been waiting for. An actual melody, not sound shaped to music but music itself, a tune that he knew. A digital arpeggio that melded with everything, brought it together—an anthem of pain. It grew loud and then louder and Gabe felt he would break.

But then some lucid part of him remembered.

He had heard that melody every day for months. It was his phone. Thinking only of how he needed to silence it, how he could take control of at least that one thing, Gabe rolled from his bed and knelt on the floor. He crawled to where he'd thrown it down in his haste to undress.

Val, said the screen.

It was so loud. He knew he shouldn't answer, that he would only make a fool of himself and scare her, that once he said aloud what was happening to him his life would change forever. But he was too desperate to resist. Regardless of what the consequences were, he understood that he had no real choice. Henry had never asked for help. Gabe didn't need to repeat that mistake. He would tell her everything and deal with what came next. He accepted the call and held the phone to his ear.

"Gabe?"

Val's voice came through clear and cool and strong as a trumpet blast. It echoed in his mind, the sound of his name coming back weaker with each repetition. When finally it went silent, everything else did too.

"Gabe?" she said again. "Are you there?"

He listened for the music but couldn't hear it. His body was still tense, his muscles sore, and his skin soiled with the accumulated nervous sweat of the day, but other than that he felt fine.

"Hey," he said. The fever had broken, the memory of it already fading away like some absurd dream.

"Are you all right?"

"Yeah," he said. And then, as if nothing strange were happening, as if he weren't standing nude and clammy in the darkness of his bedroom, shaking from the aftereffects of the strangest, most frightening experience of his life, he said, "I'm really glad you called."

ADAGIO: 41

V IRGINIA IS FOR LOVERS.
    The welcome sign said so.

"Do you remember this?" Henry asked.

"I do," said 80. He was driving, nervous eyes fixed to the road, hands tight on the wheel at ten and two.

They were headed for New Orleans, their departure timed so that they'd reach the city at about the same time as the bus that contained 29 and his bandmates. If there was a plan for what would happen once they all got there, Henry didn't know what it was.

The car 80 drove was a nondescript gray sedan, different from the one that he'd been driving when he picked up Henry. They had left that other car twelve years in the future, which meant that, in Henry's current moment, all its pieces were scattered around the globe. The metals were perhaps still buried in the ground, the plastics still waiting to be fabricated or recycled. 80 wouldn't say much about it, how he'd gotten the vehicles, or the house, or the cash that he spent freely on their gas and food. He just said that it was easy to make money when time was meaningless. As they drove, Henry gave a lot of thought to that. It would be simple enough to find a casino. Sit at a roulette table for an hour and memorize a handful of winning numbers. Find a bridge and shift back.

"So if you remember this drive," he said, "why don't we remember seeing us when we were twenty-nine?"

80 clenched his jaw, sighed through his nose.

"You don't know?" said Henry.

"Not for certain. But I do have an idea. It has to do with inevitability. Our meeting with 29 hasn't happened yet. We're driving there and we think that it *will* happen, but it hasn't yet, not in any of our realities."

"That doesn't make sense," said Henry. "You remember all sorts of things that I'm going to do even though they haven't happened yet."

"But our encounter is now fact. I didn't remember any change in my past until you recognized me. It was that recognition that changed your future. This Henry, our twenty-nine-year-old counterpart, he hasn't seen us yet."

Henry let that idea tumble through his mind. "So what *do* you remember about this drive?" he asked.

"It's strange," said 80. "My life since I was your age requires that I return you to your time. That in turn requires that you change your mind about this trip—or that I do. For instance, this morning when you awoke on the bridge, I said we didn't have to go anywhere. In that moment I remembered that you would agree with me, that I would take you back home. Everything would proceed from there much as I described yesterday. But then you stood up, told me we were leaving. A slightly different past was created then, one in which we got in the car but didn't make it out of the driveway before you changed your mind. Then we made it out of the driveway and everything changed again. Right now I keep remembering how we turned back. But so far we haven't. So we didn't. And each time we reach a point that defies my memory, I remember something new."

Henry couldn't think of anything to say to that.

"We're doing something very strange here," said 80.

"This is just occurring to you?"

"No, but…we're pushing the boundaries."

"What boundaries?" said Henry. "Maybe it's you that wants to turn around."

"Maybe," said 80. But he kept on driving.

The hotel in Roanoke was nice enough, but Henry felt too strange to enjoy it. He was a visitor from another time. The guests in the lobby wore clothes in earnest that would only be worn as a fashion statement where he had come from. It looked like a theme party.

When 80 told the woman at the front desk that he wanted to pay in cash, she asked a dozen questions and requested a large deposit. 80 obliged on all counts. The woman eyed Henry throughout the exchange, noting his silence and wondering, he was sure, what kind of fetish she was tacitly supporting by handing over the keycards. In the room, TV on and shoes off, Henry found the commercials to be kitschy and quaint, the long-canceled shows they interrupted just as irritating. He tried watching the news but grew frustrated. So little of it was important, not when it was still *news* and especially not in retrospect. He turned it off.

"What's going to happen tomorrow?"

"We'll leave at seven thirty," said 80. "It'll take twelve or thirteen hours to get to New Orleans, so with stops for lunch, gas, whatever, we should get there just in time to find a hotel and catch the ten o'clock set."

"We're going to see a show?"

"Indeed," said 80. "At d.b.a. Minerva Blanc and the Grits."

"Jesus." Henry laughed and the memories came unbidden. He pictured Minerva—Molly, though she'd insisted nobody call her that—the way he'd always seen her onstage: from behind, straddling the microphone stand, the stage lights passing through the outer fringes of her big curly hair to form a reddish-brown halo. He'd never found her particularly attractive, though he knew she was. The reaction of the crowd told him that.

He didn't ask 80 why they had to see the band. It would be good to see their younger self in action, to reconnect with him briefly and anonymously before changing his life forever. It might give them a better idea of how to deal with him. But that was a rationalization. The truth was much simpler. It was too tempting to resist. It would be fun.

The next day Henry drove. In the passenger seat, 80 was splayed in the totally uncontrolled backwards lean of a sleeping old man: mouth open wide, lower jaw swinging with the motion of the car. It was almost like he wasn't there at all. Henry glanced at 80's head, saw the graying skin and the mottled little sun spots. He understood so little about what was going on within the man's mind. Over the years, he'd had the same feeling about Val. They'd be sitting at dinner or watching a movie and the thought would hit him with the philosophical force of a tidal wave: he had no idea what she was thinking, no concept whatsoever of what it meant to *be* her. And yet he loved her, knew her better than he knew anyone else in the world. It was even stranger to apply this notion to Annie. She was—in a very real way—a physical extension of Henry's own body, and yet her mind was essentially a mystery.

Henry wondered if it would be any different when he saw his younger self for the first time. Would he see inside of this person that he'd been? Would he finally feel with himself what he'd always yearned to feel with others?

"What's that?" said 80 as he jerked awake.

"I didn't say anything."

80's body remained completely still, but his mouth, now closed, squirmed as he tried to gather enough saliva to wet his tongue.

"Hello, Georgia," said Henry.

WE'RE GLAD GEORGIA'S ON YOUR MIND, read a sign.

"You haven't turned around," said 80.

"No," said Henry. "It's time we discussed what we do when we find him."

80 frowned and sat up, loosened the seat belt from around his waist. "He'll be out of it, already a little bit psychotic. We need to get him to a bridge, travel back a few days. That should straighten him out, and it's the only way to prove that we're real."

"Get him to a bridge. Okay."

80 opened the glove compartment and pulled out an old spiral-bound map book. "There's one over a train yard not too far from the club. Another a few minutes away that crosses the Mississippi, though it's long and will offer less privacy. If we can take the time, I have my eye on a small crossing over a canal—should be quiet, a ten-minute drive from d.b.a."

"And then what?"

"Then we play it by ear."

"Great plan."

"And what do you propose?"

"If I had a better idea, you'd remember it," said Henry.

"It should be fast," said 80. "We get him to a bridge right away, then we shift back. I'll take us to an afternoon. The change from night to day should heighten the effect, make him certain that what he is seeing is genuine. He'll recognize you more readily, so you'll do most of the explaining. Then, if he's well enough, we'll get a hotel room in town and spend a couple days talking it out. He'll need time to think. As will we, to be honest. It gets… murky."

"And what if he won't go with us?"

"What do you think?"

"I think we take him. By force if we have to. Once he hears the music, he'll know. That's all that matters. We just have to get him to the bridge."

80 sucked his teeth and sighed.

"What?" said Henry. "Just say it."

"This whole plan—it's possible that it's meaningless. The moment he recognizes us, everything will be different. Everything. More than a decade of your life will be replaced instantaneously. Fifty years of mine. You need to be prepared for how confusing that might be, how potentially damaging."

"I know."

"You couldn't possibly," said 80. "You can imagine it, but the imagining is meaningless. I'm so full of memories. I met you on the sidewalk and thousands of days just materialized. A whole lifetime of moments remembered and misremembered, dull and exciting and joyful and heartbreaking—they all came to me in an instant and I don't feel as if I really lived them, but I did. I must have, because they are the pieces of me that, when put together, tell the story of how I came to be. But the old pieces are there too. They sit side by side with the new. So which am I? The old or the new? Do you see?"

"I couldn't possibly," said Henry.

From the corner of his eye Henry could see that 80 had hung his head, brought thumb and forefinger to the bridge of his nose.

"It's impossible," said 80. "I feel like a fool, like a child. I just don't have the words to say what's happened to me."

"Then stop trying," said Henry. "I'll know soon enough."

NORTHEAST CORRIDOR

I N RETROSPECT, VAL wasn't sure why she'd called Gabe in the first place. Her bumbled apology over voice mail wasn't planned. Nothing was. She supposed she just wanted to hear his voice. She needed a signal that things were essentially okay, that the weirdness of their morning-after could be forgotten.

She waited a day before trying him again, and during that time she replayed the night in her head. Gabe's sleeping face inches in front of her own. His pained look of awe when she lifted her arms to stretch in the doorway. It felt good to relive those moments. Too good. So as an antidote she tried to picture Henry crazy and lost, gone and alone. But she couldn't hold him in her mind.

Gabe answered her second call. They talked for more than an hour, but not about Henry. After hanging up Val lay on her bed and clutched her phone. It was hot in her palm from overuse. It felt like an admonition. She had meant to bring up Henry, she told herself. That was why she'd called. But then Gabe sounded so happy to hear from her. The awkwardness had apparently dissipated on its own and it didn't seem necessary to dampen the mood.

That was Monday.

On Tuesday, Val kept away from her cell as best she could. She congratulated herself almost hourly for having the willpower to restrain herself. When Gabe called her, late in the afternoon, her neck and arms tensed with guilty anticipation.

She was expecting the same breezy conversation as the day before, so she was surprised when he said, "I think I'm kind of losing it."

"How so?" she said.

"I'm hearing things. I see Henry—just, like, out of the corner of my eye. And I'm...I don't know. I'm scared. That I'm going crazy."

"You said that when Henry started acting weird he could barely talk, right? And when he did, he didn't make sense?"

"Yeah."

"Well, you're making sense to me."

Gabe laughed. "Maybe you're losing it too."

"I know it must be really hard, but you're not going catatonic or anything. Whatever you're experiencing, I'm sure it's normal."

Val could hear a faint exhale on the other end of the line. "I feel normal," said Gabe. "When I'm talking to you."

Val didn't know what to say.

"I'm sorry," he said.

"Don't be."

"It's stupid."

"It's not."

"This isn't on you, Val. It's not your job to make me feel good. But, honestly, I'm scared—really scared. The fact that I can talk to you, that we can be in touch like this, it's the only thing that feels real right now. I appreciate it, I guess. I think that's what I'm saying."

"I appreciate it too," said Val. "I was worried that I was, like, using you or something. Honestly? I've just felt out of touch since I moved here. Like nobody knows who I really am. When you called—and I know it's about Henry, and I can't imagine what you're feeling and it's really scary, I get that—but when you called

I was just really happy. And when you came over, that made me happy too. So you don't have to be too appreciative. This is good. We're good."

Gabe sighed again. "I just need him to come back," he said.

"I know," said Val. She wondered why she hadn't said *Me too.*

"I need this to be over."

It wasn't the painful confrontation with a sad reality that Val had been counting on. It didn't resolve her confusion. And when it was over, it was as if they'd purged something poisonous. Gabe lit up, even brighter than before. By the time Val hung up, the muscles around her mouth felt weak and warm from smiling.

Wednesday and Thursday passed and Val lacked all focus. She made sure to be home by eight or nine so that she could talk to Gabe. Kara teased her about it, how Val was locking herself in her room at night like a teenager, her laughter seeping out from around her door.

"But you're just friends, right?" said Kara.

It was the same question Val was asking herself as she stepped off the 5:43 New Jersey Transit Northeast Corridor train and onto the platform in New Brunswick.

She couldn't calm down as she walked up the bright, familiar sidewalk on Easton Avenue. Why did she have an extra set of clothes in her bag? What did she expect to happen now that she was in this place that she'd fought so hard to leave? More to the point, what kind of heartless bitch makes plans to sleep over with her missing ex-boyfriend's best friend?

Val's only answer was that it couldn't be wrong to spend time with someone who made her feel like herself. And Gabe was *Henry's* best friend, not hers. She trusted that friendship. If Gabe could feel okay about what they were doing, then she could too.

It was Friday evening and the streets were already loud. The weekend had taken hold of New Brunswick and it wouldn't let go until Sunday came to make everything quiet and sad again. Sundays in New Brunswick reminded Val of how she used to feel after birthday parties or bar mitzvahs when she was young. It was an empty loneliness brought on by the realization that something she had looked forward to was over and it hadn't changed a thing.

On Hamilton the street was darker. She passed the grease trucks, smelled the alluring mix of oil, cheese, eggs, and meat that poured out of the food vendors' little trailers. Across a campus parking lot from the trucks was frat row. The hair-gelled bouncers were already set up on their moldy front porch couches. As she passed the frat house closest to Hamilton she heard a moan followed by laughter. She glared in the direction of the catcalls, but the offenders were in shadow.

She made it to Gabe's place early. She'd never seen it before, so she checked the number twice before mounting the stairs and ringing the doorbell. Cal opened the door and greeted her with more warmth than she would have expected. She'd met him a few times and always thought he seemed harmless but odd. He led her through the front hallway to the living room.

"Gabe's in the shower," he said.

Val thought she heard something strange in Cal's tone, like maybe what he really meant was *The shower . . . you know what that means.* Then she wondered if it was Cal's tone or her own ear being tuned to a specific key. She sat down on a couch and looked at her fingers. The cuticle on her left pinkie nail was ragged from being picked. She made tweezers of her right thumb and index finger, but then thought better of it and slid her hands underneath her thighs.

Did Cal think this was a date? Had she been visiting anyone else the answer would be self-evident, but Gabe wasn't anyone else. He was Henry's best friend, and Henry was still missing. And as for the shower, Gabe probably showered every day.

Val's nose twitched from the sharp smell of mold and pine. She wondered if it was Henry's living room or his roommate.

"You wanna smoke?" said Cal. In his outstretched hand he held a marbled glass pipe in the shape of a mushroom.

Val smiled. "That's okay."

Cal shrugged, lit, and inhaled deeply. "So you're at NYU now, right?" he said, his vocal chords muted by the smoke.

"Yeah. I love it," she said. The words sounded strange.

"It's expensive."

"Well, it's a really good school."

"I think it's insane."

Val couldn't tell where the conversation was going, but she wasn't about to back down out of uncertainty.

"Insane?" she said.

"I mean, what—sixty thousand dollars a year? You should tell your parents to just give you that money to keep. After four years you have almost a quarter million dollars. You could just move to Argentina or somewhere and live off that money for the next thirty years or something."

Val heard footsteps on the stairs. Gabe appeared in the doorway to the living room, a towel wrapped around his waist. She'd seen him shirtless before—at the beach and in the dorms—but this time felt different. She'd always told Gabe that he was attractive, but she'd said it in a big-sister *I'm gonna find you a girl* kind of way. She puffed him up because she knew he needed it, not because she had a strong opinion about his looks. He was skinny. Not tight and purposefully skinny. Semi-starved broke-college-kid skinny. He had strange little patches of hair pushing out from the sides of his upper arms. His back, too, had sparse, long hair arranged in two splotchy wings beneath his shoulder blades. He wasn't muscled. Acne scars were just barely visible on his shoulders.

"Sorry," he said as he rushed past her. "I'll be out in a minute."

Gabe entered his bedroom and closed the door. Sitting so near to his naked body gave her a buzzing feeling. Even through the door. Even if he was flawed.

Cal continued. "I mean, for that kind of money you could make a real difference, you know?"

"Where's your bathroom?"

Cal placed the pipe on the coffee table and rubbed his face with both hands. "Go out the way we came in, and you'll see the stairs. Take them up and when you get up there on the right is my room, the next door down is the bathroom."

"So, upstairs then," she said.

Cal giggled, confused, and Val stood up. She smiled silently to herself as she walked down the hall.

Once in the bathroom she lowered the toilet lid and sat down. She needed to order her thinking, but all she could focus on was the impressive filth of the room in which she sat. Black mold carpeted the single shower curtain, and yellowed tissues sat piled around the long-overfilled garbage can. The light switch was within reach, and Val flipped it with a flick of her wrist.

She breathed deeply. Once she felt steady enough to go back downstairs, she turned the light back on and flushed the toilet for appearance's sake. She washed her hands, taking care not to look up at herself in the mirror.

By the time she got back downstairs, Gabe was out of his room and standing in front of the television. Apparently all the ease afforded by the telephone was gone, because neither of them seemed to know what to say.

"What do you think of the place?" he asked. He sat down on the couch and moved his hands from his lap to the couch on either side of his legs, then back to his lap again.

Val remained standing and picked up her coat. "Can we get something to eat?" she said.

Gabe jumped up and went back in his room to get his jacket.

Val turned to Cal. "You coming?" she asked. She knew the answer, but she wanted to see what she could learn from his response.

"No," said Gabe as he walked back through the living room. "He has plans."

Cal shrugged and grabbed the remote from the coffee table. He met Val's questioning gaze with a heavy-lidded smile before resting his red-rimmed eyes on the luminous screen.

Val followed Gabe into the kitchen. He was standing by the back door, holding it open with one hand and rubbing the hair that fell around his ear with the other.

"After you," he said.

Val followed his direction, her body propelled forward by an electric anticipation that burned from her navel to the top of her scalp. She sensed that it was strange to feel so excited, but she also knew that if she examined the sensation it would go away. So she left it alone. She was tired of feeling bad. She was tired of asking questions. Too many things had felt wrong for too long. For that night, at least, she was back in New Brunswick. It was the weekend. She was with Gabe. For once, all her pent-up angst couldn't penetrate the happiness she felt.

She bounded down the steps and into the night.

ALLEGRO: D.B.A.

THEY PARKED AROUND the corner from the club. 80 walked a block in both directions in search of felled signs that might prove that their spot was too good to be true. Henry stood on the sidewalk and peered through chain-link at the tour bus in the club's back parking lot. He hadn't seen the bus in more than ten years, but still he felt the terrifying power of it.

It was almost nine. They rounded the corner onto Frenchmen Street and mixed in with the crowd. Frat boys in plaid shorts and polos dripped beer from plastic cups. Old tourists smiled in New Orleans T-shirts. Locals were marked by their casual indifference to the out-of-towner dress code. They wore sweats, basketball shorts, baseball caps, paint-stained tees.

The sound of a four-piece band blasted through the open doors of a bar across the street. Faint traces of a robust Latin percussion section wafted from a couple blocks down. A reggae bass line joggled Henry's insides, and he vividly recalled the few hours he'd spent at Café Negril a decade before, entranced by the Bob Marley songbook as performed by a group of musicians that looked like they'd been thrown together by a tornado. The white guitar player had a science-teacher look about him. The woman on keys was dressed as if for casual Friday at an insurance office: ill-fitting straight-leg jeans, a turquoise sweater, fancy bejeweled flip-flops. The lead singer was more the part, though his dreads were thinner and better kept than the mane worn by Marley in the mural that covered the back wall of the venue. The drummer played so far behind the beat that Henry's face contracted in a grimace of pleasure. But the real object of Henry's infatuation was the bass player. If the drummer was the heartbeat, she was the blood. She was fat and dark-skinned, her short hair pulled back in tight braided rows. To Henry she was sexier than any photo spread, more enlightened than the Buddha. He'd been looking for a god, and there she was. Her ministration was the rhythm. Her disciples were all who had ears to hear.

Henry snapped back to the present. The flood of memories made him nervous, but if 80 shared his anxiety he didn't show it. Once inside d.b.a., Henry marveled at how small the place was. A long bar bisected the space. On one side was the stage, on the other a lounge with high tables and stools. The early show was just wrapping up, an all-male three-piece rock outfit. The lead singer wore the kind of checkered scarf that had been popular among hipsters for a time before once again becoming the domain of Saudi princes. Henry crossed back over to the lounge area to find 80 leaning against the wall by the door.

"Do you remember anything yet?" asked 80.

Henry shook his head. Lost in nostalgia as he'd been for the past few minutes, he'd nearly forgotten why they were there.

"Me neither."

It was difficult to hear over the din of the bar. Henry moved a little closer to 80.

"Do you think we should stay on this side?" asked Henry. "So he doesn't see us until we want him to?"

"I don't imagine he'll be able to pick us out of the crowd," said 80.

Henry tried to remember what it was like up on that stage. He had retained little of the forty-five minutes he'd spent there twelve years before, and what he did recall was slippery. He saw a crowd painted red by the lights. Now that he was here, though, none of the lights seemed to be red at all.

"When are we going to approach him?" asked Henry.

80 put his mouth directly to his young self's ear so he wouldn't have to yell. "He'll go next door to hear that reggae band. When he walks over, we approach him on the street."

"Too public," said Henry. "We should go out back, to the bus."

80 pursed his lips. "We'll have to get over that fence."

"Easy," said Henry. "My memory is better than yours. He'll go out there right after the show to change out of his sweaty shirt. The rest of the band will be in here accepting free drinks from the crowd, trying to get laid, whatever. We go out to the back before the last song is over and wait. When he gets there we call him over, have a nice quiet talk."

80 leaned away from Henry and squinted with apparent concentration. "Okay," he said. "We're doing this together. Whatever happens, we remember that."

"This was your idea, old man," said Henry. "Whatever happens, you remember *that*." He was teasing, but only just. "I need some cash."

80 put a hand deep into his pocket and came out with two twenty-dollar bills. Henry hadn't seen the old design in years, but the bills were stiff, the ridges of freshly pressed ink still tangible on their surface.

"I'm going to the other side," said Henry.

"I'll see you at the end of the show." 80 tottered to an empty stool and sat down.

The opening band finished their set in a torrent of affected wails and pained expressions. Henry sipped his beer and enjoyed the quiet of a space in transition. The house music that came on was soft in comparison to the live act and conversation got softer too. Henry remembered this kind of peace from his years of gigging. It was the quiet in which nerves took hold, the quiet that said *They're waiting.* The stage was almost clear. The drummer took the last pieces of his kit; the guitar player snaked cable into loops.

And then it was time. Phil, the bass player for the Grits, stepped onto the stage. He was followed by Jack, the guitar player, who brought out his custom-designed pedal board and lovingly placed each piece of equipment in its own perfectly calibrated position. Molly herself wouldn't bless the stage with her presence until after the band had actually started playing. It was just one of her many stolen stagecraft tricks. She was more Jim Morrison than anybody else, with her faux-deep lyrics, wry poetic commentary, diva affectation, and raw sexual aggression uncut by shame or inhibition. She wasn't nearly as charismatic as Morrison must have been, but she thought she was and that got her about halfway there.

Henry was done with his first beer and motioned to the bartender for a second. After paying up, he looked back at the stage and saw his bass drum with attached tom-tom placed in its customary position. His diaphragm tensed and his lips parted in a smile. From the side of the stage came the silver glint of a cymbal stand. The man who carried it was overweight and dressed in ill-fitting clothes. His face was serious and he never looked up from his work. It seemed like he wanted to avoid the audience entirely. Henry watched his young self set up each piece of the kit. He took pride in seeing how 29 tweaked the tom, adjusting for the sound of the room, how he carefully gauged the space between the top and bottom of the high hat. At any moment the Henry onstage could raise his eyes up from his work and see his older self at the bar. A whole new universe would be created—not with a big bang, but with a silent moment of recognition. So far 29 was too focused on his work. He fidgeted and tuned while Henry drank his beer and watched, fascinated.

Phil, Jack, and 29 all left the stage, signaling that their setup was complete. The house music faded out and the venue's manager came out. Though three out of four of the Grits lived in Jersey, he announced that they came from Brooklyn because their manager, Marco, had insisted that it sounded better. The lights dimmed to a chorus of hoots and scattered applause. 29 was the first out. He sat down, looking contemplative, then picked up his sticks and began an earthy, shuffling beat. Henry recalled that he'd worked for days on that snare drum before he was satisfied with the tension of the heads and snares. The result was half drum, half shaker. A barrel filled with beads. The bass drum was tight, the mallet on the pedal hard so that when amplified its sound was round and fierce like a kick in the stomach.

Then Jack and Phil came out, guitars hanging from their shoulders. When they plugged in, the speakers popped in time with the beat and feedback splashed out in dissonant waves that built up and up so loud that the drums were almost obscured. Then a garbled blues riff smoked out from Jack's guitar and the distortion broke. After a few measures of that, Phil completed the foundation with a bouncy bass line, and the crowd nodded, swayed, laughed and moaned as one great body.

Henry smiled. The needle was in the groove, but he knew it was only foreplay. Molly would come out when everybody was primed for her, or maybe a little after. She liked to make them wait.

Just when heads began to turn side to side, just when the audience finally got acclimated and slightly bored, Molly extended a naked calf onto the stage. She announced herself with red patent leather shoes—vintage, of course—with a modest two-inch heel. The shoes caught the eye but didn't hold it. Rather, they served to force anyone looking at her to start at the bottom and work his way up. Cutoff shorts ended impossibly high on her slim, muscular legs. A black bra showed through her white sheer shirt, the neck of which was cut low enough to bisect the top of the image that decorated it: Ziggy Stardust in halftone. On anyone else it might have seemed trite. In fact, when Molly wasn't onstage it *did* seem trite. Henry remembered walking into roadside stores with the band. With her little bowler hat akimbo, her long red hair reaching farther down her body than her shorts, she got looks that could be mortifying. But here she was where she belonged, and Henry got it. She wasn't simply sexy. She was sex incarnate. She owned the room before she opened her mouth. She owned the whole building when she breathed into the microphone. By the time she started singing, she was Minerva, and the whole city was hers.

Once the set was fully under way, Henry stared hard at 29 and tried to remember what it had been like to live his current moment as that younger man. Of this particular performance, though, nothing concrete remained. So he let it go. Grooving on his own drumbeat, he let the noise of the room converge. The babble of the crowd, the bark of the bartender, feet shuffling on dry floorboards—the sounds groped each other and conjoined before spinning off alone again. When he sipped his beer, the bubbles on his tongue seemed to mingle somehow with Minerva's voice. The sensation was pleasant at first, like a warm melting low in his gut. But then it turned sour and Henry felt something pop and fizzle deep in his sinus cavity. His eyes shot open and he looked at the stage. Where Minerva had been standing, partially blocking Henry's view of his twenty-nine-year-old counterpart, there was now an open space. Framed by two cymbals and the rise of the high tom, he could see his own face. It was younger, contorted by the effort of driving the band steadily and furiously forward. 29's eyes were open and when his gaze met Henry's the larger music of all crescendoed to an almost inconceivable wail.

And then Henry remembered.

CROSSING THE LINE

I F GABE HAD known they were going to kiss, he wouldn't have been so smooth about it.

They'd each had trouble speaking when Val first arrived at the house. She looked effortlessly amazing, which to Gabe was always the best kind of amazing. Her hair was gathered up in a loose bun on the back of her head. Auburn forks of it escaped to tickle her exposed neck. It reminded Gabe of the morning he'd woken up with her, how he'd fantasized about burying his lips in it.

Before she arrived the musical hallucinations had kept coming in unpredictable waves. And hallucinations were what they were, Gabe was sure of it by then. He hadn't yet pieced together the implications, and he didn't really want to. It was the same with how Val made it all stop. He wondered why, but the why was immaterial. She was his escape hatch and that was all that mattered.

They left the house and walked a block before Val spoke.

"Cal was trying to bait me," she said.

They both laughed. Silence resumed.

Gabe looked behind them every few minutes. Henry would know she was in town. He would follow them just as he'd followed Gabe to and from the city. If he was even real. For the time being it didn't matter whether Gabe was avoiding a flesh-and-blood time traveler or a figment of his imagination. All that mattered was that he get through the evening without seeing Henry, without freaking out or throwing up or getting overtaken by terror.

"I wasn't prepared for how being back here was going to make me feel," said Val.

"What do you mean?" Gabe was glad she was speaking. It gave him an excuse to look at her as they walked.

"Getting off the train . . . it just felt weird I guess."

Gabe kept looking at her. Was he staring? How had he walked with her before? Did he ever casually touch her? Did he make eye contact? Suddenly he couldn't recall what it was like to walk next to anyone at all. It felt as if he'd never done it before.

"It's like I just stepped into a different version of myself. The one who lives here and goes to classes on College Avenue and spends depressing nights by myself in the dorm. It's hard to remember how much has changed since then."

"A lot," said Gabe. He felt stupid.

They arrived at Gabe and Cal's go-to Indian joint on Easton.

Gabe would come to remember their meal together as a collection of thoughts and images, each one isolated and beautiful. The greasy dosa bread between Val's fingertips. How unself-conscious she was with the messy Indian food and the way her laughter rose above every other noise in the restaurant. Gabe almost didn't recognize Val that night. The shapes that made up her face seemed to exist independently of one another, and he could feel his brain putting her together. He'd seen but not really noticed the tiny dimple on the underside of her left cheek, the little dip in her hairline, the length of her eyelashes. Her smile was familiar, but nuances were visible that hadn't been before. She didn't have just one smile, she had thousands.

The green chilies in his masala dosa might have been partly responsible, but Gabe was euphoric. His lips burned and his skin tingled. Time moved in short bursts interrupted by long pauses. His face hurt from smiling and his diaphragm ached from laughing. When finally they stood up and stepped outside, Gabe put his hand in the air to give Val a high five and said, "Great dinner." The high five turned into a hand-clasped half hug. That hug ended with each of them trying to kiss the other's cheek, but they both turned an inch too far. When their lips touched it wasn't straight on. The corners of their mouths overlapped, that was all. It was chaste and quick. Val didn't recoil, and neither did Gabe, but they didn't keep on kissing. She put her cheek against his and hugged him a little harder, rocked from one foot to the other. They held the pose. Her closeness was an admission that something strange was happening, but its persistence signaled it wasn't reason for panic or fear. It was as if their bodies were talking.

Val's tense neck said *The kiss was a mistake.* The rest of her body said *But it's okay.*

Gabe's arms said something like *Mistakes are good.*

She relaxed into him and leaned her head on his shoulder, moving her lips as far from his as she could. *I can't.*

Gabe in turn rested his chin on her head. *That makes perfect sense. But really?*

She released him and smiled reassuringly.

"Let's get a drink," she said.

Gabe laughed. "This is New Brunswick," he said. "Everyone cards."

"Well, I'm from New York," she said, her voice a funny version of the mocking baby talk Henry used when he wanted to make fun of Gabe. "Everyone has really good fake IDs."

They walked downtown. Most of the bars between the train station and the ghetto catered to a more middle-aged clientele. The State Theater and George Street Playhouse brought them. Gabe had always imagined that it was the quintessential married date night: dinner in town followed by the touring company of an Irish dance troupe or *Les Miserables* starring nobody you've ever heard of. If they'd gone to one of the college bars, he'd have been carded at the door. But since they were downtown they managed to slip into a brewery-slash-grill. There was a standing table in the corner, out of sight from the bar so Val could go up and retrieve drinks without the bartender asking questions about who she was buying for.

Gabe asked for a Keystone Light but Val rolled her eyes and brought back something dark that smelled like weed and tasted like burnt rubber. She was drinking the same. Their flirtation continued, but it felt different now. Where before the banter was natural and unconscious, now it felt forced, as if they each had something to prove. It felt as if they were negotiating, but about what, Gabe didn't know.

When their conversation hit a lull, Gabe chugged the half of his beer that was left. He didn't enjoy it.

"We can't hook up," said Val.

Gabe's stomach tightened. On the face of it she was changing the subject. In reality they both knew that the possibility of sex was the only conversation they'd been having since dinner.

Gabe met her gaze and held it.

She smiled, an apology, but a sweet one.

"I know," said Gabe. He looked at the table, traced a circle of dried something with one finger. Disappointment was only part of what he felt. There was shame, too, and a bit of fear. Henry could be standing outside the bar, hidden in the dark. They had already laughed and carried on enough to show how little he was factoring into their evening.

But despite all that, Gabe was excited. Val had broken through. They were discussing *it*. They might be able to put it to rest for the night, maybe even for a few more days or weeks. But the *We shouldn't do this* conversation wouldn't end as long as they wanted each other. It was a hungry question, one that would require more and more energy to try to answer until finally it would catch them in a moment of weakness and force them into action.

"I want to," she said. "It's not just you."

"Hm."

"It's just, I thought you should know that."

"Thanks." Gabe meant it, but he sounded sarcastic.

"Hey. Gabe."

He looked up from the stained tabletop.

"I love hanging out with you. I feel like this is what friendship is supposed to be like. We just barely got this. And we can keep it. We both need it. I don't want to ruin it."

"I figured it was more about Henry."

"Henry is reason enough." She looked wounded, a little guilty. "You're right. It's just hard to remember that he's really gone. It's just too bizarre. Especially because my life—our lives—they just keep moving on. I really hope he's okay. But I can't imagine how he could be."

Henry's fine. I saw him. Gabe almost said it. He wanted to tell her. If only to explain to her that Henry didn't mind. But of course he couldn't. He didn't even know if the Henry he'd spoken to was real. If he was, Gabe had promised not to tell. It was the only thing Henry had asked.

Well. Not the only thing.

When it happens, I don't want you to think about me.

"I just have this feeling," said Gabe, "like he's fine. Not *fine* fine. I mean, obviously." He couldn't say it without really saying it. "Like he's going to be back and he'll stay, but that right now he just needs to explore a little bit. He's not in any state to do that safely, I know, but…I guess I just trust him."

Val crinkled her brow. "But Gabe," she said, "he's not himself."

"You're right. And that's another feeling I have. He's never going to be himself again. Not the Henry that we know."

Val sipped her beer. She was drinking it slowly and deliberately, like wine. Gabe wondered if maybe she didn't like it either. "You're probably right," she said. "But it feels like a betrayal, I guess."

"What does?"

"That we're even here. That we're out, having fun." And then, hesitantly, "Together."

"I know what you mean," said Gabe, "but don't you think he'd rather know that you're hanging out with me? That we're both trying to deal with this together? I mean, we're here because of him."

"That's true," she said, "but it just sounds so wrong. Boy goes nuts, his ex-girlfriend and his best friend start hanging out together. Talking on the phone. Living it up. You know?"

"It would be better if we weren't having fun?"

"Yeah," she said. "I guess it would." She smiled.

"I doubt Henry would give a shit if he knew that you and I were just sitting around crying over him for hours on end. He left Jan at home, didn't he? She must be devastated." There was anger in his voice; he could feel it, though he wasn't sure what he was angry about. "I think we've both found something here, together, that we can't get anywhere else. That's not a betrayal of Henry."

Val looked relieved. "I know you're right," she said. "But look at us. We're not just finding comfort. I mean we *are*, but that's not all we're doing."

"What do you mean?" He knew he was being coy, but it seemed important that he get her to say it. He wanted her to give voice to her desire.

"You know what I mean."

Gabe nodded gravely. "But we can't do that," he said. Not a question, but not strictly a statement either.

"No," she said.

Gabe lifted his glass and she did the same. They clinked and Gabe laughed a little.

After that they grew more relaxed. Perhaps by drawing a line they would not cross for Henry's sake they had given themselves permission to do whatever they wanted on the safe side of that line. Val retrieved another round of beers and Gabe tried to get used to the bitterness. Val said it was an "aypeeyay," and Gabe assumed it was something exotic until he looked at the drinks menu and realized that it was an acronym. He told Val as though she didn't already know. She laughed at him, her hand on his upper arm.

One more round later they decided to leave. Gabe was drunk enough not to fear the backstreets. They walked in the dark. He forgot the music, forgot to look for Henry. Val kept her hands in her pockets, but she kept leaning in to him, so Gabe slipped his arm around her shoulders. She let him. It felt natural to touch her. The alcohol made him feel like his old self, like he was harmlessly flirting with the Val whose relationship with Henry was central to Gabe's own life. But his arm sat on her longer than their previous friendship would have allowed. Then she reciprocated by wriggling her hand around his back, holding on to the fabric of his jacket. Gabe felt something ignite in the dark space beneath his sternum.

The house was dark and silent. He'd been counting on Cal to be there, if only to simplify the rest of the night. Cal would cut the tension, force both of them to act like the friends they were.

If Val noticed or cared that they were alone, she didn't show it. "I gotta pee," she said.

Gabe wondered how drunk she felt, listened for it in her heavy footfalls on the stairs. He sat down in the living room. He knew that if he turned on the TV they would probably fall asleep on the couch without any further awkwardness. It seemed like a good plan, which was probably why he had such a hard time following through with it. He put his feet on the coffee table. Then he took them down. He kicked off his shoes and crossed his legs underneath him. He was in the center of the blue couch. She would probably sit on the other sofa. The added space between them would help quiet his mind.

He heard running water from upstairs. Not just the toilet but the sink, too. For a while. She wasn't just washing her hands. Gabe pictured her checking herself out in the mirror, splashing her face, brushing her teeth. Finally the door opened and she came down the stairs, this time bounding a little, *ba-bump bum-bump bum-bump.*

"I used your face wash," she said. "At least I think it was yours."

"That's fine," said Gabe. Her makeup was gone. Without the shadows over her eyes or the mascara darkening her lashes, she looked partially naked. It was intimate, as if she was more present in the room. She was showing him what the rest of the world didn't often see.

Val walked around the coffee table and sat on the sofa that Gabe wasn't already hogging. A moment later she got up.

"I'm gonna change."

Gabe nodded and finally turned on the television. Val crossed the room in front of him once to get her bag from the kitchen, once more to get to his bedroom. The door slid shut. He turned the muffled sounds he heard through the door into images. She was slipping out of her jeans, placing her fingers underneath the band of her underwear to free the elastic where it stuck. Now she was taking off her shirt, reaching her hands behind her back to unhook the clasp of her bra, shoulder blades protruding, hands awkwardly stretching up behind her. Gabe imagined the feeling of the cold air across her chest and the weight of her breasts when they were finally released.

It hurt to want her so much.

When she came out a minute later in oversized yoga pants and a big long-sleeved T-shirt, he had to force himself to breathe. She probably thought she was dressing as unattractively as possible, but her shirt was old and worn. It hung off her body, pulling at her collar bones, falling sharply from the peaks of her nipples. She sat down. Gabe stared at the television as though it were the only thing in the world.

"I'm thirsty," she said. "You need some water?"

Gabe looked at her and nodded once. She got up again and went to the kitchen, her hands inside her sleeves and drawn up to her face. Was it cold? He couldn't feel anything resembling a sensitivity to temperature. The adrenaline had obliterated all other sensations. She came back and he moved over so she could sit down next to him. He noted where her lips touched the glass as she drank. When she handed it over he put his lips there too.

They looked at the television. Gabe stared without seeing and heard without listening until finally he caught himself falling asleep.

"You wanna sleep out here?" he asked. "Or Cal's not here. You can have his bed."

She nodded, drowsy. "You sure that's okay?"

He stood up, inviting her to follow him. They went up the stairs and he knocked on Cal's door, just to be sure. When he heard no answer he opened it and turned on the light. Val looked at the bed. A single twisted top sheet covered the bare mattress, and a stained gray comforter sat huddled at the foot of the bed like a dead body.

"Never mind," said Gabe.

Val laughed.

"You could just sleep with me," he said, though he couldn't believe it.

"Okay," she said. The couch was forgotten. "Whatever."

Gabe knew at that moment that they would not be resisting forever. They wouldn't be resisting at all. He told himself it was for the best. The longer they went without touching each other, the better it would feel when they finally did, and when Gabe really thought about it that meant that the ethical concerns underpinning their mutual resistance were more or less moot. Better to do it sooner rather than later. They'd enjoy it less. Which would in turn make it more acceptable.

Gabe chuckled to himself.

"What?" said Val.

"No. Nothing. Cal's bed. Go ahead down," he said.

Gabe brushed his teeth, and when he got downstairs Val was on the couch.

"Do you think this is the best idea?" he asked. "Given, you know. Our conversation? Earlier."

She screwed up her mouth to one side and cast her eyes down as if she was thinking really hard. They were both playacting now. Partly to save face. Partly as a form of foreplay.

"We're grown-ups, right?" she said.

Gabe wondered if that meant *We're grown-ups, so we can handle ourselves, right?* or *We're grown-ups, so doing what we're about to do is completely reasonable, right?*

"I can control myself," he said.

She laughed. "Good."

"Let me just get changed."

Gabe went in his room and closed the door. He had one pair of pajama pants, which he never wore. They were a Christmas gift from his parents, blue flannel with white snowflakes. He had to search the plastic storage bins beneath his bed to find them, but it was worth the effort. It seemed critical that he wear pants to bed. He slid open the door again.

Val's head lolled over. She looked up at him.

"I'm so tired," she said.

Gabe nodded again. He went to get more water, and when he got back his comforter had conformed itself to the shape of Val's body. She was facing the wall, her hair pushed up off her neck and splayed out on the pillow. He turned off the lights and climbed in.

It wasn't courage so much as total lack of self-control that made him find her lower back with his fingers. He dug his thumb in, massaging the column of muscle that sat next to her spine. She whimpered a little, not in a sexual way, but encouragingly. They had given each other massages before. There was a precedent. They were still on the safe side of the line.

"Could you do my shoulders?" she said. Simple and direct, not much for Gabe to base any assumptions on, but she flattened onto her stomach and he did as she asked.

Gabe listened closely to her breathing and hoped for hints about how her body was responding. All he heard was the steady, faint passing of air through her lips. His own hand moved under the covers, kneading the softness behind her shoulder blades. The rustling made its own little rhythm. It took a minute, but Gabe began to sense that her breathing and the rustling were in synch.

Val cleared her throat, punctuating the soft music of her breathing. "Can you do my lower back again, but the other side?"

He tried to move his hand to the side of her back closest to him, but he was all jammed up. "Turn on your side," he said.

Gabe lifted the covers with his arm and Val rolled to face him. She lifted her head and tried to free her hair, but it was caught underneath her shoulder. Gabe helped without thinking, his fingertips finding the base of her neck and combing outward until she was satisfied enough to rest her face on the pillow. Gabe placed his hand on what he thought was her waist, but he felt ribs and quickly moved lower. He rolled the pads of his fingers into the muscle at the small of her back, and she moaned. It sounded different from before. Something uncontrollable about it. Not a *Thanks, that's nice* sound, but something unconscious, as if her body were speaking directly through her throat with no cerebral middle-woman. It wasn't his intention, but as he pressed harder into her back, he was effectively pulling her closer to him. She was almost near enough to feel how hard he was, so he moved his hips back.

The muscles in his hand burned but he didn't dare stop. His fingers moved as if he were playing a chromatic scale up and down her back, and he began to hear it overlaid on the sound of her breathing, which was suddenly much louder than before. His eyes, now adjusted, caught the shine on her lower lip. Her breath smelled like beer and toothpaste, but strangely the combination was perfect. He wanted to taste her. The higher up on her back he went, the closer her face came to his own, and though she must have been conscious of it she didn't retreat.

Were they still on the right side of the line? Even if Val's lips were so close to Gabe's that he could have grabbed them with his teeth; even if their breath was mingling so much that he felt lightheaded; even if the only thing separating her breasts from his chest were her wrists crossed in front of her—were they safe?

Val lifted her arm and snaked it between Gabe's body and the inside of his elbow. Her hand came to rest on his back—the sound of it moving underneath the blanket swept up around his ears and was amplified and transformed. It locked in place with the rhythm of their breathing and echoed before finally resolving into a variation on the music that had been torturing Gabe for days. This time, though, it felt different. There was no dissonance. A dark memory materialized in his mind then, of Henry in a sleeping bag, the strange song that was a part of their game. Whenever that image appeared, Gabe tried his best to push it away—the shame and humiliation hadn't lessened in the years since Jan had pulled them out. But now, with Val close to him, he didn't feel the need to escape it. He simply let it float in and out, like a breath. One of millions. No more meaningful or powerful than any other. It wasn't shame he felt just then, but a beautiful sort of sadness. Henry was gone and all of

Gabe's memories of him mattered, no matter their quality. He was glad for that.

With Val's arm around him Gabe thought of how little space and cloth lay between his skin and hers, and he willed it to disappear. She had remained calm, never opening her eyes or reacting outright to the way their bodies had found each other, but she was not asleep and she was not resisting. Gabe moved his hand to her neck and prodded deeply into the muscle that he'd so wanted to touch that morning a week before—had it only been a week? He drew her face closer until the only difference between a kiss and what they were doing was the width of a hair, a minuscule protraction of the lips. Gabe increased the pressure on her neck and pulled her mouth perfectly against his own. The kiss was soft, and then it stopped. They both exhaled as though they'd been holding their breath for hours. Gabe pulled the warm, moist air from her mouth deep into his lungs. The sound of his heart—so loud, how could he never hear it?—pulsed its way into the song. He wasn't frightened or confused. He didn't need to ignore the music, but neither did he need to give it his attention. It washed through him, inseparable from the sensation in his body. The pause after that first kiss was long enough for either of them to reconsider. *Speak now,* said the moment, but they both held their peace. Val pulled him closer, her hand pressing into Gabe's back until the tops of their bodies met and he could finally feel the shape of her against him. He kept his hips swung out and away, not sure how she would react. They had removed the old boundary, but he didn't know what that meant.

Val pulled him closer.

The anthem pushed him forward.

When it was over, the music didn't stop. It became a lullaby, set to the beat of Val's even inhale and exhale. She was already asleep, her pajamas back on and her now heavy arm thrown over his chest. He wanted her naked again. He didn't know that he could wait. Val hadn't been awake long enough to express regret, but the way she draped herself over him said that she didn't have any. Still, Gabe felt a panic in his chest like a puddle of molten desperation.

Eventually the music decrescendoed and diminuendoed and, in silence, he fell asleep.

RONDO: 29

ENRY WORRIED ABOUT her. He knew she shouldn't be alone, not during the first trimester when she might be sick and exhausted, but Val insisted she was fine. It was so early, she said. Not yet a month since the test had come back positive. She was busy with work, enjoying herself while he was on tour. It gave her the opportunity to read the birthing books, see friends, concentrate on her work. She told him she was stocking up on solitude before the baby came.

But still Henry worried, and after a week on the tour bus his anxiety began to shift into something more dangerous. He couldn't sleep. He had a bed—the top bunk of a little cubby enclosed by a thick curtain—but it made him claustrophobic. So each night he retired to one of the captain's chairs up front, reclined as best he could, pulled a blanket up over his chest, and closed his eyes. There were minutes when he slept, but mostly he occupied the queer place in between. Imagined sounds awoke him while real sounds formed the auditory landscape of his dreams. The dreams themselves weren't all bad, but they were powerful and would linger for hours after he was up and about. Then the nightmares began. At first, the threat was vague, nothing more than an invisible undercurrent of violence. It pulled at him, beckoning him deeper, until soon the violence surfaced in fantastic detail. He didn't tell any-one, especially not Val. She didn't need to hear about the gruesome scenes of murder and evisceration that accompanied his fears about her and the baby. He could not bring himself to say how he awoke convinced that he was covered in blood and bits of flesh. Neither did he mention the feeling he had been getting that she was in real danger in the waking world, that he had to save her.

It seemed unfair to burden her with all of that when he was so far away.

The tour started in Louisville. It was a southern circuit of colleges and clubs calculated to give Molly some of the American roots mu-sic provenance she so desired. Nashville and Memphis, then west through Arkansas and Oklahoma before dipping down into Texas and heading back east by way of Houston and New Orleans.

There had been insurance forms to fill out. The tour manager, Marco, wasn't really entitled to know anything about Henry's men-tal health history, but Henry felt strange not telling him. It made him feel like a liar.

"Do I need to know this?" Marco had asked. "Is there some rea-son for you to be concerned about it?"

Henry had said no.

"All right, then." And that was the end of it.

Henry was embarrassed to have brought it up.

Now, after he'd had a week of little sleep and increasing inse-curity, Marco's having been so cool about the whole thing made Henry less inclined to talk to him. He didn't want to disappoint the man, so he kept his mouth shut. By the time they reached Austin, he was basically mute. Jack and Phil and Marco all assumed he was shy and left him alone. Not Molly, though. She was a self-professed bitch and extremely proud of it. Her thing—and Henry couldn't really argue that she was wrong—was that male rock stars had always gotten a free pass when it came to their attitude. It wasn't just accepted that they were assholes—it was encouraged. She wanted to single-handedly dismantle the double standard. Club promoters who did a shitty job of filling the room were a common target of her wrath. If they tried to turn it back around on Molly (and they usually did), she displayed her knack for the kind of pithy vitriol that few people have the balls to pull off.

"I thought it was *my* fucking job to bring the music and it was *your* fucking job to bring the audience. Maybe if you'd told me that this was a fucking redneck sheep-fuck rodeo bar and that there was 'technically' no fucking stage for actual fucking musicians, we could have avoided this uncomfortable fucking situation, would you agree? And furthermore"—she was college educated, after all—"don't give me this 'technically' bullshit, asshole. Me saying *Technically, I don't have a nine-inch dick* is the same shit as me saying *I don't have a fucking nine-inch fucking dick.*"

She gave it to Marco, too—about the bus, her stipend, how often she had to perform, it was something different every time—but he was a professional. He responded sensibly to her message and ignored her delivery. Jack and Phil stayed out of her way, and at first Henry wasn't even on her radar. As the tour wore on, though, Molly sensed something in him that set her off.

It was the day after their last show in Austin. The plan had called for a stop in San Antonio, but the club had canceled—something about underage drinking and a temporary issue with their liquor license—so instead they headed to Houston early. Everyone was excited for a day off and a surprise stay at an actual hotel. As they drove, Jack and Phil took turns telling war stories about a coke-fiend keyboard player they'd toured with a few years before. Marco was laughing politely, Molly was nearly hysterical. Henry watched her closely. The tank top she wore bared a dense sleeve of tattoos—dark green and brilliant magenta. Henry felt there was something intimate about them. That was her *skin* she was wearing. It belonged to her, covered her whole body, and he was seeing it. And when she laughed she was as far from Minerva as Henry had ever seen her. She was, for a moment, a shining symbol of everything right. Her teeth so white and straight. Her hair, falling across her forehead in locks bound together with the oil of her skin. She was so naturally beautiful and it was beautiful, too, that she could activate that other persona. Molly could be Minerva when she wanted to be. There was something very *old* about that, something very yin and yang and Vishnu and Jesus—

"Henry, what the fuck?" Molly was staring back.

He wasn't prepared for that. The thought that she would notice him watching her hadn't occurred to him. He didn't move, unable to recall if it was more normal to turn away or to keep on looking.

"You're staring," she said.

"Hmm?" said Henry.

"So what the fuck? What do you want?"

Marco got up to stand between them. "Come on, Mol, he's not staring—"

"Shut the fuck up, *Mar*. Henry. Hello?"

Finally he turned away. He had been admiring the yin and now he had to contend with the yang it inferred: brute force, aggression, war. Jack and Phil, per usual, shared a reaction. They sat, confused, waiting to see what happened next. They respected Henry, he knew that, but they were not exactly his allies.

"I'm fine," said Henry.

"No, you're not fucking fine, man. You're freaking me out." Molly leaned forward in her seat, as if preparing to lunge. "Looking at me like I'm a goddamn turkey leg or something."

Henry didn't know what that meant but it sounded funny, so he laughed but it came out as a half whimper.

"Marco, I swear to God," said Molly. She stood from her seat.

"Get this motherfucker sober or get him out of the fucking backup band." She stomped to the rear of the bus and disappeared into her private sleeper compartment.

"Backup band?" said Jack.

Phil laughed.

"Don't worry about her," said Marco. His eyes said that *he* was a little worried, but there was compassion in them. "You want to lie down awhile?"

Henry stood up. He walked back to his bunk, climbed in, and closed the curtain. He could feel the heat coming from Minerva, and he knew she was making preparations. She would destroy him and he'd probably let her. He didn't have the energy to fight the kind of war she seemed capable of waging. He lay with his eyes open, listening to the road.

Alone in his Houston hotel room, Henry slept deeply that first night. His dreams were sinister and circular scenes of being trapped, cornered, and broken, and the panic they inspired didn't ebb when he woke up. He walked the few blocks that surrounded his hotel for hours until finally, mercifully, it was time to get back on the bus and head to the venue.

When he saw Minerva again she was darker and more beautiful than before. That night, her voice puffed sensual flames of pain through Henry's body, and though he couldn't bear to look at her he also couldn't turn away. At the end of the show he was spent and he slept well once more, though he awoke from dreams that made him wish he hadn't. It was so much easier to control his thoughts when he was awake.

The second Houston show was worse. He stared out at Minerva, her painfully proportioned little body framed by his cymbal stands. She seduced the whole crowd, men and women alike, and Henry marveled at her power. Minerva was showing off, threatening

Henry with a demonstration of all she could do. He hated her, but it wasn't as simple as that. He worshipped her too. The only way Henry knew to fight back was through the music, so he pushed himself hard. His rim shots were brutal *thwack*s, sonic punches aimed at her throat. He drove the music faster, tried to wrest control from her through force and blistering speed. By the end of the set he was soaked in sweat and on the verge of bawling. It hadn't been enough, he knew that. She'd bested him. Rather than withering in the face of his attack, she'd drawn power from his intensity, as had Jack and Phil. The set was fevered and raucous, and Minerva fed on the frenzy.

Henry packed his gear alone, avoiding eye contact with members of the audience, spurning proffered fist bumps and high fives, ignoring even Jack and Phil. He didn't feel he could trust them anymore.

As soon as the drums were loaded Henry took a cab back to the hotel. He was supposed to stay in the bus that night, but that would have been impossible. He would pay for the room himself if it meant that he got to be alone. Once in his room he locked the door, closed the security clasp, and sat on the bed with the lights off. Through the open curtains, constellations revealed themselves in the streets below. Lighted windows of office buildings, car headlights and streetlamps—they formed a shifting milieu for a metaphysical soap opera peopled by voices and songs and poignant images of Henry's own devising. He watched for what might have been fifteen minutes or fifteen hours. His phone rang. He pulled it from his pocket and was struck by the picture that appeared. It was of Val. She sat in a chair at an airport gate. They'd been on their way somewhere—he couldn't remember now—and the sun coming through the floor-to-ceiling windows facing out onto the tarmac was incredibly bright. She wore a white T-shirt, the soft skin of her neck revealed by a deep V. Henry almost forgot that the picture on his phone signified that Val herself was trying to get through to him. He whisked his finger over the screen to accept the call.

"Hello?"

"Hey, love."

The constellations disappeared the instant her voice struck his eardrum. Minerva was Molly again. Whatever strange man had been plotting defenses and strategizing attacks was a pathetic shadow of the person Henry knew he was. It was like waking from a nightmare.

They talked for almost two hours. He told her he was having trouble sleeping, but that he was having fun.

Val told him to be careful. She said she wished he would just come home.

He told her he was staying. That he was fine. Each word burned his throat.

They talked about the tour, about Minerva and Jack and Phil and Marco. Val told him about her days, about how she missed him but found it funny how quickly her whole routine changed. She was saying yes to every invitation, reading books that had sat on their shelf for years. They talked about the baby. It hadn't really hit Henry that they would be parents soon, and he told Val so. She said she felt sort of the same way but that it was different for her. She had accepted that she was pregnant but not that she was going to have a baby. In Henry's mind those two were the same thing, but to her they were completely separate. One was something that was happening to her body. The other was something that would happen to her life.

By the time they hung up Henry had almost forgotten about the strangeness that had brought him to the hotel in the first place. The constellations outside his window and his fantasies about Minerva were like dreams he was happy to forget. He turned off the lights and took off his clothes, then climbed under the covers and spread each of his limbs as far as he could, his body forming a big X draped in cool satin.

He didn't want to sleep. It felt good to simply exist in a quiet hotel room seventeen stories above the ground. He opened his eyes and glanced at the window. The view was beautiful, for a moment.

Seventeen stories.

Some quick mental math.

That was somewhere around a hundred and fifty feet in the air.

Without warning, Henry imagined what his insides would look like as they burst out of his body upon impact with the ground. He felt the asphalt give beneath him and "Pop Goes the Weasel" began to chime in his head, the muted, thunking sound of it as if from his childhood jack-in-the-box. His fingertips vibrated with the chiming as he held the red wooden ball on the end of the lever and turned and turned and turned. He thought of Jack and Phil in the box of their bus, sleeping on top of one another in their little stacked compartments. He saw Minerva slinking out from the back, sliding across the floor, feeding on them, her naked body slick with blood. "Pop Goes the Weasel" accelerated now in time with Henry's heartbeat until it went so fast that he felt like his chest might explode and paint the walls with bits of bone and lung.

He turned on the television hoping for a distraction but forgot to look at it. Hours passed before the bright white smiles of weekday morning news anchors told him it was Wednesday. They told him the sky would be blue. They told him about thigh-trimming exercise tips and how the famous chef with the jaw of a pit bull would be coming on later to make simple summer salads. Henry turned off the television and got in the shower. The rushing water quieted his mind for a time. It told him what he already knew. He was falling into something, and though he'd beaten it before that was no guarantee he would beat it again. It warned him to take care.

He didn't notice the tears falling from his eyes until after he'd dried off. He put his clothes back on, the same ones he'd been wearing for days, and left.

Nobody asked questions when Henry showed up at the door to the bus and walked straight to his bunk. He lay down and wondered briefly why he wasn't hungry and tried to remember when he'd last eaten. He surprised himself by falling asleep, and when he awoke he felt emptied, like the fever had broken and the pus had been drained. He opened the curtain on his bunk and saw Jack across the narrow hallway. He was reading, a book propped up on his bare chest. The oversized chain he always wore had pooled itself into his armpit and then cascaded over his biceps to partially frame the wildly colorful cherry blossoms embedded in his skin.

"Where are we?" Henry asked.

"Pretty close," said Jack. He dog-eared the page he was reading and closed the book. "You cool, man?"

"Pretty close to where?"

"New Orleans."

"I'm not sure," said Henry.

"Not sure of what?"

"If I'm cool."

"Oh," said Jack. "Listen. Marco told us you had some kind of history."

Henry wasn't surprised, but it stung a little. He nodded, almost imperceptibly.

"He didn't have a right to do that," said Jack. "It's none of our business."

"Thanks for saying so," said Henry. He lay back and faced the ceiling. "It's true."

"That you have a history or that it's none of our business?"

"Both, I guess. But I don't really mind you knowing."

"Well," said Jack. And then he said nothing.

"You don't have to be afraid."

"I'm not," said Jack. "But, honestly, Molly is. She's too young to know the difference between uncertainty and fear."

Henry smiled at that. He thought of Val and how she was when they were younger. It had been *his* uncertainty back then that was scary, never hers. She was the one always telling him that he could conquer this. She liked to use words like that. *Fight. Conquer. Beat. Overcome.* They would have been empty coming from anyone else. Even Gabe. Even his mom. They empowered him only when they came from her lips.

"It's not youth," said Henry. "It's scary for most people. Doesn't matter how smart or stupid, young or old. Most people just get freaked out. The problem with *Minerva*"— and at that Jack and Henry both laughed—"isn't her youth. She's just self-centered. She thinks that's a professional necessity. So she thinks the way I'm act-ing is about her, I guess."

"She doesn't have the authority to get you off this bus," said Jack. "You're an incredible musician. Phil and I have your back. So does Marco, by the way, even if he does have a big mouth. As long as you want to hold on, we'll put Molly in her fucking place."

"Thanks," said Henry.

"It's not worth it, though. This tour. You gotta take care of your-self, man. I know it's tough to quit and all, but seriously? You think Phil or I would put the fucking *Grits* over our health? Molly would quit over a fucking hangnail. Ferreal. If we had three shows in a row where nobody showed up she'd probably claim exhaustion and make some poor suit from the label fly down here to convince her of how important she is before she agreed to continue."

Henry nodded, his face relaxing into tight-lipped laughter.

"Just do what you gotta do, that's all. I'm not saying I know what that is. I'm just saying."

• • •

Henry was watching the water of Lake Pontchartrain skim by at sixty-five miles per hour when he felt his phone vibrate. He didn't have to look. Nobody else ever called him anymore. He really wanted to speak to Val, but he was afraid he'd have to lie to her again. He decided the only thing worse than lying to her was avoiding her so that he wouldn't have to lie to her, and he answered.

"Hey," she said.

"I've been thinking about you," he said. He walked back to his compartment and closed the curtain.

"Oh yeah?" she said.

"Yeah."

Val waited in expectant silence. When she spoke Henry could hear laughter in her best mock sexy voice as she said, "So…what are you thinking about?"

"I'm sick." Henry said it fast before he could stop himself. "Fuck—I'm just—it's happening again, kind of."

"No," said Val. "What? Why didn't you tell me? Jesus, Henry, I don't even care, just—just come home, okay?"

"It's not that bad, really. Just some—interludes I guess I'd call them, but I think it's under control. I just didn't want to lie to you again. I thought you should know." He wanted to soften the blow, but the blow was the blow. If he'd really punched her, would it have mattered how hard?

"Come home, Henry. You need to be here."

"I will, I'll be home soon, but really, it's not that bad. It's under control—I just need a little more time."

"Listen to yourself, Henry. There's no more time. It only ever goes in one direction if you don't take care of yourself. Just get off that fucking bus and get a cab to the nearest airport and come home. Right now."

Henry had ensconced himself in his bunk again. He felt the bus slowing down, heard gravel beneath the wheels. Jack pulled back the curtain and mouthed *We're here.* Henry nodded.

"Are you listening, Henry? Please."

"Val, I love you, but we just got to the club."

Silence came from the other end of the line.

"I'm sorry, I know this is shitty, but we'll talk as soon as the show is over. Just a couple of hours. I'll come home."

"This is unfair," she said. "You're going to spend the night playing some fucking club and I'm going to be sitting here freaking out."

"I know. I'm sorry. I know how this makes you feel—"

"You couldn't possibly."

"Okay, but it doesn't change the fact that we're here, at *some fucking club* in New Orleans. They're unloading without me, I can hear it." The scraping of amps and cases on corrugated metal reverberated through the body of the bus. "It's one more night. I'll make it, I'll be okay," he said.

"Go."

"Are you sure?"

"That's not a real question, Henry—you know I can't stop you. So just go and call me as soon as you can. I'm going to go find a flight for you, tonight or tomorrow."

"You don't have to do that," said Henry. "Don't do that, I can take care of it. I shouldn't have said anything just now, I should have just told you later. It's not that urgent."

"But you're coming home."

Henry sucked his teeth. It was what he wanted. He couldn't even tell why he was resisting, but the resistance was strong, something innate and prideful that was unwilling to relent.

"You're coming home, right?" said Val.

"I'm fine," said Henry. "I can get help down here, maybe. I can call the doctor, get a prescription."

"Come home," she said.

"We'll talk about this later, okay? I promise."

"I love you," said Val. "Call me as soon as you finish. Please."

"I love you too."

Two hours later, Henry was in the middle of the set. He was playing well, but it seemed as though his body was doing all the work while his mind and ears were elsewhere. The sound of talking from the bar was amplified by some unseen trick of acoustics, and though he tried to ignore it, it was soon joined by the babble of the crowd and the hum of the ceiling fan and the static in the distortion of Jack's guitar and the effervescent patter of drinks being poured. He continued to play the beat that he knew he was meant to, but he couldn't hear it any longer. There was only this *other* rhythm, the one being synthesized from the ambient sound of the room.

It grew louder and Henry's fear grew with it. He opened his eyes wide and looked out into the crowd, hoping to find something that might center him, something *real* to focus on: smiling and laughing faces, bad dancing, the soft green glow of the stage lights. His body slackened, his breath grew steadier. But then he noticed the man at the bar. He was older, maybe mid-forties, unkempt. He stared right back at Henry, his eyes locked open in a horrified leer. The rest of the room receded into blurry darkness as the man's face got brighter and bigger and the deeper beat grew louder. Henry's hands and feet moved expertly, and he was dimly aware that he was still playing along with Jack and Phil, but that was incidental. The man's face and the deeper beat were everything.

Then, suddenly, as if it were the most natural thing, he knew.

It felt more like remembrance than realization. It had happened before, after all, and he recognized the feeling of manic wholeness. Just as in the practice room, he was communicating with this man.

Not words. Not even images. The messages were pre-verbal and un-seeable. Vibrations, patterns of thought, data shaped by rhythm and sound pounding in waves against the shore of Henry's mind—and for some timeless moment Henry *was* the man at the bar. He saw the stage from below and felt a strong desire for Minerva coupled with a dizzying déjà vu. He heard the music through the stranger's ears as well as his own. Then, most disorienting of all, he felt that he was remembering being onstage. He was someone else, remembering his own moment as if from far in the future, his selves kaleidoscoping inward and outward forever.

The man scooted away from the bar and knocked his beer over as he stumbled over the rungs of his stool. He pushed his way through the crowd to the back of the room and disappeared.

Henry winced, squeezed his eyelids shut. The other rhythm faded and dissipated and he was slammed back into his body so abruptly that he nearly lost the beat. Luckily it was an opportune moment—he stopped playing for a measure and Jack filled the space with a guitar lick as if the whole thing had been planned. The crowd went crazy for it. Minerva turned to Henry and smiled lasciviously.

The final note of the set was still ringing in his ears as he stepped down from the stage and into the hallway outside the greenroom.

"Great fucking set," said Marco. "Unbelievable."

"Who was the man at the bar?"

"The man at the bar. Uh...which one?"

Henry shook his head fast and sweat flew in droplets from the ends of his hair.

"What the fuck, man?" said Marco, laughing as he took a cocktail napkin from beneath the glass in his hand and wiped his forehead. "There were lots of people at the bar. The house was packed! It's a good night."

"There was a man at the bar," said Henry. The next act was already bringing their gear onstage, and the spot where Marco and Henry were standing was a bad place for a conversation.

"You have to get your kit offstage," said Marco.

"Who was he? You need to find out."

"You need to get your shit together, pack it up, and get it on the bus." Marco looked scared, but he managed to push out an authoritative "Right fucking now" before turning around to step out the back door of the club.

Henry went back to the stage and focused all of his attention on the crowd as he worked. He scanned the face of every person there but saw no sign of the man. Molly was working the room. Men stared and waited for a chance to talk to her, to touch her, to try to make her laugh. She wasn't well known but she exuded fame, and it was funny to see people who'd previously never even heard of the Grits become starstruck in forty-five short minutes.

Jack and Phil were on their way back into the club as Henry approached the bus with the last of his things. He slid his stick and cymbal bags into the storage compartment, then stood outside the door at the front of the bus. Marco would be inside changing his shirt, combing his hair.

Henry had made a decision, and though he knew it was right, he was afraid of turning back. Standing in the parking lot and waiting felt easier than marching up the steps.

Marco emerged.

"I'm done," said Henry.

Marco looked at him with a haggard mixture of pity and frustration. He tensed reflexively as Henry approached him.

"I'm sorry, Marco."

Marco nodded. "What happened? After the show—you looked terrified."

"It doesn't matter. Find the nearest hospital. Please. Now, before I lose my nerve. I can't go back on the bus. Please get my bag, leave whatever isn't packed, except my phone, which should be in the compartment by the head of my bed."

Marco went back on the bus and Henry waited outside. He hoped he was early enough to put an end to it before the roots took hold. It was strange how little time seemed to have passed since the last time he'd given in to his sickness. It made him sad to think that all those years, all his time with Val, it hadn't really healed him.

But he was relieved, too. He was keeping his promise to Val. He was going to get help.

THE PORCH

V AL LEFT THE next morning. Gabe wanted to beg her to stay, but he settled for walking her to the train station. They stopped at an upscale diner called Old Man Rafferty's that served mediocre food and bottomless coffee. Gabe's omelet was oily and he envied Val's Reuben from across the table until she gave him a bite.

They didn't talk about what had happened. Gabe sank a little deeper into his pit of anxious longing with every tooth she bared through her perfect grinning lips. She told stories about her friends. Gabe wasn't really listening. He was instead imagining her train ride back to New York. He hoped she'd fall asleep. If she stayed awake, he feared what an hour's worth of quiet introspection might do to her, what it might take from him. There had to be some gesture, he thought, something he could do to lock in place whatever they'd started the night before.

A dollop of Russian dressing sat fat on the corner of her mouth. Her hair was a messy knot. He had never wanted anything as much as he wanted her.

The diner was just up the hill from the train station. They walked down and froze when they reached it. It seemed that neither of them could think of the appropriate goodbye, but after a moment

Val made the decision for both of them and kissed Gabe lightly on the cheek.

"I'll call you later," she said. She disappeared up the dark stairwell that led to the platform.

Gabe still felt her as he turned up the hill to get back home. The dried sweat on his skin wasn't all his, and his lips were raw, his muscles sore in strange places. It was comforting proof of what had happened between them hours before. While waiting at the intersection of Easton and Hamilton, he lifted his arms, clasped his hands behind his head, and stretched from side to side. Perhaps that was when the music started again, or maybe it had been there all along and he just hadn't noticed it. As he moved his head the timbre of the ambient noise modulated. It grew and shrank as his steps took him past restaurants with open doors, cars blasting dance music, the muttered mantras of panhandlers. And this time, instead of resisting, he let go. He was too tired. Too happy. It was as disorienting and scary as always, but Gabe felt free. He floated along the sidewalk as if in a dream, and he thought of nothing but Val while the song swirled around him. By the time he got home he felt wonderfully weak, ready to sleep for as long as his body would let him.

"Hey."

The voice echoed its way into the music. A second after hearing it, Gabe recognized it as a word. A second after that, he looked up to where it had come from and found Henry—that *other* Henry—sitting on the porch in a camping chair, his feet resting on the railing.

"Are you okay?" said Henry.

Gabe trudged up the steps and sat down at the top. He didn't know how to answer, wasn't even sure he was capable of speaking.

"You look like shit," said Henry. He laughed.

Gabe fought to focus, pushed the music further away with each breath. He listened for the sound of air passing through his clenched teeth and let it drown out all the rest. When his mind was clear enough he stood up, brushed past Henry's knees, and sat in the other chair on the porch.

"What did you do to me?" he said. He'd meant it as an accusation, but the words left his mouth with a calm curiosity.

"The music?"

Gabe squinted and took a deep breath. "Mm," he said.

"You get used to it."

"I don't think so."

"That wasn't the proverbial 'you.' I mean you, Gabe. You will get used to it."

"That's not fair."

"It's the truth. A few years from now I'll be sick again. Years *ago* for me. I'll be spouting nonsense about conspiracies and the song of the world, how it's going to break everything apart, how it will steal me away. You'll be trying to console me and you'll tell me—as if it could help—that you've heard the music too."

"I don't want to know," said Gabe.

"I think you do," said Henry. "You'll try to tell me to fight it. You'll say it'll get better. You'll even try to teach me how not to get lost in it. *We don't need to understand it,* you said. *Just don't let it take over and it'll go away*. Like it did for you."

Gabe could picture that.

"You'll think you're doing me a favor, I guess. Sympathizing like no one else can. But it won't be a favor. It will only make me think that you've somehow broken into me, that you're just another voice in my head. That in turn will just feed my paranoia, and instead of centering me your compassion will send me back over the edge. At least you had the wisdom not to tell me about *me*. The park and the bridge. God knows how much worse it would have made things. Doesn't matter. I'll go back to some hospital. Which one I don't even remember—there've been so many. Lost track."

"You're not even here, are you?" said Gabe. "Somehow you gave me something. Before you disappeared. I'm sick."

"I didn't mean to. Maybe the bridge did it. Just proximity. Or maybe there is some huge mystical force at work, the universe itself fighting against me to make things right. I don't claim to know. But I don't think you're sick. That's what you're teaching me now. For a long time I've thought that my illness was the source of the music, that the two were intertwined. Now I'm not so sure. There's the one thing—the thing we share—and then there's the other. You don't have what I have. You never will."

Gabe kicked off his shoes and curled his toes around the railing in front of him. He thought of Jan, how she'd sat where Henry sat now. It seemed like an impossibly long time had passed since then. "You're not here," he said. "You don't want me to mention you to Val or your mom—really, *I* don't want me to mention you—because you're not really here."

"Hmm." Henry tilted his head back, rested it against the filthy aluminum siding of the house. "Where does that line of thinking end, I wonder? The music isn't really *there*, I'll give you that. Or at least it's not vibrating the air in quite the way you're hearing it. But let's say Cal comes home. You introduce me to him. He sees me too, so I'm really here, no doubt about it. Then I leave again. You get in bed at night and wonder whether Cal was really there, whether he really saw me. Maybe Cal's not real either. He's a pretty unlikely guy all around."

Gabe didn't see the point in responding.

"So where does it end?" said Henry. "What about this house? Or this town? What about your memories of me from when we were kids?"

"I had those before you showed up. I've had them forever," said Gabe. But he knew that in relation to Henry's line of questioning it was an indefensible supposition. All he had was his memory of remembering. And memory could betray him.

"And last night, with Val—was that real?"

Gabe stood up and walked to the front door, checked three pockets before he finally found his keys and stepped inside, closing Henry out on the porch. He sped through the house and collapsed on the bed. On the pillow, inches from his eye, sat a single strand of Val's hair. He picked it up and twirled it around the smallest joint on his pinkie. She'd been there. He knew that. But then the music had started again. He was touching her. She was touching him. Eventually they were all mixed up together. He felt parts of her that he'd been dreaming about, she pressed her naked body against his. The music played throughout, synchronizing itself with their shared breathing. It dripped off her and into Gabe's ears. It sang a song in the shape of her.

His memory of the night before was perfectly aligned with the fantasies he'd fostered before Val came over. Perhaps too perfectly aligned. Gabe shifted on his side and closed his eyes. He concentrated on the images. He wanted to relive them and inspect them while they were fresh in his mind.

She woke up in the same clothes she'd gone to bed in.

So had he.

Had they put them on afterward, or had they never taken them off?

He hadn't used a condom, she said it was okay, she was on birth control. So there was no wrapper, no sad wad of latex. No proof.

Gabe jumped at the sound of rapping on the thin glass window that separated his room from the porch. If this Henry was a hallucination, he was a persistent one.

"Come on." The voice was muffled but easy to make out.

The window again rattled in its frame, and Gabe sat up. He lifted his bare foot from the ground, then drove it down onto the floor. A shock of pain ran up through his shin and into his knee and he did it once more, then again. *This isn't real,* he thought. *Not real not real not real.* He heard footsteps on the porch, then the small creak of the hinges of the front door followed by the sound of it closing. The turn of the lock. *All imagined,* he thought. *Not real.* The footsteps advanced along the wall next to Gabe's bed until they stopped in the living room, just outside his door.

"Jesus." Henry laughed. "This is…unbelievably weird."

Gabe levered himself upright. When he reached the doorway of his bedroom he found Henry standing in front of the coffee table, turning slowly to take in the room.

"Get out," said Gabe.

Henry was still smiling. "No." He stepped around the coffee table, inspected the room from this other angle. "My God, this place. It's even worse than I remember."

"You're not real," he said.

"Maybe," said Henry. He sat down on the couch facing Gabe's bedroom. "She was here last night. You guys were right here, huh?" He patted the cushion next to him. "I'm probably just imagining things, but it's like I can feel it."

"We talked about you. That's what she came here for," said Gabe.

"I'm sure that's true, but that's not what she got, is it?"

"We talked about how we couldn't do anything because of you, how you might come back, how fucked up it made both of us feel. But then…I don't know."

"You did it anyway."

"Yeah, we did it anyway. I think."

"You think."

"I think. It was as real to me as you are. So I guess I don't really know."

"To not believe in things that actually exist is sometimes worse than being convinced by a good hallucination. Trust me. I'm an authority."

"So it happened."

Henry fixed Gabe with a stare. "You two will be together. It wasn't a mistake, understand? Don't fuck it up, because it's the only thing I have left to feel good about."

"I *don't* understand," said Gabe.

"Me neither."

Somewhere down Hamilton a stoplight must have changed from red to green, because a procession of cars wailed past the house and brought the music back. Gabe shuddered.

"Why does it have to be her?" Henry's voice was so soft that Gabe almost didn't hear it. The words betrayed no anger or fear, only sad resignation. "That's the question I keep asking myself. It was always going to be her. You were always going to have her. It's the only constant. I came back here, found you—God knows what that's done to you—I don't regret it, because it was necessary. But still. Why her?"

Gabe didn't know where to begin, but he felt obligated to at least attempt an answer. "At first," he said, "before you came to me on the train, I didn't think it was going to happen. It wasn't planned. We slept in the same bed. That was it, and for your sake I guess I wish it had ended there."

"But then," said Henry.

"Val and I know each other really well. You disappeared. Your mom—I mean, she just cut me out—and I can't talk to Cal without feeling like he's trying to dissect me." Frustrated, he sighed. He'd started in the wrong place. He stepped farther into the living room and sat on the floor, leaned against the wall. "Everything was all fucked up. You went nuts and disappeared and then I'm having weird experiences that I can't explain. It was like everything I ever cared about was just gone. But then Val and I get in the same room together, and it's like nothing's changed. I'm just—I'm *myself.* Something good is happening for the first time in months."

"It was always that way," said Henry. He was busying himself with a cellophane wrapper he'd found on the table. "So simple. I kind of figured. But thank you. For telling me that."

"It should have been enough that she was my friend," said Gabe.

"It was never going to be enough."

"It was the music, too."

Henry looked up from his hands. "What about the music?"

"It stops," said Gabe. "When I talk to her, it just goes away. It's the only thing that's kept me from losing it this week. I mean, I'm getting to be okay at ignoring it or whatever, but with her it's like everything just goes silent." Gabe didn't want to discuss the exception to that, the way the music had become a part of Val's body, how it had driven him forward, coaxed him inside of her.

Henry eyes were alight with curiosity. It made him look younger, more like the friend Gabe knew.

"I thought you knew all this stuff."

"We only had one conversation about it. Years from now." Henry dropped the cellophane on the table. "But you didn't—wait. When you see her it's just *gone?*"

"Pretty much," said Gabe.

"What do you mean, *pretty much?*"

"Calm down—"

"What do you mean, *it stops?*" Henry was a stranger again, his eyes laying Gabe bare with spiteful acuity.

"It just goes away," said Gabe. "Like it was never there."

Henry stood. He pulled the hair up off his face with both hands and laughed, the same joyless sound that had months before rearranged his person into some unrecognizable specter.

"Jesus," said Henry. His eyes were wet, he was breathing hard, and a thin stream of spittle flew into his beard. "It's so obvious. I've wasted—you should have just told me."

"I just did."

Henry pointed a shaking finger. "No, you fucking didn't. Not when it mattered." He relaxed, then, and seemed to collect himself. That made it all the more surprising when he bent over, grabbed the lip of the coffee table, and heaved it up with an animal scream. Glass hit the wall and the floors followed by ash and dust, and Henry continued his yell as he drove his toe into the now exposed underside of the table, over and over. "You didn't fucking tell me!"

"I did, I just did!" Gabe screamed back. "I don't understand!"

Henry leaned forward to rest his hands on his knees, then lifted one foot from the ground and hopped awkwardly on the other. "She fixed you. You knew that. You said I should just fight it, that I could make myself better, but you knew, you knew she could fix one of us and you chose yourself. You could have told me. Everything could have been different. I would have remembered before I started any of this, and I never would have come to you!"

"I don't know what you're saying."

"I came back here, I gave up everything, literally everything, just to come back here—to give her to you! Do you know that?"

"*Give* her?" Gabe was standing, his back against the wall in the corner of the room, and Henry closed the distance between them with three heavy strides.

"I came back here to give her to you. Yes. That's what I said." His hot breath washed over Gabe's eyeballs with each labored exhale.

"You can't *give* her to anyone." Gabe said the words with much more courage than he felt. He was certain he was going to be hurt, his skin prickling with the expectation of it.

"She *was* mine to give. You have no idea what I gave up. I came here to make sure. To set her free, to set you free. It was the only thing I had left. But you knew. When you told me about the music, how you fought it, you knew. You knew it was her and you lied. You wanted to keep her and you left me alone. Every single time you left me alone."

Henry stepped away, then out of the doorway and out of the house.

Gabe looked at the floor. Sensation was everything—unfiltered and overwhelming but also insubstantial. The seismic beating of his heart. Breath fast but so little oxygen. The glass, the empty bottles, unknown liquids painting the upholstery, the table overturned, the ash and dust in the air, how it caught the weak beams of sunlight sneaking in through the shades and took their shape in wide, thin planes.

Gabe bent to pick up a bit of paper, then dropped it again.

He went to the kitchen, got a garbage bag from the open box on the counter. Cal would be back sooner or later. He didn't want to have to explain, didn't know how he ever could.

NOCTURNE: 80

ENRY DIDN'T KNOW what had happened, couldn't remember why he was on the floor, one arm being lifted by a bearded man in a Harley-Davidson jacket, the other grasped by a goateed kid in a striped polo. Then he was standing, and the bearded man's hands were on him, patting his shirt to dust him off. He opened his eyes wider, as if by expanding his field of vision he could also expand his understanding. He saw 41 approaching.

The bearded man saw him too and said, "This your dad?"

41 seemed dumbstruck, too confused to do anything but stare back at the man, who mistook the glare for a challenge.

"I didn't do nothing," said the man. "One minute he's just sitting there, then he blacked out or something. You should take better fucking care of him."

The goateed boy laughed and turned to his friends. "Old guy's wasted!" he said.

41 grabbed Henry's elbow and guided him out of the bar, then pushed him along the sidewalk until they'd reached the corner and turned off of Frenchmen. Each step aggravated a deep ache in Henry's shoulder. As they got farther from the clubs the music receded, but Henry could still hear the song of the world ringing out and up and on and on.

They stopped. 41 turned to face him. "Do you think we can stop him?"

"Stop him? I don't know."

"Don't say you *don't fucking know!* We're going to try. He's going to that hospital, and the second he gets there and some nurse calls Val—"

"I know what happens," said Henry, though that wasn't exactly true. He could tell that something was wrong, but he was too confused to understand what it was.

"Then do something," said 41.

Henry held up his hand and backed away. The life he was just beginning to remember came to him in random impressionistic chunks of sensory recollection. A sunny day. A rainy one. A pair of pants he bought at a department store. A restaurant he liked. A song he'd written. The time he drove to Poughkeepsie. Val's wedding. *Val's wedding?* Each bit was confusing, the transition harder than either time before. Henry couldn't keep anything straight, so it took him a few seconds of concerted effort to think of Annie—but where was Annie? *Oh God oh God oh God oh God where is she?*

"Wake up!" said 41. "Do something."

"You think I wanted to lose her? That I wished for this?"

"We have to fucking try!"

80 looked up, tried to focus the flow of memories, tried to pick out the ones that mattered. "It doesn't...it didn't work. It can't work." He thought of the time he'd spent trying to come up with a way, all the ideas he'd abandoned in the face of the only logical conclusion. "We can't get her back," he said. "She hasn't *gone* anywhere, she *never was.* Even if we could somehow convince 29 to come with us—"

"But you changed my mind, right?" 41 squatted on the ground, a hand on either side of his head. "I made a decision you didn't remember, it didn't work—it never worked—and then it did, so we just have to do the same thing. We have to get to him now and stop him from going to the hospital, stop Val from finding out. We can stop her. If we can't stop Henry we can go back up there and stop Val from...from...God, I can't even say it."

"That world is gone," said Henry. "Even if we can make it so Annie's born, she won't be the same, not really. She won't be Annie." He swallowed hard to hold back tears. To hold back a scream. To hold himself together. He swallowed again and breathed, breathed, breathed, then said, "It's all gone."

41 jumped up and rushed him, grabbed two fistfuls of his shirt, and swung him hard into the fence that separated the sidewalk on which they stood from d.b.a.'s back lot. "You don't get to give up." He held Henry there, pushing and lifting and it hurt, it hurt so much, and he was afraid. "I should...I should kill you," said 41.

Henry remembered saying those words, remembered meaning them. He imagined his own body breaking against the pavement. It wouldn't take much, really—he was old, too old, *how old was he?* There were too many years. He was old even before he'd lived them three times over. He reached up and grabbed 41's wrists. It was a strange embrace. He knew he wouldn't die, not that night—that's not how it happened.

"I should just fucking kill you," said 41 again.

"Maybe you should," said Henry. "But you won't. It wouldn't change this. It wouldn't get her back. We can replace the past, but only with something new." The words came out in a high whisper. "Everything else is gone."

"We have to try," said 41. "Do you understand me?" He again pushed Henry against the fence and the sound it made was like little bells. The ringing washed through Henry's mind, taking some of the music with it as it dissipated and disappeared. 41 let go and Henry felt himself sliding down toward the sidewalk as he wept.

"We have to try," said 41. He stepped back and pointed his face at the sky, slack-jawed.

Henry lay down on his side, his sobs growing louder.

"Shit," said 41. He was looking back toward Frenchmen. "Get up. Get up right now."

Henry moaned in protest.

"People are watching us. We can't— We have to get out of here."

41 knelt beside Henry and cradled him, lifted him up. Somehow despite the pain in his shoulder, the burning in his back, the ache in his knees, Henry stood. They got in the car.

The drive back to Esopus passed like a daydream. 41 didn't want to sleep, so he drove through that first night and all through the next day.

Henry himself was in too much pain to stay awake for long, hard though he tried. He was afraid to fall asleep, afraid of what 41 might do. He had told 41 that they were immortal and in a philosophical sense that was the truth. But he didn't feel immortal. Death felt certain in a way it never had before. He could feel it getting closer. Henry didn't want to die, and given all that had happened he didn't trust his younger self with his life. He remembered getting back safely, true, but he also remembered what 41 was thinking. He remembered the great black vacuum of sadness that had surrounded him those first weeks after losing Annie. He remembered the anger, how it seemed to demand violence, how it prevented him from thinking in a straight line about anything at all. His mind was a snarl of dead-end regrets, a broken machine, a faulty program, and though Henry hadn't run off the road and killed them both when *he* was 41, that offered little comfort. He didn't know the rules of his existence anymore. He wasn't even sure there were any.

They pulled into the gravel drive in front of the house and immediately walked to the wooden suspension bridge to shift back to 41's present. Then, exhausted, they both went to bed.

The next day, 41 began a cycle that would last for more than a month.

Wake up early.

Drink.

Rage by himself in his room until he cried out all his energy and fell asleep again in the early afternoon.

When he woke up in the evening, they would eat. The only thing thicker than the tense silence between them was the smell of 41's unwashed body. After a couple weeks it permeated the house even when 41 was upstairs, a fulsome reminder to Henry of everything he had come to regret. It was his penance, and as inescapable as the stench was, it bound him to his shame. As did his loneliness. Even with his years of living alone, he was totally unprepared for the desperate isolation he felt in that house with 41.

He often thought of driving down to Jersey. There he'd find the Val he knew forty years before. Perhaps he would spy on her through the kitchen window of the house she shared with Gabe—maybe she'd look out and recognize him, invite him into the house and offer him coffee. Henry imagined he would apologize. Val wouldn't understand what for, but she would accept the apology. He would stay for dinner. Gabe would greet him when he got home from work, and like the old friends they were, they'd talk for hours about all they'd missed in one another's lives.

The Val that was living in New Jersey right then, in 41's present, had been married to Gabe for seven years. She was the Val that had gone to her obstetrician a decade before to request that her pregnancy be terminated. In another world—the one they'd destroyed—Henry's twenty-nine-year-old self would have stayed on the road another week. When he left the tour he would have gone home before finally heading back to Lung-Ta.

In the world as it was, 29 saw a man sitting at a bar in New Orleans and the music returned. It scared him so badly that he sought treatment right away, and Val, by herself in New Jersey, pregnant with a fetus that a weekly email newsletter told her was only the size of a blueberry, made a difficult decision.

Val must have known that Henry would feel responsible, so she told him that she'd miscarried. It was a mercy, Val must have thought. She was sad—of course she was—but hopeful. She was only thirty. They had several years in which to try again. And they would, when Henry was better.

Henry stayed in Louisiana for three months, and when he arrived back home he didn't recognize the place. It hadn't changed—that wasn't it. It just no longer seemed to belong to him. He was sane but detached to the point of cruelty, bitter about the great leap backwards he'd taken, self-pitying and angry. Val tried to coax him out of his depression, but there was nothing she could do that he would not resent. He lashed out. Eventually fights were all they shared, but even their battles lacked passion. Henry didn't fight to win. He didn't care if Val saw things his way. The only thing he really wanted was the freedom to not want anything.

At some point during this long dissolution, Val must have realized that the truth about her abortion was like a big red eject button. Finally, in a moment of hopeless anger, she pressed it.

They were divorced within a year.

Gabe tried to be helpful to both of them, but Henry was incorrigible. So Gabe gravitated to Val until they were in each other's orbit for good.

Now, looking back, Henry knew that he would have lost them both no matter what. He was always losing them. In fact, he might have done Val and Gabe a favor. The first and second time around,

Val had suffered for years before giving in to the knowledge that Henry couldn't be saved. And through all of those years Gabe had been made to wait.

The mistake Henry and 41 had made in New Orleans may have erased Annie from the earth, but it had also sped up the inevitable. It had set Val and Gabe free. Henry himself was the only one suffering for that.

In the early afternoons, when 41 was back asleep and the house was quiet, Henry sat on the porch, at the kitchen table, in the living room, it didn't matter. Sometimes he read. Every few days he went to the grocery store for food and alcohol. He spent hours cooking elaborate dishes that 41 would eat with the same bored expediency as always.

Henry's fantasy about visiting Val and Gabe rusted and disintegrated as if oxidized by the unavoidable truth. Annie's flesh and bone had never materialized in the dark quiet of Val's womb. All the bits that would have become her were out in the world somewhere, wasted. In Henry's own present, a time he would someday have to return to, Val was long dead, and if he were to drive down and see her now she wouldn't share any of his memories of their family. She would feel no pain at the loss of their daughter. She would be a stranger.

So instead of fantasizing, he recalled worlds that no longer existed. As the sole survivor of those worlds, he felt he had a responsibility to keep them alive.

He'd remember a moment and ask, *Which life was that?*

An afternoon at the beach that ended in a violent thunderstorm. Annie wrapped in a towel and shivering as she hopped her way from one puddle to another in the parking lot, how she giggled with fearful excitement. That was his first life.

The heat and humidity of his first apartment after the divorce.

The way it felt thick in his lungs and made all his clothes seem damp and dirty even before he put them on. The way summer felt like sadness for the rest of his life. That was his second.

As for his third life, the world as it was since the disaster with 29, something strange was happening. Henry could remember becoming 41; he knew what it was to be the man that was even then drinking himself into a suicidal stupor in a fetid room upstairs. Eventually 41 would demand to be taken back home and Henry would oblige him. From there 41 would deteriorate fast. Without a life worth maintaining, he wouldn't bother fighting his sickness. Soon he'd be wandering just as he had when he was nineteen. The music would follow him everywhere, so loud that he couldn't hear anything else. And though he'd vowed not to tinker with time, though he'd told himself that he would never become the old man who had ruined him, eventually 41 would wander onto a bridge and be overtaken by the light.

That was where Henry's memory started to fail. Trying to see what came after was like trying to see the blades of a fan while they were in motion—there was the generalized blur, and if he moved his eyes fast enough a crystal-clear image would appear and vanish so quickly that he couldn't be sure he'd seen anything at all. The bits and pieces shifted.

He recalled, for instance, attending Val's funeral in this his latest life, but when he tried to remember details it was as if every possibility had been scrambled together to form a void. Sometimes she was in a casket. Sometimes she was cremated. Sometimes Gabe embraced Henry when he arrived and sometimes he spurned him. Sometimes Henry didn't go in at all but sat in his car outside. There was a universe of these possibilities, every moment a divergence into millions of possible outcomes.

What this meant Henry couldn't be sure, but he had a strong sense that it was linked to 41's feelings about him. He recalled the dark hopelessness. The fear and the infinite rage, how it seemed to fill every cell in his body. And all of this directed at the *old man* who'd ruined his life and killed Annie. 41 blamed him for all that had happened, and Henry recalled how clear that conclusion was, back when he was younger. How much better to blame his elder, to avoid any responsibility of his own. And how easy when the old man had all the power. So, when 41 developed his own abilities, when he was able to shift on his own, why wouldn't he try to escape the manipulative son of a bitch who'd taken everything from him? How he'd managed it was another question, one that Henry hoped he would never have to answer.

He didn't bother to think through all the implications of what he planned to do next. He was well past trying to predict exactly what changes would occur with another intervention. New Orleans taught him that. Once he took action, everything would be different. And that was all that mattered.

He had to get 41 back on his side. It was the only way he could think of to escape his amnesiac terror. Even if it meant lying. Even if it meant becoming that manipulative son of a bitch he'd so hated when he was 41's age.

It was a gray and muggy day of the kind that occurs only in late summer when the earth has begun to express its longing for fall. Henry spent the morning in the usual way, but he had a feeling that something was different. He remembered that day better than the rest.

When 41 woke up from his afternoon nap he came downstairs and rinsed his face in the kitchen sink, then took a long drink from the faucet. Henry watched the whole thing from his place at the end of the kitchen table. When 41 was finished he gasped for air, turned off the sink, hobbled to his customary chair, and sat down with his arms folded protectively in front of him.

Henry was scared, but he tried to look stern and inscrutable.

"I want to go home," said 41.

"Take a shower," said Henry.

"I'll shower at home."

"You'll shower here."

41 was so still that he looked like he wasn't even breathing.

"Once you're cleaned up," said Henry, "we're getting you out of the house."

"To go home."

"There's nothing for you there. You know that. You can spend the rest of your life regretting this, hating me for it. Hating yourself. Or you can try to get it all back."

"You said that was impossible." He wore defiance like a mask. But he was curious, Henry knew. How could he not be?

"I did say that. And it probably is," said Henry. "But it's like you said. We have to try."

THE SULLIVAN ROOM

I T WOULD HAVE been so much easier if the sex had been bad. Val might have told Gabe it was a mistake and simply moved on. But she had liked it, despite her guilt. She wanted more.

Her relationship with Henry was never centered on sex. He was so sensitive, always afraid of doing the wrong thing. Gabe was different. There was nothing apologetic about the way he touched her. He did what he wanted, and it made her feel grown-up in her desire.

Comparing the two of them made her queasy. They were so much like brothers. Now she'd lost her virginity to one and fucked the other. She could put it in nicer terms, but *fuck* was the only word that applied. What she and Gabe had done was too hungry and clumsy to be called anything else. That first morning after, a few stops away from New Brunswick, the guilt was so strong that she nearly convinced herself to get off the train in Secaucus. She could transfer there to a line that would take her just a few minutes from her parents' house. Her mom could pick her up, and when she got home Val could curl up in her old bed and sleep for days. When she awoke she could take down all her old posters. Paint the room. Go through all her old notebooks and journals. She wanted to wallow in nostalgia, to swim deep in it and allow it to swallow her whole.

But she stayed on the train. She relived the night in her imagination until her body got loose and rubbery.

That night she couldn't sleep, so she gathered her laundry and a couple of textbooks and went down to the basement of her building. She read while the machines clicked and whirred around her. Whether out of exhaustion or distraction, she couldn't let the sound be. Usually the machines provided the kind of white noise that made it easy to concentrate fully on her work, but that night there was a different quality to the sound. It asked for her attention and she found herself identifying with it, personifying it. There was a voice in the room, and it spoke in long, meditative moans punctuated by the ticking of buttons against metal.

From then on, her days were spent waiting. Not for him. Maybe for him. Not *only* for him. Really, Val was waiting for the hours at night when she could be herself. She was quiet in class, politely refused invitations from the girls who thought they were her friends. Nothing compared to the ease she felt with Gabe. And though she knew that some effort might yield the kind of friendships she really wanted, it seemed like so much unnecessary work. She talked to her roommate, too, but Kara focused on Val the way she would a soap opera. She grew strangely attached to the stories Val told, as if she were feeding on them. And then, whenever Val was done speaking, Kara spoke in platitudes. *If it's meant to be . . . You can't beat yourself up over it . . . The heart wants what the heart wants.*

Val would just nod. It would have taken too much effort to disagree.

She was happy, but her guilt persisted. She preferred thinking of herself as the college girl who was in love, but Henry still hadn't been found. Each day that passed made it more likely that he was never coming back, and Val felt a responsibility to be the mourning ex-girlfriend. She saw proof of her iniquity everywhere. In Kara's eyes for certain, though Kara couldn't help it. Val was more worried that she'd begun to see that same reproachful look on the faces of strangers. As if the whole world just knew.

She never talked to Gabe about her guilt. She would suffer alone. That was what she deserved. But that was being too generous. Really, she didn't tell Gabe how she was feeling because she didn't want to ruin her time with him. She wanted to laugh and eat and drink and have sex. She saved her regret for when it wasn't interrupting anything more enjoyable.

It was a Thursday night, a month after Gabe and Val's first night together. Kara was getting ready to go out to a party at the Sullivan Room—a party that she'd begged Val to attend with no success. When she first started at NYU, Val was one of the ringleaders, always doing internet research on the right places to go, suggesting groundbreaking destinations like the Upper East Side or even *Brooklyn*. Kara had only ever been invited along because of Val. Now Kara was fully a member of the tribe Val had basically started, and Val herself was on the outskirts, the subject of whispers and rumors. She tried not to mind. She deserved all that, too.

Kara walked out of her bedroom. She had recently been experimenting with variations on the Mormon dress code. She still wore knee-length skirts, but the wider denim ones she'd always favored had been replaced by stretchy skintight numbers that hugged her hips and thighs. And as for her initial ban on sleeveless tops, it had apparently been lifted. Kara was wearing a semi-sheer blue tank, her black bra showing through.

"Damn, girl." Val laughed and gave a low whistle. "Look at those arms."

"Shut up," Kara said, smiling.

"I thought you were saving those arms for marriage."

"Maybe I'm getting married tonight."

They laughed. Val was on the couch, eating from a brown paper takeout container.

"You should come tonight," said Kara. She tried to sound casual. "No."

Kara went to the bathroom to do her makeup. When she came back a few minutes later, she grabbed the remote control from the coffee table and the sound of reality show contestants screaming at each other went mute. Val looked down into her food and sighed.

"You're coming tonight." Kara literally put her foot down with a petulant stomp. Val thought it was cute.

"I don't want to."

"You've been sitting around for weeks. When Gabe is here you're all excited. That's great and everything, but when he leaves you act like your whole world is tumbling down."

"That's not true," said Val.

"I'm not judging you, okay? I don't think I can understand what happened with your ex, and I don't think I can understand what's happening with Gabe."

"You're right. You can't—"

"Don't be mean to me, Val. Please."

Val threw her head back and rolled her eyes. "Sorry."

"I'm trying to help you. When you first got here all you talked about was wanting to experience something new. Something that you'll never get the chance to experience again. I think you'll have plenty of opportunities to watch VH1 and eat leftovers."

Val thought about the evening stretching out in front of her. She couldn't imagine feeling much different regardless of where she was, but she knew Kara was right. For all the joy she was taking in her life in the city, she may as well have been living in New Brunswick.

It was that thought that got her up off the couch.

• • •

Val powered through her getting-ready routine in just under forty-five minutes, but they were still late getting to the restaurant. Even so, their group waited almost an hour to sit down to tapas. Val wasn't hungry, but it irked her. She might have once found it charming and exciting and adult to wait that long for a table, but now it seemed ridiculous. She pushed her way to the bar and ordered a drink. Once she was back among her friends, the conversation eventually turned to her. She could tell that Kara had been keeping everyone up to date, because there was a reluctance to their curiosity, as if a question as simple as "How are you?" might be too personal to ask.

When they finally sat, Erica insisted on ordering for everybody. When Val had first met Erica she thought they might turn into best friends. Now they hadn't spoken in two weeks. A parade of small plates appeared before them and Val picked absently at the meatballs, the crispy boquerones, the bacon-wrapped dates. She drank the wine, too. It was cheap and too spicy. Her throat burned. By the time they completed the exhausting process of splitting the check, getting change, and actually paying, the room felt fuzzy and thick. Val heard herself laughing and offering up opinions she hadn't known she held. Her mind was mercifully quiet, and she felt relaxed and happy and completely removed. Best of all, she was only dimly aware of the guilt that had been plaguing her since she'd started seeing Gabe.

They relocated to an NYU hangout on the same block as the Sullivan Room. Val drank sangria and danced. College boys made their way into her pulsing circle of friends as if by osmosis. Val felt no connection to the dancing, slurring animal through whose eyes she was watching the world, but that didn't bother her. A guy finally managed to break her away from the pack. He was respectful, his hands going no further down than her hips.

"Do you have a boyfriend?" he yelled.

It hurt Val's eardrum, and she pushed her shoulder against the side of her head. The only answer that she could think of was *I don't know*, but she didn't dare say something like that out loud.

The boy went to get her a drink, and she gravitated back to the girls. They enveloped her and laughed teasingly. She smiled and continued to sway, held upright by the bodies around her. Another drink was placed in front of her and she felt a hand on her waist. She leaned into the touch and felt the hand grip her in response. It felt good. She took a large sip of whatever was in the cup. Its chalky aftertaste reminded her of the candy necklaces she loved as a kid.

"What is this?" she shouted, to no one in particular. A voice from behind her said something about bulls and vodka. She giggled.

"I hafta pee."

She was suddenly in a bathroom stall. It was quiet and dim, the single lightbulb over the mirror obscured by the stall door. She closed her eyes and put her face in her hands. Her elbows dug into the flesh right above her knees, and she could feel her feet tingling from the lack of circulation. Some timeless moment later she found herself at the sink, drinking water from her own cupped hands. When she lifted her face to the mirror she saw a pretty girl who she knew to be herself. Water trickled down the girl's chin in a single line that reached all the way into her cleavage. Val tried out a few different expressions and watched as the girl in the mirror followed suit. She laughed, then set her nose close to the surface of the glass and stared deeply into her own eyes.

She opened the door and smiled warmly at the girl who had been waiting to get in. Walking back to her friends, Val wondered if she looked as off balance as she felt.

Kara grabbed her by the arm.

"Where have you been?"

"I had to pee."

"You've been gone for, like, fifteen minutes." Kara rarely showed anger, but Val could feel it in the force of her grip.

Val shrugged. "Let's just go." She walked away.

Kara called after her. "Don't be mad at me."

"Come *on*, Kara, just stop."

"Stop what? See? You *are* mad at me."

"Don't get all fucking weepy. We're having a good time. All right?"

They made their way out onto the sidewalk. The rest of the girls were out there already, blowing smoke into the street. Their bodies were all configured in precisely the same way. One foot angled out. Hip crooked with an air of impatience. One arm crossed in front of the torso beneath the breasts, its hand pinned against the body with the elbow of the other arm, which reached up and ended in the glowing point of a burning cigarette.

Val struck the pose, brought two fingers to her mouth, blew a few fake puffs. She laughed.

"Is she gonna be okay?" Kara asked, but nobody heard her. She put her arm around Val's shoulders and they followed the group down the block.

Under normal circumstances Val would have walked away the minute she saw the line to get into the Sullivan Room. But drunk and tethered to Kara, with nowhere to escape, she waited patiently. The chill felt good, and she was slightly sobered up by the time they got to the door. Inside, a soft green light emanated from the walls, but the roiling center of the room was in shadow. Val squinted through the dark. Someone handed her a drink. She didn't want it, but then Kara said, "You don't have to drink that. Just come dance with me," and Val put the cup to her lips and downed it with irrational defiance. As soon as she finished swallowing she wished she hadn't.

She pushed into the crowd and danced with her eyes closed, her stumbling body held aloft by the party but removed from it. The music was so loud. Voices yelled from all around her, struggling to fight with the noise from the speakers. It all converged into a single, endless crashing like the sound of a wave from underneath the water. Val felt a hand on her back. It pulled her body forward until she was nestled against a man's chest. She liked the way he smelled. When she opened her eyes she saw that the shirt against her face was a pale blue. Chest hair, thin and brown, showed at the open collar. She hadn't looked at his face yet and was embarrassed to do so now. She didn't really care. She was being held without any expectations or responsibilities. She hummed softly and swayed to the endless progression of indistinguishable beats until it occurred to her that she'd perhaps been asleep.

"Let's go," said a voice. It was coming from the mouth of the man in the blue shirt, not a demand but too forceful to be a polite invitation.

As the man pulled away to lead her, she finally looked at his face. He didn't look like she thought he would. She wondered what she'd been expecting and surprised herself by thinking of Henry. The hand on her back had, briefly, been his hand. She thought of Gabe, too. The chest had been his chest. It was funny and sad, but then Val remembered that she'd just been propositioned and that she was painfully, blissfully drunk. She let go of Henry and Gabe and everything that had brought her to this particular moment. It was easy. The blue-shirted man was handsome enough, and older. He had just a trace of a beard and his hair was somewhere between clean-cut and shaggy. Little curls framed his ears and he was smiling, she thought. It was difficult to get a full picture in the shifting light.

They made it to the wall and wedged themselves between two other couples. "I didn't mean to be forward," he said. "I just thought—"

"I thought it too," said Val. "But let's rest here and then keep dancing."

"Okay. That sounds good." The man smiled. The black-light glow of the room brightened his teeth and the whites of his eyes.

"And buy me a drink."

He left and she was alone again. A few of the girls danced toward her, arms outstretched, hands digging between bodies to clear a path. Val didn't move to greet them, worried that if she went too far the man wouldn't find her again.

"What's his name?" Erica said. Her voice was hoarse from shouting.

Val smiled.

"You don't even know?" said Erica, laughing. "You slut!"

Val laughed, then pursed her lips. Just as she was thinking how glad she was that her roommate wasn't there to make her feel guilty and different and strange, Kara appeared at her side. They locked eyes.

"God, Kara. *What?*" said Val.

"I think we should go home."

"Why would we do that?"

Kara leaned in closer, her lips almost touching Val's ear. "You know why. You're wasted. That guy is creepy, okay? Let's just go."

"You think God doesn't like fucking?" Val turned her head just far enough to see the hurt in Kara's eyes and the shake of her head. "I'm not coming home tonight, so if you want to go, go. But leave me the fuck alone."

Val tried to storm away but the bodies were too close. She got four paces before she slammed into a guy with thick hair sculpted into the shape of a meringue. The beer that had been in his cup was now on all over his brilliantly white T-shirt. She pushed past him just as he was calling her a dumb bitch.

The man in the blue shirt was working his way toward her, a

drink in each hand. When he reached her she took one of them and gulped it, stopping only once for air. She looked at him expectantly until he did the same.

"I don't want to dance anymore," she said. She grabbed his hand and led him away.

VARIATION: 41

"Y OU'RE LYING," SAID Henry.

80 contorted his face into a passable facsimile of disbelief. "Why are you lying?"

"I'm not lying," said 80. "I can't be lying, because I don't know the truth. It's impossible for us to get back the life we had, but perhaps we can remake the *kind* of life we had. We can have Val. We can have a child with her. It might not be Annie, but we'll love it just as much."

Henry's head hurt. He'd had his share of hangovers, but this was different. He'd been on a bender for weeks. His gut was sour, his muscles burned. He felt as if his body had been scraped out, his insides replaced with wet garbage and the maggots that fed on it. He wanted to go back to bed, but here was 80, propositioning him again. "You don't care," said Henry. "You don't care about getting Val back. I can feel it. You lost her years ago. She's dead to you."

"That's not—"

"So what do you *really* want?"

80 feigned frustration.

"And why are you acting?" said Henry. "What do you want, 80? What do you want, huh? Henry?"

"A house divided—"

"No fucking sermons!" Henry slammed his palm on the table and regretted it when the sound hit his ears. "You remember being me. Which means you remember how I feel about you. You remember how I feel right now, this fucking hangover…Jesus." He closed his eyes, laid his forehead on the wood surface in front of him. It was comforting for a moment, but bending over made him want to puke, so he sat back up. "If you respect me at all you'll stop treating me like a child and just tell me what it is that you want. What's the new future? What terrible fate are we trying to avoid next?"

"You think this is all my fault, but you're wrong."

"I don't think so."

"You're wrong. You did this with me. We did this together. We're the same person—"

"We're not. No more than I'm still five years old or ten or twenty."

"But we *are*, whether we like it or not, whether we agree or not. I didn't kill Annie. I regret it, what we did, more than I regret anything. But it's done. And now that it's done, you have a question to answer."

"Please," said Henry. "No more questions—just say what you mean."

"Do you want a future or not?"

"No," he said. The answer had come with frightening ease.

"You want to die."

The corners of Henry's mouth trembled. "Yes."

"I was ruined because I couldn't forgive myself for what I'd done," said 80. "At first it was just the older me that I couldn't forgive. That was the easy part. But then I saw my own responsibility and it only got worse."

"No."

"You think you're mad at me. You should be. You are. But you don't want to die because of what you lost. Or because I took it from you. You want to die because *we* are responsible. And we are not two people. Not really. We're both you. We did this. You did this. And now that it's done we can either kill ourselves over it—and you'll choose a slow and painful death over a quick one, I'm proof of that—we can either kill ourselves, or we can find a way through."

"There is no through. Without Annie, there's no way through. It will only get worse," said Henry.

"There is no worse. What could get worse?"

"Your goddamn rhetorical questions—just tell me what you want already."

"I want us to get 19."

Henry laughed. "Why? Flames of glory? Is that what you're thinking? Do as much damage as possible?"

80 hesitated. Henry thought he looked scared.

"Up until now," said 80, "we've been concerned with fixing specific wrongs. And—I know this isn't the right moment for this—it's going to sound dismissive of your feelings, like I don't understand what you're going through—but I—"

"Please," said Henry.

"I know." 80 licked his lips. "We've taken a fantastically narrow view of this situation. Out of a lack of imagination or courage, we've been stuck on the idea that we could improve our lot in bits and pieces. But now we've nothing left to lose. Courage—it doesn't come into it. To have courage you need to have fear, and whatever else we are right now, we're fearless, because we've already lost everything. We *want* to die. Perhaps we can find a way to be with Val again, maybe even Annie. But if not, we could at least endeavor to make that sacrifice more meaningful, couldn't we?"

"It can never be meaningful," said Henry.

"We are a totally new kind of human. That in itself was bound to cause some suffering. But the worst is over, and the only way to make that suffering worthwhile is to do something with this gift we've been given. Something extraordinary."

"And abducting 19, that's extraordinary?"

"We come from worlds that are gone. Memories are etched into our brains, memories of things that no longer exist and never will. And they're torturing us. But for 19, Annie will never be. He'll have Val for a time but he'll go on tour, get sick, she'll leave him, and he'll descend into sickness for the rest of his life. You know this. You remember it. His future is no future at all. If we change it, the only thing we're taking from him is the certainty of pain.

"And if we can teach him, teach ourselves, to control this gift we've been given, then we'll have a whole lifetime to explore the possibilities. All that we've lost, it will never be worth it. I know that. But it's done. The past is the past. Most of our past never even was. But we can still have a future. 19 can have a future. He doesn't have to suffer as we have."

"So you want to teach him," said Henry. "You want him to have the power that you have."

"I want *us* to have it. I want to have spent at least one of my lives exploring it to its fullest. Yes."

"And Val and Annie—they're just collateral damage? What you had to lose in pursuit of this grand fucking goal?" Henry found it just unflattering enough to believe.

"It wasn't planned," said 80. "I never would have done that damage knowingly. Never. But it's done, it's done already. And like I said—19 is our best chance at getting them back. I loved them just as much as you did. You must know that."

"I still love them."

Chastened, 80 looked up and at the window above the sink and chewed the inside of his cheek. "Henry," he said. "I love you, too."

Henry closed his eyes, shook his head.

"You're me. We're one, whether you like it or not. Seeing you like this, it's absolutely devastating. But the years will ease your pain. That's just the way life works. I understand that it's difficult to confront right now, but you can't hate me for having healed, for having the capacity to look at this situation with fresh eyes, to see opportunity in the loss. I am just trying to share that opportunity with you. With myself. I'm trying to forgive myself and move forward. I'm offering us a way out."

Henry ran the tips of all ten of his fingers from his forehead to the back of his scalp, as if by rubbing his skull he could massage order into his thinking. "If we succeed," he said, "I'll have that power too." 80 nodded, jaw clenched, eyes on the floor, and Henry saw something there that he hadn't expected. "You're afraid of that," he said.

"I am," said 80.

"Because of how much I despise you. And what I might do."

"Yes."

"You should be. And more than any of your other bullshit rationalizations, your fear makes me want to do this. You must already know that. This is just another manipulation."

"I'm not manipulating you."

"Then why? Why do this?"

"I want you to trust me. In my experience, the best way to earn trust is to give it. Even when I shouldn't. Even when it scares me."

"A house divided."

80 nodded.

WASHINGTON SQUARE

IT STARTED IN a dark corner of the club. Val and the man kissed on a couch, their writhing bodies feebly lit from above by an old-fashioned wire-filament lightbulb that sat fat like an illuminated bird in a bamboo cage. With her eyes closed, Val could almost forget the smell of sweat and beer. The sound of the room had long since merged into a single endless blast like the roar of a waterfall.

She pulled her face away, gasped for breath. "Is there anywhere else we can go?" she said.

The man nodded and took her hand. They were on the street then, though Val wasn't sure how. The air was dry and cold, almost painfully quiet.

The man walked ahead of her. She wished that Kara had tried one last time to keep her from going. Now she was on her own, headed toward a kind of oblivion. She would go wherever the man was taking her, despite her fear, and something about that felt cleansing.

They entered Washington Square Park. Val tried to remember if she had ever seen it at night. She looked up as she walked and saw milky orange streetlamps flooding through densely crosshatched tree limbs. Beyond it all was the sky, brightened to a pale purple-blue by the combined light of all the buildings in the city.

"Where are we going?" she said.

The man stopped and turned around. "I'm just in town for the weekend," he said. "I'm staying at the Washington Square Hotel."

Val couldn't think of what to say. She was dizzy from the alcohol and from looking up at the sky, so she lowered her gaze to meet his.

"It's just on the other side of the park. Look." He pointed down the path. "You can see it right through there."

"A hotel?" she said.

He laughed. "Unless you want to stop right here."

"Okay," she said.

"Okay what?"

"I want to stop here." She stumbled toward a bench, then let herself sink low on the wooden slats until the back of her head was planted on the top rung.

"What's wrong?" asked the man.

"I don't even know your name."

The man had stayed standing. His face was in shadow, but Val thought she saw in it a half-hidden reflection of her own sad confusion. He looked left and right, surveying the path.

"I don't know yours," he said.

"I'm Val."

"Val." The man looked down and pushed a pebble with the toe of his shoe. "I'm Ed."

Val swallowed and it hurt her throat. The man sat down next to her.

"How old are you?" she asked.

"You picked an interesting time to start asking questions."

"Maybe it was the fresh air."

"Listen, I don't want to stay in this park."

"I don't want to go to a hotel with a man I don't know."

"So…"

"So tell me about yourself." Val closed her eyes. Her body felt as though it might spin apart and disintegrate. She swallowed again.

"There's not much to say, really."

"Are you married?"

"Not anymore."

"Divorced?"

The man's upper arm was pressed into Val's own. He shifted, perhaps in a shrug,

"Widowed?" she said, then regretted it.

"No."

"So divorced, then."

"You need some water," he said. "Maybe this was a mistake. I don't usually do this."

"Ha," said Val. "That's one of those things, you know? Like you say that because it's one hundred percent true or one hundred percent not true. Never anything in between. Never, never, never."

"I guess," said Ed. "In my case it's true."

"That makes two of us, then."

"We don't have to do anything. I can put you in a cab. In fact, I should probably do that. This was a mistake." He stood up from the bench.

"I need some water. How old are you, anyway? Ed, how old are you?" She opened her eyes.

"Too old for this." He paced a small circle, and when he'd completed a full rotation and was facing her again he said, "I'm around forty."

"Around?" Val laughed. "So vain. I'm around twenty. Don't you think that's weird? You look good, don't get me wrong, and I like how you kiss. But, Jesus"—she laughed—"what am I doing?"

"I really think you should get in a cab. Just, please, let's get out of this park."

"I think you should shut up and take me to the hotel bar to get some water."

"If I do that will you get in a cab?"

"But don't you want to fuck me, Ed?"

Ed sighed, his shoulders dropping with each cubic inch of air that left his lungs.

"I'm sorry," said Val. "That was...I guess that was rude."

He offered her a hand. Val looked at it as though she was confused by its meaning. "Let's get you some water," he said.

He grabbed both her wrists and pulled her to her feet.

The hotel had an Old Hollywood art deco vibe. Black and white marble floors, rich red wood paneling, lots of ornate ironwork filled in with stained glass. Ed had made Val take her arm off his shoulder before they walked in, and he insisted that she attempt to walk straight.

Val tried. At least she felt like she was trying.

The concierge greeted them with a polite hello.

Val smiled brightly. "Good evening," she said, drawing out each syllable in a childish approximation of formality.

Ed fixed her with a glare that only barely hid his amusement. They proceeded to the lounge. Wrought-iron screens with gold-painted accents stood between the tables. Sepia-toned images of long-forgotten starlets stared down from the walls. Above the bar hung a massive reproduction of a de Lempicka painting. Val congratulated herself on being able to identify it from her art history class. She felt older walking into the room, but also younger— grown-up enough to be there but not enough to belong.

A long leather bench reached around the perimeter of the room on one side. Val slipped behind the first table she came to and sank into the banquette. The leather was cool to the touch. She fantasized about putting her face on it.

A waitress came. She was about Val's age, and she smirked as she handed them menus before stepping away.

"This place is ridiculous," said Ed.

"It's beautiful."

Val greedily emptied the tumbler that had somehow material-ized in front of her. She took Ed's and drank half before placing it back on the table.

"Feel better?" said Ed.

"I think I should have more."

The waitress returned. Ed ordered more water, guacamole from the snack menu, and a Maker's and ginger for himself.

"I feel weird saying *guacamole* in here," he said.

"You wanna see who can say it louder?"

"No."

"Guacamole," she said. She laughed. "I think I'm feeling a bit better."

"Eat some. The longer you stay up, the better you'll feel tomor-row. Believe me."

They talked about hangovers and their cures until their order came. Ed swirled a red plastic mixer through his cocktail. Val eyed the condensation on the outside of his glass. She wished she were that cold.

"So if you don't do this often," she said, "what were you expect-ing to find at that club? Women your own age drinking martinis? A jazz trio?"

"And what were you expecting to find? A desperate older guy who would put up with any manner of bullshit just as long as he thought he was getting some?" He stared into Val's eyes until she looked away. "More water?" he asked.

Val tipped her glass until the ice crashed down onto her lips, sending rivulets of frigid water down her chin. She sucked a chip out of the glass and bit down.

"I don't know what I was expecting to find tonight," said Ed. "I'm not a widower. The truth is I'm not divorced, either. But my marriage is over. She cheated on me. I found out. So." He took a sip of his drink, stared into the glass once it was back on the table. "We were young when we got together. Younger than you are, even, and there are a lot of things I didn't do. So I guess I just wanted to be in a place filled with people your age. I just wanted to get a taste for what that was like. The simplicity of it. To be without responsibility. I don't know. It's stupid."

Val crunched the ice in her mouth.

"Then I saw you dancing and you were so...unself-conscious."

"That's a good euphemism for *wasted*."

"I didn't know that's what you were. I thought you were just kind of oblivious, and it made me happy. So I took a chance, danced next to you. I surprised myself, actually. I hadn't planned on that. I thought I would just see you there and go."

"I left with you because I'm confused," she said. "My life is weird."

"Tell me."

Val looked at him. His short cropped beard had spots of gray, the hair on his head still thick. He was attractive, more so than she had thought before. She stared at him, fascinated. "It's hard to explain," she said. "Things don't make sense. I was all excited to move to the city and I had all these plans, like everything about me was going to be different, like I was going to find out that I wasn't the boring girl with the high school sweetheart and the obsessing parents. New York was just going to pop that right out of me and the next minute I would be everything I'd ever wanted to be. I just wanted to want to be something. I guess it never occurred to me that I'd need to know what it was I wanted to become. This must sound so stupid to you."

"No."

"Yes, it does. Don't humor me just because I'm drunk. But you don't know. You don't know how real things are for me right now. I mean, I wouldn't be sitting here if things weren't pretty real."

"Real?" Ed smiled and shook his head.

"Don't laugh."

"It's not that."

"What is it then?"

"It's just 'Real.' I don't think I know what that means."

"Well, it's slang. American. Means super deadly serious or completely genuine, depending on context. Has this not made its way up to your generation yet?"

"I know how you meant it. I just don't know how I mean it, when I think about it. I was just musing."

"Musing?"

"I was just musing. Yeah."

Val grabbed Ed's drink and took one large swallow.

He leaned back fast, his hands up as if she'd pulled a gun. "Jesus, why did you do that?"

"I want to go upstairs."

"I'm putting you in a cab."

"I won't get in a cab."

"That's not my problem."

"It is if I tell the concierge I'm fifteen and you got me drunk and stole me from my parents' house and please oh please could he call them for me." She laughed, and Ed looked as if he were trying not to. "I'm fine," she said. "I don't want to go home, but I can't sit up on this thing anymore."

Ed sighed and placed his chin on his sternum. He took a deep breath in and held it, then looked back up at Val.

"Look at me," he said.

Val tightened her face into a faux-serious glower and tried not to smile.

Ed didn't reciprocate, and Val saw that he wasn't playing at anything. He looked afraid. Val softened her own features and examined his wide-open eyes. Back and forth, one at a time—strange that she couldn't focus on both of them at once. She noticed a little quiver in the muscle beneath his eye. It stirred something in her, as if she were hearing a song she didn't know she remembered. The room receded and Val's whole world filled up with the strange, familiar face in front of her.

"Can I get you anything else?"

The waitress's voice made Val blink, but it didn't interrupt her focus.

"No," she said. "Just the check."

The waitress walked away.

"Do you understand?" said the man.

No, thought Val, but she said, "Yes."

"I'm sorry." He looked as though he might cry.

"Take me upstairs."

When they got to the room Val sat on the bed and nervously smoothed the white duvet until her fingers felt numb. The man sat down on a chair next to a marble-top table with the phone and hotel binder on it.

Val had too many questions to pick just one. She looked at him and willed her eyes to see something other than what she'd first seen in the lounge just moments before.

"Am I crazy?" she asked.

The man shook his head.

"Are *you?*" she asked.

"Not right now," he said. He shrugged. The tears that had been forming for minutes finally fell, tracing a path from the corner of his eye to the edge of his lip.

Val lifted herself from the bed and slipped off her shoes. She went to him and placed a hand on his head, traced her fingers over his ear and down the side of his face until the pads of her fingertips came to rest underneath his chin. She applied just enough pressure to lift his face. Looking up at her like that, he seemed younger and even more familiar. She lowered herself onto his lap and grazed her lips across his forehead, his cheek, his mouth. They'd been kissing not even an hour before, but the electricity that gathered on Val's skin made her feel as though she'd never kissed anyone before.

The man exhaled. Val felt the air rush out of him and across her face, and she leaned her lips against his. Finally he placed his hands on her. One found her back, tracing the bones of her spine, the other rested softly on the top of her thigh.

Val stood up and stepped back to the bed. She turned away from him long enough to pull back the tightly tucked sheets, then turned back.

"I don't know if we should do this," he said.

In response Val lifted her shirt over her head and placed it gently on the floor. She unbuttoned the tight black jeans she was wearing. She tried to peel them off gracefully but then lost her balance, tipped back, and sat on the bed so she could get them past her ankles and feet. They both laughed. She stood again and reached her hands behind her back to unhook the clasp of her bra. She slipped the straps from her shoulders.

The man still sat in his chair. Val thought he looked shocked, scared, even, yet undeniably pleased.

"I've missed you so much," he said, and he rose to meet her. He ran the back of one finger down her navel, then grabbed her hips with both his hands. He kissed her.

It was too late by then for Val to do anything but kiss him back.

DA CAPO: 19

8 0 STOPPED TO rest every few minutes. The forest floor had been too much for the old man's feeble footing even before the excitement of the morning. Henry didn't want to help him, but any satisfaction he got from watching 80 struggle was far outweighed by his annoyance at the delay. He took the man's elbow with one hand, held him around the waist with the other. They didn't speak, and it felt like hours later when they broke into the clearing. 80 slumped against the boulder and pressed his cheek to it as he caught his breath. Henry was happy to be unencumbered but in no mood to sit down, so he paced the rock's perimeter and tried not to look at the car in the gravel drive. He wondered where the keys were.

"What do you want?" said 80.

Henry stopped walking. The question was so vague that he was forced to consider all its possible meanings and the answers he might give for each.

"When you go home," said 80. "What do you want? What do you wish would be waiting for you?"

"I don't—it feels like enough to just be sane. I can figure the rest out from there."

80 laughed. He bent forward on the rock and kicked first one leg, then the other as if trying to shake out cramps.

"What's so funny?" said Henry.

"What is sane going to be like for you, I wonder? After this, I mean. That's where I think we went wrong, where I went wrong every single time. We thought it would be good to provide evidence for this, our most incredible delusion. We looked back and we thought, *If only I'd known it was real.* Hindsight is not twenty-twenty. We were blind."

"I'm not sure this *is* real," said Henry.

"*If only I'd understood back then,* we thought, *I could have controlled myself.*"

"And when I get home, like I said. Even if I remember this and think it really happened, as long as I'm not hallucinating—"

"But we were never going to control ourselves. We can't control anything. 41, I'm sure he thinks he's in control, just like I did—"

"—as long as I'm not afraid of everything, as long as I can think straight, I'll figure it out—"

"—but don't you see?" said 80.

"I don't. I don't understand. I don't care. I just…I need to go home."

"And I need to sit down." 80 started walking toward the house. Henry followed.

"You won't be well," said 80. "41 is off somewhere, some time. He's playing with your future. He must be. And in order for you to become him someday, you'll have to hear the music again. You'll have to cultivate that ability. And that means that no matter how sane you feel, you'll eventually pursue the insane. You'll get lost in obsession. Just like I did. Just like 41. And once you start traveling, who knows?"

Henry trailed behind the old man. He knew he should care about what he was hearing, but he felt too angry, too bored, too confused. The old man's words spewed out in a torrent, but before they penetrated Henry's mind they hit a wall, crumbled into their constituent letters, fell to the ground like ashes.

"You'll always be alone." 80 took the stairs up to the screen door one at a time. Like a toddler, he placed both feet on each step before mounting the next.

Henry watched from behind and was grateful for the windowless room that awaited him, grateful that he'd soon be cocooned in its darkness, asleep on cool sheets. When he woke up he'd find the keys. 80 couldn't stop him, and Henry didn't care if 41 found him. He hoped he did.

"You have me to thank for that," said 80.

"For what?"

"For being alone," said 80, and he opened the door, stepped inside, turned to hold it for Henry. "For all of this. It's my fault."

Henry walked up the steps. When he was at eye level with his older self, he said, "I just want to change my clothes and go to sleep."

"Listen to me," said 80. "I'm sorry."

Henry ignored him. He stepped over the threshold and into the relative dim of the living room.

"He's not," said a voice from the kitchen.

Henry looked at 80 with a silent question written in the folds of brow. But 80 had no answer. He looked even older than before, so pale and scared, his jaw trembling. Henry stepped through the living room and turned the corner onto the linoleum floor of the kitchen. At the head of the table, where 80 had been earlier that morning, was a man that Henry recognized despite his shorn hair and clean-shaven face.

"Go ahead and change," said 41. "The clothes are in the basement, just where you left them a couple hours ago. We're leaving."

80 entered the room behind Henry. "No," he said.

"It's over," said 41.

"We can fix this."

"There's nothing to fix. Let's go, Henry. "

"I don't understand," said Henry.

"He doesn't hear the music," said 41. "He can't take you home, but I can. So come on, get dressed. We're going back to the bridge."

"What?" said 80. He advanced on 41, who sat back in his chair and slumped down. He looked bored. "Where are you taking him?" said 80. He leaned down and pressed a knobby index finger against 41's sternum.

"Home," said 41.

"No," said 80. He whirled around and paced back toward Henry, eyes wet with despair. "We didn't take you anywhere, Henry. You're in your own time. You're already home."

"He's lying," said 41.

"Think about it," said 80, "we got you from the bridge and brought you here, that's all."

Henry shook his head. "I was unconscious on the bridge. And just before, in the woods. I just asked you when I was and you wouldn't answer. You were lying then or you're lying now and either way you're a liar." He turned to leave the room, but 80 caught him by the arm and held tight.

"I'll prove it," said 80. "Come with me—I'll drive you to Mom's. I'll show you. You can't go to the bridge with him. I don't know what he's doing, but, God..." He let go of Henry and staggered to the sink, where he rested his arms on the rim and lowered his forehead to the curved faucet. "Where are you taking him?"

"Henry," said 41. "He doesn't remember being you. He doesn't know what you're thinking or what this has done to you or what it has yet to do. I do. You have to trust me."

80 laughed and tapped his head against the metal spout.

"You wanted oblivion," said 41. "Maybe you didn't even know it, but all you wanted was to destroy everything, to disappear, to remove us from the world piece by piece. You should be thanking me. In the time it took you to walk back to the house I've spent months making sure that you get your wish. As soon as I get 19 back to where he belongs, this is over."

80 shot upright and slammed his hands on the edge of the sink. "And where do you think he belongs?" he yelled. He stepped back between his two younger selves and Henry flinched as 80 stepped toward him. "Wherever this man—"

"*This man?*" said 41. He laughed and the sound was thin and caustic. Henry suddenly felt afraid.

80 took one more step forward and opened his eyes so wide that it seemed they might fall out of his face and hit the floor. "Wherever this man is taking you, it's not your home," he said, slowly, as if to ensure that he was being understood. "It's a mistake to leave with him. You must understand that."

"I don't understand anything!" said Henry. "How many times do I have to say it? You're both fucking crazy."

"You're right," said 41, "and if you come with me now you'll be rid of us forever. Go with him and I'll be knocking on your door a day from now, a week, it doesn't matter. I'll find you, Henry. I'll always find you. And the truth is, I'm not really giving you a choice about this, because that choice would be a lie—the same lie that 80 told me. Go change. Now."

80 spoke with the same grave cadence as before. "Listen to him, Henry. Is that who you want to become?"

"Fuck it," said 41. He jumped up and rushed forward, tossed 80's body aside as he passed. The old man hit the refrigerator and crumpled. Henry turned to run, but 41 kicked his ankles out from underneath him and jumped on top of him. Henry thrashed but 41 had him pinned on his stomach, the side of his face pressed into the cold kitchen floor.

"Stay still," said 41. "It's almost over."

Henry felt a sharp pain deep in his thigh. He cried out, placed his palms on the ground, and pushed hard until he'd lifted both himself and 41 off the ground by an inch—just enough to give him leverage—but just as he was about to try to turn his body to the side, his arms collapsed beneath him. He felt cold and rigid but somehow warm and loose, too. A shiver jackhammered his jaw and then relented, and when it was over he was still. Everything was still. He could hear breathing, labored and loud, and for a moment he recognized that it was his own, but then the idea of *his own* lost its meaning and he felt himself dropping down fast toward blackness.

A voice echoed through the dark. *"What did you do?"* it said, and Henry felt with dreamlike intensity the absolutely overwhelming need to respond coupled with the urgent fear that he didn't know the answer.

Another voice interrupted his anxious searching. *"Say goodbye,"* it said.

Henry tried to move his lips in response to the command, but he couldn't. He descended faster and a rushing sound like the wind through leaves gave way to silence. The black overwhelmed him and he disappeared.

THE CONFESSION

G ABE DIDN'T KNOW why Val was frantic on the phone. It was a Friday afternoon. They already had plans for later that night. But then she called from the train, told him she was on her way and please could he be at the house when she got in. Gabe called the Dragon and said he was sick. It was a lie when he said it, but by the time he'd waited an hour and a half for Val to show up at his door, it had become the truth. What started as a seed of suspicion blossomed into horrific, illogical certainty. She would end it. It had been a month since they got together. He loved her. That it was too good to be true was a given. He'd expected her to break it off before, but she hadn't, and now she would. It seemed obvious.

Gabe wanted to leave his house, make her find him, or maybe just never talk to her again. Maybe just disappear altogether, like Henry had.

And yet up through the pain and fear a strange little bubble of relief was rising from deep in his gut. It was wrong that they should be together. Henry was still missing.

The man hadn't appeared again either, not since that afternoon in the living room. The music had continued intermittently, but Gabe hadn't told anyone. Whatever was happening to him, he was sure it wasn't the same as what had happened to Henry. Gabe was in control. He had adjusted.

He prepared for what he was sure would be his emotional evisceration by doing absolutely nothing. He sat on the porch so that he could watch her walk down Hamilton from downtown. Each solitary figure in the distance started out as her before resolving into some stranger. With his eyes so engaged, Gabe's peripheral vision caught the movement of every bush, tree, bird, and neighborhood cat. Everything was Val until he looked at it carefully and proved that it was not. Finally he saw a smudge approaching on the other side of Hamilton that moved in a familiar way. The bounce looked right, and the general color scheme. She approached, making no sign that she knew she was being watched, and Gabe understood that he'd never seen the way she carried herself when she was alone. He let himself imagine her as a stranger. She was pretty, but not shockingly so, her gait purposeful. She came closer and Gabe could see that she held her head low, her eyes fixed on the ground in front of her. He wanted to remember the moment, perhaps one of the last during which she would be his.

She stopped on the opposite corner and waited for an opening in the steady flow of traffic. When she saw her chance, she jogged across the road, hands still in her pockets, then came to an abrupt stop at the bottom of the steps. She looked up at him and he could see from her darkened eyelashes and rosy nose that she'd been crying.

"Can I come in?" she said, but just barely, the words aborted by a shuddering, pathetic little sob.

Once inside, they sat on the edge of his bed, as far from each other as it was possible to be. He didn't ask her what was wrong. He didn't want to know yet. Val opened her mouth to speak, but it closed itself and tightened into a wide line. She cried with her whole body until it collapsed and she slipped off the edge of the bed and onto her knees. She shuffled toward him awkwardly and lay her face on his thigh while hugging him around the waist. Gabe felt a tinge of anger. He was done with this histrionic prelude.

"Please just say you'll forgive me," she said.

"What happened?" He was surprised to hear the comforting tone of his own voice. He tucked some loose hair behind her ear and wiped a tear from the bridge of her nose. Another fell in its place. "Just tell me. Whatever it is we'll work it out."

"You can't know that."

"Not until you tell me."

She lifted her head from his leg and peered up, her eyelids swollen like flower buds, the corners of her mouth turned down. She looked perfect that way, Gabe thought, but that made no sense and it made him feel horrible.

"I need something to drink," she said.

He gently pushed her arms from his lap and went to the kitchen, thinking of their first real night together, how it had started with their lips touching the same glass. He wondered if this would be the last time he'd touch her like he had a right to.

He returned with water. She was nestled into the corner of the bed with her legs crossed underneath her. He handed her the glass and crawled up to sit across from her. Their knees touched.

"I did something," said Val. "I need to tell you everything. I'll understand if you hate me, but I can't not tell you. There's nobody else I can talk to. I know how unfair that is."

"Just...please," he said, fighting to keep his patience.

She took a long drink of water and then handed Gabe the glass. He leaned back and snaked his arm over the edge of the bed to set it on the ground. He sat back up. "Tell me."

"So these girls, they go out every Thursday." She stopped. Gabe put a hand on her leg and she grasped it. "I've just been feeling really lonely, you know? Not when I'm with you, or when I'm talking to you, but all the time besides that. I feel like we're doing something real, and I want it, but I'm not paying attention to the life that I fought to have. A life away from fucking New Brunswick, and Henry, and you." She glanced up into Gabe's eyes, gauging his reaction. He was still. "When I'm not with you I'm a mess. I don't think you know that."

"I'm a mess too," said Gabe.

"You're just saying that."

"No, I'm not. I told you I thought I was losing my mind. I wasn't exaggerating. It's gotten much better, but for a little while I was really scared."

She breathed in deeply and nodded. "But don't you think it's weird? We're both living these lives that are all fucked up and broken. Then we come together and act like nothing is wrong? We don't talk about Henry at all, at least not since those first few times we hung out, and even then it was like we were afraid that he would pop out of the closet or something."

"There are these girls, you said. What does that have to do with it? What happened?"

"I don't know. It's hard to explain." She motioned vaguely to the desk. He understood and leaned back to get the roll of toilet paper that he kept there in lieu of tissues. Val blew her nose, the loud trumpeting incongruent with the stillness of the room. "So we went to this club. I just—we went to this club and I don't know. I was so drunk, Gabe. So drunk."

Gabe felt a spark of understanding. Then pain. He was torn between needing her to continue and desperately wanting her to stop.

"It was really dark and I just started thinking, like, what did I come here for? Who am I supposed to be here if not somebody that can just take advantage of the kind of—but I didn't mean for it to happen. Please, Gabe, believe me. It wasn't because I wanted to hurt you. If anything it was because I knew how much I wanted this and I was afraid of what that meant. It doesn't make any sense, but that's how it feels. I just—God, what's wrong with me?"

"What happened?" said Gabe. "Stop crying."

"I can't," she said.

Gabe was mad then, but still he saw her vulnerability and pain as something beautiful. His disgust at that only made him angrier.

"There was a man," she said. "He was older. He was buying me drinks." Val took a moment to catch her breath. "I was just really drunk, and I felt like—God, it's so embarrassing. It's probably something he's perfected, some technique he uses with younger girls who are too fucking stupid to know any better. Or maybe I was just too drunk. But at the time, he made me feel in control, like I knew what I wanted."

Gabe turned away from her and dangled his legs over the edge of the bed. "What happened?" he said. He wasn't sure what it was that he was feeling, but he couldn't look at her anymore.

"We had sex."

Gabe leaned forward, elbows on knees, the heels of his hands digging hard into the hollows of his eyes. He wanted to get away from her. He wanted to break something. Anything. The walls, Val's perfect fucking nose, the bed frame, the bones in his hand. He lifted his fist, then brought it down hard onto the flesh of this thigh. He heard Val gasp, but at least she didn't touch him. The pain was too brief so he did it again. It hurt more the second time, and he closed his eyes to give the sensation his full attention. His breath, so hard to control a moment before, came easier after that.

"Nothing else about it matters, Gabe. Nothing except that as soon as it was over I felt worse than I've ever felt." She cried, uncontrollably this time. It was an ugly, wet cry. Gabe hated her for it. Seeing her spasm and wail, hearing the sounds of drowning from her tensed throat, he wanted to slap her and shake her like men did in old movies.

Get ahold of yourself.

It was funny.

Val kept crying. Gabe turned around again and watched her as if from far in the future, as if it wasn't happening at all. The longer it went on, the steadier his pulse became. Eventually he wasn't angry anymore, just sad. And though it was humiliating, he began to pity her more than he pitied himself. Her legs were still crossed beneath her, but she was bent over at the waist. It made it difficult for him to hold her, but he got as close as he could and slipped his hands around her belly, rested his cheek on her shoulder.

Val's crying was all Gabe could hear for a time. It didn't mix with any other sounds, didn't meld and merge and take flight into a symphonic hallucination. It was a song unto itself. Gabe listened with his eyes closed as it peaked and, eventually, quieted. Val rose up and Gabe lifted himself off her. She found the roll of toilet paper and blew her nose again, then interrupted her sadness to fixate with disgust on the disintegrating paper that was stuck to her finger. Gabe took the used wad and pulled a new sheaf off the roll. Val took it with a grateful nod.

"As soon as it was over, I just knew I only wanted you." She lifted her head and put her face close to Gabe's, so close that he couldn't focus his eyes and she remained doubled up, a tangle of loosely connected features. "It's like I've been resisting it, like I didn't want to admit that we were really doing this. I knew I wanted it but I couldn't give in, because of everything that's happened."

"Me too," said Gabe.

"That's it?" she said. "Please, just say something else. I know you're mad, I know I fucked up. Just say something."

She was right, of course. He was mad. But feeling her that close to him, breathing in her distinctive smell, he knew he wouldn't hold this mistake against her. He was too weak for that. Or maybe too strong. He wasn't sure. Whatever it was that she'd done, it had brought her to his door, professing that she didn't want to be without him. Did he really care to know more? And if he would soon forgive her, as he knew he would, what could be the point of the kind of heat-of-the-moment outburst to which he felt inclined?

"It hurts," he said. "I'm angry. But you're here."

Val started to cry again. Gabe felt manipulated, a specific blend of impotent inner violence and futile resentment that always accompanied the knowledge of being played. But she cried and he held her. She felt so good crumpled up against him. Val released herself from his arms and lay down on her side. Gabe lay down too. He pushed his body against her and squeezed her from behind harder than he thought she could take.

Val gripped one of his hands, her bony knuckles tightening painfully on his own. She held her breath.

"I'm a bad person, I guess," she said.

"Me too."

After a long silence, as if it were a completely natural extension of their conversation, Val said, "Henry might not be back." Whether she said it for Gabe's benefit or for her own, he couldn't tell. It was just the truth, bald and naked and horrible. But for all that, it was undeniably attractive.

ALLEGRO: 41

THEY TOOK EVERY possible precaution. Henry made sure of that. 80 didn't share his conviction that they could avoid mishap through preparation, but the old man conceded that it couldn't hurt and played along. For weeks they recounted each moment of that morning on the George Washington Bridge. They mined every recollection for details that might make their task easier and planned the extraction down to the second.

As for what to do with 19 once they had him, it was Henry's idea to rebuild one of the downstairs bedrooms. They needed it to be ready for their young self in his own time, twenty years before, so they shifted back before carpeting the room, buying new furniture. Henry measured and cut drywall to cover the window. 80 objected at first, but Henry was adamant that the boy be introduced to his new reality slowly, each revelation carefully controlled. When they were done they went back to the bridge, shifted forward to Henry's time, and found the room still in place. It was eerie. Dust covered everything but there were no signs of wear. Nothing had been touched or moved in over twenty years.

Henry didn't feel ready. He insisted on covering every permutation they could imagine, every direction their past might take once 19 was in hand. 80 cooperated for several days, but eventually he'd had enough. Their plans were likely to be meaningless, he said, there were too many variables. They'd done all they could and it was time to act. They'd leave in the morning.

On the day of the extraction Henry awoke in the dark and put on his clothes. He walked down the steps, shoes in hand, careful to be as quiet as possible. 80 would have remembered creeping downstairs—it was impossible for Henry to do *anything* without his older self's knowledge—but he hoped he would at least be left alone to say goodbye to the world as it was.

The sky was just beginning to lighten as he sat down on the top step of the porch. His bedroom had been silent, a soupy stillness containing only himself and his thoughts, but now that he was outside he could hear the distant sound of the creek. Birds chattered tentatively, as if whispering to see who else was up. He untied his shoes, loosened the laces. It made him think of how he'd arrived. Barefoot. A filthy robe draped over his shoulders. His feet raw from running on the asphalt and concrete of his neighborhood. Henry was not the same man he'd been when he'd arrived. That man was gone.

He stepped off the porch and began walking to the woods. He passed the boulder in the backyard and, as habit demanded, slapped his palm against its rough bulk. By the time he got to the bridge it was roughly sunrise but hard to tell. With all the hills around, Henry wasn't sure what sunrise meant. Was it the theoretical moment when the sun would cross the horizon were he on a flat plain? Or was every sunrise truly in the eye of its beholder? How could something as irrefutable as the beginning of another day be so subjective? He sat down on the bridge just as he had the morning before they drove off to find 29. And, just as on that morning, 80 evenutally approached him from the forest and said nothing. He conjured the sound of time. Henry acknowledged the fear and nausea, the blood-boiling *everythingness* of the sound, but he let himself go until, for a timeless instant, Henry wasn't anybody. He wasn't even an "it," let alone a "he," and that was the best feeling in the world. But then he saw hands gripping a twisted steel cable and began to recognize them as his own. He was a man again, a single entity alone among all others, and he wondered why anyone would ever subject himself to something so terrible as that.

He stood.

It was the middle of the night. The dark forced them to take their time getting back to the house. A hundred miles to the south, their boy was still stewing in his bedroom. The seething green vibrations from across the street were packing his body tight with the sickening nausea of anticipation. For the first time since they'd hatched this plan Henry could sense 19's proximity. It was comforting to know that soon his young self would be released from the pain.

They entered the clearing, passed the boulder—both of them touching it softly as they went by. They checked that the room was ready and gathered their gear. 80 had somehow procured the sedatives, a syringe filled with a wicked-looking milky liquid that Henry was scared to even look at. 80 had also bought clothes of the size and style he thought appropriate for 19, but Henry thought his choices were strange—a pair of pajama bottoms, an oversized T-shirt. Henry didn't like thinking about how out of touch 80 was with his nineteen-year-old self.

They got in the car.

Henry felt a wave of panic and he imagined that he was an astronaut strapped to the point of a rocket filled with high explosives. It was too late to turn back, too late to do anything but grit his teeth and fly. He closed his eyes while 80 turned the key in the ignition, and they were off.

"It feels like something is ending," said Henry.

"What do you mean?"

"You don't remember?"

"No," said 80. "I'm barely awake."

Henry reclined his seat a little and settled in. He tried to imagine forgetting this strange feeling or divorcing it from this monumental moment. But then he thought of Val, how he had held her hand as she pushed Annie out into the world. The long labor before was undoubtedly filled with strong, disorienting emotions, but he could only guess at what they actually were. Those hours were gone, obscured by the brilliance of what came directly after.

"What *do* you remember?" he said to 80.

The old man seemed not to have heard him. He squinted out into the bright circle painted by the car's headlights. Then, when Henry had almost forgotten that he'd spoken his question aloud, 80 said, "I remember seeing him from afar, when I was you. Watching him pass through the gate to the walkway on the upper level."

"And then, what? We turned around?"

"We know what that memory's worth."

The road was suffocated in the deep country darkness of a moonless night. Henry wished he could see into the forest on either side. *One last time,* he thought, but he didn't know why.

"We'll be back through here in just a few hours," said 80. "You'll see what this is like. Watching yourself sleep in the car. Nothing like it."

"I know."

"You saw 29. But this is different. You're going to have to talk to this one. You're going to remember having already heard every word you say. Or some of it, anyway."

"We've talked about this," said Henry, not sure why he wanted 80 to shut up. It was an urge that he didn't care to examine.

"We've talked about the psychological effects," said 80. "I'm just talking about how it feels. You'll find a lot about it to like, I should think."

Henry pondered that and watched the darkness roll by.

Dawn came looking like an old watercolor, its tints faded and washed out. Downtown Fort Lee glowed colorlessly in the gathering light. More than half of the storefront signs were in Korean. It added to the otherworldly feeling of the place. It was a town built on the banks of two rivers, one of water and one of cars, neither of which ever stopped flowing. The entrance to the George Washington Bridge was like a great asphalt heart. The on- and off-ramps the left and right ventricles, all the looping underpasses and overpasses the arteries. Henry knew he should be concentrating on 19, on what he was about to do, but he was overwhelmed by memories. The bagel shop he came to with Gabe on Saturday mornings when they were in high school. The twenty-four-hour diner where they'd stop on their way out of the city after a show. His old drum teacher who lived at the bottom of Grand Avenue and who was even then asleep in his bed exactly as Henry remembered him.

They parked in a little gravel lot directly across from the entrance to the pedestrian walkway. Above their heads hovered the beginning of the bridge itself, and in front of them, across four deserted lanes of local service road, was a wide path leading directly to the chain-link fence that kept people off the bridge between sunset and sunrise.

"I hope we have the right day," said 80. He put the tip of his thumb against his front teeth and chewed.

"It's the right day," said Henry.

A police car parked on the sidewalk across the road. The officer that stepped out was tall, widely built, his gut hanging over his leather belt. Henry and 80 watched as he sauntered to the gate, unlocked the padlock, and pulled the chain through. It rang the fence like a triangle until it got stuck. The cop pulled lightly at first. When it wouldn't budge, he set his feet at shoulder width and pulled hard. When the chain came free he jolted back and just barely stayed on his feet, then swore at the chain as he kicked it with the toe of his boot.

Henry laughed through his nose, a single exhale of amused disbelief. "I don't remember that."

"Me neither," said 80.

The cop put the chain in the trunk, lowered himself into the driver's seat, and drove away with his siren on.

Henry focused on the long road to his right. It led up a gentle incline to a stoplight about a hundred yards away. As if willed into existence by his gaze, there appeared in the distance a teenage boy. The boy jerked as he walked, and the toe of one of his shoes scuffed the ground with every other step.

Henry looked on with a glimmer of a smile on his lips. There was no stone. 19 was kicking at nothing. It made perfect sense, but Henry hadn't known that before. It was sad but strangely empowering.

"How do you feel?" said 80, whispering.

Henry didn't answer, but he acknowledged the question with a short, choked moan and a deep breath in. He exhaled until there was nothing left.

19 reached the fence. He was beautiful, Henry thought, with his small body framed by the impossibly large towers of the bridge. He had come here to escape the bright green spastic low vibration, to outrun the end of the world. But now his world really *was* going to end—Henry and 80 were there to make sure of that—and it made Henry sort of sad.

Henry and 80 opened their doors and eased out of the car. 80 went around to the trunk. Henry joined him and together they pulled a brand-new folding wheelchair from where it was stowed. Henry opened it, unlocked the wheels. 80 gripped the handles. They waited, watching, as the third Henry trudged his way to the now open gate and walked through it, the invisible stone pulling him along as it had for hours.

The rest went quickly. By the time Henry and 80 reached the gate, 19 was well ahead. The boy had already lost his stone guide companion and he was looking out over the railing that separated him from a two-hundred-foot free fall. Henry recalled the concentric rainbow circles, but just like the stone they weren't really there. 19 faced the other end of the bridge. He looked up and cocked his head.

The first clarion tone of the music hit Henry's eardrums like a lance. 19 started to run and as Henry ran after him his feet pounded out the driving rhythm of the bridge's anthem just as they had years before. The theme was so powerful that he couldn't believe he'd ever forgotten it, so complex that it was ludicrous that he'd ever tried to re-create it. As he ran Henry felt lifted out of his skin, as if the vital part of him was shedding its human shell and rising into the sky, carried aloft by the noise. 19 was past the first tower now. The walkway angled around that tower in a switchback so the boy was out of sight. Henry ran harder. He struggled, out of breath, but the pain seemed to belong to someone else. He reached the tower and made a quick right turn into the steel-encased corridor. Two sharp lefts and another right later, he was spit back out onto the long middle expanse of the bridge, and there in the distance was 19. He'd fallen and was struggling to get up. Henry kept running with the music until he reached the spot where the boy lay in a haphazard pile of limbs. Henry was supposed to have taken the syringe from his pocket. According to the plan, he was meant to have jammed the thing into 19's thigh and depressed the plunger the instant he was able to. But he'd forgotten. Of course he had. Momentum carried him forward and he fell. His hands touched the boy and the music bled to white.

There was a sound like the ocean.

It whished and whirred before resolving into the familiar beat of cars on concrete. Beneath Henry was a body. Its face was his own. 19's. He looked to be at peace. The sun was an afternoon sun and there was no chill to the air.

Henry lifted his head. In the distance, he saw a person walking toward them from the New York side. There was very little time. Henry had to either rouse 19 and get him standing or take him back to the time they'd just left. They could not be confronted by this stranger. He took the syringe from his pocket, removed the cap, and sank the flared tip through 19's pants and into his thigh. The boy didn't move as Henry depressed the plunger. Too late, he realized his mistake. If he couldn't get 19 back to when 80 was waiting for them with a wheelchair, he would be stuck with a sedated body instead of one that might have stood up and walked on its own. He couldn't lift 19 alone, and even if he could it would attract attention. That left only one option. He needed to get back to the morning. He needed 80 and the car. Most of all he needed that wheelchair.

Something big, most likely an eighteen-wheeler, passed underneath them on the lower level and honked its massive horn. The sound was momentarily overwhelming—deep and full like an ancient battle horn reverberating off the walls of a cave. Henry held on to the sound. It was such a simple thing. Instead of allowing it to fade into the distance with the truck that produced it, Henry simply kept the noise in his body. A car passed in the nearest lane. Its high, airy *whoosh* rose and fell, and Henry found that he could stretch the sound indefinitely. It wasn't just the one car. It was all of them. Henry let their collective sustain build and build. He tapped his fingers against the cement next to 19's head and heard the deep resonance of the bridge. He didn't question what he was doing or why, and he wasn't overly excited by it either. It was familiar, totally natural. He pictured the gray-blue morning and the car. He focused on 80 walking toward him and the wheelchair and the storefronts of Fort Lee, their neon signs just beginning to blink on. The images piled onto one another, then blended together to create a single, infinite expanse, a bright and audible shine that grew and grew until the present could no longer hold it.

Henry let himself disappear into the brimming void.

When his eyes could see again, it was just after dawn. The boy was still underneath him, and he smelled terrible. A broad band of acne stretched across his forehead like the Milky Way. His mouth hung open and Henry could see his own teeth inside, a little whiter than he was used to and still lined up nicely from the braces he'd worn as a teenager. And then he remembered. The memories didn't hit him with epiphanic force. They had always been there. Henry had lived them—he'd long since categorized and prioritized them, and they made up the story of who he was. But in another sense, in some old part of his mind, they were new, too.

He looked up to see 80 emerging from the darkened corridor around the western tower. The details of their plan came back to him, except now they were overlaid with his own memories of waking up in strange clothing in a pitch-black room in the Catskills. The moment was no longer just the present. It was the future and the past, too. It was all so confusing that it took Henry a moment to understand that he'd shifted himself back. He'd brought the boy to the right moment in time. And, more surprising, Henry suddenly recalled that it wasn't remarkable that he'd done that. Not at all. He'd known how for years. He laughed just as 80 was finally tottering close enough to make his voice heard over the sound of early rush-hour traffic.

"Get him up," said 80, his urgency matched by his volume.

Henry couldn't move. His new past was still coming to him and his mind became a dark kaleidoscopic swirl of chaos that churned inward and inward.

"What are you doing?" said 80. "Get him *up!*"

Henry's body responded. He grabbed 19's hands and pulled his torso forward and up off the ground. The boy's head lolled back so far that it looked like his neck might snap, so Henry lowered him again. He maneuvered his way around 19's back and grabbed him underneath his rancid armpits.

"He's deadweight," said Henry.

They hadn't practiced this part, and it made Henry feel stupid and utterly unprepared. If they'd forgotten about something as simple as their likely inability to lift 150 pounds of unconscious human, what else must they have overlooked?

80 rolled the wheelchair closer and put the brakes on. Clumsily, precariously, they got the boy's prone body up and wedged it into the seat. Henry released the brakes and pushed 19 back toward New Jersey at a trot. 80 kept up, but he looked like shit, his colorless lips parting as he gasped with each step. "Was he awake when you first touched him?" he said, and then he breathed in and out, hard, before gathering enough air to speak again. "Did he see you?"

Henry glanced back at 80. "Just move," he said.

They reached the western tower and went single file through the walkway—a left, two rights, and a left—then moved as fast as 80's aged body would allow toward the car. Again the old man managed to draw enough breath to speak. "Are you curious," he said, then took a jagged breath, "...are you curious about why we haven't remembered anything yet?"

"No," said Henry, and he walked faster. He didn't know where the lie had come from. It was immediate, completely natural. He didn't question it.

"Well," said 80, "as soon as he wakes up, then, I suppose."

"I suppose," said Henry. "Move faster. We're almost there."

SYMPTOMATIC

I**T STARTED WITH** a single white hair halfway between his chin and lower lip. Gabe smiled when he first saw it in the mirror. It felt like the beginning of something, a glimmering beacon of maturity, but even so the urge to pull it out was simply too great. He found his tweezers amid the mess of rolling papers and mysterious knick-knacks on Cal's bedside table (the table itself was mysterious: an overturned clementine crate emblazoned with a green and white hornet and Spanish slogans). When he'd last seen the tweezers, Cal had been using them to dig deep underneath his large toenail. Gabe washed them with soap and water. Washed them again. Then he heated the tips with his lighter. Once he was satisfied that they were sterile, he leaned close to the mirror and dug into the undergrowth of his beard to locate the root of the offending hair. But before he could, it fell out on its own and descended into the toothpaste-grouted sink.

Gabe hadn't felt anything—no pinprick, no tug to indicate that the hair had ever even been attached. He laughed at how much energy he'd put into the whole thing, then forgot about it. But two days later he saw more of the ghostly strands growing from the same spot as the first one. These fell out, too, and they were followed by others until within a week the bald spot had grown to be the size of a dime.

Val told him it didn't matter, he looked fine, but that maybe he should go to the doctor. Gabe went to the internet instead. *Alopecia areata.* He concentrated on the parts of each article that focused on the autoimmune implications, the unknown source of the disease, and its various treatments. He skillfully ignored any passage detailing the ailment's relation to stress and trauma.

He rubbed at the spot. He thought about it all the time. He watched strangers' eyes to see whose would land on the spot before making eye contact. When a new colony of the offending hairs started to develop lower down on his chin, his heart started beating so fast that he thought he was going to throw up. He grew to be absolutely certain that the spots were a warning of some horrible tragedy to come. Cancer. Hepatitis. The tropical flesh-eating virus that made the news when he was a kid. AIDS.

Late one night he and Val lay awake in his bed. It had been four long days since the last time they'd been together, and neither of them wanted to waste time on unconsciousness. They fooled around, talked, fooled around some more. Apropos of nothing, Val said, "I want you to see a doctor."

Gabe moaned in frustration.

"I'm going to go too," she said.

Gabe furrowed his brow in the dark. "Why?"

"I haven't been feeling that good either. Just little stuff. Like, I'm not that hungry. I just don't really want to be near food at all, actually."

"I'm sorry," he said. "I didn't know."

"I was looking up some stuff about alopecia. Seems like it's something that comes up when people are really stressed out."

"Hm."

"Same with my appetite," she said. "I had this feeling right before I broke up with Henry. When I think about it now I feel stupid. Like my body was telling me something was wrong but I just wasn't listening."

"Are you saying you want to break up?" said Gabe. "Like I give a shit."

Val pinched his arm and he laughed. He had hoped the joke would be enough to divert their conversation, but then she said, "We don't talk about him. I don't want to, not always. I know you don't either. It's painful. But it feels wrong, like we're lying to ourselves. He's been gone for three months and nobody is doing anything. Nobody is saying aloud the thing we all know."

"There's nothing we can do for him," said Gabe. "That sucks but it's the truth. I feel better about it when I'm with you."

"Me too," said Val. "But ever since that night, since what I did…"

Gabe threw his arm over her, pulled her close. "I just want everything to be okay," he said.

She gently lifted his arm and rolled over to face him. "We don't talk about Henry. And we don't talk about what happened with me. It's weird. It's like ever since I told you that I cheated on you things between us have just been more amazing. Don't you think we need to talk about it? It's like neither of us wants to ruin this by bringing up anything bad."

He rolled onto his back and held his breath. "I'm confused. You want me to be mad at you or something? I was. I still could be. But you're with me. You love me. I'd rather just forget it, really, and I don't know what's wrong with that."

"I think it's making us both sick," she said. "Literally, physically sick."

Gabe let his body go slack. Dozens of sentences began in his mind, each one too confused, muddled, or unflattering for him to actually express out loud.

"The more time goes by, the more I feel like this could work. Like we could really be together," said Val. "At first I was afraid."

"I was petrified," Gabe sang.

"Stop," said Val. "At first, I think we were both just reaching out for something."

"Maybe," said Gabe. "But that was just at first." He touched his lips to her brow, brushed them back and forth on her skin.

"What we're doing," she said, "if it's going to keep working, this can't be taboo, you know? We have to own it. That there's still something really uncomfortable about all this. We have to just live with that and not be afraid of it or else it will just get so big that we won't be able to deal with it anymore." Val drew herself up on one elbow and placed her forearm on Gabe's chest, her fingers scratching their way into his beard. "I mean, think about it. What if he doesn't come back?"

"What if he *does* come back?" said Gabe. *What happens if he's already back?*

"It doesn't have to be tonight, but we need to find a way to talk about this. There's got to be a place for it."

"Okay," said Gabe. But it wasn't, and they didn't talk about it any further.

Val had to leave the next day after breakfast. Gabe went to the bathroom as soon as she was gone and stared at the growing colonies of strawlike hairs on his chin. He dug under the sink for the electric buzzer and reduced his beard to fuzz. Val always left a razor and travel-sized shaving cream in his shower. Gabe found them and lathered up.

Each stroke of the razor revealed another inch of his naked face, and once it was all gone he did feel a bit better. He could outsmart the disease. Beat it at its own game. He thought of the research he'd done, all the pictures he'd seen online of men and women with pink bald patches all over their scalps, and turned on the buzzer again. He didn't think. He took a tentative jab at the side of his head and watched a thick clump of hair drop down into the sink.

"Oh," he said. "Shit." He laughed.

Ten minutes later, much of what Gabe had come to think of as his actual head was in the sink, clinging to his shoulders, or on the tops of his feet. He looked in the mirror at what was left. He was pale. Shiny. The continuous plane of bright white skin between his chin and the back of his head made him look like a worm. His lips looked bigger too, his eyebrows comically prominent. It was strange how changing the context could make those unalterable features seem so unrecognizable.

Still, he didn't regret it. He felt clean and controlled. He felt new.

REQUIEM: WAKING UP

I DON'T UNDERSTAND," said 80.

The words represented the starting point of a conversational loop. Henry had allowed it to repeat five times since maneuvering 19 into the backseat and driving away, but now he was losing his patience. "Just wait until he wakes up," he said.

"It shouldn't matter," said 80. "It was one thing with 29. We were in the same room, nothing changed until he saw us—that makes a kind of sense. But 19? He's in the car with us. That he will wake up and encounter us is inevitable, don't you think?" said 80. "Our intervention has begun. We should be remembering something by now." He tapped the door, looked to Henry, out the window, back to Henry again, glanced at the backseat.

Henry was glad to be driving. It gave him an excuse to avoid eye contact, to guard his own reactions until he'd had a chance to contemplate his next move.

"What if the dosage was wrong?" said 80. "What if he's about to go into cardiac arrest? There has to be some reason we don't recall anything new."

"He's fine," said Henry. "Just wait. He doesn't know that we've taken him yet. When he does, things will change. We'll remember."

In those first few moments on the bridge Henry had concealed the truth out of instinct. The more 80 talked, the more Henry appreciated that instinct. He knew the music now; he could take himself whenever he wanted to go. And for some reason that he had yet to understand, he could remember being 19 though 80 could not. He was in control, and that control was all the more total due to 80's ignorance.

They were in the mountains by then, the broad switchbacks of the road soothing in their regularity. Henry purposely took each curve just a bit too fast. His stomach turned pleasantly, as if in free fall. 80 didn't notice. He licked his lips and gazed unblinking at the dashboard. "Something's really wrong," he said.

"We're almost home," said Henry. "There's nothing you can do but wait, right? I don't know exactly why we don't remember being him yet, but I feel okay. I'm calm. So maybe you should just try to remember how you felt when you were *me*. It might help."

Henry took his eyes off the road momentarily, fought a smile as he watched the old man's face screw itself into a look of barely subdued horror followed by a deliberate softening of his features, the first indication of the lie to come. Next 80's jaw clenched, stretching papery skin around the bulb of hard muscle beneath his ear. He swallowed, dipping his chin. "Of course," he said. "If I could be calm about this once, when I was you, I can be calm about it again."

The remaining twenty minutes to the house passed in silence.

19 wouldn't wake for hours, so Henry took his time experimenting with different methods of levering the boy's body up onto his shoulders. When he found a hold that felt sustainable he carried 19 up into the house and through the doorway to the white bedroom. He and 80 tucked 19 in, then sat together in the kitchen to wait.

80 hadn't spoken much since they'd arrived, and Henry didn't press him. The earth had shifted underneath both of their feet, and

now that Henry was on higher ground for once, he could watch and wait. For all 80's talk about them being together, about trusting each other and acting with a single purpose, Henry was curious how the old man would play it.

He was disappointed but not surprised when 80 said, "I think I remember something." The old man had just refilled his coffee mug, and he sipped with eyes squinted in concentration.

"Yeah?" said Henry.

"Yes. It's not quite a memory. More like a feeling. I have this sense welling up within me that I've been in that room before, in the dark. That I heard voices through the wall."

Henry thought about that for a moment. 80 was likely just making an educated guess. But it was possible, he supposed, that he was wrong about the old man.

The coffee in Henry's own cup was cold, but he liked it. It reminded him of all the times he'd let coffee go cold before. It usually meant the end of an evening well spent, he and Val laughing about the day and the unbelievable things that Annie had said and done of her own spectacular free will. Back then it was decaf with lots of milk. After a few more minutes of silence, a less pleasant association occurred to him. Cold coffee didn't belong just to his first life—it also belonged to his second and third, to his years spent wandering in the spaces of his mind, so overmedicated that time itself seemed to exist elsewhere. He spent hours sitting alone at the diner by his apartment near Lung-Ta. It was common at that time for Henry to start a thought and find that its conclusion—seemingly instantaneous to him—had taken five, ten, fifteen minutes by the hands of the greasy clock mounted above the diner's kitchen door. When that happened, the contents of his mug would have gone cold as if, it seemed to him, by magic.

Henry snapped back to the present. A remarkable expanse of time had filled his memory the moment he'd touched 19. It was possible that the old man could remember nothing but the briefest impression of having been in a room and hearing voices through the wall. Perhaps it was 80's age, or his general confusion at having lived so many times. Maybe he was suffering from dementia.

Much more likely, he was full of shit.

Henry took a deep breath and said, as loud as he could without yelling, "I think he's awake."

80 looked at him uncertainly.

"I'm pretty sure of it," said Henry, even louder this time.

"Yes," said the old man. "I remember it now. That's so strange."

Henry gave him a look with nothing in it, his face brutally indifferent. "We should go see, don't you think?"

80 nodded slowly and looked down at his coffee cup as if there were answers to be found in its murk.

"You're the one who opens the door," said Henry. "Whenever you're ready."

From the room came the bubbling of 19's laughter.

"I actually *do* remember it," said Henry. "Sitting in there, giggling like an idiot."

80 looked up from his cup and stared into Henry's eyes. His face was half pleading, half defiant. He hadn't put the pieces together, but he knew that the finished puzzle would not form a picture he wanted to look at. "This is cruel," he said.

"Do you know why I was laughing?"

80 shook his head, his lower lip trembling like a baby's. He looked down again, any pretense of anger now completely destroyed. He carefully folded his shaking hands around the mug.

"I laughed because when I woke up in that room I was sane again. I felt like myself for the first time in months. And I thought, *I don't care that I don't know where I am, or how I got here. I don't care that I don't know what's coming next, or that the last thing I remember is the sound of the whole universe crushing me to death. None of that matters because here I am in a comfortable bed in total darkness and I feel like* me."

80 was still nodding, the motion so small that it almost wasn't there at all, an octogenarian tremor.

"Really, I was laughing because I thought things couldn't possibly get any worse than they'd been. Somehow I'd escaped. Everything was going to be better, always."

The legs of 80's chair screeched across the floor as he pushed it back and stood up. "Let's go in already."

"It is funny, actually. I was right to laugh. It's funny because I was so wrong."

80 walked away from the table. Henry stood to follow him and, on the way through the kitchen, grabbed the dish towels that hung on the handlebar of the oven. 80 stood in wait outside the bedroom. He removed a key from his pocket and placed it into the knob, then opened the door, but just barely.

"You're going to want these," Henry whispered. He shoved the towels in to 80's chest.

80 looked at him, eyes burning with disdain. "And why is that?"

Henry just motioned to the door.

80 grimaced. He knocked softly. "Henry? I won't hurt you. You have to trust me," he said. "I want you to close your eyes until I say. Are they closed?"

He opened the door slowly, the light from the hallway illuminating first the side wall and finally the corner where 19 sat staring at them through eyes wide with horror. The boy's mouth curled into a grotesque crater, his lips trembled as he sat up to get a closer look. Then he bent forward, heaved, and went slack.

"Do you remember how long he'll be out?" 80's question was monotone, void of any subtext. He just wanted to know what would happen next.

"We're going to give him some more sedatives," said Henry.

"He's barely slept in days. You'll change him, clean up the vomit, get his clothes in the wash. And I'm going to go to bed. He'll sleep through the night."

80 nodded his agreement.

"Don't worry," said Henry. "You'll have plenty of time to lie to him in the morning."

"I'm going to die," said Henry. The dark of his bedroom had no answer.

Downstairs, the boy slept. 80 might have been sleeping too, though Henry doubted it. But asleep or awake, 80 was still downstairs. He hadn't ceased to exist, and yet Henry himself would never become him. The link had been severed, and if not by death, by what? It was the only explanation that made any sense.

"I'm going to die," he whispered. Repeating the phrase in his mind didn't seem to have the effect he was looking for. He was saying it aloud in the hope that he could somehow force the idea into his psyche.

He sat at the head of the bed, his back leaning against the wall. The vinyl paint stuck to his bare skin. Tomorrow he would leave 19 and 80 behind—that's what he remembered from when he was nineteen. In doing so, he would be making sure that 19's life was essentially destroyed. Henry remembered the years of treatment ending in failure. How 19 would never get over this experience in the Catskills, how he'd never cease believing in its truth. That insistence would guarantee his institutionalization. It would separate him from everyone in his life until one day, fifteen years into 19's future, he'd walk out onto a bridge over the Connecticut River in Northampton, Massachusetts, and hear the song he'd been yearning for. He'd become immersed in that song. He'd use it to seek oblivion.

If Henry took 19 back right away, he could perhaps improve the boy's future. But he wasn't going to do that. He wanted 19 to be free for a while, free from the responsibility of being crazy among people who wanted him to be well, free from the pressure to lie, even to himself, about what he knew to be true. 19's time with 80 would be a vacation from the hell that his life would become.

He thought of Val and then, inevitably, of Annie. Her small face was always smiling, proudly displaying the ridiculous spaces between her teeth. Those spaces were still waiting to be filled when he'd erased her. 80, though—he remembered a woman. Henry envied him. He hated him. Then he thought of Gabe. His only friend, one who had proven three times over that he would choose his love for Val over his love for Henry when the opportunity arose. A familiar anger seeped into Henry's body. It filled empty spaces, expanded blood vessels. Val and Gabe would carry on without him. Once he disappeared, their bodies would fly together and adhere like magnets. It was the only consistency between all of his worlds.

But that was not *exactly* true.

Since touching 19 on the bridge, Henry remembered that in the world as it was now Val and Gabe would come together only briefly. Their loneliness would push them into each other's arms for a time, but then, when Henry returned, they would break it off. After a few years, Gabe would tell Henry all about it. He would confess, expecting forgiveness, maybe even appreciation for the sacrifice he'd made for Henry when he let Val go.

So now, finally, Henry had destroyed everything. It had taken lifetimes, but it was all gone. Annie had never been. Val's love for him diminished with each new past he remembered. Gabe grew more distant. And now even the connection Gabe and Val had with each other had been reduced to nothing but a mistake, an inadvisable hookup.

Henry felt he could come to terms with the fact that he'd die. It was much harder to accept that he would leave the world as broken as he was. He wouldn't accept that. He didn't have to.

With exhilarating ease he came to a decision. He knew where he would go the next day. He knew why 19 had to be gone from his own reality for so long. And he felt at peace, a kind of confident calm that he hadn't experienced since his days spent gathering noise with Annie.

He knew what he had to do.

THE CUTICLE

V AL NIBBLED THE cuticle of her right thumb and stared into her television's bright void. It was only three o'clock. Gabe was just finishing his shift and it would be another few hours before he showed up at her door. She wanted him to be there *right fucking then*, but she also wished he would never come at all. She didn't want to tell him. She wondered, for the hundredth time, whether she had to.

But of course she did. Not telling him? It wasn't even worth fantasizing about. She didn't want a lifelong secret. It would kill her. It would come out. Something horrible would happen. She wanted to stand up, go to the bathroom, dig through the garbage to take another look, because maybe there was a mistake, maybe she'd read it wrong. But no, she'd already done that. She'd bought a three-pack of the tests and taken each one. She forced herself to stay on the couch. She sucked her cuticle. She'd gone too far, nibbled too much, but it was too hard to stop, so she bit harder, tasted blood, took her hand from her mouth and shook it, shoved it under her thigh to keep herself from starting on another finger.

The television flickered as she changed the channel. Images reached her eyes but seemed to get scrambled on the way to her mind. As had happened so often since that night in the Washington Square Hotel, unwelcome memories of the man flooded through her. Not his face—she could never quite remember what he looked like and was disturbed to always find herself imagining Henry—but the way he made her feel. The thrill and the fear. The way her heart beat when she took off her clothes and saw her own desire reflected in his eyes. Her blood scrambling like a wild animal as it fought its way through her body. Then, afterward, how she was so pleasantly tender from alcohol and sex. The way the king-sized bed took her shape and cradled her.

Val slid her hand from beneath her and found the raw spot just above the nail on her thumb. It stung as she pushed against it with her tongue. She changed the channel, not because she cared what was on but because she thought that maybe if she found the right show Kara would emerge from her room and sit down to watch. They hadn't spoken much since Val's outburst at the Sullivan Room. Val had tried to apologize, but it seemed of little use. She had long known of Kara's deepest fears—that she was merely being tolerated, that she was a joke, that people thought she was prudish and boring—and Val had exploited those insecurities to wound her. Had it been anyone else Val might have been able to blame it on the alcohol, but Kara didn't drink. Any excuse based on drunkenness would only make her respect Val even less.

And Gabe? *Jesus,* she thought. Gabe. How would he respect her after this? He loved her. She knew that. She wondered if it was possible—in light of what she'd done and what she'd kept from him—that she loved him, too. And what if she did? Even that was fraught and fucked up. There was still Henry to think about, wasn't there? He deserved some kind of consideration, even if, or maybe especially if, he never came back.

No.

Val wouldn't think about that. Not just then.

How much longer until Gabe arrived? She looked at the clock and had to keep herself from groaning in protest. Three minutes had passed since last she checked.

Val wondered what it meant about her that she was more embarrassed than ashamed. She just felt so incredibly stupid. So out of control. Who was that girl, she wondered? Who was that reckless stranger who had taken over her body and wreaked impressive havoc in just a few short hours? At least she'd had the sense to walk out in the middle of the night. She thanked herself for that. It would have been so much worse to wake up in that hotel room. Small talk about all that she and that man had in common would have lasted no more than a few minutes. And after that? Breakfast in the lounge. Or, worse, room service. Some server coming in and discovering her there, removing those silver covers with a flourish while secretly imagining what had happened the night before. No, Val was glad she'd left. The only thing she regretted about her escape was the note. She'd known it was a mistake even as she was writing it by the light of her cell phone screen. Halfway through she'd considered tearing the paper off the pad and leaving, but then she thought the man might notice an indentation on the pad itself and scratch it with a pencil to reveal the proof of her cowardice. She could have taken the whole thing, but she didn't want to be remembered as the girl who'd absconded with the hotel stationery in the dead of the night.

So she wrote. She apologized for leaving, though she knew that was ludicrous. She shouldn't have been apologizing at all. Better to have written YOU'RE WELCOME in big block letters and sign it *Valerie* with a cute little heart dotting the *i* the way she did in middle school.

A commercial came on, obnoxiously loud. As designed, it grabbed Val's attention. Toilet paper and cartoon bears. She took her thumb from her mouth. A large angular patch was now the glossy pink of new flesh tinged with blood. It didn't hurt too badly yet, but she knew that the pain would soon get worse. Maybe by the time Gabe showed up. Maybe by the time she'd told him the full truth about that night.

She changed the channel.

CODA: THE NOTE

HENRY WATCHED THE girl he'd married and raised a child with crawl naked across the rich plush carpet in the dark. Val swept her arms across the floor as if swimming. She was looking for something. Her clothes? Her bag? Henry could have turned on the light. He could have said something or offered to help her. But he didn't. He would have had to see her and hear her voice, and he didn't feel ready for that. Not yet.

He thought of how it began. The way she'd reached behind her back to unclasp her bra. The small round bones that protruded from the front of her shoulders, her slender rib cage, her smooth skin made sublime by its imperfections, the freckles and scars—all those delicate parts of her summoned a lifetime's worth of desire. There was no music, no great white light, but still Henry was transported. He was nineteen again and Val's body was a miracle to him, a present that he couldn't believe he had the fortune to unwrap. The future was only an idea, a cosmological certainty that nevertheless held no real power or meaning. The moment, the present, the very fact of Val's existence—that was all that mattered to Henry, and to want her so badly was to experience a pain better than pleasure.

But Val's youthful delicacy did more than turn him on. All those parts of her that had yet to be swollen and stretched and softened by time reminded him of another young girl. An eleven-year-old that he'd lost. Henry had pushed the thought from his mind as soon as Val kissed his lips, and he ignored it again now. That deep, dark Freudian hole was best left unexplored for the moment.

Val found her underwear and slipped them on without standing up.

What Henry could not ignore was the question of what to do next. He'd been trying for months to push Gabe and Val together. At first he enjoyed the self-righteous assuredness that his goal provided, how it justified his every action. But that certainty faded as he realized that his plan wasn't working. No matter how much time he gave them, no matter how much encouragement, Gabe and Val's tryst would end soon after 19 reappeared. It didn't make any sense, and Henry was running out of ideas.

And then Gabe revealed his secret.

Except it wasn't a secret at all. Or it needn't have been, anyway. It was an obvious fact of Henry's life and it was his own fault that he'd neglected to notice it before. NYU, the Minerva Blanc tour, the *Bridgesong* travesty—he'd understood that Val's absence was related to his decline, but he'd always seen it as a symptom, not a cause. But once he understood the truth, it seemed obvious that it was he and not Gabe who was fated to be with Val. The music came to him first and Val could silence it completely. She was the normalizing force of the universe, the antidote to his poison. They were both a part of some larger scheme then, and without Val nearby Henry had no hope of discovering what grand purpose they were meant to serve.

So he went to her. He prepared for weeks. The initial approach would decide everything, he figured, so he had to get it right. He headed back to New York. On the basement level of the George Washington Bridge Bus Terminal was a convenience store kiosk that sold scratch-offs. It was open-air, no walls or doors, so Henry could easily watch over it from a bench nearby. He begged for change from passing commuters, ate junk food, washed himself in the public bathroom. It took three days, but finally someone hit a five-hundred-dollar jackpot. Henry got close enough to see what game the lucky customer had been playing, then walked up to the street, climbed the circular ramp to the bridge, and shifted back a few minutes before heading back to the basement to cash in.

He got a haircut. Some new clothes. A shared room in a hostel in the East Village. And then he set to watching her.

Days passed. He sat outside her building. Waited for her outside of class. He almost spoke to her on a few occasions, but each time he lost his courage at the last moment and told himself that there would be better opportunities to come.

One evening, she left her apartment building with the roommate. He followed her to a restaurant, then to a bar, where he had to fight the urge to pounce on some kid whose hands kept finding their way to the small of her back. Then to a club, where he bought a ticket and went inside. From a distance he watched her dance, her body growing more and more slack from the alcohol. An hour later her friends carried her outside and encouraged her in cooing tones to throw up on the sidewalk. Two, three, and then four cabs refused her entry, but at last a black car opened its doors and spirited her away. On the walk back to the East Village, Henry's plan came into focus. Early the next morning he walked to the Williamsburg Bridge and shifted back a day, then set a course for the Washington Square Hotel.

And now it was over.

From the floor of the hotel room came the sound of short, labored breathing. Val's head appeared just beyond the edge of the bed, then her torso, and Henry could tell by her vague silhouette that she was holding her jeans out in front of her. She bent over to slip her feet into the legs, then shimmied the waistband back and forth and up as she rocked her hips. Henry smirked. How many times had he watched her put on pants? He knew her body so well. He'd seen it through countless illnesses and held it every night for almost twenty years. He'd seen it give birth.

Now, mostly dressed, Val stepped into the bathroom and closed the door. It seemed clear that she was getting ready to leave, and Henry had no idea what that meant. He tried to remember some change in his past, something that would help him understand where this night was leading her, but nothing came to mind. The bathroom door opened. Val stepped toward the desk and pulled out the chair before lowering herself into it. Her profile was illuminated by a soft electric glow, and a small, methodical tremor moved through her. She was writing something. Soon the light dimmed and went out. Val grabbed her bag from the desk and pushed the chair out behind her.

The door opened, flooding the room with light, then closed. Suddenly Henry saw the fantasy he'd been entertaining for what it was: the self-indulgent wish of a teenager, a figment of a manic imagination. He had allowed himself to hope that Val would know who he was, that all doubt would leave her, and that she'd allow herself to be taken away into a life so strange and beautiful that she would need nothing but him forever.

With so many emotions vying for his attention, Henry was surprised to be overwhelmed by something as ordinary as embarrassment.

He groaned and sat up, pulled the comforter from his body, and stood. He stretched, yawned, put on his underwear and the thick terrycloth robe he'd taken from the closet—anything to delay the moment when he would have to read the note and know for sure that Val was gone forever. When he couldn't put it off any longer, he walked to the desk and turned on the lamp.

Ed—, said the letter.

That one word was enough. He shut off the light.

Over the next few hours, as Henry waited for the sun to make its way back to the city, he replayed the night. It hadn't occurred to him that Val would doubt what she'd seen. Her body had understood. He felt sure of that, and he thought it would be enough. But all those drinks—once she sobered up even a little it must have been easy for her to write the whole thing off as an alcoholic delusion.

He opened the curtains and sat on the bed. The room had a beautiful view of the park. Its glowing lamps looked cheerful, but they only made Henry feel lonelier. He could hear a garbage truck crunching its way down the block.

Given enough time, he would move past all this. Henry knew that. Like a few of his other worst memories, it would be regrettable but ultimately meaningless. But how would Val interpret this night? What would it mean to her?

The letter.

He couldn't bring himself to read past *Ed* before, but now he crossed to the desk and lifted the pad, brought it close to the window so that the paper reflected the iridescent purple of the bright city sky.

Ed—

I'm sorry I had to leave. I have a boyfriend. Sorry I didn't tell you, but I figured you wouldn't have really cared either way. We're pretty serious, actually, and I don't want to mess it up. I hope you understand. —V

Again Henry sorted through his memories of Val. This time, a vertiginous moment came and lingered, and he felt a strange crackling deep in his skull as his knowledge of the world rearranged itself. He lay down on the bed, covered his head with the cool sheets, and grinned wide.

There were many more memories to examine than he'd expected. New memories. Of Val as a woman. And of Gabe. Then, surprisingly, of someone else.

CADENZA: GABRIEL

G ABE STEPPED OFF the A train and onto the platform. The early-December chill had permeated the subway tunnels by then, robbing them of the heat they'd banked over the long summer and fall. As he bounded up the steps and onto the street, his body tensed in preparation for the more acute cold of the outdoors. It was worse now that his head was shaved clean. He had yet to adjust to that sensation, a kind of nakedness that was altogether new. Val still didn't know. They'd spoken every day since he'd taken it all off, but he had wanted it to be a surprise. Now that he was getting closer to her place he doubted the wisdom of that. If she didn't like it, would she be able to hide it?

His anxiety went far beyond the haircut. Val had persisted in bringing up Henry. She even mentioned her one-night stand a couple times. Gabe knew she was right to be concerned about how closed off they were being, but he had no desire to talk about the pain that had brought them together and kept them close. His avoidance only validated her point, of course, but he couldn't shake the feeling that they could forget it—all of it—if Val would only allow it. They could be free.

It was a childish wish, he knew, maybe even a dangerous one

given all that was at stake. But no more dangerous than the alternative. Up until weeks before, he'd been hallucinating a whole human being. And the music—the never-ending racket of all things—it still lingered in his ears, giving no indication that it would ever leave him alone. So Val might have the luxury of confronting head-on all the strangeness of the past few months—it might even be good for her, Gabe could see that. But he didn't think the same was true for himself. If he admitted any of what had happened to him since their first night together, she'd force him to get help. She'd have to. She'd be right to. And after that? Whatever romance they'd shared would be as good as dead.

He couldn't tell her—not then, not ever. He'd dug in, and if he wanted to preserve what being with Val had given him, his only choice was to dig deeper.

A couple of blocks from Val's apartment Gabe slowed his pace. He wanted to enjoy the neighborhood, this particular flavor of New York that he'd never known before. There were no numbers on the street signs in the West Village, and navigating the quaint labyrinth had confounded him at first. But recently Gabe had taken pride in his ability to understand the meaning of august-sounding combinations such as Bleecker and Barrow, Bedford and Morton, Hudson and Christopher. The trees without their leaves framed rich red brick and sculpted iron. He willed the beauty of the neighborhood to spirit away some of his anxiety. It worked for a few moments, but the closer he got, the more his tension grew.

Gabe signed in at security and took the elevator to Val's floor. Despite all that he was feeling, the anticipation of seeing her took over. He smiled uncontrollably. When the doors opened he stepped into the empty hallway and skipped to her door. He imagined the security guard downstairs, watching this jubilance on a black-and-white screen, thinking, *That kid's about to get laid.*

Gabe knocked. Silence. He knocked again. The door opened a couple of inches.

"Hello?" he sang. "Can I come in?" There was no answer. He pushed the door with the tips of his fingers and stepped inside. Val was right next to him, he saw, leaning against the wall in tears, her face compressed in agony. As soon as Gabe closed the door she let out a little wail and he threw his arms around her. She slumped, her face in her hands, until they were both on the floor.

"What's wrong?"

She didn't answer.

He held her and spoke question after question until the meaning of his words grew vaporous. When finally it was just sound, Gabe stopped asking. He pulled her upright and led her through the kitchen and onto the couch in the living room. He waited, assuming that she would reach a state of exhausted resignation, but fifteen minutes later she seemed no closer to calming down than when he'd first walked in.

"Val," he said. "Stop crying. You need to tell me what's going on."

He placed his fingers on the back of her neck and tilted her face toward his own.

"Now," he said. "Just say it."

Val lifted her eyes. Her lips trembled and curled, just barely under her control. She seemed to fight with impossible effort to shape the sound of her voice into words. "I'm pregnant," she said. And then she went back to whimpering.

Gabe was actually relieved. He wasn't sure what evil he'd been expecting, but a pregnancy? It didn't seem so bad.

"Okay. It'll be okay," he said, though he wasn't sure what, exactly, the *it* was that he was referring to. "It'll be okay. Okay? No matter what you decide."

Val cried harder. Gabe examined his own words, questioned whether it was insensitive or valiant to leave the decision to her.

"What *we* decide?" he said. He hadn't meant it to be a question.

Val shook her head, the meaning unclear. She looked up at him and her grief was momentarily suspended. "Your face," she said. "Your hair."

Gabe smiled. "Later," he said. "It was dumb."

Val placed a palm on either side of his head and brought his face close, kissed his cheeks and his mouth with tight lips.

Gabe pushed her back, gently. "What about the ring?" he said, referring to the plastic loop that he sometimes felt when he was inside her. He called it her magical hair tie.

"I guess it didn't work," she said. The way she looked at him then made it clear that what Gabe had assumed was the climax of their conversation was only the preamble. His dread returned.

"What?" he said. "What is it?"

She kept her gaze fixed on Gabe. Her glistening eyes moved back and forth, frantic, as if searching his face for something she'd lost. Later, he'd understand. She was trying to fix him in her mind, trying to hold on to the last moment she would have with him before everything changed.

"I have to tell you something," she said. "I didn't use a condom. With the man. That night. I got tested after—I thought it was okay. I didn't *know*."

Gabe threw her hands off his own and got up from the couch. Inside he was pacing and pounding and yelling at the top of his lungs, but none of that was making its way to his body. He just stood there, staring.

"Please," said Val.

"Absolutely not. Please *what?*"

"I don't know what happened that night. I still don't know."

"Why is that?" Gabe said, his voice loud in his own ears. "Is it because you were too fucking wasted? Or because your shitty fucking friends were there? Egging you on?"

Val stood, tried to embrace him, but he stepped back. "I'm really sorry you're so confused, Val. But I don't actually give a shit."

"Please—"

"You asked me to accept that you made a mistake and I did—I tried to. And now you tell me this? What am I supposed to say? You want me to feel bad for you? About how confused you were?"

Val sat down, lifted a couch pillow from beside her, and jammed it over her face. Gabe could see her shaking. It pleased him. It hurt him. He hated himself. He hated her.

"We're all fucking confused," he said. "You think I'm not confused? You think I don't care that Henry is gone? Of course I do. But I don't go around trying to fuck my way out of it."

Val slammed the pillow back down on the couch. "God, Gabe! That's what—I don't know what happened. Yes, I was drunk, I told you that. I don't know why we didn't use protection, it didn't occur—" She stopped, as if surprised by her own words. "Jesus, what's *wrong* with me?"

"Don't do that. Okay? You don't get to pity yourself right now. I'm not going to console you. That's not fucking fair." But he wanted to. It was the only way to keep her. But he wanted to run away, too. He backed up and lowered himself to the floor, then leaned against the radiator. "Just—I don't get it."

"I thought it was Henry," said Val.

The words came out so fast that Gabe almost didn't understand them. Then they registered and he felt like he was cresting a hill at high speed, his intestines hitting some inner wall.

"I saw this guy," she said. It seemed like her body was fighting to prevent her from saying more, and her voice went from mezzo piano to fortissimo as her diaphragm forced all the air from her lungs. "We were dancing, I didn't even see him at first, actually—I was just really drunk, and all of a sudden I was dancing with him. My mind was playing tricks or something—I can't explain—I looked at him and I just felt like I knew him. And then I tried to figure out how and without ever actually saying it to myself, I just *knew* it was Henry." Val took a deep breath in. "This isn't supposed to help. It's not an excuse. If anything it's whatever the opposite of an excuse is. I'm fucked up. I'm scared, okay?"

Gabe considered it. Questioned whether it was possible—

"Then we left and walked through the park, like some dark wilderness, then this bright, opulent hotel. It was like it wasn't really happening. Like something out of a movie. A place that didn't really exist at all. Then I sobered up a little—maybe that was the problem. I thought I was okay, like I was thinking clearly, even though now that seems absurd."

Gabe felt a cold horror spreading out from the space between his shoulder blades.

"He told me to look at his face and I did. We didn't say anything. I just saw him and I thought—I didn't really think it, I just...I saw something there. I saw Henry again. I didn't *say* it, I never *said* it out loud. It was a trick of—I just thought I didn't need to say it. Like he understood."

"I have to go."

"What?" Val sat up, so fast that her hair whipped up over her head and landed in the shape of a haphazard crown. "No, Gabe, please don't. Just talk to me. I don't care what you say, just stay."

"You don't want to hear what I have to say right now."

"I do," she said.

"You don't," he said, and he stood.

"Please, Gabe, just say whatever you want to say."

"And what am I supposed to say, exactly? The facts are worse than anything I might have to say about them. I mean, you tell me about this guy weeks ago and I forgive you, I try to forget it. But then you come out with this?"

"*This?*" she said. "The fact that I'm *pregnant* is not a *this*. I love you, I want you to stay. I could have just kept this to myself, made you think this...that I'm pregnant because of you. I'm telling you because I want to be honest."

"If you'd wanted to be honest you would have told me before. But if you'd told me then? That you hadn't used any protection, that you'd fucked him because he looked like *Henry?* Jesus, Val—I might not have comforted you, right?"

Val looked down and folded her arms in front of her chest.

"And *now* you stop crying?" he screamed.

"Don't leave," she said.

It didn't stop him from walking toward the door.

The overlit hallway, sterile and nondescript. Each door a carbon copy of the one before. A hall of mirrors.

The elevator, the whir and dings, the feeling of falling.

The blast of cold air when he left the front door of the building.

The calm, quiet streets of Greenwich Village giving way to the rush of Seventh Avenue and then Sixth.

Gabe's senses detected each detail, but there was no cohesive picture. He was walking through a dream. Then, an hour later, he was on the train again. He felt like he was always on the train. He wanted to return to her. He should never have left. The fact that he did would be hard for either of them to forget. His phone hadn't chimed. The screen hadn't told him that Val was trying to reach him. Finally, he wrote a text.

I'm sorry. I need to think. I love you.

He erased it.

I need to think.

He sent it.

The rhythm of the train on the seams of the tracks formed the familiar backbone. Screeching. Footsteps down the aisle. The reverberation of the words he'd spoken to Val sat atop that clunking foundation. *Secaucus Junction. Newark.* The stations passed like dim apparitions; landscapes blew by without leaving any impression at all. *Elizabeth. Linden. Rahway.* The conductor's voice a familiar punctuation, egging the music on, pushing it closer to some gruesome climax. When the train stopped in Metropark, Gabe realized he hadn't been fully conscious since the last stop. Maybe it was sleep. It didn't seem like it, but that was the only thing it resembled. Really, it was more like a trance. He was so tired of the song, the incessant fevered refrain. He got up and stood in the entranceway to the train car. The quaint central Jersey suburbs rolled by.

I can survive this, he told himself. *I can even be a father if I have to be.*

It sounded like what it was: an empty reassurance. Above all else, he thought, he was a hypocrite. He'd spent hours talking to a man he thought was Henry. He'd been seduced, just as Val had, by the idea that there was a way back to how things used to be. They were both wrong, but equally so. No, not equally. Gabe's fantasy hadn't lasted a few hours—it had lasted months. It had lasted so long that still, in the aftermath of Val's revelation, he had an insistent little voice inside him saying that perhaps Val hadn't been confused at all, that she'd seen Henry just as he had. He stood with his eyes closed and the music swelled and burst open, a relentless chantey, a storm of sound. Gabe didn't have the will to fight it anymore. It painted vivid pictures of the losses he'd experienced and the pain that was still to come. He surrendered more completely than ever before, and his body swayed with the movement of the train, his forehead resting on the window. The world streaked past in wintry striations of slate and brown.

Metuchen.

Edison.

Finally, thank God, *New Brunswick.*

Gabe stepped off the train and ran the length of the platform, his footsteps clumsy and forced, then down the steps. He grabbed the banister as he descended, the steel so cold that it felt like flame. Past the Burger King and the college bookstore, past Old Man Rafferty's, the booth he always shared with Val, past all the chicken joints and pizza joints and bagel joints and sandwich joints. The smell of fried miscellany. The laminated photographs in the windows, close-ups of the greasy food, larger than life and oversaturated. The back of Gabe's throat burned with bile that he imagined was the color and consistency of tar. Finally he made it off the main strip and onto the residential Hamilton Street, where he slowed his pace. The relative calm shaped the music from jack-in-the-box frantic to moody and sweeping. He would have to call Val when he got home. He dreaded it, but he desired her voice, needed it to counteract the noise. This time he would be completely honest. He'd tell her about the music and the Henry he'd known. They'd have to make some kind of decision about the pregnancy, and he couldn't let her go through that without knowing the whole truth. That he might be sick too, or worse, there might be another Henry haunting their world. In either case, something was deeply wrong.

But first, he needed to quiet himself. He focused on individual houses as he walked down Hamilton, tried to erase his recollection of them and instead just *see* them as they really were. The sky was a smoky shade of white but still bright, the clouds kindly diffusing the sunshine instead of blocking it out. It was a beautiful winter day. Lucidity came slowly, but soon Gabe felt almost normal again. He began to rehearse what he would say to Val, and that task took him the rest of the way home.

There was a man on the porch.

Gabe stopped at the bottom of the steps. The man was sleeping in one of the camping chairs, his chin on his chest. Gabe ascended a few steps to get a better look. It was Henry, but he had thick, short hair. It was ruffled and pushed up in a way that was either purposely boyish or completely accidental, and on his face grew the beginnings of a beard. Had he cut his hair to rendezvous with Val? Gabe couldn't picture this Henry being so vain, but he couldn't be sure. He knew nothing about the man sleeping on his porch aside from what he *used* to be, and that was almost like knowing nothing at all. Then still, as always, it was possible that this Henry was a figment, an apparition that was now mocking Gabe, mirroring his own cleanly shorn head or simply showing Gabe what he wanted to see.

Gabe charged up the steps and roared. Henry awoke, confused, and Gabe grasped his shirt with both hands, pulled him up out of the chair. Then he hesitated. He had no plan. A few seconds before he could have strategized, thought it through, but his rage hadn't allowed him to wait. He'd never been in a real fight before, and having just instigated one, his options were limited. Henry began to fight back. Their hands wrestled awkwardly, they shoved each other, Gabe grunted, Henry just kept saying *Gabe! Gabe! Gabe!* over and over again, and when that failed to slow Gabe's pathetic on-slaught, Henry laughed, tore Gabe's hands from his shirt, and spun him around by his wrists. Gabe struggled, tried to use the heel of his foot to scrape down Henry's shin, but he couldn't get any real purchase and ended up just stepping on Henry's foot.

"Ow." Henry laughed. "Calm down."

"You fucked her?"

"I said calm the fuck down!"

"I'll throw you off this fucking porch."

It was a mistake to have given Henry the idea. Gabe felt himself rise and kicked his feet in the air, tried to push back against the railing. But Henry quickly swung all of their combined weight forward and let go. Gabe's foot caught the wrought iron and his body spun as he descended into the low shrubs just in front of the house. He felt the branches poking and scraping, and then he landed on the small patch of grass between the bushes and the sidewalk.

For just a few seconds, everything was blank. Gabe forgot to remember why he'd been fighting, who he was fighting, Val's pregnancy, everything. There was only the pain in his body. He held his breath.

The quiet of the street seemed to amplify the sound of Henry's laughter.

"Fuck," said Gabe. "My fucking leg." He rubbed his hip and thigh with both hands.

"Calm down now," said Henry.

Gabe looked up. "Fuck you."

"Are you okay?"

"Fuck you!" yelled Gabe. He could feel tears gathering in the dark space behind his eyes and nose. He fought them back and hissed through his teeth as he sat up. "Why are you doing this to me? You told me I should be with her, you acted like it's what you want or like it's meant to be or something, and I actually believed you. And then you...you *fuck her?* Why? Why would you do that?"

"I could ask the same of—"

"It's different!" said Gabe. He tore a fistful of grass from the ground and threw it at Henry, but it only made it as far as the bushes. "Don't even try to compare this to what I did. Because you left. You went fucking crazy and left me here alone and she was the only person in the world that ever gave a shit about me besides you. Of course we started talking, of course we started seeing each other. There was nobody else, all right? Can't you see that? You're not like other people. The three of us? We all had something that nobody else could ever understand. Val and I got physical, but it wasn't because we didn't care about you. It's fucking different, all right? But you—you come here and manipulate me, infect me with some sickness that I don't understand. You act like you know me, like you care what's best for me and then...I mean, the coffee table—what the fuck? And now *this?* There were so many times when I wished you would come back, but now? Just…" Gabe swallowed, shook his head. "Just leave me the fuck alone."

Throughout Gabe's outburst Henry had stared down from the porch, his face steely and impenetrable. Now he sat back down, and Gabe's view of him was obstructed by the floor of the porch and the bulk of the bushes.

"Nothing?" said Gabe.

"I'm sorry," said Henry.

"Oh, God," said Gabe, "you're sorry. Is it yours?"

"I don't know," said Henry. "I'd like to think she's mine, but I'd also like to think she's not."

Gabe lay back on the ground and laughed. "*She?* So she's going to have it, and it's a girl, and you don't know whose it is? I don't believe you." He stood up and tested the weight of his body on each leg. He was unharmed. Better than that, actually. He felt clearheaded. Still, not wanting to miss a chance to chastise Henry, he limped dramatically toward the stairs and sat down. "You threw me off the porch," he said.

"I'll do it again."

Gabe couldn't stop himself from smiling. There was the cleansing effect of the fight and the fall, but it wasn't just that. He and Henry had fought like brothers their whole lives. It was familiar, comforting even, to hear this man goad him the way he always had.

"Just tell me the truth," said Gabe.

"I said I don't know. I remember watching her grow up. There's a lot of you in her. Not the way she looks, necessarily—she has so much of Val—but the way she *is*. And in the past, the one I remember now, I didn't know it was even a possibility that you *weren't* her father until—you know. A few weeks ago. But of course I've thought about it. The time line. It's possible."

"Just *tell me*." Gabe had meant to sound stern, but all that came was a desperate mewl. "You know things. You have to know things. Just tell me."

"I'll always love Val. Somewhere else…she loved me back for a long time. But she always loved you, too. This is how it's supposed to end. That's all that matters."

"So it doesn't matter if the baby she's carrying is mine or yours? You can't actually believe that."

"I can. I do."

Gabe looked at Henry. He was more recognizable without the beard. It was comforting.

Henry looked back and smiled. "You always loved her, Gabe. This is what you wanted, and now you get to have it. You'll take care of that child because you love Val. It'll be yours because she loves you back."

"This is all bullshit," said Gabe. "We're just supposed to move on after this? After all this?"

Henry smirked.

"You can't just come into my life and distort everything." Gabe shook his head. "You can't fuck Val and make me crazy and act like you're being noble about it. It's not fair."

"I'm not being noble about anything."

"I don't want to hear any more," said Gabe.

Henry stood up from the low canvas chair and stretched his hands high up into the air. "Then I won't say another word," he said. He crossed the porch to the stairs and placed his hand on Gabe's shoulder as he walked down to the sidewalk, where he turned around.

"Don't show up here anymore," said Gabe.

"You won't be seeing me again. Not like this, anyway."

"Good," he said.

"Her name is Annie," said Henry, and he turned and walked away.

The music had returned—Gabe didn't know when. It was such a constant presence that it was hard to keep track of its comings and goings. As he watched Henry saunter down the sidewalk toward the center of town, the song swelled to a plodding requiem. Gabe didn't try to quiet it. Fighting only made him tired. He lifted himself up, got his keys out of his pocket, and entered the house.

Shoes off by the door. Bathroom. Glass of water. Gabe went through the coming-home routine as though his world were not dissolving around him. As if his girlfriend—was she his girlfriend? would she ever be *his* anything again?—as if Val weren't pregnant, possibly with the baby of a man from another time. As if he were not having aural hallucinations and Henry weren't still missing somewhere, his future self haunting a depressed pocket of New Jersey like the Ghost of Homeless Future. The water gurgled through the pipes. The floors creaked. The bathroom mirror reflected Gabe's image just like always. Finally he was sitting on the couch with one hand curled around the remote and the other gripping his phone.

He would call Val soon, but not before he decided how to tell her everything he meant to say.

Sorry.

I'm an asshole.

Forgive me. I'll come back.

The man you were with, I think I know him.

Maybe we're both insane.

And then, unbelievably, *You're keeping the baby. And her name is Annie.*

I'm yours now, and you're mine.

He slipped his thumb over the well-worn power button on the bulky black TV controller, lifted it to get a line of sight between transmitter and receiver. Just before he was about to turn it on and escape for however long he could, he heard something. A muffled snort or a heavy sigh from his bedroom. He set the remote on the couch cushion and placed his glass of water down among the rest of the filth on the coffee table.

He heard it again, right on the other side of the doors. He stood, slid one side open just enough to poke his head in, expecting to find Cal sleeping in the wrong room at this odd hour for some predictably odd reason.

There was a body in the bed, but it wasn't Cal. He was turned away, a man, his face close to the wall. Gabe opened the door wider so that he could step inside. The man wore unfamiliar but clean clothing. His beard and hair were uncut, probably since the day he'd left his bedroom at the top of the stairs nearly seven months before. Gabe had no problem recognizing this Henry. He was the real Henry, the one who'd been missing, and now, incredibly, he was found.

Henry snored again and it was all Gabe could hear. The music was gone. The house seemed to shrink around him. It was familiar and safe. He was home. He left the bedroom and slid the door closed behind him. He found his phone and looked for Val's number in his recent calls.

Then, thinking better of it, he opened his contacts menu, and touched Jan's name. He would talk to Val later. They had the rest of their lives.

EPILOGUE

The Daily Targum

September 12, 1983

State police say a car crash involving three vehicles on Route 18 in New Brunswick, NJ, has left one person dead. New Brunswick Police Sergeant William Pilgrim told the *Targum* that a motorist struck an unidentified male believed to be between 35 and 45 years of age and that the man was announced dead on the scene.

The accident occurred at approximately 3:40 p.m. on Monday at the intersection of New Street and Route 18.

The motorist has been identified as 23-year-old Mark Williamson. His statement indicates that he was on his way to work in Piscataway when the victim "landed on the hood of [his] car."

At least one other witness, 43-year-old James Gore of Highland Park, corroborates this account. Gore is one of a team of workers currently installing the foundation for the New Street footbridge, the much-debated public works project that has been mired in delays since construction began in September of last year. In an interview with the *Targum*, Gore claimed to have seen the victim "fall from the sky." Gore states that he didn't see where the victim came from but is certain that he was not standing in the road when he was struck.

After colliding with the unidentified man Williamson briefly lost control of his Oldsmobile Cutlass, hitting two other vehicles before coming to a stop. Damage was minor and no other injuries were reported.

ACKNOWLEDGMENTS

I will not save Vanessa Wingerath for last. Thank you for your grace, intelligence, humor, and positivity. I love you more every day. It's impossible not to.

This book has had many lives. It took ten years to write, but that should not imply that I wrote it for ten years. Mostly I ignored it for eight years and wrote it for two.

It was only after the first meeting of the Escriben Cartel that I started writing every day, so I mean it when I say that this book would not exist without EC. Special thanks are owed to Zachary Marco for starting the group and for being a particular kind of man. I'm no less grateful to Ryan Dodge, Alex Woodson, Sam Ferguson, and Zachary Scheer. Also, to the Monday-night bartender at Tom & Jerry's in New York: You are a beautiful freak. You may not care, but you are the enigmatic glue that holds the Escriben Cartel together.

Thanks to my former work-spouse Erica Barmash. Even after our marriage ended, your support was ongoing and instrumental. Special thanks to the staff at the Chipotle on Fiftieth between Park and Madison.

Long before I got serious about finishing *The Lost Boys Symphony*, it was Hanna Karsevar who helped me to find this book's emotional backbone and gave me the confidence required to keep typing.

It's my opinion that an exceptional high school English teacher is the absolute best thing that can happen to a teenager. I had two. There will always be a John D'Ambra inside my head challenging me to be succinct. There will always be a Mark Wright in my head reminding me to pursue my interests with as much curiosity, vigor, and joy as possible.

Roald Dahl, Kurt Vonnegut, Philip K. Dick, and Paul Auster taught me that books can make you a better, more interesting person.

Mark Vonnegut's beautiful writing about his own mental illness was invaluable.

To my HarperCollins family: I became an adult while working at 10 East Fifty-Third, and in that time I learned more about the business of books than it's advisable for a writer to know. I'm especially grateful for all the love I felt when I decided that it was time to leave.

Jean Naggar, Jennifer Weltz, Alice Tasman, Jessica Regel, and Mollie Glick were my first ever real-life bosses and coworkers, and I couldn't have hoped for better. Alice in particular has been a warm and savvy ally during this publication process. Thanks also to Tara Hart and Laura Biagi.

Jessica Regel gets a new paragraph because she is now my agent. Jessica, thank you. Thank you so much. Your intelligence, level head, and good taste make you the ideal representative and friend. I hope that your obvious and emphatic belief in me will someday be warranted. Thanks as well to everyone at Foundry.

A note to the reader: Wes Miller at Little, Brown is the reason that you finished reading this novel instead of lighting it on fire. Thank you, Wes, for helping me shape this beast of a convoluted story into something resembling a page-turner. You have a fantastic sense of direction and your instincts have taught me to trust my own. Thank you also for suggesting that I cut down on words like *vomit* and *cum* and *masturbate*.

Thanks also to Miriam Parker, Carrie Neill, Peggy Freudenthal, Anthony Goff, Megan Fitzpatrick, Nancy Wiese, Tracy Williams, Kapo Ng, Reagan Arthur, and anyone else at Little, Brown who had a hand in bringing this book to market. Alison Kerr Miller copyedited this book and obliterated *many, many* repetitions and errors. Before, it was just alright. Now it's all right, except where I insisted that it shouldn't be.

Others with whom I discussed this book and whose thoughts and positivity are notable include Dan Forst, the incredibly talented and charismatic Julia Weldon, Andy and Analiese Wilcox Marchesseault, Katie Clarke, Jody Avirgan, Brandon Contarsy, Caitlin Clarke, Amanda and Luke McCormick, Brianne Halverson, Joshua Cristantiello, Olivia Wingerath, Tamini Wingerath, Joe Sackett, Leah Wasielewski, Angie Lee, Kathy Schneider, Jonathan Burnham, Matt Calhoun, Christian Larson, Cyriaque Lamar, Mike Milnes, Andy Weeks, Pete Calautti, Scott Farah, Jamie Peterson, Mackenzie Firer-Sherwood, Victoria Loustalot, Charlotte Ross, and Jonathan Janeway.

This book was written using Scrivener, the only software for writers that makes any kind of sense. It was written while listening to Steve Reich, Max Richter, Miles Davis, Brightblack Morning Light, white noise, and Medeski, Martin, and Wood.

Thank you, Megan Clary.

Deep gratitude and love to the artist, poet, and musician Dan Ovadia.

Finally, thanks to everyone in my Ferguson and Wingerath families for their love, humor, and acceptance.

Mark Andrew Ferguson is a writer, graphic and web designer, and novice farmer living in eastern Connecticut. *The Lost Boys Symphony* is his first book. He is @thefergusonian on Twitter and Tumblr.